Praise for On Bear I

Reviewer's Choice Nominee, Best Conten
— *Romantic Times Book Club 2003*

Nominee, The 2002 Townsend Prize for Fiction

Reviewer's Choice Nominee, Best Mainstream Romance
— *Romantic Times, 1997*

"Characters as intriguing as the abstract sculpture."
— *Atlanta Journal Constitution*

"I highly recommend On Bear Mountain . . . a deeply touching tale."
— *Romance Reviews Today*

"A delight."
— *Hollywood Behind The Scenes*

"Rich, complex."
— *The Romance Reader*

"Beautifully written . . . A shimmering web of sorrows and joys."
— *Booklist*

"Readers of the novels of Anne Rivers Siddons will welcome into their hearts Deborah Smith."
— *Midwest Book Review*

"A fine and gentle tale"
— *Publishers Weekly*

"Charming and heartwarming"
— *Library Journal*

"Smith's best novel yet."
— *Kristin Hannah*

Other Novels by Deborah Smith

The Crossroads Cafe
A Gentle Rain
Charming Grace
Sweet Hush
A Place to Call Home
The Stone Flower Garden
Blue Willow
Miracle
Silk and Stone
Alice at Heart
Diary of a Radical Mermaid
Just a Little Bit Guilty
Soul Catcher (writing as Leigh Bridger)
Solomon's Seal (writing as Leigh Bridger)

On Bear Mountain

by

Deborah Smith

Bell Bridge Books
PO BOX 67
Smyrna, GA 30081

ISBN: 978-0-9821756-6-8

Bell Bridge Books is an Imprint of BelleBooks, Inc.

Printed and bound in the United States of America.

A hardcover edition of this book was published by Little, Brown & Company in 2001
A mass market edition of this book was published by Warner Books in 2002

We at BelleBooks enjoy hearing from readers. You can contact us at the address above or at BelleBooks@BelleBooks.com

Visit our websites – www.BelleBooks.com and www.BellBridgeBooks.com.

10 9 8 7 6 5 4 3 2

Cover design: Debra Dixon
Cover photo: Mountain Ridge - © JulietPhotography - Fotolia.com
                  Rusted lettering - © Dana Sitarzewski, Jaguarwoman Designs
Interior design: Hank Smith

Lw:00:

Dedication

Every book grows into its own unique structure, its bones forming the shape of some mysterious animal no one—not even the author—has ever seen before. This story evolved in wonderful, unknown patterns, sometimes sprouting unneeded parts, then reabsorbing them, sometimes lumbering along on a dozen feet, then sprinting on two. I want to thank the following loyal, caring, and extremely talented friends for helping me ultimately birth a creature strong of backbone, proud of head, and tender of heart: Sandra Chastain, Gin Ellis, Debra Dixon, and Martha Shields.

This book is for every roadside Picasso who paints heaven on a weathered board, for every sculptor of *found objects* who twists a tin can or a rusty timber saw into an *object d'art*, and for all the other dreamers who have the courage to create something wonderful out of nothing.

This book is for Ma. *I will always miss you.* And for Hank, who told me exactly what a crankshaft and a buggy spring look like, how hard it is to bend rebar, and how to rust-proof a rusty iron pot. For those and so many other wisdoms shared in thirty years of marriage, I love him.

www.deborah-smith.com * www.leighbridger.com

Show me a hero and I will write you a tragedy.
F. Scott Fitzgerald

PROLOGUE

I vowed to embarrass Quentin Riconni if he died in my arms that day, there on that Georgia mountaintop under a cold, winter sky. "Powells don't grieve the way ordinary people do," I whispered in a voice that shook against the wind curling over the high mountain glen. A hard night was coming; the frost would kill every vulnerable living thing, including him.

"I'll spend the rest of my life telling everyone I meet who you were and why I love you and why I was never the same after you died. And I'll make you sound a lot better than you were, stronger and kinder than you ever had any intention of being. People will say you must of charmed me with big talk and good looks. I'll have to tell them you didn't talk that much or look that good. Do you really want me to lie?"

His eyes remained closed and his lips slightly parted, his breath now making only a faint mist in the frigid air. It had been at least an hour since he'd answered any of my questions. I lay beside him, trying to keep him warm. Light flickered on his face from a fire I'd built. In the towns and homes, the farms and resorts in the valleys below us, fireplaces sent decorative warmth into the air. But here, high up where only the hardiest souls could survive, fire meant life, and only promises spoken out loud could keep the darkest fears away.

"Arthur believes in you," I said. "Now you have to believe in *him*. You taught him to be a man, and he's not going to let you down." The sky had ripened into cold purples and golds over the forested rim of the Appalachians. The gray-blue dusk of a fading sunset drew the last minutes of Quentin's life below the horizon. I was praying for just one small miracle. My brother, Arthur, had gone for help hours ago.

I pressed my hand tighter to the spot low on one side of Quentin's rib cage, where the bullet had torn through him. *If we'd only gotten here an hour earlier*, the rescuers would say. A minute earlier. A second earlier. It was always the small pieces of time that ruined people. I knew that help would come eventually, but by then it would be too late. He'd never survive the long trip back down the mountain. I touched his lips, searching for even the faintest trace of breath, but couldn't find it.

He was leaving with the sunset.

Some choices are made for us before we're born. Some traditions are set in hard patterns we're expected to follow, their seams welded, their strengths and weaknesses hammered into place. We don't cast our own shadows until we know who we love and where we belong. Only then do we understand.

Sometimes you've got to break the mold that's been made for you, or die trying.

PART ONE

1

When I was a child it seemed to me that our secluded farm lay at the end of a path to a magic land where only Powells and legends could survive. Even by mountain standards the land at Bear Creek was too rocky to farm, too steep to log, and too isolated to hunt. There was only one level spot of any useable consequence, and that was our five-acre hilltop overlooking the vast woods of the creek valley. The soft ribbon of our narrow dirt road dipped and wound through the woods for a mile before reaching a paved county two-lane. The approach to our homestead managed a hardy fringe of decoration only where the sun hit it. At those places it burst into wild daisies, morning glories, old-fashioned, ruffled roses that had escaped from some long-dead Powell's arbor, and buttercup-yellow jonquils that had migrated from tamer beds. I lived there with parents who knew we were special. I was born on the day that our destiny began to find us.

On a cool March morning in 1966, a Southern Railways freight train finished its long trip home from New York. The big engines and their long line of cars lumbered out of the last moss-dappled granite tunnel beneath the ancient Appalachians, then chugged up a steep grade bordered by enormous firs, rhododendron, and wintry hardwoods, before leveling out on a high plateau near the Georgia-Tennessee line.

Looking east over a breathtaking vista of gray mountains still waiting for spring, the engineer might have glimpsed the distant smoke from the Powell homestead's hundred-year-old chimney, if the wind were right. Inside that whitewashed farmhouse I was five hours old, safe in my mother's arms, and unaware that my future was rolling into town.

The train slowed with the great grandeur of industrial might as its horn saluted the Tiber Poultry feed mill, the Tiber Poultry Hatchery, and the Tiber Poultry Processing Plant on the outskirts of town. A mile further, it eased down a shallow grade, its horn blaring even louder, as it entered the very civilized environs of Tiberville.

Beneath the town's canopy of bare, winter trees, cars and pick-up trucks lined the handsome streets as if a festival were underway. At the Tiberville depot, several hundred people waited. The college marching band played *Dixie*.

A crowd of notable town citizens stood in the prime front spaces on the depot platform. The rest of the county stood below the level of the loading platform, consigned to the depot's graveled parking lot along with the town dogs. This caste included Tiber-contracted chicken farmers, chap-handed employees of the bloody Tiber chicken processing plant, wild mountain folk who made their livings in rebellious ways involving liquor, hunting, and cars, and my father, Tom Powell.

At 11:52 a.m. the train rumbled to a stop at Tiberville's historic depot, which had survived Sherman's firebug troops during the Civil War. Inside a box car sat a sculpture of a native Georgia bear. Our town matriarch, elderly, eccentric Betty Tiber, who was Powell kin by virtue of being the daughter the notorious Bethina Grace Powell Tiber, had commissioned it for the campus of Mountain State.

The sculptor was an unknown Brooklyn artist named Richard Riconni. No one in Tiberville or Tiber County had any idea what to expect from him except Miss Betty and my art-loving Daddy, who had cooked up the plan for a bear sculpture made from local *mementos*, (as Miss Betty called them,) or *junk*, in Daddy's simple terms. *This silly idea came from her Powell blood,* some Tibers insisted, and it wasn't a compliment.

The Tibers and their friends nurtured desperately hopeful pretty-postcard visions of classic statuary that could pose grandly on Mountain State's manicured lawns. Or, at the very least, a piece of modern art that would not embarrass old ladies and ministers. So when the door of the box car was pushed back, everyone crowded forward to see Tiberville's first piece of Yankee sculpture. They quickly backed up.

The abstract black bear towered over them, touching the roof of the box car with its rounded backbone. It had soaring, see-through sides of iron bar and short, thick legs of twisted metal, swirling down into black-iron paws with elegantly curved claws. The head was noble and massive, made from hammered sections of thick iron that merged into an amazingly engineered star of seams above the sculpture's muzzle. Two smooth black holes in the head gazed out at our world with the startling effect of mysterious, all-knowing eyes. The sculpture didn't resemble a bear so much as a playful Omnivore of the Universe, some serene spirit with the power to amuse, annoy, or enlighten.

Daddy loved it at first sight. Deep inside its see-through ribs, suspended on steel wires, was a heart-shaped clump of melted metal that had once been the carburetor of his Grandpa Oscar Powell's 1922

Ford tractor. That tractor had faithfully plowed two generations of garden earth and hay pasture at Bear Creek. Centered around such an earth-loving and loyal core named for the ursine population of the world, the Bear sculpture instantly became a member of our family.

"It's plain beautiful," Daddy said loudly, a lone voice in the stunned wilderness. People around him either gazed up at the enormous sculpture in speechless awe or embarrassment. Mountain State College officials nearly strangled. The Tiber family had founded the college in the late 1800's, and since then had endowed half the buildings on campus. Betty Tiber herself had funded the new concession stand and concrete bleachers for the campus baseball field. They couldn't reject her terrible junkyard joke. Betty was in the hospital recovering from a mild stroke, but had sent word she'd come by ambulance to view her pride-and-joy that afternoon.

Every Tiber on the depot platform sent dark scowls toward my father. "Tommy, come up here," John Tiber ordered in his most magisterial Rotarian-president tone. "Tell me that you and my grandmama didn't know this goddamned thing would look like this."

Daddy bounded up on the platform, grinning. Behind him, the whole crowd burst into loud guffaws. John Tiber's heart turned black with impugned authority and loss of dignity. His father had died young, a genteel Tiber drunk, and his mother had simply faded away. John had spent his youth overcompensating for his parents' dishonor, and so he didn't abide humiliations very well. Now, for the first time in the history of Tiberville and Tiber County, his family was being turned into the butt of a very *public* joke. From that moment forward Mr. John, as everyone called him, would loathe and fear the sculpture's effect.

Daddy sank his hands into the pockets of his threadbare coat and grinned wider. "Johnny, the sculpture looks like it's *got* to look," he said to his red-faced cousin. "It's *supposed* to make folks think twice. It's made up of good things and bad things—ruination and joy and hope and loss—it's *life*, Johnny."

"Life is not made up of junk and nonsense." Mr. John, not even thirty but already balding and fleshy, was the perfect captain of small-town society in a brown suit with a gold Tiber Poultry tie clasp anchoring his thin black tie against the brisk March breeze. Daddy, about the same age, was dirt-poor, hard-labor lanky, and sweetly homely, dressed in his best overalls and white dress shirt, a well-worn brown fedora slouched comfortably on his auburn hair, his warm eyes filled with awe as he studied his and Betty Tiber's ursine abomination. "It's perfect," he said.

Furious, Mr. John took a step toward him, halted, and clenched his fists. Only their lifelong affection for each other kept him from punching him in the mouth. They were cousins, after all, and that meant something, even if Powells were no longer formally recognized or invited into Tiber society. As boys they had been devoted friends, and they were, each in his way, the keepers of the community. One word from Daddy could settle disputes between Tiber Poultry and the county's contract chicken growers. "Tommy," Mr. John said in a low voice, "You've just set back our family relations another hundred years."

"The bear's got heart," Daddy insisted. "It's got a soul." Heart and soul. Those were Daddy's brands of art critique—a dead-on judgment that summed up the library books he checked out about Picasso and Salvador Dali, or a 'Jesus Saves' warning painted on a homemade billboard, or a kitchen garden bursting with bright red tomatoes planted in whitewashed tires. "Now this town's got a real piece of art to ponder over and discuss," Daddy went on. "It could change our lives, make us see the world with fresh eyes."

"It's got about five goddamned thousand dollars of my grandmother's savings," Mr. John replied. "I should have taken over her power of attorney before she cashed in her Coca-Cola stock and started talking to New Yorkers."

He motioned brusquely for the dock men to close the freight car's door, and the Bear disappeared from view, at least temporarily. The show was over. The people of Tiberville and Tiber County went back to their jobs, their homes, their college classes, their lives, either laughing or sputtering with indignation. Life would never be the same.

When Daddy returned to our farm that day he loped upstairs on our creaking, white-washed stairs, yelling, "Victoria, the sculpture was a glorious sight! It's gonna change the way people look at the world around here!" Mama was snug in the bedroom, wrapped in quilts to ward off the drafts that lived like happy ghosts in the isolated Powell farmhouse. She said devotedly, "I reckon I don't doubt so, if'n you say it," as she cuddled me to her bare breasts. She'd given birth to me at home because hospitals were against her religion. New Testament fiddle faddle was not for her.

Daddy sat down beside her on their pine-slab bed and with great patience told Mama all about the second wonderful work of art he'd seen now that their daughter had come into the world. He kissed my forehead and Mama's smiling lips, and then they talked about my name.

"It's got to be a bear name, because of today," he said. "I'd like to call our girl 'Ursula.' I've been studying on the name. Ursa Major and Ursa Minor, you know—the star patterns in the sky? The constellations? Ursula means Little Bear. I figure that oughta keep our family bear spirit happy. And it's in honor of the Iron Bear, too. That's what I'm calling that sculpture. I just got a feelin' this is important in the big scheme of things! I'd like to meet Richard Riconni and shake his hand for building it! He's a man who knows you gotta reach down inside yourself and pull out your own bones to see what you're made of!" Daddy stroked his thick, callused fingers over my head. My hair was auburn and unruly, like his. "That's what I'm gonna teach this little lady! To be an iron bear!"

Mama, who could see the sacred structure inside Daddy's whimsical ideas, merely nodded her loving acceptance. Nursing at her breast, I was contented and unaware of the responsibility I'd just been handed.

For better or worse, I and the Iron Bear had arrived.

*

Five states and one thousand miles to the north, Quentin Riconni huddled next to the radiator in the chilly living room of his parents' small Brooklyn apartment. The room was crowded with cheap vinyl furniture, and the bookcases overflowed with encyclopedias, art texts, and novels. A dozen of his father's smaller sculptures perched on the coffee table, on the lamp stands, and in the corners of the floor, like weird metal elves. On the living room windowsill, a plaster copy of Picasso's Head of a Woman looked down on a street of bedraggled trees, littered apartment stoops, and shops with barred windows.

Quentin scribbled feverishly in his journal, a spiral-bound notebook on which he had pasted the Greek symbol for infinity, a fanciful picture of H.G. Well's time machine, a picture of a gleaming Marine dress sword, and a newspaper photo of Muhammad Ali, then known as Cassius Clay. At the top of the notebook cover, outlined in precise block letters Quentin had drawn in ink, were the words, *My Credo*. He was no ordinary eight year old. He was telling the story of his life so far, and of recent events which were about to *change* his life.

A couple of years ago, when I was still just a kid, I thought Brooklyn was the whole world. Mother says as long as Brooklyn has libraries we ARE the whole world. She is a librarian, so she knows what she means. She says

I can stand on the beach at Coney Island and see all the way to Europe, if I think about it hard enough. Our part of Brooklyn is ugly but the rest of the city is okay. Ugly is only how you look at things, Papa says. I don't know about that. I see ugly on our street, and it just IS. And it is going to get worse.

Today I found out that Papa can't live with us, anymore. He is going to a town three or four hours in the car from here, where a man who bought one of Papa's sculptures has an empty warehouse Papa can use for a studio, so he can have plenty of room to work on his sculptures all the time. All Papa has to do is take care of the building. We don't have the money to rent any place like that around here. It's real big, I hear.

Papa says people used to store stoves and mattresses and other things at the warehouse before the man that used to own it got in trouble with the FBI. Now the warehouse belongs to Uncle Sam and it is in *limbo*, Papa says. Our upstairs neighbor, Mrs. Silberstein, told me there are probably some mob guys buried in the floor. Mother says Papa won't mind mob guy ghosts. He grew up around them.

We will only see Papa on the weekends, until he gets to be rich and famous with his art. He says it will only be a year or two, he bets. But that feels like forever and I don't know what we will do without him. I caught Mother crying in the kitchen, (My Mother NEVER cries) and she swore it was because she opened the bag of onions on the table. She pretended to beat the bag with her cane. Take that, onions, she said. I pretended to laugh.

I AM NOT GOING TO CRY, EITHER. I HAVE A MOTHER TO TAKE CARE OF.

Until last week, Papa worked for Mr. Gutzman. GOOTS MAN. Papa calls him Goots. Goots is a German. He has a big fancy garage where he fixes dents in nice cars. He says Papa is the best body man in New York State, and he is sorry to see him go, but he is sure Papa will come back as soon as the money runs out. Mother told Goots we live like Spartans and don't need much money. We need great art and great ideas, instead, she says.

For a long time Goots let Papa use a corner of his garage to build art out of metal. Sometimes Papa took me there, and I helped him. "We're making metal talk to us," he said. "Telling us what it wants to be. We're like God. We're giving it life." Father Aleksandr at St. Vincent's (my school) wouldn't like Papa talking that way, but I'll never tell on him, not in Confession, not anywhere, even if I burn in hell. He is the best father and the greatest man in the world!

He made a big twisty thing out of a metal staircase once and Goots said Awck! What is THAT? It has been caught in a bad storm? A truck ran over it? What? Papa told him it was supposed to make you think of something broken and what it means to be broken, but Goots shook his big fat head and said Awck, again. Then a rich man from the Heights came in to pick up his car and he *bought* the sculpture for 200 dollars!

He put it in his office waiting room.

He was a back doctor.

Papa and Mother got excited after that but Papa did not sell even ONE other sculpture for so long he almost gave up. I could tell he felt bad. He is real quiet anyway and sometimes I am scared when I can't get him to talk. Not like he would hit me, but like he wants to hit himself. He wouldn't even go to museums on Sundays with us, anymore. Mother hugged him all the time. She is his heart doctor, Mrs. Silberstein says.

But then last November he got a big customer for his art, and everything changed! A lady paid him 5,000 dollars to make a bear for her! A BEAR. He put it on a train and sent it to the lady a couple of weeks ago. ALL THE WAY TO GEORGIA. I checked on the map.

Papa said the bear is special, and that it taught him some lessons. You can sort of tell it is a bear, and THAT'S SURE SPECIAL, because most of the time people don't know WHAT Papa's sculptures are trying to be. Mother says it is the spirit of life. She says it means that Papa has found his calling. It just looked like a bear with all its bones showing, to me.

This bear means Papa is going to be important, that's what Mother says. Even if he never finished high school! She should know. She went to college! Papa doesn't care about school, but he loves to read, so she and him get along fine. Except he hates church. He grew up in a mean church home for orphans and he has a belt scar on his shoulder, I saw it! But he made me be an altar boy, et cetera, because Mother wants me to and St. Vincent's is a good Catholic school and I get in free since her nutty Aunt Zelda left St. Vincent's all her money. I'm even named after an old priest who taught Latin there.

Riconnis have been trying to build something important for about 150 years now and so far, it has not gone real well. Great-grandpapa died working high up on the Brooklyn Bridge. Grandpapa died building pontoon army bridges across a French river during WWII. Riconnis die pretty easy, and don't get too old.

So Papa wants to build art that will make people remember our name and our GRAND ideas. He has to hurry. There aren't many of us Riconnis left in America. Just me, him, and Mother, I guess. And she started out as a Dolinski.

Now he is going away. And it's all because of his art. Because of that 5,000 dollar bear. That DAMN bear. It is a BIG damn fucking bear. It looked down at me at Goots shop like it knew I was not as big as it is. Papa says his sculptures talk to him. (He's not crazy. We have some crazy bums on our street, so I can tell.) He says the Bear told him to Go For It. Quit his job and become a real, live sculptor.

I am having a lot of trouble understanding what this Bear thinks it is doing. This is not fair. I'm worried.

But I am not crying. Not! Crying!

I just feel like I am rusting inside. And that hurts.

*

On a bright, cold April morning, Richard Ricconi threw a duffel bag of clothes into the back of his old truck, alongside welding equipment, a box of pots, utensils, and dishes, an army cot, a sleeping bag, and a box filled with his books—a much-read collection of tomes on art and sculpting. He was a tall, big-shouldered man with thickly knuckled hands, dark Italian hair, and brilliant gray eyes. He drew admiring glances from the women who walked past him on the grimy sidewalk, carrying their groceries or their laundry, hurrying to shops with bars on the windows and shabby brownstone apartments with heavy locks on the main doors. This was a tough neighborhood, and getting tougher. People walked fast, these days. If he'd had any choice, or enough money, he'd never have left Angele and Quentin there.

Richard had a love-hate relationship with his sculptures, and they mirrored his uneasy battle with life in general. He constantly tore the works apart and started over, or left many of them half-finished in disgust. The metals he used—pried from junked cars, from appliances, from corroded iron fences and ancient tin roofs, and from all the other flotsam and jetsam of the society that had so often rejected him—refused to conform to the shapes he imagined. Only the Iron Bear had come easy. He never forgot that.

Until that moment, when he finished packing his battered old truck, he had willed himself not to look up at the fourth-story window of the small apartment building. He knew they were watching him. Now he raised his head, slowly. His look-alike young son and beloved

12

wife gazed down at him, and his heart twisted. They waved, feigning smiles.

Angele Dolinski Riconni kept her hand raised, pressed her fingertips against the glass, and held him still with dark, consuming eyes behind black-rimmed glasses. Her wavy brunette hair was still tossled from his own hands. She looked taller than her medium height, more sturdy than her slender build. She always seemed larger than life to Richard, always elevating him and herself with her deep reverence for knowledge and ideals.

Angele despised pity, self-pity or otherwise. She had had enough of that in her life. Her right leg had been crushed as a child in a car accident that killed her mother. Her father had deserted them years before. Angele had memories of painful therapies and years of lonely recuperation spent at her Aunt Zelda's eccentric Manhattan apartment, where hundreds of porcelain dolls and antique Teddy Bears filled the chairs, the sofas, even the china cabinet and bathroom closets.

Angele had grown up immersed in books to escape from Aunt Zelda's crowded, miniature world. After Aunt Zelda died, leaving Angele nothing, she moved to Brooklyn, drawn there by her job at the imposing Brooklyn Library, which Angele loved. She rented a room at a boarding house for Catholic women, and settled into a life that was satisfying but all too lonely.

She was straightening shelves at the library one day when she met Richard. "Miss, I gotta find a book on modern sculpture theory," he said in a deep voice straight off the meanest streets in the city. He was looking at her through an open space between books. Dirty, muscular, and dressed in a mechanic's jumpsuit, he hardly resembled a book patron. Yet his eyes seemed gentle to her, silver and unmalleable, and he also seemed sincere.

Just as she was about to answer him, a security guard walked up. "Outta here," the guard ordered. "Get cleaned up if you want to hang out and pester the librarians."

Richard had straightened with the ferocious pride of the often disregarded. His eyes flashed, and his fists tightened. The guard put a hand on the club at his belt. "I'll vouch for this patron, Charlie," Angele said quickly. "He's an acquaintance of mine. He's just come from work. We're looking for a book."

The guard frowned, apologized, and left. Richard looked at her with searing intensity. She was not accustomed to men eyeing her that way. She wore glasses and walked with a cane. Her plain skirts and white blouses said frivolous fashion disrupted serious goals. A vivid thought or extravagant paragraph could send her lithe hands into her short brown hair excitedly, as if pulling on it opened more room in her brain, so that she always looked disheveled. Until that moment she had believed no man would ever find her sexy.

But this one looked at her as if he wanted to eat her alive and make her like the process. "Why'd you stick your neck out for me?" he asked.

"You're here to find answers. It's my job to give them. No one should be made to leave a library."

He walked slowly around the end of the shelves, and slowly up to her, giving her a chance to back away. She didn't. "I could use all the answers you got," he said. Her eyes never strayed from him. He handed her a sketch on notebook paper folded in his pocket. It was a wildly convoluted concept for some sculpture he hoped to build, when he had a better place to work. "I want to see if I'm only copying a Boccioni I remember. Boccioni was a sculptor, a Futurist—"

"How fascinating!" She studied the drawing, and then him, as if she'd found a diamond. "That specific movement focused on twentieth century technology, did it not? It was the first significant step toward total reverence for the machine age?"

He could only gaze at her with complete and instant adoration. No one had ever understood or shared his obscure passion, before. "Did you ever want to *be* somebody," he asked slowly, "and suddenly you figured out *who?*" She caught her breath then nodded. "I'm good for a cup of coffee and a sandwich," he went on gruffly. "If you got some time."

"Oh, *yes.*" She met him after work that day. Ten years had passed since then, and they'd always been together. She would always have faith in him, and in the ideals they treasured.

Standing below the window of their apartment ten years later, Richard looked up at her and thought, *She could've done a lot better than marrying me.* He loved her because she believed she *had* done better by marrying him.

Perched between her and Quentin on the window sill, the plaster copy of Picasso's Head of a Woman gazed down at him, too. Angele had given it to him for a birthday, years ago. *Head, heart, soul and dreams,* she wrote on the card. *All yours. You're the only man I know who understands the gift.*

He lifted a hand and gestured for Quentin to come downstairs. He and Angele had agreed on this plan to give Quentin some time alone with him. Quentin disappeared from the window like a shot. Richard continued to hold Angele's devoted gaze. Ten years of love, marriage and impossible dreams—a collision of his streetwise world and her genteel one—posed on slivers of iron and steel.

Quentin popped out of the apartment building's heavy front doors and raced down the steps of its concrete stoop, then jerked to a stop and made an obvious effort to compose himself. "Papa, I'm ready," he said firmly. "I've been reading about the Roman Caesars. When they went off to war their kids lined up and gave them gifts." He reached under his pullover sweater and retrieved a packet of postcards he'd made from index cards. Each was already addressed to Mr. Quentin Riconni, and bore a stamp. On the opposite side of each card, he'd pasted headlines from the newspaper. *Surveyor Satellite Finds Safe Home On Moon. War Protesters Say Bring Soldiers Home. Star Trek TV Show Voyages Far From Home.*

"So you can write to me. And to remind you of home," Quentin said, holding out the cards.

Richard took them reverently. "These are great. Just great." He admired them for a moment while waiting for the tightness in his throat to relax. "Come on, let's sit in the truck for our man-to-man talk."

They climbed inside and shut the doors. Richard carefully laid the cards on the cracked vinyl seat, then lit a cigarette and hung one hand out the open window, watching the cool spring air carry the smoke. "I want you to know which bad guys to look out for. You see that guy down there on the next block? The one hanging around that old yellow van?"

"Yes, sir."

"He's a junkie. Sells drugs. He's new around here, but I think he's not the only one."

"I won't talk to him."

"What if he talks to you, first?"

"I'll ignore him, just like Mother says to do when kids make fun of me for going to St. Vincents. I use my brains, not my fists. I've got a good mind, so I don't need to have a big mouth." He recited his mother's litanies dutifully.

"What if the junkie keeps trying to talk to you? What if he tries to give you some drugs? What if he says something he shouldn't say to your mother?" Richard looked at him grimly, and waited. Quentin hesitated, but not from lack of confidence. The kid was brilliant, a real student, and thanks to Angele he was never going to have to work in a garage or worry about money. He'd be somebody slick, maybe a doctor or a lawyer. He'd have a title and letters after his name.

If he survived the neighborhood. Richard had to make certain he did. Richard watched him and thought worriedly, *Me and Angele have put the kid between a rock and a hard place. We teach him different things. He's confused.* Quentin sat silently, still thinking.

"Don't tell me what your Mother wants to hear," Richard ordered. "Tell me what *I* wanna hear. What are you gonna do to that junkie if he gets in your face?"

Quentin exhaled. His eyes narrowed and he smiled. "I'm gonna punch him in the balls."

"That's right. Then you go tell Alfonse Esposito, and he'll have the bastard arrested." Alfonse, a good neighbor, was a New York police detective. "Same rule goes for anybody who causes you and your ma trouble. Like Frank Siccone. He's a goddamned loan shark and his kids are thieves. Don't take any shit off them. *Capice?*"

"*Capice.*" Quentin nodded, and Richard watched him lift a hand to his chin. He suspected he'd been walloped a few times already by Siccone's son, Johnny, who was older and bigger.

Richard grunted. "Your ma wants you to be a good altar boy who doesn't fight and talk trash. I know you try. You talk good, you study, you're really smart. I'm real proud of you. You keep acting the way she wants you to act, anytime you're around her. 'Cause she's right. You're gonna be somebody, someday." Richard leaned toward him. "But when you're out here—" he jabbed a blunt, fight-scarred hand toward the street—"you act like me, okay? You talk like your old man, you fight like your old man, and you make sure people know they can't mess with you—or with your ma. 'Cause these punks out here don't care if you can speak Latin. They don't care how smart you are. They don't give a goddamn what the Roman Caesars did. And hey, I know they give you a lot of grief over your school uniform and the tie you gotta wear, and all that. I figured."

"Aw, they're just a bunch of dumb *schmucks*," Quentin assured him, with great disdain. "That's what Mrs. Silberstein says."

"Yeah, but you let them take advantage of you, and one day they'll kill you."

Quentin straightened proudly. "They won't mess with *me*," he vowed. "And they won't kill me. And I'll take care of Ma. I swear."

Richard grabbed him and pulled him into a deep hug. They clung together for a long moment, then he kissed his son's dark hair and pushed him away. "You be the worst ass-kicker on the block, all right? And the best student. And I'll see you every other weekend. I'm getting a phone put in, so you can call me if you need me."

"*Capice.*"

"Here. I'm no Roman emperor, but I got a gift for you." He pulled a slender, gleaming object from the pocket of his wool jacket, then held it out. Quentin whistled under his breath. He gingerly picked up the long silver handle, thumbed a clasp on one side, and flicked a long, stiletto blade into place. "This beats my pocket knife all to heck," he whispered. "Thank you, Papa."

"Tell me how you use it."

"Never pull it out for fun, 'cause it's not a toy. Never show it to Father Aleksandr. Or to Ma. Never cut some guy unless he tries to hurt me, first."

Richard nodded. Quentin slowly folded the deadly blade and slipped it inside his jacket. He looked up at his father with pale misery and a clamped mouth. It was time to say goodbye. "Do you have to go way up there to work?" he asked. "It's almost in Canada."

"Yeah, I gotta go. It's a free place, it's big enough, and I got the money from the bear sculpture to finally get me started. Your old man's not a bum. No matter what it takes, I'm gonna make you proud."

"I'm already proud."

He ruffled Quentin's hair. "You're a good kid," he said in a gruff tone. "Now gimme a line or two of Latin then get the hell out of here and go upstairs. Be the man of the house for your ma, okay?"

Quentin got out of the truck, shut the door, then leaned against the passenger window. He took several deep breaths, and Richard saw painfully that he was disciplining himself not to cry. *The kid will be all right*, he prayed, *if he can just walk the line between soft-hearted ideas and cold-blooded facts.*

"Ars longa," Quentin said, finally. "Vita brevis." *Art is long. Life is short.*

Richard smiled. "Okay, smart guy. What's that mean?"

"I want you to live forever," Quentin said gruffly, then turned and walked away before the tears showed.

2

Dozens of Mountain State students (and more than a few upstanding alumni) made midnight efforts to burn, cut up, or deface the Iron Bear, but it stood inviolable and dignified, four paws firmly on the earth, in a place of besmirched honor on a circular brick patio between the daffodil bed and the azalea hedges of the administration building.

The Tibers' loathing of the sculpture grew stronger each year. A disgruntled employee at the Tiber plant would snipe at Mr. John, *Go stick your pecker up your Iron Bear*, on his way out the door. A chicken farmer who had been shorted on hatchlings might mutter, *If that ain't a double dose of Bear balls*. A catty friend at the country club could be overheard saying, *My house might not be as fine as the Tibers', but at least I know the difference between art and scrap metal*.

I often sat in the sculpture's shadow while Daddy scraped graffiti off it. He taught me that life was a work of art we build on crudely welded turning points and hopeful imagination. He said every birth, every death, every joy, and every heartache shaped our destinies from thin air, while we were busy pretending we were in charge of our own construction.

"The world is full of ordinary riches," he said as he cleaned and painted his beloved Bear. "There's nothin' money can buy for you if you aren't happy. Better to do without it."

We did without.

Daddy didn't care about money, and as long as he could make enough for our basic needs and the mortgage payments on his chicken houses he gladly gave the rest to neighbors with even less than us. Mama didn't have any use for money and comfort, either. Her soft brown hair hung in a braid to her knees, she wore no makeup around large eyes the color of a new green leaf, and she was always scented with fresh cornbread and talcum powder, her only perfume. She'd been raised in a family of snake-handling, faith-healing tent evangelists from the hot swamps of south Georgia, followers of a small fundamentalist sect so strict in their avoidance of the modern world that they made Luddites look soft.

She met Daddy during her family's traveling revival show, which set up at the state campground on the outskirts of town one summer. He grew outraged during a sermon when her parents held out a box to her, filled with rattlesnakes. Mama had just turned sixteen. In their eyes it was time for her to test her faith. Daddy watched her put her shaking hand in the box. She didn't make a sound when a snake bit her on the finger, but Daddy yelled.

He pushed his way to the pulpit, grabbed her in his arms, and rushed her to the county hospital with her whole furious family in hot pursuit. He stood off her murderous, faith-healing kin until Mama woozily admitted she wanted a doctor to treat her. Regardless of being a lost soul, she wanted to live. Her family disowned her on the spot. She married Daddy a week later at the county courthouse, but she vowed never to set foot in a hospital, again. She had to honor her lost heritage as much as she could.

She not only didn't care about money, she distrusted the slightest hint of greed as an evil worthy of Satan's worst demons. "Hold one end of this here dollar bill," she said to me when I was five years old. I held the paper's edges, wide-eyed. "Hold on tight! Shut your eyes."

"They're shut! I'm holding on, Mama!"

"Feel the pull on the other end?" She was doing the pulling, but under the spell of her drama I didn't notice.

"Yes!" I was hypnotized.

"That's Satan!"

I dropped the bill, stared at it in horror, and refused to pick it back up. "He can have it!"

Mama nodded proudly. "The harder you hold onto money, girl, the harder him and his demons pull. And they'll pull until they suck you down to the fires of hell with them." I didn't touch cash money for years after that.

Tibers, she said, were to be pitied; their lust for money and acclaim doomed them. They tempted the devil every day with their fine homes and luxuries. "Their good works are naught but ashes," Mama insisted, "because they cain't beat down the sin of pride, and no gift is godly if'n it's give with a reward in mind."

It was true that Tibers branded everything they built for the town with their name, and the walls of Mr. John's office at Tiber Poultry were crowded with plaques and certificates praising his charitable work. But it was also true that Mama had come from people so downtrodden that they used religion like an opiate to dull the pain. I didn't feel poor, and so none of this made any difference to me.

I had the most incredible home in the universe. Our farm house, barn, pastures, and outbuildings sat at the end of a trail so ancient that

I found arrow heads along it far older than any Cherokee had left there. Before the settlers hunted them to distraction, bears had wintered in the farm's impenetrable creek bottoms and inviting granite caves. I could scoot under rock overhangs and crouch in an imagined cloak of fur and claws, the ruler of every wild soul.

Including me. There were many untamed places both inside and out where children have to find their way, alone.

*

There was no kindergarten in Tiberville when I was a child, no pre-school or daycare centers sporting candy-colored playground equipment built of pliable plastics with rounded edges. Daddy began dropping me off at the community center playground behind the Tiber Poultry plant one day a week. There I rampaged happily with about three-dozen other five-year-olds, risking my life on the sharp metal swings and steep metal slides.

This glorious weekly event, called Little Citizens Playtime, was created and sponsored by Tiber Poultry, which provided cookies, punch, and indoctrination. Little Citizens Playtime was designed to lure the most isolated farm families into the civilized world of town, where their children could be brainwashed into believing that Tibers were benevolent and progressive employers.

I suppose John Tiber insisted that his five-year-old daughter Janine attend Little Citizens Playtme because he wanted everyone to believe that Tibers, despite their virtual control over the town, were just ordinary folks. But Janine already understood her place in the world. She was a princess of poultry. The rest of us were mere peckers.

She wore beautiful jumpers and playsuits, her blonde hair was swept back in perfect ponytails, and she screeched when the least speck of grime dusted her ruffled socks. She snatched anything she wanted—a cookie, a place in line at the swing sets, or another child's toy. "Mine," she'd say firmly, and shove the victim out of her way.

I tried not to notice her. Pitiful, doomed sinner, that's what she was. I was better than her, more righteous. When the ladies handed out packets of jelly beans—my favorite food in the world—I gave mine away, elevated by a vow of poverty, self-sacrifice, and a meandering hope that god would be so impressed he'd give me more jelly beans. It didn't happen.

At first Janine seemed to sense that I was someone to leave alone. I was a tall and strongly built child, with muscles already honed by hours spent helping Mama and Daddy shovel out the chicken houses. But Janine was fast, small and shrewd, so when she finally moved in on me one day, she was able to snatch the one belonging that no one should ever try to pry out of my possession. My *Twas The Night Before Christmas* book. The little hardcover book of the classic poem had been a gift from Daddy on Christmas Eve. I'd already memorized the entire poem. Christmas was six months past, but I carried the book everywhere.

"Mine," she hissed, then grabbed my book and ran. I chased her to the door of the community house, where she darted inside. Her mother, John's elegant Atlanta-socialite wife, Audrey Tiber, stopped me from entering. "Now, now," Mrs. Tiber cooed, waving a diamond-backed hand holding a long cigarette, "you stay out in the yard. You're too dirty to come inside."

"Janine took my book, ma'am." I said.

"Well, I'm sure she'll bring it back." She shut the door.

I waited urgently near the swing sets, my mind a silent, seething volcano. I was surrounded by a hubbub of unsuspecting children at play, none of whom realized they were future Tiber contract farmers and plant workers. That was my destiny, too, or so the Tibers believed. My stomach knotted in fury and anxiety. My book. My beloved book. Books were sacred. Daddy said so. Finally, Janine wandered back outdoors. My book was nowhere in sight. "Where's my book?" I demanded in a low voice.

"It's mine," she said, and flounced away.

I went blind with vengeance. I pulled back a heavy metal swing as far as I could, and let it go. It caught her in the back of the head, knocked her down, and *knocked her out.* I ran over and stared down at her. She didn't move for a few seconds. Blood stained the blonde hair beneath her ponytail. *Not a creature was stirring,* I thought, petrified. *Not even a Tiber.*

I'd given Janine a concussion and put a gash in her head that required ten stitches. Mrs. Tiber permanently banned me from Little Citizens Playtime. In the midst of the hysteria and accusations that were hurled at me that afternoon I earned a reputation as a stubborn, tearless, unremorseful soldier for literary justice, although in fact I was just so worried I could barely speak.

But far worse than anything else was the way Mrs. Tiber humiliated my father when he arrived. "Tom Powell," she lectured, "If you know what side your bread's buttered on you'll teach your child to behave. A measure of goodwill and gracious manners is little enough to ask from employees of my husband's business."

"Ma'am," he said in his deep, raw-cream, mountain voice, "I'm sorry for my daughter's choice of methods."

"That's an excuse, not an apology!"

"All I can grant you is the *unbuttered* side of my bread, Ma'am."

"I'll have your grower contract canceled, mister. We'll just see how you feel when you can't pay your bills and the sheriff comes out to take your farm!"

"There's no need for that kind of talk, Mrs. Tiber," Daddy replied calmly, but I remember the worried look in his eyes and the way he held his sweat-stained straw hat in his hands, as if he were standing before a judge. And I knew I would never, *never* again commit an act that might put him at the mercy of a Tiber, again.

On the way home in his truck, I burst into tears. "Here, now, you didn't do anything so bad," he said gently, not understanding at all. "Let's go over to campus and talk to the Bear."

The sculpture was his inspiration in all times of trouble. That day its pot-headed face was smeared with a sickly spray of purple paint, and someone had hung a dead mouse from its behind. Daddy tossed the mouse carcass aside, and we sat down on the administration building's lawn beside the Bear's feet. "You think the Bear's ashamed of itself for looking this way?"

"I don't know."

"It knows what it's made of. Nobody can change that." Maybe he did suspect that I'd seen him humbled. Daddy lit one of the cigarettes he carried in a soft leather sack tucked in his shirt pocket. He smoked contentedly, as if sharing a peace pipe with the sculpture. "On the inside, it's fine."

I stared up at the hulking creation. I could imagine the sculpture coming to life and lumbering down the roads toward Tiber Crest, the large white-columned home where Janine lived. I pictured it eating her in one squeaking, rattling gulp. After a moment spent savoring that sinful fantasy, I took my father's hand. "I'm going to hell," I said.

He smiled. "No, you're not. The Bear's says you're righteous."

"You really think it can talk?"

"Sure. But it says there's power in silence and power in *stillness*. The power of keeping your own thoughts, and walking your own path. The Bear doesn't talk to us the way you think. It tells us ideas we're too stubborn to believe. The Bear won't put up with ignorance."

New tears stung my eyes. I hid them from Daddy and silently asked the Bear a question. *Tell me how I can make people proud of us.* There was no answer, or at least none I was ready to hear.

22

Later he asked Mr. John about my book, and it turned out that Janine's mother had *thrown it away*. Mr. John didn't offer to replace it, either, because his wife had yelled at him for making their daughter play with white trash, and she had stormed off to her mother's house in Atlanta after he refused to cancel Daddy's broiler contract.

"I just wanted my book back," I told Mama. "It's not fair."

She fixed her stern green eyes on me as she kneaded biscuit dough in a wooden bowl. Her strong hands worked the soft dough with an unerring determination, just as she worked my soul. "The Lord is teachin' you a lesson about want and need, girl. You ain't lost your book—it's still in your head. It don't matter that Janine Tiber's got hold of its body, because you've still got a-hold of its spirit. Nobody can take that away from you. If you give your heart to physical belongin's you will always be worryin' about them and hatin' somebody for messin' with them."

"Yes, ma'am," I said dully. Her lesson was hard to swallow. A person had to be raised in hopeless submission to believe that martyrdom was a substitute for justice. Rationalized acceptance of oppression was the meek way out. I wasn't a pacifist.

Janine Tiber was a speck of rough gravel who would remain stuck in my craw, seeding layers of unfulfilled revenge. She went out of her way to say hateful things, and do hateful things, to me, which I tolerated with the sly patience of a hibernating flesh-eater. But I came into an understanding of my low place in the world of people like Janine Tiber, and there were days when I was miserably convinced that whole world sniffed the chicken shit of poverty on me.

I formed a shield of bony attitude. Badly camouflaged by hair that exploded in energized curls, a serious face with a clamped jaw, and blue eyes that were always narrowed in a shrewd squint, I quietly made plans to conquer my fate. I took heart in the fact that I was a small hero to every poor kid Janine had victimized, and that buoyed me to keep trying.

My reputation as a Powell had begun, a fact of no small consequence in Tiber County. Powell notoriety stretched back across the generations like a rubber band. One snap and the old stories returned to people's tongues.

It started with a Welshman and a mule.

*

In 1847 Erim Powell walked off a ship from Wales, traded a book of his poetry for an elderly mule, then headed inland from the Georgia coast. A month later, using up a last, large dollop of his good luck in a card game, he won a hundred acres of land in the mountains above Atlanta. In the old country he'd earned his living as a schoolteacher, but preferred writing poetry. Yet he dreamed of prospering in the American wilderness. Of owning land.

He rode the mule to a mountain crossroads, where the Tiber family and their slaves had already built several large cabins and a general store. The Tibers were well-educated gentry, from long-established English Tiber clans in South Carolina. Already they'd begun busily lining off streets and lots.

The mule collapsed and died. Erim walked the last five miles to his land, following a trail that for centuries had led bears to their winter sanctuaries. Not being a farmer, he didn't mind that most of his property was dotted with caves, hooded in craggy, laurel-shrouded hillsides, or consumed by tiny glens where blackberries grew in tall, thorny thickets every summer.

The Tibers could have their civilized town; Erim named his kingdom Bear Creek. Who can say whether fate or poetic justice had brought him there to begin our American dynasty?

Sometimes, it's just a matter of where the mule dies.

*

Our first real trouble with Tibers came within a year of Erim's arrival in Tiber County, when Erim seduced their cook. Her name was Annie Walker. She was three-quarters Irish and one-quarter Cherokee Indian, and had been trained in the culinary arts by a Frenchwoman from elegant coastal Savannah. Annie's frontiersmen brothers kept the Tibers from hanging Erim when he married her.

Undaunted, Erim and Annie built a homestead. He made and sold superlative corn whiskey, wrote dozens of epic poems that somehow didn't survive on paper, then set up a log schoolhouse and began educating every child and adult who wanted to learn to read and cipher. Anyone could come—white, black, slave or free, and the few mixed-blood Cherokee natives, such as Annie's family, who had managed to hang on after the government removal in the 1830's.

Again, the Tibers were unhappy with him. They had brought with them a slave named Daniel Washington, and his family. Daniel was a skilled blacksmith, and therefore commanded a certain respect. Slaves easily disappeared into the mountains and could never be found, the Tibers had already discovered. To make certain Daniel remained happy they allowed him to set up his own forge and keep the money he earned. Daniel promptly bought land beside the Powell farm at Bear Creek.

Erim and Annie welcomed the Washingtons, and Erim secretly taught Daniel's children to read. The Tibers, who probably suspected that Erim was a provocative influence, quickly started the private Tiberville Academy in town, and allowed Daniel's children to be taught there—a stunning compromise. That academy later became Mountain State College.

Erim and Annie birthed five babies, one of whom wandered away as a boy and was never found. For years after that Annie and Erim carved heartfelt messages into trees throughout the Powell homestead, as if their lost son might still be trying to find his way back. Sitting in our living room was a section of trunk Grandpa Joshua had cut from the last surviving messenger. *Dear boy we are waiting*, it said.

Around 1900, when she was an old woman of at least seventy, Annie disappeared, herself. A group of Oklahoma Cherokees were passing through town on their way to a reunion on the North Carolina reservation, so maybe she went with them, since she had kin on the reservation. Or maybe she went for one of her long, tree-carving walks and collapsed in some hollow, or stumbled over a cliff.

Erim, heartbroken, insisted he knew the truth. She'd turned into a mother bear. Annie came from the Cherokee bear clan, and considered the bears sacred. Hadn't she made him and their children promise years ago that no Powell would ever hunt them? So she'd transformed herself before his eyes and disappeared into the blackberry thickets of Bear Creek, where she would watch over all the Powell children to come, always searching for her own lost boy.

Erim's penchant for storytelling helped establish this news all over the county. The Tibers said, *Oh well, you know how a Welshman sees things when he drinks*. Bear or wife, Annie never came back. After Erim died, a joking account of his tale was chronicled in the Tiberville Weekly News as part of a history column titled Old Ways and Crazy Days. The columns were eventually collected, along with other disrespectful tall tales about Powells and other mountain families the townsfolk thought of as quaint, and the Tibers published a book in the 1930's. The book had been sold in local shops ever since, a matter of insult that no Powell would forget.

*

Bethina Grace Powell Tiber was Erim and Annie's youngest daughter. By Powell family accounts she was strong, smart, and beautiful, and had been driven to despair by a Tiber husband who beat her and dragged her by her auburn Powell hair down the hall of their big Elm Street Victorian. By Tiber accounts she was shrewd, conniving, and a social-climbing harlot. Whatever the truth, she was her mother's daughter, an adventurer looking for a lost soul, and the soul happened to be her own.

Bethina Grace turned 41 years old in 1910, when she packed her bags, climbed on a passenger train, and left town, deserting her Tiber husband, who was president of the Tiber County Bank, and their half-grown children, including Miss Betty, who remembered her kindly, nonetheless. The Tibers hired detectives to track her down. Those investigators discovered that she had gone to Brazil with a man, and the man was one of our own—Nathan Washington, Daniel Washington's eldest grandson. A black man, of course.

He and Bethina Grace had grown up a short walk away from each other at Bear Creek, playing together as children, probably in love with each other as teenagers, but knowing that love was hopeless. Nathan left home for Cuba as a young man and became a sea captain, but never forgot her, or her, him, obviously.

The uproar that followed word of this scandal roused the Klan and brought misery on the whole county for several years. Crosses were burned at Bear Creek, the school house Erim had built went up in flames, the Washington's lost a teenage boy to a lynch mob, and the shunning of Powells became a Tiber family tradition.

Powells did not prosper, after that. Only the toughest and most stubborn stayed to carry on, and there wasn't much to draw the rest back.

*

As time went by, Miss Betty was the only Tiber who refused to blame us for her Powell mother running away with black Nathan Washington. Tall and stocky, with ruddy skin, red hair and a laugh like a clarinet, Miss Betty did not look like a prophet, but she knew the depths of human misery, and she did not want to see such misery visited on any other soul.

In her younger years she had led a reasonably ordinary Tiberville life—attending the Young Women's Academy at the college, taking a graduation voyage to England, bringing home an English veterinarian she'd married during the long sea trip back. He started the Tiber poultry business, and together he and Miss Betty hatched a house full of children.

But in the summer of 1928 he died from polio, along with three of their daughters. Heartbroken, Miss Betty embarked on a crusade to protect the rest of her brood and every child in Tiber County. She chaired the mountain volunteer health society and she built a polio clinic in town, so that local victims would not have to be shipped away for treatment. She drove the rutted country roads distributing hygiene and prevention pamphlets to every family, and read the pamphlets to those who were illiterate. She had the local swimming ponds drained or fenced off, and she formed a chapter of the March of Dimes.

All of those were reasonable civic actions, in light of her loss and the desperate situation in general. But she also stopped going to church, began studying Buddhism and other eastern religions, brought in a Cherokee shaman from North Carolina to hang protective talismans all over her house, consulted numerous psychics and palm readers, and engaged in various and sundry other worrisome rituals to ward off the cycles of epidemic death and fear that possessed Tiberville and the entire county. She became an embarrassment to the Tibers. She had gone funny. *It's the Powell in her,* they said.

By the time Daddy was born in 1940 her reputation for oddity had become the stuff of local legend. She firmly believed that her potent combination of science, faith, and outright magic had saved Tiber County from a plague of biblical proportions. After all, the county had the lowest polio rates in the south, and the disease had not dared strike her family in a generation. She had raised two healthy sons and many healthy, growing grandchildren, including her favorite, John.

Despite the disapproval of Tiber relatives who would just as soon the last few Powells fell off the county map, Miss Betty took Daddy along during her and John's regular car tours of the county, and so he and his cousin grew up sharing the front seat of a dusty Cadillac and helping Miss Betty collect March of Dimes money.

The summer of 1953 was hot and steamy, the land seeming to shrink from the sun. Dogs hid under cool porches, deer retreated to the deepest coves, flower beds shriveled, young chickens suffocated by the thousands. Daddy's gentle father, Joshua, who taught high school English, and his younger brothers, Davy and Albert, came down with polio, and all three died. A month later, both Daddy and John Tiber became feverish, as well.

Miss Betty and Daddy's mother, Mary, waited in agony to see whether the teenagers would recuperate or sink into fatal paralysis. Miss Betty drove to the farm and walked down to the creek bottoms.

She had played at Bear Creek as a little girl, roaming the laurel thickets with her Powell cousins and the neighboring Washington children until her mother's infamy exploded in their lives.

She knew the legend of Granny Annie's restless ghost-spirit. "I'm searching for help in the spirit world," she told Mary. "If Granny Annie really is roaming around down there, I intend to ask her for protection. It was said she would always look after our children. She didn't save my girls and she didn't save your Davy and Albert, so she must have some quarrel with us. I intend to find out."

"Well, all right," Mary said carefully, because she was afraid of Miss Betty. "I'll make some iced tea while you talk to the ghost."

An hour later Betty staggered back up the hill waving her arms and shouting. Her face was flushed with excitement, her graying hair, wild. Briars and leaves clung to her dress and nylon stockings as if she'd been magnetized. "Our boys will live," she told Mary. "I've seen the bear spirit! Granny Annie spoke to me! Tommy and Johnny are going to be all right! And there's a cure for polio coming soon! I've promised to honor the bears, you see! We have to bring the bears back to Bear Creek, Mary! The curse is over, Mary!"

She was right. Within a week, Daddy and John Tiber were well. But there are other kinds of curses, and my poor future father, who was only thirteen, would have to live with them. Miss Betty wanted to keep him in school and eventually send him to college to study art, but my proudful grandmother said no. He was the man of the family, now, so he would have to work. There were bills to pay.

Miss Betty reluctantly co-signed a bank loan so Mary could build two chicken houses at Bear Creek, and got her a grower's contract. Tiber Poultry supplied the chicks, their feed, and medicine. The farmer supplied the chicken houses and the unending, back-breaking work. After mortgage payments and general expenses, a year's income would barely pay a family's bills. Daddy and his mother became two more Tiber indentured servants, shackled to a mortgage and a long-term broiler deal.

A few weeks later, Daddy painted his first artwork—bears trapped in circus cages—on the side of a chicken house. Grandmother painted over them and whipped him as if he'd lost his mind. He painted the bears again. She whipped him, again. He couldn't help himself—his grief, his frustration, were too great. The third time he painted the bears, she realized that he wouldn't survive without decorating the grim future he'd been handed.

Within a year, the Salk and Saben vaccines began to eradicate polio, just as Granny Annie had promised. Miss Betty began a full scale campaign to restore the hunted-out bear population to Tiber County. For more than a decade she hired men to capture bears higher in the mountains and turn them loose in our midst, to the absolute horror of her family and most other citizens. Daddy became her stalwart young assistant, putting out corn for the newcomer bears when the winters were hard, and trying to ward off hunters, to no avail. The bears were quietly killed or driven off, often under the discreet direction of Miss Betty's own relatives, including Mr. John. With every passing year Miss Betty and Daddy grew more disgusted and despairing of ever fulfilling their mission.

But then they got the idea for a sculpture. In a booklet published by the national office of the March of Dimes, they discovered a short article about charity volunteers from other parts of the country. One of those volunteers was Richard Riconni. He'd recently donated a modern art sculpture to a charity auction. He'd made it from the leg braces of polio victims. The sculpture, tellingly, was not described in anything but the vaguest and most diplomatic terms, with no account of how much it sold for, or if it sold at all. But when Daddy showed Betty the pamphlet, he and she both lit up with inspiration. She wrote to Richard Riconni about her ideas for a bear sculpture. She wanted to place it on the campus of Mountain State College.

"I wish to celebrate the victory of science and technology over ignorance and fear," she wrote. "I wish to celebrate our oneness with Mother Nature, and thus pay tender homage to the grand black bear who watches over us all. I want to make people THINK. And I intend that there will be at least one bear in this county that no one can EVER get rid of."

Richard Riconni wrote back excitedly. "I've been waiting for a chance like this all my life." Soon Daddy and Miss Betty sent him a freight car filled with local junk and iron lungs.

"That's the Powell in her," her Tiber relatives said darkly, when they learned what Betty had done.

The rest was history, just waiting to catch up with us.

3

Quentin's mother almost never raised her voice, but when the scores were announced in the structural design category of the Junior Regional Engineering Competition, she shrieked. Then she cupped her hands around her mouth and yelled like a dockworker across the crowded floor of the Boston convention center. "He won! Father Aleksandr, Quentin won!"

Father Aleksandr hustled outside the hall to the men's room, where Quentin had just finished washing his face and rinsing his mouth at a sink. "Quintus the Magnificent, aren't you done throwing up?" the cheerful Polish priest joked in a thick accent, pulling a packet of tissues from his black trousers. "Hurry up! *Carpe diem!*"

Quentin wiped his mouth with the proffered tissue then asked hoarsely, "Who won?"

Father Aleksandr chortled. "You did!" Quentin yelled in amazement. The priest grabbed him by one arm and they ran back to the huge hall, where high school students from all over the northeast were gathered with their projects. Now thirteen, he was almost six feet tall, a heartbreaker with long-lashed gray eyes, dark, almost black hair, and fine, golden skin marred only by two fine scars from fist fights, one that bisected the edge of his lower lip, and another at the bridge of his nose. He had already begun to develop his father's lean-hipped, broad-shoulder physique, and he played football for St. Vincent's.

Mother threw her arms around him and they posed for pictures beside a gleaming steel model of the expansion bridge he'd designed. "We have to call Papa!" Quentin said.

"No you don't," his father said, behind him. "I made it."

Quentin spun around in surprise and saw his father standing there grinning at him, his coat dripping melted snow, his dark hair flecked with ice. The truck had broken down a mile away, and he'd walked. He and Quentin grabbed each other in a brawny hug, his father slapping his back joyfully. Quentin had spent all of Christmas break at the warehouse with him, building the contest model under his father's careful supervision. In a sense, it was a shared victory.

When the officials handed Quentin a trophy, a certificate, and a check for a thousand dollars he stared at the check, his heart pounding so hard that he could barely believe it. Mother had said that any money he won would go straight into his college fund, but he desperately wished he could buy presents for her and his father. Just knowing that he could was a rare satisfaction.

He had been the youngest competitor to make the region finals. No one but them had expected him to win. "My two geniuses," Mother said proudly, with one arm around him and the other around his father.

"Yeah, he's got his old man's talent with metal," Papa added, and looked at Quentin with joy.

Quentin nodded and hugged him, again. He would remember that night as one of the few truly happy moments he shared with his father.

*

Life was not going as Papa had planned. Six years after leaving home he still commuted from upstate New York, spending an average of only four days a month at the apartment in Brooklyn. His sculptures sold barely enough to pay his expenses, and often didn't. "It's just a matter of time," Angele insisted. But there had not been another triumph like the bear sculpture.

"Dreamers," their blue-collar neighbors said of Quentin's parents. "What do they think they'll accomplish?"

"Ars gratia artis," Quentin said grimly, in return. Art for the sake of art alone. He had learned to speak up but to speak softly, never giving his emotions away. He had very little trouble with the bullies in his neighborhood, now. He'd put his knife to Johnny Siccone's throat one night and warned in a low, clear tone that he would slit it from ear to ear if Johnny ever fucked with him, again.

Johnny left him alone, after that.

With every passing year Quentin was growing more like his father—quieter, less patient, his eyes more intense, his moods bleaker. Without Papa's income at the garage, life in the apartment veered from one money crisis to the next. Mother never let Papa know, and he thought she was managing. *Nil desperandum*, she scribbled on a bill folder Quentin happened to see. Never give up hope.

"I can get a job delivering groceries after school," Quentin told her. "And I bet Goots would hire me to sweep floors and clean paint filters." Quentin didn't add that Goots had already told him he could have a job at his *other* garage when he was a little older, if he wanted it. Mother didn't know Goots ran a chop shop in the basement of an old building a few blocks over. When Quentin thanked him but turned down the chop shop offer, the big German shook his head sadly and said, "Your papa always turned me down for that work, too. He could have made such good money working with, hmmm, *used* cars! What do you Riconnis expect? A miracle?"

Quentin had laughed and said nothing. Yet his family did need a miracle.

"I could sweep floors for Goots," he repeated.

Angele shook her head firmly. "Your job is to be the finest student possible. Your job is to earn a full scholarship to an excellent college."

"I can do that and still sweep floors or deliver groceries."

"No. We can make do with the money we have. We *can't* make do with half-measures when it comes to your education." He looked at her mournfully, but she didn't waver.

At every opportunity he secluded himself in his bedroom, at a desk Papa had made for him out of corrugated steel roofing with slender legs of corroded rebar. He wrote in his journal, rubbed his hand on himself and fantasized about dark-haired, teasing Carla Esposito, who was a budding sexpot. Carla's mother had died when Carla was small, leaving Carla to design her own role model for womanhood. In Carla's world, most men and boys were just like her doting, widowed father, Alfonse. They could be wrapped around her little finger at will.

She kept luring Quentin over to her brownstone when Alfonse worked late at the precinct, and Quentin didn't put up much resistance. Yet when Carla had him and herself half-naked in her frilly bedroom, he suddenly said, *We can't do this, yet,* and got up. She was a year younger than him, only 12. He felt courageous for his self-control. She flung a fit and called him *queer,* but apologized later and admitted she had been afraid her father would kill them both. Quentin had thought about that, too. And what his mother would do.

He told himself he was a *man,* with all the noble connotations of the word. A man had to control himself around women. No matter how crude or rough Papa behaved in the company of other men, Quentin had never seen him treat women with anything less than gallant concern.

So Quentin channeled his energies into school and books, contemplating heroic futures, reading constantly, but also sharpening the switchblade his father had given him. He lived with a gnawing worry that his family was in danger from forces he couldn't predict or even describe. Papa's moods and struggles formed a vague, dark cloud, always promising rain.

In a box under his bed were old toys his father had made for him years earlier— rattling monsters of steel wire, nuts, and bolts; take-apart cars with small pulleys for wheels, and dozens of intricate building blocks in fantastic shapes and forms, all made of pipe, big brass washers, and other odds and ends Papa had scavenged from the dumpster of a machine shop.

This uneven metal world clanked and shifted and refused to stay in one place, just like the real world. Quentin got out the building blocks sometimes and tried, to no avail, to build even one thing that wouldn't fall down when he turned his back.

Yet, like his father, the ability to see patterns and discern hidden structures came instinctively to him. As a child he'd pried apart his wobbling nightstand and glued it back together. When it no longer wobbled, Mother thought his bedroom floor had settled. While Quentin watched in strangled amusement, she checked all the baseboards worriedly. "Oh, you," she said proudly, when he confessed. "You're a born builder. I'm just sure."

He announced he would become an architect, and his mother looked at him without a shred of doubt. "A *master* architect," she corrected. As his need for order grew stronger he studied each piece of the metal contraptions endlessly, as if playing chess with strange pieces. One wrong move might send the whole game tumbling—his whole life, out of control.

Don't let it fall, Quentin prayed silently.

*

"Hey, Riconni!" Meyer Bratlemater yelled with a grin of cruel delight on his scrawny face. Meyer was the kind of pipsqueak who lobbed taunts from a distance, then scurried away. "Your old man better sell some freakin' art pretty soon, 'cause you got kicked outta your apartment!" Meyer ducked inside the door of his parents' bakery.

Quentin had just rounded the corner of the street in front of that bakery. He had been at the library studying, and was carrying an armload of books home for a physics test. He looked down the street and saw with horror that Meyer hadn't lied, the annoying little prick. Piled on the sidewalk in front of the apartment's stoop was a small mountain of Riconni possessions—furniture, Papa's table sculptures, clothes, Mother's books, pots and pans, and so much more—spilling into the street like garbage.

He broke into a run, tossing his books onto a bin of apples outside a grocery he passed, dodging people going about their afternoon business on the crowded sidewalk. Those people drew aside, clutched their belongings, looking around hurriedly for a policeman. He was fifteen years old now, more a grown man than a boy, muscled and tall. The look on his face frightened them.

Mrs. Silberstein, old and plump and dressed in a bright flower-print housedress with soup stains on her apron, stood guard over the belongings, using a closed black umbrella as a weapon. Mother had done a thousand kindnesses for the elderly woman, looking in on her when she was ill, bringing her food, running errands. Quentin had often helped. Mrs. Silberstein was the closest semblance to a grandmother he had.

"Get back, get back!" she shouted at a trio of brawny young men. They grinned at her and darted their hands out, as if dueling. "How dare you?" she told them. "I'll whack you if you break anything else!" Papa's plaster copy of the Picasso *Head of a Woman* lay in chunks on the pavement, like some burst-open melon with dusty white innards.

Quentin plowed into the group with a low growl of fury, fists swinging. Two of the men landed on their backs, one with a bloody nose and the other clutching his groin. The third, however, caught Quentin with a fist to the side of the head, and he went down on his knees. By the time his vision cleared all three men were gone, and Mrs. Silberstein bent over him, cooing in Yiddish and anxiously stroking his face.

"Poor boy, oh poor *boychik*," she moaned. "I called your mama thirty minutes ago. She'll be here any time, now."

He staggered to his feet. Determined, dizzy, swaying, he pulled off his denim jacket, gathered the broken plaster sculpture, and wrapped the pieces for safekeeping. "Please don't tell her I was fighting."

"Of course not! But those dirty *gonifs* got what they deserved!" Mrs. Silberstein made a spitting sound of disgust.

A cab pulled up. Mother got out, fumbling the handful of quarters—her lunch money—that she poured into the cabbie's impatient palms. Quentin braced his legs and handed the ruined Picasso to Mrs. Silberstein, who cradled it like a baby. When Mother saw him, and then looked at their belongings, her face went stark white, her eyes tragic. He was embarrassed for them both, but the ruined look in her eyes tore his stomach out.

"I'm going to take care of this, Mother," he said firmly, as if he had any way of doing something.

Moving like a statue, she held out both hands, pushing the air as if she could contain the terrible pile of intimate belongings. She plucked a jumbled book from the mess, straightened its bent pages, closed its cover, then drew herself to her full height with viselike willpower.

"You stay here and look out for our things," she told Quentin. "I'm going to talk to someone about a small loan. Enough to cover the back rent. Then we'll get these things upstairs somehow, and we'll be fine. Your father won't ever have to know. Mrs. Silberstein, I can't thank you enough for helping."

"How can I not help? You're like family. I'm sorry I don't have the money to loan."

"Just thank you for caring."

Quentin stepped forward as his mother turned to leave. He churned with misery and frustration. "You're going to MacLand's, aren't you?" Bertine MacLand was a pawn broker and loan shark, worse even than the Siccone's.

She nodded. "Money is money. Just a utilitarian necessity. Be calm." She put a hand along his face, met his gaze with quiet command in her own eyes, then pivoted and limped down the street, leaning heavily on her cane, her worn brown overcoat flinging back like the wings of a sparrow.

By nightfall the apartment resembled itself, again. Quentin carefully fit the Picasso's pieces back together with glue, while Mother watched him with exhausted but satisfied eyes. Then she lay down on the living room sofa and he sat in his bedroom staring at the floor. The silence was a toxin.

"I'm going to work for Goots," he announced the next morning. "I'm too old for you to tell me I can't. I have to get a part-time job, or we'll get evicted, again."

She put down the bread she had been slicing for toast. Laid the serrated knife aside carefully. Sat down at the table with its cracked ceramic top, its fading yellow painted legs. She gazed, hollow-eyed, at a peanut-butter jar filled with fresh carnations. For as long as Quentin could remember she had kept fresh flowers on the kitchen table, in a small crystal vase that had belonged to Aunt Zelda. "My vase was broken yesterday," she said in a low, empty tone. "I found it under a chair."

Quentin winced. "Where are the pieces? Maybe I can glue them back—"

"No. I threw it away. Not everything can be fixed. No matter how hard you try." She looked up at him wearily. "I have failed to fix my family."

He sat down across from her and grasped her outstretched hands. "You can't fix our lives without my help. You've done your best. If the old man really cared—"

She stiffened. "What did you just call your father?"

Quentin looked at her for a long moment, his jaw tightening. "It's just the way guys talk. I'm sorry."

"In this house, he's your father, your papa, and you show respect for him."

"We're not exactly close, anymore."

"I know that, and it worries me all the time."

"He's been up at that warehouse for seven years. *Seven years.* It's time for him to quit kidding himself and come back. Get a real job. Make your life easier."

"But you know it's always been my choice not to tell your Papa about our money troubles. He has enough on his mind. He has a gallery opening next month, and two buyers coming to visit—"

"And it's my choice to go to work for Goots. If I have to let Papa go on believing he's not ruining us—then you have to let me help. It's only fair."

She shut her eyes, removed her glasses, and steepled her hands to her forehead. When she looked at him again her mouth was set, her decision made. "I want your classes to come first. I expect you to quit work if your grades drop."

"You've got my word. And my word's good, Mother. I won't let you down."

"You think your father has?"

He said nothing, but she could see the stark answer in his face. She bowed her head in defeat.

And so he went to work at Gutzman's garage. "You want to work at my other place?" Goots asked slyly. "Five times the money, half the effort."

Quentin flipped a rubber mallet into his hands, expertly swinging it, as if it were a sword. "I just want to fix dents and paint scratched fenders. Thanks, but the other place isn't my kind of game."

"Just wait. It will be," Goots said, and laughed.

*

The next autumn there was a breakthrough in Papa's career. He told them the widow of a businessman in a posh upstate town had fallen in love with his work. The woman decided to host a party at the warehouse, to introduce Papa to her friends in the arts community. Papa sent Quentin and Mother enough money for bus tickets, and on a warm September afternoon they left for the night's event. Mother was excited. Quentin's mood was lighter than it had been in years.

The warehouse was a hulking metal and wood building aproned by a dingy parking area of cracked concrete. It squatted in a fringe of anemic pine trees at the edge of an old industrial park. But on that autumn night the big windows glowed with golden light, and cars filled the lot. The sounds of a band could be dimly heard, and inside, almost a hundred artists and art patrons milled among Papa's statues, as waiters served them champagne and hor d'ouvres. Mother was nervous and ecstatic. Papa looked grim and incredibly handsome in a new black suit. Women could not take their eyes off him.

Papa's hostess, his *investor*, he called her, was not exactly old, as it turned out. Mother had just assumed, because he said she had white hair. She was a stately woman in her late fifties or early sixties, dressed in a slim black pantsuit that showed off her body, and her hair, while white, was cropped in short, fashionable layers. *Damn, she's not some wrinkled old lady*, Quentin thought with surprise when he was introduced to her. "Oh, you look so much like your handsome father," she said in a throaty voice, and stroked the palm of his hand with a manicured fingertip.

Remembering this, and thinking how funny people turned out to be when you least expected it, Quentin leaned against the fender of a car in the deepest shadows beyond the building's lone security light. His head buzzed from a glass of champagne Papa had presented to him with manly ceremony, and with the effect of another glass he'd lifted from a tray when Mother wasn't looking. He grinned in the darkness, then took a cigarette from his jacket pocket and lit it after expertly flicking a match against his palm. His mother would have plucked it from his lips and forced him to eat it if she'd caught him. She had done that once before. "I read doctors' warnings about tobacco all the time," she said.

"Aw, Ma," he'd replied, cocky and rebellious and still gagging on crushed tobacco. "If you listen to the screwy docs you'll think everything'll kill ya. Hey, I don't booze it up and I don't smoke dope, so whatz' your problem with a cigarette or two?"

She had stared at him in stunned silence, her ice-cold eyes like onyx. "My title is *Mother*," she said finally, "and in my home you will speak *correctly*, enunciating your words and *avoiding* slang language, because you are an educated person with self-respect and respect for *me*. I realize that you have learned to conduct yourself like one of the neighborhood gangs when you're outside my presence, but I will *not* have you turn into a street thug before my very eyes."

He had been embarrassed enough to apologize sincerely, but he had continued to sneak an occasional cigarette. That night when he heard people coming he quickly cupped one hand over the glowing tip and eased further into the shadows. He was frugal with his vices.

Several of the patrons, a mixed group of men and women, strolled by and paused near a car, while one of the men fumbled in his jacket for his keys. Quentin heard a hoot of laughter. "Riconni's work is quite good and may even be brilliant," a woman said, chortling. "But you *know* she picked him for his work in *bed*, not as an artist." There was more laughter.

Quentin dropped the cigarette and came to rigid attention, listening. "Maybe he's a *legitimate* discovery of hers," one of the men suggested. "No strings attached. Art for art's sake."

There was more laughter. "She never invests her money without screwing the poor SOB, first. *Never.* It's part of the allure of the whole art scene to her. She *told* a friend of mine so over a few martinis one time. I *guarantee* you, Richard Riconni earned his keep between the sheets before she ever wrote a check to him."

The group said no more and climbed into the car. Quentin stumbled out of range before the vehicle's headlights could find him. He flattened himself against the wall of the warehouse, breathing hard, his mind churning.

This was bullshit, mean gossip, a goddamned lie. Papa would *never* cheat on Mother, not for money, not for his art, not for any reason. *Just a lie* circled in Quentin's mind until his breathing slowed and his brain cleared. All right, *think*. Mother preached logic and methodical analysis. Patterns came easily to him, like stacking the building blocks with their fragile connections. He had his father's eye for perspective, for visualizing forms, context, how a joint fit together, how a welded seam knit metal to metal at the strongest points.

He made a simple plan. Then he lit another cigarette, squatted on his heels, and smoked in silence, his hands growing so calm that he could have cut his father's heart out with surgical skill.

They had splurged on two tiny rooms at a motel only a quarter mile from the warehouse. At midnight, Papa was still ushering out the last of his guests and closing up the building. Quentin and Mother strolled to the motel. She insisted on taking long walks as part of her daily routines, even slowed by her limp. She hummed in the pleasant September air, laughed at the moon, pointed out constellations with the tip of her cane, and wondered aloud about theories of the universe and creation, while Quentin could only manage fractured replies.

Mother slumped contentedly in a chair by the door of their room, her simple black dress swirling around her, her shoes off and her bad leg propped on the bed nearby. "It was wonderful, seeing your father surrounded by people who understand and appreciate his work!" She sighed happily. "He sold five pieces! Five! Not for huge sums, but that doesn't matter. The people who came here are quality collectors. They'll talk. Word will get around."

Quentin stood in the center of the room. He could not sit down. Dark energy coursed through him. His skin tingled. The walls were closing in. He went in the bathroom and changed into jeans, an old football jersey, and a jacket. Even his ordinary clothes felt coarse, as if the slightest rub could bring his blood to a raw surface. "There's a game room around the corner," he said. "We drove past it coming in. It's full of kids and people—it looks fine. I think I'll go play a couple of pinball games, all right?"

"Oh, Quentin, it's so late. Don't you want to see your Papa when he gets here?"

"I won't be long."

She studied him shrewdly for a moment, then gave up. "All right, but please be careful."

He went out into the night, walked a dozen yards toward a corner brightly lit with a service station, a small grocery, and the game room, in case his mother was watching, then pivoted in the shadows and headed down the road that paralleled the industrial park. In a few minutes he reached the warehouse, and saw his father's old truck parked outside. There were no other vehicles.

His heart rate calmed slightly. At least *she* wasn't here. His worst fear had not come true. Yet. The broad windows high on the buildings sides showed a faint glow of light. Quentin angled to a side door, found it unlocked, and ducked inside. He entered at a dark corner where his father stored materials. Piles of sheet metal, stacks of automobile chassis, and other items surrounded him. He began to pick his way through when he heard the crash and his father's garbled yell.

Quentin leapt forward then halted, staring. Papa had stripped off his jacket, tie, and dress shirt, and now stood in the middle of the floor wearing his slacks and t-shirt, stained with huge splotches of sweat. His face was contorted with fury and despair. He held a sledge hammer in both hands, and as Quentin watched he raised it over his head and slammed it down on a sculpture made of curving bands of metal. The relatively delicate piece collapsed, a huge dent appearing in its fragile design.

Papa made a roaring sound in his throat and swung the sledge hammer again. The look on his face was diabolical, livid, blind with emotions so painful and so stark that Quentin hunched over slightly, holding his own stomach, feeling as if he'd been punched. What was torturing Papa? The night had been a success, he'd sold his work, he'd made a few thousand dollars, and gotten attention from people who mattered in the arts community. Why was he tearing everything apart?

Quentin had come there to confront him, to ask him for the truth, but now he could only stare with fear at the raging sight. His father continued to utter incomprehensible moans and shouts of anger as he pounded one sculpture after another. He finally slung the massive hammer aside then grasped some of the smaller works and hoisted them, staggering, yelling, then throwing each one into the tumbled confusion of other sculptures he had beaten or turned over.

Quentin took a step forward, thinking, *I'll hold him before he hurts himself*, but then, *You can't! You can't let him know you saw him this way!* The dilemma stopped him. His father's face streamed sweat or tears or both. He ran to his welding equipment in one corner, and began to pull tools from a wall covered with neat rows of hangers. He hurled wrenches, tongs, whatever he could grasp next.

Quentin could take no more. Right or wrong, he stepped carefully toward his father, who did not see him, but instead drew back one powerful arm and slung a heavy pry bar as high as he could. It struck the bottom panes of a window, and the thick industrial glass shattered into glittering pebbles, falling like a hard rain. Papa sank to his knees, suddenly quiet, and bent his head into his hands.

"Angele," he groaned.

Quentin's head reeled. This was about Mother, and this was about the other woman, too. About shame and frustration. Whatever he'd come to say to his father was useless, and the question he'd come to ask had been answered. Quentin backed up slowly, silently, and left the warehouse through the door he'd entered.

He was shivering. He dragged his hands over his wet face. "Goddamn you, Papa," he said brokenly, both hating and loving him, wanting him to suffer and wanting to save him from himself.

In the end, Quentin simply walked back to the motel, then past it to the game room, where he feigned an interest watching other people play the machines. When he returned, his father's truck sat in the parking space out front and his mother peeked out their darkened doorway. "Your papa's sound asleep," she whispered. "He's *exhausted*. I gave him some aspirin and rubbed his back. He pulled a few muscles moving some sculptures around after the crowd left. We'll see you in the morning, all right?"

"Fine," Quentin said, and went to his own room.

He lay fully dressed on the unmade bed, sleepless in the dark, numb, composed, dying inside. He would never ask his father about this night, and his father would never tell him. But it would always be there, between them.

4

Out in the ordinary world, hippies were said to be running around everywhere, the Arabs were said to own all the oil, every major public event (even the Mountain State graduation) featured a naked man streaking, and President Nixon was about to resign. I had my own problems.

I hid in the ferns by the creek, accompanied by the farm cats, a few of Daddy's particularly adventuresome pet hens, and the shaggy farm dog, Bobo. I carried Daddy's small box camera on a strap around my neck. I was hunting for photographic proof of Granny Annie.

I heard mad rustling in the laurel on the opposite creek bank and snapped the camera. Our neighbor, Fred Washington, popped his black, grizzled head out of the laurel, grabbed for a spindly limb that wouldn't support his rotund bulk, then lost his balance and sat down hard. Mr. Fred had been heading to the creek to catch minnows for bait. His bait bucket landed in the laurel, like a tin crown.

"What in the world you doin', child?" he bellowed at me.

I was only eight years old, extremely bright but no match for the social horror that gripped me at that moment. "Bear!" I yelled, as if I'd seen something. He looked around wildly. "Run, child!" I dropped the camera and fled, scrambling up the steep hillside to the safety of our small pasture, rimmed in good, strong, barbed-wire fence.

Later, Daddy and I walked over to the Washington farm and I presented Mr. Fred with one of Mama's homemade pound cakes and an apology. He accepted both with good grace. Mr. Fred was a widower, and childless, retired from forty years of milking cows for a white farmer who owned a commercial dairy. His hands were knotted with arthritis from all those decades of squeezing teats, and his stiff knees remembered every long day sitting at a milk stool.

We sat on his porch awhile, eating sliced pound cake and drinking glasses of rich, raw milk from Mr. Fred's milk cow. It was his teenage brother whom the Klan hung during the bad years after Bethina Grace and his uncle Nathan ran away together. There had been a lot of Washingtons in the county then, but the Klan bullied most of them into leaving, until only Mr. Fred's stubborn parents were left. They vowed that they would raise their other two sons in Tiber County to spite their boy's killers, and that those sons would triumph.

When the boys grew up there was only enough money to send one of them down to Atlanta to attend Morehouse College. It was decided that Jonah, Mr. Fred's younger brother, would go. Jonah had earned a PhD in history and was now a professor at Harvard. He sent money and gifts to Mr. Fred but hardly ever returned to visit their old home.

Mr. Fred gazed at me somberly. "I ain't no kind of bear, child, and don't you try to take no more pictures of me." I nodded urgently. "Yes, sir." He spotted a long briar scratch on my arm, went inside, and came back with a can of salve. "Doctor Akin's Udder Balm," he said, and smeared some on my arm. "Good for sore cow teats and briar scratches."

Teet salve. I suppressed my giggles and solemnly sniffed my arm. From then on, the mentholated scent of the ointment would mean forgiveness, to me.

"Thank you, Mr. Fred," Daddy said quietly. "Why don't you come on over and have dinner tonight, if you want." He always offered, and Mr. Fred never accepted. He didn't accept, now, even though we probably had kin somewhere if Bethina Grace and Nathan had managed to produce even one child, together. Our blood might be mixed in caramel-colored people dancing a rumba under a Brazilian sky, but Mr. Fred and my family would never share a meal.

I thought about that as Daddy and I walked home. The Powells' and Washingtons' only legacies lay in the land and a notorious ability to think up interesting ideas and wander away on adventures, like Granny Annie and the others. So one way or another, we shifted shapes and disappeared.

I vowed that I would never do that.

*

Miss Betty was dying. Everyone knew it, including her. She waited peacefully in bed at the stately house where she had been born, listening to the inviting whispers of her lost mother, daughters, and husband. Daddy and I went to see her, and I stood beside her canopied bed, trying not to look at her shrunken face, but instead at the mementos of her life. I was ten years old, now, old enough to have mastered the art of pretending to be nonchalant when I was scared to death of death.

On her wicker nightstands were black bear dolls, black bear statuary and photographs of the Iron Bear. Beside those were sepia-tinted miniatures of her husband and lost daughters, and of John, her favorite grandson, whom the bear spirit of Granny Annie Powell had saved from polio, whether he believed it or not.

"I've got some news for you, Miss Betty," Daddy said gently. "Victoria's going to have another baby. We're not going to lose this one. I can feel it in my bones."

"Oh, how wonderful," she murmured weakly. "You all have wanted more children for so long. I bet this one will be fine."

I beamed. "I'm hoping for a sister."

"I hope you get your wish. A sister as fine and strong as you are." Miss Betty was so blind with cataracts she could barely see me. She put her thin, cool hands on either side of my face, examined my features with her fingertips, then confirmed her findings to Daddy. "Tommy," she whispered in her elegant up-country drawl, "you were right about her."

"That's so, Miss Betty."

"She's a wise child, Tommy. She listens." My silences were often mistaken for thoughtful reverie when they simply seethed with bound-up anger and fervent schemes. As usual, I couldn't help myself. I had always wanted to ask her a question on matters of Powell pride, and this might be my last chance. "Do you hate your Powell mama for running away?" I asked.

Her cloudy eyes gleamed. "Hate her? Oh, my dear girl. I'll tell you a secret nobody else knows. Not my brothers and sisters, not my children, or my grandchildren." Miss Betty held my hands and looked straight at me. "She told me she had to leave," she whispered. "And I told her to go."

I gaped at her. Beside me, Daddy said in low wonder, "Miss Betty?"

"Papa was mean to her. There was no other escape."

"But she was your mama," I insisted.

"I knew she loved me. Just because someone leaves or disappoints you doesn't mean the love is gone. Sometimes that's when it's the strongest. When you feel it so much it hurts." My silence made it clear this explanation was beyond me. The weakest smile crept across Miss Betty's wrinkled face. "You'll understand some day, I'm afraid. Everyone comes to that conclusion whether they want to or not. Our Bear knows, doesn't it, Tommy?"

"Yes ma'am," he nodded.

I blinked. "Miss Betty, do you think the Iron Bear talks to people?"

"Of course. How do you think I got so wise?"

"It doesn't talk to *me*."

"Oh, my, yes it does. It's full of *life*, darling. It's teaching, and you *are* learning. Never stop trying to hear what it's telling you to remember. Never stop listening to your heart." She sighed deeply. Her nurse and Mr. John's middle-aged sister, the stately and stout Luzanne Tiber Lee, who was not that friendly to us, entered the room and bustled around. "Time for her nap," Luzanne said brusquely, trailing the fragrance of Chanel No. Five and the faint odor of dog. She held her beloved beagle, Royal Hamilton, named for her sons—Royal and Hamilton, RH for short. RH, a retired field trial champion, wagged his stubby tail at us, at least.

"You take care," Daddy whispered to Miss Betty, bending to kiss her forehead.

"You take care of yourself and all you love, including our Bear," she whispered to him, but looked at me.

"I will," I whispered back.

As we walked down the shady sidewalk to the truck, I caught Daddy wiping the corner of one eye. "Don't cry," I said urgently, squeezing his big, work-roughened hand, as tears filled my own eyes.

"You first," he said, and smiled.

"Where do you think people go when they die?"

He thought for a moment as we walked, and I found myself counting the rhythm of our feet as if it were a time meter. "I think we can go anywhere we want," he answered. "I'm betting that Miss Betty will go down to the creek bottoms and keep Granny Annie company."

I still believed that I'd look up from skimming rocks across the creek one day and see Granny Annie gazing back at me with a snout and black fur, so this news made me feel better. "Then I guess I'll be watching out for *two* old lady bears." He laughed, picked me up, and kissed me on the cheek.

*

Miss Betty passed on near midnight, without ever waking up. I camped out with Daddy and about twenty other men around the Iron Bear. Rumor had leaked that Mr. John intended to send a crew with cutting torches to dismember the sculpture before dawn, now that his grandmother was dead and had left the sculpture to him, trusting him to do what was right. This was right, in his eyes.

My head buzzed with fatigue. I leaned against Daddy, who had wrapped me in a blanket against the late-summer dew. I kept nodding off or seeing weird shadows on the Bear from the light of the lanterns the men had set around it. These men were rough-looking characters, a few chicken farmers but mostly grim backwoodsmen, modern outsiders who'd rather piss on a town than live in one. They smoked, they chewed, they spit, and some drank from small flasks. They had come there because they heard Tom Powell needed help.

I didn't comprehend any of this, and was about to say so when a truck arrived. All the men stood. Me, too. I clutched my blanket and watched as Mr. John and several workmen strode towards us. Mr. John looked grim and waved both hands in firm gestures of dismissal. "Tommy, that sculpture's going back where it belongs. To the junkyard. Get out of my way."

Daddy stepped forward. "I can't let you do this, cousin." All the men around him closed ranks, staring evenly at Mr. John. One tall, bearded frontiersman said in a guttural drawl, "What Tom Powell says, goes."

Mr. John's face got redder by the second. He halted, nervously glancing at the hands of the men with Daddy, knowing that every one of them had a pistol or a knife hidden in their overalls or their hunting trousers, and that they wouldn't be shy about pulling the weapons out. "Now, look here, boys, this isn't a fight and it isn't your problem. I own this sculpture. I have a right to do with it as I please. And I intend to get it out of my sight forever."

"I'll take it off your hands," Daddy said. "I'll cart it away. Move it tonight. I'll set it out at my place. You can tell everybody it turned into thin air, if you want to."

"I want it destroyed."

"Your grandmama isn't cold, yet, and you're willing to tear down something you know she loved?"

"I honored her by allowing it to stay here for ten long years. I've done my duty."

"A duty like this isn't ever finished, Johnny. If you tear up this sculpture there'll be hard feelings around here for years to come. You're not thinking real good right now."

"What would you do with the thing?"

"I'd look at it, think about it, *feel* about it. You may hate the Bear, but that's okay, too. You want to know the only thing that's unforgivable about a work of art? When it doesn't make you care one way or the other."

Mr. John said nothing. A man built security. He built a name for himself and his family. He didn't go around *feeling* one way or the other about art.

"I'll sell it to you," he said suddenly. "If you believe in it so much, then you'll pay for it."

Daddy had earned the value of the Bear with his devotion and caretaking for ten years, but he quickly said, "I'll pay. Name your price."

"Two hundred dollars."

"I don't have that kind of money up front. I can pay you twenty dollars a month."

"Forty a month. Take it or leave it. And the bear stays here until you make the last payment."

Mr. John was carving out his pound of flesh, reclaiming the authority Daddy had taken from him in front of the men. Daddy swallowed hard. "Forty a month. Agreed. And I take the Bear with me in the fall." They shook hands in the lantern light, as the chorus of wild-looking men stood witness to the strangest deal in the history of Tiberville. I felt woozy with surprise, and I had a bad taste in my mouth. Forty dollars a month seemed a fortune, and what if Mama needed medicine? She'd lost three babies before this one.

The world was moving too fast for me, and I was afraid, for some reason. Miss Betty had passed on to who-knew-where. I tried to imagine her gently roaming Bear Creek in spirit form, united finally with her family of all kinds, including the bears. But what good had come out of all this misery? I looked up at the Iron Bear. *Tell me*, I begged. But I heard nothing.

*

Fall finally arrived, after an eternity, and the Bear came to live at Bear Creek. We'd done without even the most ordinary pleasures and necessities to scratch out the forty dollars Daddy gave Mr. John each month. In the early weeks of her pregnancy Mama seemed to get by well enough and often placed my hands on her stomach. "You feel our baby moving, Honey?" she would say. "That's your little bubba or sister in there. I got the light of angels inside me, again." But now she was seven months along, bloated and pale. She and I sat cross-legged on the ground under a backyard oak tree that shed brilliant red leaves on us with every whisper of breeze.

Mr. Fred put his tractor in high gear and pulled the Iron Bear down the ramp of a borrowed flatbed timber truck parked just beyond our backyard shade trees. "A little more to the left," Daddy shouted over the chug of the tractor engine and the scrape of the Bear's massive metal paws on the wooden ramp. Sweat ran down his face.

His overalls were covered in gray concrete dust and mud. Only that morning he'd put the finishing touches on a pad he'd poured for the Bear. I had blisters on my palms from helping him stir batches of concrete in a wheelbarrow and specks of white paint through my hair.

He stood atop the pristine white foundation, his legs spread and his arms raised in the air as he guided Mr. Fred's towing progress. A huge smile lit his face. He was conducting a symphony. He was standing before a Degas in the Louvre. He was giving thanks to heaven. He was a holy man invoking all the unappreciated beauty of the world to settle there, on our farm, because we were special.

I never loved my father more than I did that day.

Low afternoon sunshine cut through the Bear's sides, casting its weird, skeletal shadow our way. Mama drew back. She clutched my hand atop one knee of my overalls and prayed silently, her lips moving as her worried eyes stayed on Daddy. She stroked her other hand over her bulging stomach, as if soothing the baby inside.

Each time the wind shifted, more leaves rattled down and our personal stink rose up. I smelled the pungent nastiness of chicken house chores on her brogans and my dirty tennis shoes—the scent of hard work, low returns, and grim reality. I worried that the scent might make her vomit, again.

Her dazed attention never left Daddy. "I reckon the man who made the Bear is off somewhere laughin' at us for carin' so much." It was the first and last time I ever heard her say anything less than obedient and supportive. Not that Daddy asked her for submissive loyalty. It was just how she'd been raised to treat a husband. "I just hope it's not got the evil eye," she said, then pulled her frayed sweater tighter over her stomach.

I squeezed Mama's hand patiently.

Twilight came. I was soothed by the glorious hail of yellow sparks floating upward like a thousand dancing fireflies as Daddy welded the Bear's black iron paws into permanent promenade on its new foundation. I watched the welding sparks rise and fly away among the stars in the purple-black autumn sky.

"Why did you marry Daddy?" I asked Mama. "Do you think he's got moon dust in his head?" Someone at school had said that to me.

"If'n he's got moon dust, then the moon oughta be proud," she told me. "Some men's got great big empty heads and hearts like shrunk-up tomaters. Your Daddy's got a heart as big as the world. That's why I married him."

"Do we have any money left? Daddy's giving money to people right and left."

"Why, sure." She looked away from my scrutiny. "We got more than enough."

I overheard Daddy tell an old man one day that his dream was to turn the chicken houses into working art studios for all his friends to use.

How would we pay bills? I thought. *How would we eat?* I began to gnaw my fingernails and count pennies I saved. I wish the Bear could have warned me that this was the last autumn my sorrows would be that kind.

*

It was the coldest December in years. Ice rimmed the drinking water in the old bathtub Daddy had set in the pasture for the milk cow we'd bought from Mr. Fred. Daddy thought it would be a good idea to have our own supply of rich milk, now that there would soon be two growing children in the house.

That Saturday he got up before dawn, and so did I, and together we fed the chickens and milked the cow. Mama was almost due, and so tired she hadn't gotten out of bed in a week. She wouldn't let Daddy take her to a doctor, and he not only abided by her wishes, he celebrated them. "Everybody's got their own idea of god," I remember him telling me. "Your mama walked as far out on the limb of worldliness as she is ever gonna go, back when I took to have her snakebite treated. In her way of thinking, she can't rile god, again."

"Maybe you oughta *make* her go to the doctor," I said worriedly. "And then god could just fuss at *you* about it. How's about I tell god that I made her go to the doctor? I betcha god wouldn't pick on a kid."

Daddy laughed until he cried. "Do you know that god is a work of art, and you can't paint god any color you want? Your mama's god is red in the face right now, from grinning over your good sense."

On that Saturday he signed up for a day's work loading hay for a farmer in a neighboring town. The job paid well, though of course Daddy never said we needed the money. Anything that took him away from chicken farming gave him pleasure. Before he left that morning he posted the boss's phone number on the big black wall phone in the kitchen.

"If your mama gets sick," he told me, "or anything about her makes you scared that she's not feeling good, you call the man I'm working for, and he'll tell me I'm needed at home, and I'll come right along."

"I'll take care of Mama," I promised firmly, trying to appear a little bored by the anxiety is his eyes, although my heart was racing with the fear of being left alone with such responsibility. After he left I made toast in the oven and took Mama a plate full, with gobs of her homemade scuppernong jelly and a glass of fresh milk. She nibbled half a piece of toast and sipped the milk. When she refused the rest I stared at the leftovers as if they'd betrayed me. "I'll make you some pancakes," I said to Mama. "Pancakes won't turn your stomach."

She saw the look on my face and held out an arm. "Baby," she rebuked in a weak, tender voice, "Come on here and keep me warm. I'm just fine."

"Pancakes, Mama," I repeated firmly.

"No. Com'ere, Baby."

I gave into emotion and curled up beside her, under the covers. I massaged her enormous stomach over her nightgown. She hummed in appreciation, then fell into a light sleep, frowning. I put my hand on her chest and counted her heartbeats. She felt so frail, compared to me. When the sun was high in the windows, I dozed off.

Her jerking movement woke me. The sunlight was still cascading into the room; not much time had passed. But now she was wide awake and sweating, her eyes half-shut. I bounded out of bed and watched her grip the covers. "Mama? Mama?" I said loudly. "I'm calling the doctor."

"No!" Slowly, she relaxed. Her eyes went to me. She managed to smile. "I'm just fine. I'll tell you what you do. You go call Miz Maple. Her number's in the phone book. I'm gonna have her come over and set with me."

Roberta Maple was a stout older woman who had helped deliver me when I was born. Daddy hadn't mentioned anything about calling Mrs. Maple. "I . . . I better call Daddy," I insisted. "Daddy told me to."

"But I'm not sick. Wouldn't I tell you if I was?"

"Mama—"

"Shoo. Call Miz Maple."

"I thought she only came around when people had babies. Are you—" I halted, afraid. "Are you?"

"I'm not having no baby, today, Honey," she said quickly, smiling too brightly at me. "Our baby's not supposed to come 'til after Christmas. Now go call Miz Maple. I just need some company."

Caught in a dilemma of conflicting information, I went downstairs, climbed onto the foot stool that helped me reach the wall phone, and called Roberta Maple. She said she'd come right over. I took down the note about Daddy's work number, and studied it as if secret advice might reveal itself to me.

I put the note in my overalls' pocket and went back upstairs to watch Mama until Mrs. Maple came. That was the worst decision I made, that day.

*

Horror stiffened my bones. Mrs. Maple and Sue Tee had banished me to the kitchen for the past three hours, and I'd strained my ears listening for sounds. I heard Mama cry out. I leaped on the stool and grabbed the phone, fumbled for the note in my pocket, and called the number. When a man answered I yelled, "Tell Tom Powell to come home quick!" and then I slammed the phone down. I pulled the Tiberville phone directory from a shelf. My hands were shaking so badly I could hardly plant a finger on the listing for the doctor.

Mama's god could be pissed off at me for the rest of my life, I didn't care. I was dialing when Sue Tee Harper intercepted me and wrestled the receiver out of my hand. Mrs. Maple's assistant was wiry, buck-toothed and dressed in a bloody apron over a floppy brown pantsuit. She had the hardened eyes of a poor mountain woman who had no illusions about life's realities. "Girl!"

"I'm calling the doctor!"

"Callin' the doctor?" She mimicked me in a high-pitched drawl. "Lord Jesus, girl, your folks ain't got no money for a doctor!"

"He'll come anyway!"

"You do what you wuz told. You leave that phone alone. God's takin' care of your mama. You go sit out on the porch and pray."

"My daddy's gone to make some money. I AM CALLING THE DOCTOR."

"He ain't makin' enough to pay for no doctor." She pointed in the general direction of the pasture. "He spent his doctor money on that bear contraption out yonder. If you want to squeal you squeal at it, you hear? Your mama cain't afford no doctor and she sure wishes she had one now. But she knows your daddy put all his doctor money on that evil idol."

I stumbled backward, gaping at her. What to believe? Ponderous footsteps hurried down the stairs. Mrs. Maple waddled into the kitchen, carrying something wrapped in a bloody sheet. "Get her out of here," she said to Sue Tee.

Sue Tee grabbed me by one arm but I wrapped a hand around a thick iron towel bar bolted to the wall beside the sink counter. Fred Washington's ancestors had forged that towel bar, and like them it was stong, black, and built to stay. "Girl! Damn you, Girl!" Sue Tee yelled, pulling as I held on. I stared at the little bundle that didn't move, the bundle that Mrs. Maple placed on the kitchen table. "Get her outta here, I said! I have to get back upstairs!"

Sue Tee grunted, jerked, and I fell to the floor. As I scrambled to my feet she shoved me outside, tossed me my cloth coat, then locked the door. Sue Tee ran to the table and pulled back a bit of the sheet. Through the wavy door panes I glimpsed a tiny, still face. When she covered that face with the sheet again I was stunned, then filled with rage. What was she doing! Mama's baby would smother like that!

Picking up a piece of firewood from the long stack against the porch wall, I smashed a pane of door glass. Sue Tee swung around and threw up her hands as I reached inside and unlocked the latch. "Out! Out!" she yelled as I darted back inside. "What kind of thinkin' do you *do*, girl?" I dodged her and she grabbed me by the coat collar. I swung the piece of kindling still in my hand, and hit her in the chin. She yelped, whirled me around and pointed furiously at the bundle. "You want to get in the middle of this? All right! Your little brother's *dead*. That's his body right there! Now, will you listen to me and take yourself outside?"

I froze. The stick of kindling fell from my hand. I couldn't register everything at once; my mind refused to hear what she'd said. "Sue Tee!" Mrs. Maple yelled from upstairs. "I need you!"

"I'll be right back, and you better be gone," Sue Tee said, then ran out of the room. I forced one foot in front of the other, gaining momentum as I neared the table. I shot out a hand and pulled on the sheet. It fell aside. And there he was, my baby brother, bluish-pink, his eyes shut, his tiny face as still as a sleeping kitten's. I didn't see a dead baby. I saw my brother. My brother. Not dead. Not this one. He was full-sized. I wouldn't let this baby be born dead.

I gathered him and the sheet in my arms, and ran outside. When young chicks were smothered in the masses as the Tiber delivery people unloaded new flocks into the chicken houses, Daddy would gather as many of the limp bodies as he could, and I would help. We'd rush them to the livestock trough and dunk them in the water.

Sometimes the cool shock revived them, sometimes it didn't. But we tried.

That's where I headed with the baby. He was limp, he felt hopeless, but I ran as fast as I could. I knelt down and shoved him, sheet and all, between the strands of barbed-wire fence that fronted the trough, and I sank him in the icy water for a second, then lifted him out, and dunked him again.

There was no response. I unwound the sheet and submerged him, naked, one time. I couldn't bear to do that, again, it looked so hard and cruel on his tiny, wrinkled body, and he was still as limp as a bean-bag doll.

What to do, what to do? I clutched him to my chest, opened my coat and tucked him inside, then stumbled across the yard. Courage was giving way to fear and misery; I was suddenly blinded by tears. I hit something hard with one foot and tripped, sprawling on my side. I had run into the Iron Bear's concrete pad, and now, looking up and gasping for air, I saw the Bear looming over me. I lay beneath it's jutting head, gazing up at the mesh of pieces and parts shielding me from a cold gray sky.

"It's all because of you!" I shouted. "You got the doctor money!" Under my coat, pressed tightly against the bib of my overalls and the sweaty flannel of my shirt, something moved. I sat up, shaking, and opened one side of coat. My brother curled one miniature hand against my shirt, opened his mouth, and began to mewl. I stared up at the Bear. Had it heard me and felt guilty?

I was afraid to move, afraid I'd hurt the baby, stop him from living, now that he was. I huddled there with my coat drawn closely around him, staring at the house, my mind a blank wall waiting for someone to please, please come and tell me that Mama was all right, too. The Bear had saved the baby. The Bear would save her. Nothing else would make sense.

Soon Daddy raced up the driveway, left the truck's door standing open, and ran into the house. I tried to get up and follow him, but my knees shook too badly. I sat back down on the Bear's concrete base, and waited. The baby continued to make soft sounds and began to wiggle.

Daddy finally came out of the house, saw me, and half-ran, half-stumbled toward me. The look on his face made me hunch over in pain. When he reached me I began to cry; I opened my coat so he could see the baby. "He's not dead, Daddy. Isn't Mama okay, too? I tried to call the doctor." Daddy sank down beside us and wrapped one arm around me. He slid his shaking hand inside my coat and curved it behind the baby's head. "One miracle is all we could hope for," he whispered, then his voice broke and he cried, too, holding me against his chest, his other hand still cupping my brother.

I was stunned. He didn't have to tell me that Mama was dead. I could feel the emptiness under my skin, between my veins, around my heart. There was no money for a doctor because Daddy had been foolish, and Mama's idea of god had killed her, and he and the Iron Bear had let god do it. Dry-eyed and in shock, I looked back up at the sculpture. It hadn't saved my brother. It had killed my mother.

5

Quentin sat on the brick stoop of the apartment building in the growing autumn darkness, trying to study under the light of a streetlamp. He took a cigarette from his jacket then put it back. Mrs. Silberstein and the neighborhood's other old ladies would report him to his mother if they caught him smoking. They never seemed to notice the drug dealers and panhandlers who occupied every corner, but they'd notice Quentin Riconni puffing a filter-tip. They still took care of their own.

Staying out of trouble, even small trouble, had become his mantra. He was one year away from graduating, and the teachers at St. Vincent's said he had a shot at any scholarship he wanted. He pictured himself at the Massachusetts Institute of Technology. MIT. As far as he was concerned, it was the best engineering school in the country.

He slapped a calculus text on his knees and opened it. Lost in brooding concentration, at first he didn't hear the firm tap of Carla Esposito's wedged high-heels on the sidewalk. "Oh, Quent, *shit*. Not *again*," she called softly. He looked up, startled.

The shoes made her almost as tall as he. Her black hair overflowed from a Farrah Fawcett mane of teased layers. She wore denim bellbottoms and a bright pink blouse beneath a long leather jacket. There was no bra under that blouse. Her eyes were rimmed with thick black mascara, her lips bright pink, like her nails. At fifteen she was going on thirty. If Alfonse had caught her looking like that he'd have put her in a convent school.

She sat down on the step beside Quentin's legs and sighed deeply, thrusting her substantial breasts against his thigh. He and she had recently gone far past the bounds of honor and chastity. Their mutual deflowering had occurred with speedy, awkward intimacy under a tree in a nearby park. Since then, they'd improved their skills at every opportunity. "Electricity turned off again, huh?" Her voice was gentle.

After a grim moment spent staring at his book, he closed it hard. "Yeah."

"I thought the bills were under control."

"Ma's been sending more money to the old man than I realized. She was hiding it from me. He's shipping his work to galleries out of state. Not that he sells much. Hell, he barely covers the cost of shipping. Then he had to replace his welder, and some other equipment. That's why she's sending him extra money. I shoulda known something was up when she took a second job. She's working two nights a week at a bookstore."

"You could come over to my place. Pop's working late."

"Thanks for the invite, but I'm not in the mood."

"That could change." She slid a hand between his legs and groped until he caught her hand in warning. Yet Quentin studied her with pure greed. Feisty, loyal, and ambitious, Carla always wanted to make him happy, whether it was good for him, or not.

She grinned wider. "Gotcha. Wow." Her grin faded when he shook his head. "Come over where there's lights, please, please, please, or I could come up to your place before your ma gets home. Let's play doctor in the dark."

"That's how everybody else around here ends up with babies they don't want."

"Not me." She patted a pocket of her bellbottoms. "I stole condoms from Tivolii's. That old Russian turned her back and I swiped them from behind the counter."

"Some detective's daughter."

"I'm not getting pregnant. I'm gonna be somebody. I don't care what it takes. And so are you. We're getting out of this place. We'll live on the other side of the bridge—we'll live all the way over at Central Park—in a penthouse. With a chauffeur! I got the looks, you got the brains." She had won a dozen community beauty pageants, and had even modeled dresses for a department store catalog. Carla pulled on his thigh, sliding her fingers higher. "Don't worry about the electric bill. It doesn't matter. Come on. I can cheer you up. I don't like it when you're like this."

"I want to bash my head against a wall. I want to explode."

"It's only lights!"

"I hate having the goddamned electricity turned off. I hate the way Mother hangs her head when she reads the bills. I hate when she won't look the grocer in the eye because he won't charge anymore on her account. I hate the way my old man promises her every year'll be better. He got a big gallery in Soho to show some of this pieces last month. People laughed at them. There's always a few people who rave about his stuff and buy something, but never enough. He's ahead of his time, they tell him. Who knows? Who cares? He didn't sleep for a week. I want things put right, you understand? I'll never make promises I can't keep. I take care of my responsibilities." He was almost yelling, now, and gripped Carla by the shoulders. "I'm a man, a *man*, and I've got duties. I can't do anything about the electricity, but I'm not a bum!"

She slammed a fist into his arm. "You know I love you! I want to help!"

"And I've told you a dozen times I *don't* want you to love me and I *don't* want your help. *Capice?*"

"You got another girl! That's why you talk this way! I'll fuckin' kill her when I find out who she is!"

He scrubbed a hand over his face and sighed. "There's no other girl. I just don't want anybody to love me. *Anybody. Any* girl. Not you or anybody else."

"*Why?*"

"I don't need love. What good is it?"

"I'm gonna marry you some day!"

"You want to get married? Find a husband. Not me. Never. I don't believe in marriage."

"You're a liar!"

"You think whatever makes you happy. But enough about it. *Enough.*" He straightened ominously, warning that one more word would send him to his feet and walking away. They had had this argument, before. She never believed him, and he never gave in.

Carla popped to her feet, her face livid and her hands clenched. "Fuck you. *Fuck you.* I know what this is about. You think you're gonna go away to some big college next year and never come back here, and I'm just some Brooklyn wop cop's daughter you're gonna forget all about. You don't know everything, Quentin Riconni. You don't know *nothing*. You don't even know where your ma really works at night!"

He got to his feet, instantly on alert. "What are you talking about?"

Her face paled. Her eyes filled with tears, and her anger faded. "Shit," she said under her breath. She hadn't meant to say anything.

"What are you talking about?"

"Quentin, I . . . damn. *Damn.*" Carla's shoulders slumped. "Pop found out, 'cause detectives always hear stuff about those operations. He tried to talk her out of it, but she made him promise not to tell. She says it's just for a little while."

"What?"

Carla's mouth trembled with remorse. "She's doing office work for MacLand's."

The loan shark. MacLand was scum under a rock. He sent guys out to break knees and fingers. He was a merciless piece of shit.

Quentin quickly walked Carla back to her brownstone and kissed her in the darkness beside the steps. "I've got things to do," he told her, and left her standing there, crying.

He watched the stars for comfort as he strode down dark city streets no one should be walking alone. This part of Brooklyn was squeezed under strips of sky, the smell of diesel oil and subways and spilled garbage scenting the night. The streetlights beamed like yellow eyes. He hunched his shoulders menacingly under his coat and shoved his hands deeper in his jean pockets, clamping one fist around a small automatic pistol, the other around a switchblade.

A man appeared from the shadows of an alley. "Hey, what you doing, what you got for a friend?" the man asked in a slurred voice. He reached loosely for Quentin's arm.

Instantly Quentin pulled the knife, flicked it open, and thrust it up, stopping the slender point just below the man's breast bone. "I'll cut your heart out," he warned softly.

"Hey, hey now." The stranger backed into the alley, hands up, then turned and staggered away.

Quentin put the knife away and continued walking fast, his knees weak. A sleek, jacked-up black Camaro pulled up at the corner. Quentin strode to the door and got in. Johnny Siccone, swarthy and thick chested, with shaggy black hair, sneered at him. "You still got the balls to do it?"

"Hell, yes." Quentin's chest felt like a balloon filled with water. He spread his hands on the knees of his jeans, letting his palms dry. Johnny drove him to the Heights, and they quickly perused the expensive cars parked along a street lined with nice old homes. "Go," Johnny ordered. "Get that one."

Quentin leapt out and ran to a small, dark Mercedes. With a flick of the tool in his hand he was inside the elegant sedan, and with another twist, its engine roared to life. He drove blindly back to his own familiar haunts, with Johnny following, and pulled the car into the sunken driveway of Goot's chop-shop garage.

"Jesus God," Goots said, when he opened the garage door and saw the Mercedes. Laughing and muttering praises in German, he peeled off several hundred-dollar bills from a wad in his pocket and looked at Quentin. "You want to bring me more?"

"Yeah."

Goots hesitated. "Listen, call me a fool, but I have to say something. Your papa wouldn't want you to do this."

"You gonna tell him?"

The icy tone in Quentin's voice settled on the slow, heavyset Goots like a layer of warning. He never prodded a problem that was not his own. He liked peaceful larceny. His jovial smile returned, beneath shrewd eyes. "I say nothing. What you do with your life is between you and your papa." He shrugged.

Quentin walked back home with the money in his pocket, his knees shaking and vomit rising in his throat. *De minimus non curat lex. The Law does not concern itself with trivial matters.* He hoped not, because he was a car thief, now. Not a dreamer like Papa, who was turning into one of his own stark, skeletal works of metal before Quentin's eyes. Now Quentin would be just a guy looking out for his family, divining patterns that needed to be broken.

He told Mother that Goots had promoted him to assistant machinist at the shop and given him a hefty raise. He told her he knew about her job at MacLand's, and he wanted her to quit. He could cover the difference with his salary increase.

She looked helplessly relieved. She hated the job for MacLand, and had lived with the fear and shame of anyone finding out. Quentin's help was a necessity, now, she couldn't deny it. He'd made good on his promise to maintain his grades while he worked, so what harm was there in a promotion from kindly old Goots? She was worn out, lonely, depressed all the time. Richard's deepening despair terrified her. Sometimes they talked on the phone for hours at night, her trying to soothe him, to encourage him.

The world was closing in on her. "I'll have to thank Mr. Gutzman," she said with tired dignity.

"No need," Quentin answered with a strange little smile. "He's getting his money's worth."

From then on, Quentin stole cars. He was good at it. He gave his mother as much money as he could without making her suspicious. The rest he stashed in his room. Carla found out about his thieving through a girlfriend of Johnny Siconne's. She was scared for him, but also excited. He handed her a hundred dollar bill and she forgave him for everything.

He lay in his bed at night wishing he never had to shut his eyes. When he slept he had nightmares about being shot in the street. He wrote a long letter to his parents, telling them everything and asking their forgiveness, then sealed it and hid it among the military novels and war-history texts that filled his bedroom bookcase. This was a recent fascination of his—men and machines of destruction, their heroics, their epic ideas—their honorable deaths saving god and country. His grandfather had died in WW II, a hero.

Not a car thief.

*

Quentin walked outside Goot's shop – the legitimate body shop – during a break. He was soaked in sweat. Speckles of black paint dotted his jeans and t-shirt. He rinsed his face at a water faucet outside the garage. His father drove up in the truck.

Quentin straightened slowly. Papa was in his early forties, now, and starting to go gray at the temples. His face had weathered the hard years like a craggy rock. All the softness had been eroded from his features. His eyes were as cold as steel. "Get in," he said. "There's somebody I want you to meet."

For a minute, Quentin didn't move. Papa had driven down in the middle of the week, with that look on his face, to make him meet somebody? He felt the hairs rise on the back of his neck. Something was very wrong, here. Then he tossed back, "Yeah, whatever you want, it's not like I've got a job," and climbed in the truck without another word.

Papa didn't speak again during the drive. His old plaid shirt and khaki trousers were flecked with tiny burn marks where his cutting torch had cast flecks of hot metal. His hair was singed around the front. He must have walked out of the warehouse on short notice.

Quentin steeled himself for trouble. He was dimly aware of traveling through Brooklyn communities better or worse than their own, a landscape sometimes dominated by black faces, sometimes by white, bleak or comfortable, the uneven terrain of a sprawling city that engulfed people. Finally Papa turned through the gates of a huge cemetery so crowded with tombstones and small mausoleums that there was hardly any room for the living to walk among them.

Quentin's puzzlement grew as his father drove down one narrow, paved lane after another, coming to a stop deep inside the forest of the dead. "It's just a few dozen feet that way," he said, and pointed toward an area of low, plain markers. Quentin followed him in speechless curiosity, sidestepping flat grave stones. Papa dropped to one knee beside a stone and brushed flecks of mown grass from the beautifully carved surface. Quentin stopped beside him and looked down.

Jeanne Louise Riconni, the stone read among swirls of carved roses. The dates said she was only eighteen when she died, and that she had been dead for almost twenty-five years. Papa smoothed his large, coarse fingertips over her name. "She was my sister."

Quentin dropped to his heels and looked from the stone to his father incredulously. "Why did you keep her secret?"

"I don't like to talk about her. It won't bring her back. She died when I was about your age. She was a saint. The gentlest soul I ever knew, until I met your mother. If you want to understand anything about me, then it's here." He pointed to the stone. "I grew up fast, that year."

"How did she die?"

"Polio. She couldn't breathe. They put her in an iron lung. Like a casket. Only her head showed at one end. I'd sneak into the clinic and sit with her. I didn't care if I got sick from being around her. She was all I had in the world. Looking at her inside that machine, it was as if she'd been eaten alive. And it wasn't making her better."

"The machine kept her from dying sooner, though."

"That's the helluvit, isn't it? You never know whether to hate a thing like that, or love it." He paused, then raised his dark, scalding gaze to Quentin. "I built the bear sculpture for her. She's the reason I got the commission for it." Quentin could only shake his head in confusion. Papa's sister had died a long time before the bear. His father went on, "The lady in Georgia who ordered the bear read about me in a March of Dimes newsletter. I did some volunteer work for them in Jeanne Louise's memory. Repaired leg braces, fixed crutches. They wrote an article and mentioned I wanted to be a sculptor. This lady, Betty Tiber, that was her name, she saw the article and sent me a letter. She'd lost family to polio. She wanted a memorial." He explained how that had translated into a sculpture of a bear, but Quentin could barely listen. Where was this leading? The old man had driven home to tell him this story? Was his father a little crazy?

When Papa finished Quentin stared at him carefully. "What's going on? Why do you want me to know all this?"

"Because life isn't a goddamn *choice.* It's a gift, and if you fuck it up there aren't any second chances. I'll never understand why Jeanne Louise died and I lived. I decided to earn my life. Did I deserve to live?"

"Sure. It was her time to go, not yours."

"Don't recite what the fuckin' priests tell you."

Quentin raised both hands in a gesture of emptiness, and suddenly years of anger boiled up in him, frustration and disgust blistering his brain. "What do you want from me? You want me to say your life has a purpose and a meaning and you're doing a great job living the life your sister didn't get? You want me to lie?"

His father's expression tightened into a stark mask. The push-pull of anger electrified the hot air. They stood. "I didn't come here to talk about me, or even about me and you," Papa said between gritted teeth. "All that matters right now is *you*. You, and what you gotta take responsibility for before you flush your life down the toilet."

"I've been taking responsibility for my life and *our* family since I was old enough to understand you wouldn't be around to do it."

His father hit him—just drew back a fist and punched him in the mouth. It happened with such power and speed Quentin had no time to react. He sprawled backwards over a tombstone, lay still for a minute until his vision cleared, then propped himself on one elbow. He put his other hand to his mouth and wiped blood from his cut lower lip. Papa dropped to a squat beside him and looked at him with merciless intent. "You're a goddamned car thief," he said.

Silence. Quentin didn't move, didn't speak, just stared back at him. He tasted his own blood, accompanied by a wave of shame. "How did you find out?"

"From old friends who know Goots. When you went to work for him I knew what might happen, but I kept my mouth shut. I said to myself, *My son has honor. His mother has taught him the letter of the word and I think I've shown him the spirit. If Goots offers him the wrong choice, he'll say no. I gotta let him prove himself.* But you didn't."

Quentin slowly wiped his hand on the leg of his jeans. He trembled with disgrace. He still wanted his father's approval, and when he realized how little that need had changed he was filled with bitter shock. Yet years of pain and resentment boiled out of him. "Who are you to lecture me about honor? You're a lousy father and a lousy husband. I steal cars to pay our bills. Ma's always hidden our money problems from you. And you never bother to look that close."

He confessed in grotesque detail about the bill collectors, the eviction, the job for MacLand's. And finally, the worst. "I know you fucked that woman who sponsored you," he shouted. "I know you did it to get her money."

Papa's rage gave way to a stunned look, then despair. He shut his eyes and bowed his head.

"Don't tell me about honor," Quentin continued into his awful silence. "Just stay out of my business! You're killing Ma, and I stopped giving a shit about you years ago! Go be a fucking artist and follow your dream, but leave me alone!"

Silence. Slowly his father stood. He held down a hand. Quentin shoved it away. "I can take care of myself. That's what you wanted, that's what you got."

His father left him sitting there, walked numbly to the truck, and drove out of the cemetery. After a moment, the sounds of birds and distant traffic filled the ordinary quiet, and Quentin looked around, blinking, dazed, as if just waking.

He crawled to Jeanne Louise's grave. There was no victory or wisdom in anything he'd said. He flattened a hand on his aunt's marker, the only symbol of a long-dead girl who had inspired Richard Riconni to be more than he'd imagined possible.

"What did I just do to him?" he asked brokenly.

The silence of the dead was his only answer.

*

"What a mess. You're fired," Goots said the next day. "Fired from the garage, fired as a thief. Fired. I'm very sorry. Believe me."

Quentin had just arrived for work, and stared at him as if this were a joke. "What'd I do? Look, about yesterday, my old man came by with a problem, and I had to go. Yeah, I should've told somebody I was taking off, but—"

Goots waved his beefy hands for silence. "It's nothing you did. Your papa came to see me last night. Said either I fire you or he'd shut me down. He could go to that goddamned Alfonse Esposito and *do* it, too. So I have no choice. On the other hand, I respect your papa and I know he's only looking out for you."

"There are other places to work. You know what I mean. I won't stop."

"*Och*! Have some common sense. You're not like the others who steal cars. You're no Johnny Siccone. You've got brains, you're going to college. Don't risk it all. God sent you a message yesterday. An angel. Your own papa. Take the hint."

"My old man's no angel, and it's too late for me to change." Quentin walked out.

*

But in fact, Quentin didn't steal another car during the rest of the summer or into that fall. Goots had run a relatively secure, efficient operation. Quentin knew of others who were rumored to be just as trustworthy, but he took his time, checking them out. He caught himself thinking Papa would approve of his methodical technique, though he knew the idea was ridiculous. He thought about his father constantly.

And then the news came. In Father Aleksandr's darkly paneled office, Quentin was handed an envelope from MIT. As the priest grinned Quentin opened it and read that the university was offering him a full engineering scholarship. He planned to graduate early from St. Vincent's, and could start at MIT in the spring, if he wanted. A weight eased from Quentin's shoulders. He was surprised to feel so astonished. Mother's faith in him, which he had often taken at face value, had been right.

And if she were right about him, then maybe she was right to believe in Papa, too.

On that cool October afternoon he waited outside the massive doors of the Brooklyn Library's main branch, flicking jaunty looks at girls who looked back, mentally daring grown men to cross his path, but in fact so excited behind his cool exterior that he could barely stand still.

He jostled the switchblade in his pocket like a talisman as he leaned against the library's towering walls beside enormous, bronze Art Deco doors that had made him feel, as a child, that he was an ant hurrying inside to steal bread crumbs. Now he defied any symbol of learning and power to make him feel ignorant, again. When Mother walked outside the massive building with a heavy book satchel dragging on one thin shoulder and her purse dangling awkwardly around her cane, Quentin leapt to her side. He took the encumbering items from her, dropped them carefully beside her feet as she gaped at him in confusion, then threw his arms around her in an enormous, grinning hug.

"What is it?" she asked breathlessly, looking at him wide-eyed, her question magnified by her glasses.

He stepped back. "I'm going to MIT next spring," he answered.

Her eyes gleamed and filled with tears. She shrieked, then hugged him and held him. But what began as a joyful moment quickly turned desperate. She held on, and began to shake, then sobbed into his shoulder. Quentin was so startled he began to say *Mother? Mother?* and to pat her on the back.

She tried to calm herself, choking down soft sounds of misery, shivering. "Sorry, sorry, oh, sorry," she managed. "It's not you. I'm so happy. It's a dream come true. But . . . I wish your papa were here. I wish . . . I'm so worried, Quentin. Something's wrong." Quentin grabbed her satchel and purse, then guided her along the plaza in front of the library. "Sit down, take a breath," he urged, and they sank down on bench. "What's going on?"

"He didn't call last night. And I've been trying to reach him all day." She bent over and quickly wiped her eyes with the hem of her pale blue sweater. When she straightened she grasped Quentin's hand and shook her head. "I'm sure it's nothing. I don't want to ruin this moment for you. Really."

"It's okay. Tell me more about Papa."

"He's been so depressed. Since the summer his ability to see some hope for the future has evaporated – he's *changed*, Quentin, he's lost a spark that kept him going. Always before, no matter how much he agonized over his work and his career, no matter how often he felt success was impossible, he still believed in what he was doing. But lately he seems to have given up. *Given up.*"

Quentin listened to all this with a sick knot growing in his stomach. *He* had done this to his father—he had punished him, broken him. And he'd never wanted to do that. "I'm going to borrow a car and drive up there tonight." He paused, then, "I can get a car from Goots."

"I'll go with you."

"Would you mind if I went alone? I'll even spend the night there. Hang out with him, talk to him. We've got some issues to settle. Just the two of us."

She squeezed his hand and studied him intently. Anxiety merged with restored hope, and he watched the color creep back into her ashen face. "If you could do that," she said softly, "I would consider it as worthy of celebration as your scholarship."

"I'll talk to him. I promise."

"He told me he's thinking of coming home."

Quentin grew very still. "You mean, quitting?"

She nodded. "And God forgive me, I *want* him to quit. I never thought I'd say that, but I miss him so much and he's worked so hard up there, alone—it hasn't been good for him. If we can just get him home we'll take care of him. He'll find some other place to use as a studio, and we'll get by. It could be a new beginning. He's just so isolated up there."

Quentin held her gaze without wavering. The scholarship was a prize he could hand to his father as proof Riconni men had a future in the world. *Both* of them had a future, and the past could be put aside. He stood. He felt sure of himself, and almost light-hearted. "I'm going to bring him home," he vowed.

*

He arrived at the warehouse just after dark, driving one of Goots' personal cars, a sleek red 1959 Corvette. "For good luck," the German had beamed. "College boy."

Ahead, the glimmer of yellow streetlights around the warehouse filled Quentin with anticipation, although he could see no light from the warehouse windows. Papa was probably huddled under a lamp at his drafting desk. Papa's truck sat in the parking lot.

Quentin repeatedly pressed the buzzer at the side door, but there was no answer. Frowning, he circled the building, trying the mechanisms on a pair of enormous roll-up doors, checking another side entrance, finding everything locked. He went back to the first door and spent five minutes jabbing the buzzer uselessly.

Goosebumps scattered down his spine. He began to list all the possibilities. Someone had picked Papa up for dinner. Papa was sound asleep in the small living area he'd built, and simply didn't hear the buzzer. Papa was deep into a sketch or a model for some sculpture, and was ignoring all visitors.

Papa was with a woman.

That last idea sprang into Quentin's mind unbidden. No matter how much he pushed it away, it galvanized him. He couldn't just drive back to Brooklyn and tell his mother Papa wasn't there. He didn't want to sit in the dark waiting for Papa's return from a meal, either.

Most of all, he didn't want to stand there contemplating the thoughts that were going through his mind. Quentin pulled a pair of long, slender tools from his trouser pocket and carefully slid the tips into the door's key lock. After a minute of expert jiggling and twisting, the bolt clicked back. He eased the heavy metal door open, stepped inside the vast darkness, and shut the door behind him. The steely echo made him uneasy. Papa no longer stored his working materials in that corner.

Quentin moved carefully along the wall until he found a light switch. When he flicked it a hanging work lamp illuminated the plywood cubicle Papa had built as an office and apartment. The twin bed he used was empty, and neatly made. There were no dishes, no sign of a recent meal around the old sink and stove Papa had installed. On the wall behind a scuffed metal desk hung a yellowing photograph

66

of the bear sculpture, with a copy of Betty Tiber's check framed next to it.

Quentin glanced up at bare girders and a dingy skylight, as if Papa must be sitting on a cross beam, playing some kind of joke. He cupped his hands around his mouth. "Hey! Papa! You gone, or what?"

No answer. Quentin peered around a corner into the darkness. He took one step back toward the door then stopped because he felt something slide under his tennis shoe. When he scooped it up he saw it was a sealed envelope.

Papa had written in tall block letters on the front: FOR JOEY ARAIZA. JOEY, READ THIS AS SOON AS YOU COME IN. DON'T TAKE ANOTHER STEP. READ THIS FIRST.

Joey Araiza was an art student from one of the local colleges. Papa let him use space in one corner. Joey built boxes out of steel plate, and then he stacked them. Steel boxes were his entire artistic *oeuvre*. He worshipped Papa.

Okay, so Joey would be here in the morning. Quentin put the envelope on the office desk, then went to a fuse box on a dark wall just outside the cubicle and switched all the breakers. The warehouse's interior flooded with light from industrial fixtures high overhead. Dozens of his father's weird metal sculptures looked back at him, gleaming and cold, yet unnerving in their personality. Maybe they *did* talk, as Papa had claimed when Quentin was little.

He walked warily through a narrow pathway in the maze, squinting into the jungle of twisted metal, feeling foolish. Papa would laugh to see him treading so silently, as if the sculptures could hear.

Papa separated his working and welding area with a makeshift screen built of chain-link fence on a two-by-four frame. The screen was covered with heavy canvas. Quentin went to it and crooked his head around the edge. All he saw was a wall hung with hand tools and welding gear, and in the middle of the floor his father's welding unit, cutting torches, and heavy work tables. Not a thing out of place. He blew out a breath of relief and wandered forward.

"Okay, so I'm just gonna crash on your bed and wait," he said aloud. "You're somewhere, and you'll be back." Quentin snorted in disgust, turned to go to the cubicle, then noticed the warehouse's bathroom just across the work area. The door stood open. He walked into the dark space and flipped the light switch.

His father lay on his back on the cracked tile floor, his face turned toward the door, and thus toward Quentin, his eyes open and blind.

He wore one of his tan work shirts, a pair of his jeans with burn marks on them, and leather work boots. His hair was only slightly ruffled, his long legs were splayed out casually, his left arm was draped across his chest. His right arm was flung out, his strong fingers still and relaxed, ending at the butt of a pistol he always kept in the truck.

The floor beneath him was covered in congealed blood. The smell rose up like a slaughter house. At the center of his chest was a thick hole rimmed with gore. Tiny pieces of flesh had spattered his shirt and jeans.

Quentin would never be able to fully recall what he did or felt in the minutes after that. Eventually he realized he was sitting outside on the stoop of the open warehouse door, sitting there quietly in the darkness, not making a sound, not crying, not moving.

His hands were covered in rusty flecks of dried blood. Like a crazy man he'd tried to feel a heartbeat in his father's chest and, simply by touch, to fix whatever had pushed him over the edge of the cliff he had always walked. But he knew the answer.

I killed him, he thought.

6

Quentin feared his mother would die from grief. He watched her constantly. She did not talk about his father, she did not look at pictures of him, she could not bear to discuss his unsold work sitting in the warehouse, yet. She went to work and returned with barely a word passing her lips, her silence so profound that strangers at the library wondered if she were a deaf-mute. Bone thin and sleepless, she often sat up all night before a small television in the living room, her books open but unread on her lap. Her eyes were always hollow, with a thousand-mile stare.

Inside the drawer of her night stand she kept Papa's suicide note. He had sealed it in a separate envelope inside the letter he left for Joe, which instructed the hapless art student to call the police, tell them they would find his body in the restroom, then walk out and not look back.

To Angele he had written: *I'm empty of ideas and hope. There are no more shapes inside me waiting to be formed. I haven't kept my promises to you, me, or Quentin. Sell everything for scrap and get on with your life. I'm sorry I did this to you and our son. It's no one's fault but mine. I love you both too much to keep dragging you down with me.*

In the end, he had lost faith in himself long before Mother ever would have, and before Quentin could understand that leaving them was his father's truest act of creation, a twisted sacrifice built on love. Quentin would always blame himself.

Joe Araiza kept track of inquiries about his sculptures. Several articles were written about Papa in important art journals. Papa's admirers bought more of his pieces in the six months following his death than ever during his life. *Dead artists are more collectible*, Quentin thought bitterly, when he allowed himself to think about Papa at all. Papa came to him in nightmares, tired, bloody, his chest torn open, holding out his hands, speaking without words. Quentin always woke up with tears in his eyes, frustrated, trying to hear what Papa wanted to tell him. Or warn him about. The same fate?

No. *No.* Mother would always be shackled to Papa's legacy, but Quentin rejected it. Life was about getting the job done, keeping your distance, and looking for the patterns that could kill you. *Don't love what you can't save, don't want what you can't have, don't need what you might have to die for.*

Even Carla couldn't get past this wall. She'd been there for him every day since the suicide—loyal, caring, and always certain that sex, love, and greedy ambition would all work together in his favor as well as hers. He didn't think about her when she wasn't with him. He examined his face in mirrors and wondered how he could be so cold-blooded. It was a sign. Not needing other people would protect him from his father's curse.

Joe Araiza dutifully brought Mother boxes of Papa's files. She began to sort through his sketches and notes, jotting references on long legal pads. "I intend to manage and promote my husband's legacy," she told Joe, who was in awe of her. "Not only will that legacy survive, it will flourish. I promise you."

"They'll say he was a genius," Joe assured her.

She looked at him without blinking, and nodded. She was able to go on because she could convince herself of absolutes. She wrote a letter to Mountain State College in Tiberville, Georgia.

I am so pleased to think of my husband's favorite sculpture gracing your campus. I'm sure it has been an object of great admiration and discussion over the past decade. My husband recently passed away, but his work, his goals, and his legacy will live on forever in monumental creations such as the bear. In going through his files I discovered that he had given the sculpture a name: Bare Wisdom. The whimsical name reminded me that he was a man of gentle humor as well as brilliant artistic talent. Could you please let me know how Bare Wisdom is doing? I would greatly appreciate any photographs and anecdotes you could send.

Quentin returned from a long walk one night to find her sitting on the apartment stoop with Mrs. Silberstein, who had a consoling arm around her. His mother looked shell-shocked. "What's wrong?" he asked.

"What those stupid *schmucks* at that *cockamamie* college did, that's what," Mrs. Silberstein answered hotly. Mother handed him the letter that had come from Mountain State's administrative office.

Dear Mrs. Riconni, we're sorry to inform you that following the recent passing of Mrs. Herbert J. (Betty) Tiber, her commissioned sculpture of a bear was removed from campus and has since been destroyed. No photographs or other information regarding the sculpture will be available now or in the future from Mountain State officials.

"I had dreamed of seeing it again," Mother said quietly. "I had dreamed of seeing it be celebrated and revered."

Quentin laid the letter on her lap. "I'd get it back for you, if I could," he said hoarsely.

All those years, all those hopes, his father's life, his own honor. He'd give it all back to her, if he could. Everything. His childhood began and ended with the bear.

*

He took a Jaguar on a frigid night in early March. He went all the way to Manhattan, slipped the sleek, steel-gray car from a parking garage, and wondered aloud, during the drive back over the bridge that had taken his great-grandfather's life, if he was asking to get himself caught. When he pulled down into the alley of a chop-shop garage on his home turf he blew the horn, then got out as always and lounged in the shadows nearby, waiting for the owner, a black man named Marshall, to open the garage's heavy steel doors.

Marshall was slow that night, he thought. Quentin pulled a cheap silver cigarette lighter from the pocket of his black jacket and idly flicked the top. The soft metallic click seemed to echo on the brick walls around him, or to call up an answering sound, not an echo. Quentin frowned and straightened, the hair rising on the back of his neck. He realized too late he'd just heard the sound of a revolver being cocked.

"Police! Don't move!" someone yelled, and then a second voice repeated that. The beam of a flashlight blinded Quentin and he heard the rush of several officers as they leapt from a doorway further down the alley. He bolted three long strides toward the street, operating on sheer instinct before he saw another trio running toward him from that direction, too.

By the time he slid to a stop the first group was on him. He was tackled and slammed to the ground, pain shot through his jaw, and he tasted blood in his mouth. Men were sitting on him, standing on him, grinding their heels into the small of his back, jerking his arms half out of their sockets as they wrenched his hands together and cuffed them.

Suddenly they moved back, and he could breathe a little. He raised his head enough to look at the tips of Alfonse Esposito's polished wingtips. Carla's father dropped to his heels beside Quentin. Alfonse had a long, serious face, gray sideburns in his black hair, and a nose that had been fractured a half-dozen times. Yet he dressed and spoke with an elegance that was unnerving.

He spoke in a low, utterly dispassionate tone. "I've had my suspicions for a long time, but I didn't want to tell your mother.

Yesterday I caught Carla with a fistful of your money. She wouldn't confess the truth, but I'm not stupid. You'll get out of this with your nose clean—I'll do that for your mother's sake. But it's going to be on my terms, I'll make sure of *that*. Your mother's a classy lady and she trusted you, and now you're going to break her heart just like your old man did. And I ought to kill you for getting my daughter involved in this."

"Go ahead," Quentin said quietly, filled with stone-cold apathy. He rested his head on the bloody pavement.

*

"Did I teach you a code of honor so complex that you could not follow it?" Mother asked in a voice so soft he had to strain to hear it. They faced each other at the kitchen table after he was released on bail. His mouth was swollen, one cheek turning bright purple. He sat with hunched shoulders, his large and capable young hands in front of him on the old Formica tabletop, as if still cuffed together. "I helped you pay the bills," he rasped. "I saved the rest."

"Alfonse is sending me the money Carla hid for you in her bank account. Thousands of dollars. I intend to donate it all to charity."

"That money was my way of taking care of you and me. And Papa, if he hadn't given up. For the future."

"You felt your papa always let you down?" Her voice shook with emotion. "You believed he'd never prove himself?"

"Yes."

"So you became a thief. And a liar. And a cheat. And you allowed Carla Esposito to act as your accomplice. A girl who loves you dearly. All of those choices were an honorable balm for your pride?"

He winced at her description of his judgment. "I take responsibility. I did what I had to do."

"No, you did what came easiest, and you called it necessity. Your papa died for us, and this is what you gave him in return. Shame."

He said nothing. She raised her chin. Her eyes glittered. She looked ragged, her clothes disheveled, her brown hair in wild rivulets and feathered with gray. "I've been weak since he died. Allowing myself to mourn endlessly when there was work to be done, and trusting you, depending on you, to take charge of your own life, to be the man I thought he had inspired you to become."

Quentin's head, already bowed, sank lower. He didn't ask for her forgiveness, or shout that his father didn't deserve any defense. He simply hurt, deep in his soul, for everything. "I'll make it up to you," he promised, the words graveled.

"You'll make it up to *him*," she corrected, and left him sitting there, more utterly alone than he had ever been in his life.

*

Alfonse was able to get him a deal with a judge who owed Alfonse favors. The judge would keep Quentin's arrest off the record and have the charges dropped, but only on one condition: Quentin would have to join the army.

The punishment seemed quaint in a post-Vietnam world where military service had become a dubious glory but not a life-threatening one. Yet it meant the loss of his prized scholarship, banishment from home, and the fierce tragedy of his mother's disappointment. Now he had destroyed another of her dreams.

"My son will go into the army and redeem himself," she said, when Alfonse gently told her. "I have no doubt." She hurt too much to let anyone know she was devastated, and she feared she would fly apart if she admitted the destruction of her family, her goals. So she began to school herself to show no outward emotion at all. Quentin could never come to her for a smile or a soft hug, again. He knew he deserved her rejection, and he knew he had to earn her respect, but it nearly killed him.

He opened a box in his closet, took out years of notebooks filled with his writings, carried them downstairs, and burned them in an alley. He saved only one, the first one when he was eight, to remind himself that he'd started out loving and being loved as simply as anyone could imagine.

On the day he left to join the army, Mother stood at the apartment window just as she had done when Papa moved upstate. Almost ten years separated those days, and she no longer smiled. Dressed in a slender black dress, she raised one hand in formal farewell. From the sidewalk, Quentin gazed up at her in agony and homesickness and self-loathing so thick he went numb. He had visited Alfonse the night before. "I'm asking you to look after my mother," he said to the stern detective, who quietly smoked a pipe and watched him with shrewd, dark eyes.

"I will. You have my word. In return, I ask that you break off with Carla. No letters, no phone calls. Let her forget you." Alfonse had sent her to the suburbs of Chicago to stay with an aunt. Quentin heard she was practically locked in the aunt's house. He'd received one letter from her, smuggled through a friend. *I'll always love you. I'll wait for you forever.*

He sent her a thousand dollars he had managed to keep, and wrote on a slip of paper, *I'm sorry for everything. Don't wait.*

Quentin now winnowed his goals to a brief, blessed few. Survive. Earn the right to live. Never be hurt by a loved one or cause hurt to a loved one, again. He had to fit Alfonse's order into this new structure. As his silence stretched out, Alfonse's eyes narrowed. "Tell me something. Honestly. Do you love her?"

After a moment, Quentin answered simply, and truthfully. "No."

"Thank you. Then you'll be doing her a favor."

Quentin exhaled slowly. "I won't contact her. You have my word."

So he had settled all the scores with his old life, his childhood, as much as he could. He raised a hand in goodbye to Angele Dolinski Riconni, his mother, and to the only home he had ever known. Then he got in a cab and didn't look back.

When he could no longer see her, Angele pressed her hand to the window, and cried.

*

Mama shouldn't have died; the baby shouldn't have been hurt. I thought I would become transparent and float away from rage and pain. I convinced myself that Mama would have told me to call the doctor if we'd had the money to pay him—if Daddy hadn't bought the Iron Bear. Her strict religion, her peculiarities, her own stubborn backwardness evaporated completely from my mind. She became sacred, perfect, an angel who could not be held to account.

Daddy named the baby *Arthur*, saying it was a heroic name, coming from the old Welsh language, from a time of myth and fantasy, an old Celtic legend. In old legends it paid homage to bears, like my name. Arthur was a hero on the day of his birth, and he was definitely a miracle—because I couldn't hate him for causing Mama's death. I think I knew right away that he wasn't quite as he should be, that he'd been damaged. A doctor told us he might be mentally retarded.

Daddy said it didn't matter, that there was room for all kinds of creations in the world. I stared at Daddy with vengeful misery. I wanted to yell, *You ought to care. It's your fault*, but the words remained inside me, festering. I loved Daddy so much that the fury and the disappointment had no place to go but into the bones of my own soul, where they would harden and constrict.

At school, the double horror of the truth sank in, again. Janine sidled up to me one day and whispered, "You better be nice to me or I'll tell my daddy to have your mama *dug up*, because you're just a charity case and my daddy had to pay for her funeral." I immediately said, "You're a liar," but she repeated it smugly and I stared at her in blind rage, knowing in my guts that even Janine Tiber wouldn't lie about something like that. I drew back a fist and punched her in the mouth, regardless. She lost the last of her front baby teeth thanks to me, but she never told anyone I'd hit her, which was even more proof that she hadn't lied. She wouldn't risk explaining why I'd been provoked.

I never asked Daddy about the funeral costs. If it was a loan from Mr. John, he paid it back and never told me, but the damage was done. He mourned Mama endlessly, but I punished him by never crying in front of him. He wore her little gold wedding band on a chain around his neck. I slept in her shirts, burrowed in her sweaters, enclosed myself in everything of hers that would fit me in any form. Even then, in those first weeks and months, I was changed, angry, distant. Daddy would begin to sense all that as I grew older, but not yet.

I sneaked after him on clear nights and watched him stand by the Iron Bear with his tear-streaked face raised to white, lonely moons. His grief for Mama surpassed my own, and made it easier, somehow, to learn to hide how much I missed her and faulted him. We couldn't afford two moon gazers in the family. I knew my own strength, now. I saw Daddy's world—his art, his gentle whimsies—as selfish and short-sighted. After all, it was me who had rescued Arthur, and saved his life.

After Daddy stumbled back inside the house on those nights, I crept to the Bear. I always found a small tree limb to bring with me. With all my might I flailed at the sculpture's unbreakable prongs and swoops and angles, furious because the heartbreak of lost magic and betrayed trust made not even one dent, not even one shiver of sympathy from the one creation that had the power to steal everything I loved. *Liar, killer, thief,* I chanted. Hard and fast rules began to take root where fantasies had played. I would escape from this kingdom ruled by forces I couldn't control. And then I'd become just as unbreakable as the uncaring thing I tried to tear apart.

PART TWO

Twenty-two years later

7

Angele kept a scrapbook of her son's accomplishments, though she didn't tell him. Pasted in that volume was an article she'd found in a veteran's magazine. The writer had interviewed a soldier who'd served with Quentin in the 1991 Gulf War.

The captain in our Ranger company was a career officer named Riconni, but we nicknamed him X-Ray because he had a weird ability to see inside things. I mean this captain could take things apart, fix them, and put them back together like new. He didn't even need a diagram or anything. Guns, cannons, hell, probably even a whole tank if you asked him—there musta been nothing Capt. Riconni couldn't memorize and take apart.

He came from a tough neighborhood somewhere around New York, I heard— he had that whole mean-street attitude going when he needed it, but he was real sophisticated and educated, too. He had this look in his eyes that told you he'd seen something he couldn't put back together or forget, so maybe that's why he'd been in the army forever. He didn't have much to go home to. He was easy to get along with, but nobody messed with him. He liked to read poetry and shit like that. He could speak Latin, for godssake.

But he was there when we needed him. When a Humvee drove through an Iraqi mine field we had five guys hurt bad, screaming. They were stuck in the damned camel-humper desert where there wasn't even a bush to use as a guide or landmark. Nobody else woulda set a foot around the Humvee. But Capt. Riconni took a long look at the spots where the mines blew up, and then he picked his way out to those guys—five trips out, five trips back, while the rest of us stood there all ass-knotted so bad we could taste our own shit. Officers usually sent the lowest dumb-cluck in the platoon to do a job like that. They didn't risk their own hide.

But Capt. Riconni carried all those guys out of the mine field, and he never missed a step. Man, it was creepy and awesome. The colonel asked him later how he did it, and Capt. Riconni just said, Everything fits a pattern. All you have to do is find it.

When our company got back to the States the Army gave him a couple of medals, and he got some write ups in the news, and that's when we learned that his pop had been some kind of artist—sculptor or something—so we thought maybe the Captain had inherited a knack—an eye for seeing stuff, you know, like a photographic memory or something. But one of the guys got the nerve to ask him about it, about having a talent he got from his father, and Capt. Riconni got this closed look on his face and said the only thing his father had a talent for was pulling a trigger. We never knew what the hell he meant by that, and nobody had the balls to ask him. He quit the army not too long after that. Guess he'd proved whatever he wanted to prove. I've always wondered what happened to him since then.

A lot of hard-assed guys have off-limits places inside their heads you wouldn't want to visit without a bodyguard. That captain was the bravest man I've ever seen, but he'd walked some heavy-duty minefields before he ever went to war.

Angele felt heartbroken every time she read that last part, though she never told Quentin how much she worried, how much she still grieved for the words she and he never spoke, anymore. He, in return, had never told her he'd saved men's lives, and had been called a hero.

*

The incredible year that ended in blood on a wild Georgia mountaintop began, for Quentin, in a private viewing room of one of the biggest auction houses of Manhattan. He stood at a discreetly tinted two-way mirror, gazing down on a packed audience of wealthy art patrons with the cool intensity of an amused wolf. He would turn forty on his next birthday, and the slightest hint of gray tinged the hair at his temples. But he was still muscled and lean, a disciplined man of spartan but elegant tastes, the strong set of his weathered face as clean as the line of a rifle.

Dressed in a handsome gray winter suit, his black hair gleaming under the soft lights, he might have been one of the wealthy men sitting in the room beyond the window, except for his heavily callused hands, the army tattoo hidden under his shirt sleeve, and a deep, watchful reserve that spoke of something far less elegant than the suit promised.

The seven years since his return from the military hadn't been soft or easy, but they had been successful. He owned an architectural salvage company. Dreams of becoming an architect or a builder had long since faded. With blunt precision and a certain compassion for lost treasures, he dismembered other people's homes.

In the pocket of his fine gray trousers he still carried his father's gift, the thin silver knife, spring-hinged and razor-sharp. He kept it more for nostalgia than need, though there were still times when he palmed it discreetly behind his curled fingers.

Angele sat nearby, straight-backed and proud as she gazed at the auction beyond the window. A Manhattan stylist kept her graying hair short and perfectly formed. Her face was lined with the soft signatures of sorrow and wisdom.

She had long-ago given up her glasses for contact lenses, and her plain skirts had become simple, tailored, suit dresses. She wore no jewelry except tiny gold earrings and the plain gold wedding band Richard had given her. She walked with a handsome wooden cane fitted with a brass handle that Quentin had made for her from metal left in his father's supplies. Everything else she had made of herself— image and substance—was designed to reflect well on Richard's sacrifice and his work.

In the art world she was gently known as The Steel Angel, a respectful joke that indicated how much fame she'd earned as a one-woman promoter of her husband's work. Over the past two decades she'd written countless magazine articles about his pieces, persuaded museums to display his sculptures, organized gallery exhibits, and bombarded the art critics for endorsements.

She had even persuaded a small publisher to issue a handsome book with pictures of the sculptures and excerpts from Richard's notes. Even now she went regularly to the bookstore at the Museum of Modern Art to check their inventory and secretly, when the clerks weren't looking, turned the Riconni book face out on the shelves.

Finally, she'd staged an amazing promotional *coup*. She'd talked her way into a meeting with brawny, mercurial *Lucca*, the current darling of the Italian fashion designers, and had convinced him to use a few Riconni sculptures as set pieces in one of his smaller Parisian showrooms. Richard's erotically masculine sculptures fit perfectly in the *Lucca*-centered world. "What life, what lust, what a consuming *need* for satisfaction they inspire, *so much like my own work*," he said of the Riconnis, when interviewed by *Vanity Fair*.

Soon Riconni sculptures had been seen in his showrooms across Europe, and then, New York. As one after another of the sculptures sold to high-profile buyers, the art world began to take notice. Suddenly *Riconni* was the name every serious collector of modern art must possess. An auction was announced. The entire collection of remaining Riconnis would be sold at one of the most talked-about events of recent years.

Today.

"They're selling the piece your papa titled Absence," Angele said to Quentin. Another sleek creation rotated into view with slow, grand presentation on a circular platform. The audience's numbered placards flashed like military signals, and the auctioneer's elegant chant rose with theatrical excitement.

"I watched him build that," Quentin said. "One summer."

A long canine tongue licked Quentin's hand, distracting him, and he was grateful. He stroked the head of the large, front-heavy, ugly blonde dog who then settled back down at his feet, pillowed on the long gray coat Quentin had tossed there without caring. Hammer affectionately licked Quentin's polished shoes for a moment then returned to gnawing a beef bone the auction house's staff had hurriedly acquired from a restaurant. No amount of pampering was too extravagant for Richard Riconni's heirs, including pets.

"Hope And Light, item one-fifty-seven, *sold*," the auctioneer intoned, slapping a gavel on a gleaming wooden podium. "For two-twenty-five." The sound of the gavel filtered into the small private room through a speaker, which lent it an appropriately surreal quality. Two hundred and twenty-five thousand dollars.

"Why couldn't your papa live to see this?" Angele asked. "I know he's with us, watching over us in spirit, but still. *Still.*"

Quentin inclined his head in acknowledgement but refused to be drawn into his mother's musings. She wanted to believe Father Aleksandr's gentle view of suicides. He'd told her Papa was watching from a special place granted by the Pope. Religious faith was one of many supports Quentin had removed from his life. He regarded it as a curiosity, not a need.

She grew more rigid at his silence. "Don't you ever wish your father had lived?"

"I wish Papa knew how much you love him."

"And you?"

"He was my father. I try not to think about it."

She looked at him angrily, as if some younger and more easily damaged version of herself were about to escape. On the delicate antique table near Quentin sat a stack of glossy catalogues prepared specially for today's massive sale. The title was embossed in gold. *Richard Riconni: Icons From the Industrial Millennium.* Angele opened one of the auction catalogs and made herself look at the one page she'd avoided until then.

On it was printed a grainy, black-and-white photograph of the bear sculpture. Art critics were calling the sculpture *a turning point conception.* Beneath the photograph, a single line of text summed up the sculpture's fate: *Unfortunately, this magnificent and unique early masterpiece of Riconni's was destroyed in 1976. (Owner: Mountain State College, Tiberville, Georgia.)*

She touched the page with her hand. "This deserved better than a scrap pile. This is the one that mattered the most to him. And to me."

Quentin's cool reserve wavered for a moment and he spoke gently, as he had as a grieving teenager all those years ago. "I'd get it back for you, if I could."

Suddenly tears slid down her face. She turned away, her back quivering with restraint. Since he'd left home as a teen she'd rarely acknowledged his help, his sympathy, or his affection. Quentin searched for tissues, saw none, and ripped two thick blossoms off an arrangement of roses. He handed them to her.

"Roses?" she said. She made a garbled sound over the clumps of satiny red petals, then pressed them to her cheeks. Hammer sat up, anxiously cocking his head at her noises. He rested his huge, friendly head on her lap and gazed at her with worried brown eyes. Quentin had rescued him from a dumpster. He was perpetually grateful to all Riconnis.

"Item number 158, *sold!* Sold at one-point-one," the auctioneer's disembodied voice said. *Million.*

The last word, unspoken but implied, made a silent echo in the room's stunned silence. The amounts were beyond comprehension. The bleak irony of it all was beyond words. Angele's years of lonely devotion, Quentin's endless, bitter remorse, and Richard's agonized sacrifice had finally paid off.

At a very high price.

*

Ursula, you don't make it easy for a man to be a man. You're too self-sufficient. You're a small business with no interest in outside investors. A professor said that to me in graduate school after our third and last date.

He was right. I had grown up determined to make ends meet and to never accept the Powell-anointed middle ground of make-do. No half measures for *me*, even though some of the reserve people assumed about me simply came from a childhood spent in poverty at Bear Creek. My cool confidence was really just a protective stillness learned from standing downwind of chicken shit.

While I was a student at Emory University I worked sixteen hours a day, seven days a week to buy a tiny old bookstore in an aging Atlanta neighborhood. For the first few years after I graduated I made up for the store's losses by moonlighting part-time as a midnight-shift manager at a canning factory in the flat suburbs south of Atlanta. I was driven by a need for security—not money so much as dependable goods and ideas. I scared away the men who might have helped me— challenged them, overwhelmed them, sent them scuttling back down the sides of my personal mountain as fast as they could run.

Good-looking women don't usually want to be left alone the way you do, one ex-boyfriend said to me as he packed his apartment for a move to Europe.

Smart women are all good looking, I answered.

I liked to think of myself as classic, like a statue of a Roman noblewoman. At the age of 32 I had topped out at almost six feet tall, with long hair the color of an old penny, a strong-boned body of reasonably jiggling proportions, and a square-jawed face with deepset blue eyes surrounded by stubby brown lashes.

And I finally *had* found a pleasant, dependable, likable man to *keep time with*, as the old mountain women put it. He was a researcher from the Centers for Disease Control. Very brilliant, very logical, very clean. I met him when I rented the garage apartment behind his bungalow. I continued to live there and pay him rent even after several years of intimacy and rejected marriage proposals. He was not happy about that. But I was.

I would never be my mother, I vowed. Never love a man so much I let his dreams kill me. So I'd put distance between the people and memories that hurt me or might hurt me—most of all, Daddy. At least I told myself I had.

I liked to think of myself as happy and *right*.

But I was all wrong.

*

The "Save the Shops of Peachtree Lane" rally, which I organized, was held on a perfect day for public protest: Bright, blue-skied, and sixty-five degrees, a sunny vacation in the middle of a chilly Atlanta winter. I carried a clip board among the crowd with all the humor of a smiling commandant. I looked like the tall, sturdy warden of an elegant female prison, dressed in black silk trousers, a black sweater, and a brown wool blazer, with my hair swept back in a tight French braid. People gulped and did what I told them to do. I handed out SAVE PEACHTREE LANE decals and presented children with silver pencils from the local literacy group. *Read, Learn, Grow*, they ordered.

The normally quiet, tree-lined, two-lane streets leading into the Peachtree Lane community were choked with parked cars and people. I'd hired a pair of off-duty police officers to direct traffic around the shops. The crowds spilled into a small park across the way, picnicking on the soft, faded lawn or dancing in the golden sunshine to the music of a house band from an upscale nightclub in Atlanta's Buckhead district. The band, which had donated its services, played a mixture of old ballads, swing, and top-forty.

I grimly hummed Nat King Cole's *Unforgettable* under my breath. Life should be about matters of substance, lasting values, ideas and accomplishments built to withstand any test. I had settled in a neighborhood of age and character, and now I was fighting to save a block of small, aged brick shops that had been lucky to escape a bulldozer long before then.

"Signature, please? Oh, bless your heart. Thank you so much." Armed with that southern-belle mantra, I was unstoppable. I knew how to be polite yet intimidating, a style I'd learned from the late Edythe Ellis, my bookstore's famous former owner. Edythe had come from silver-spoon Atlanta gentry encased in generations of shrewd, Old South manners.

Over in the parking lot, two dozen authors sat autographing their books at long tables. A part of the proceeds would go to our merchants' association's legal fund. I'd purposefully positioned the tables in the center of the crumbling, pot-holed parking lot to draw attention to the graceful old peach tree at its center, inhabiting a small island in the cracked concrete, circled by granite stones big enough to sit on. Several hundred fans waited patiently in long, roped-off lines to get their books autographed. I had placed a large sign on the shops' namesake peach tree, where everyone in line would see it. I'LL BE THE FIRST TO GO, IF YOU DON'T HELP. I was shameless.

As I moved down the line of book-toting autograph seekers, plying them to sign my petition, I heard a voice, meek and gentle, but rising in a trill. "Please don't take another cookie... really, won't you please sign the petition, at least?"

I turned in time to watch a well-dressed woman shake her head as she took a gingerbread cookie from Harriet Davies. Harriet, a small, round woman in soft tweeds, ran the Magnolia Tea Room next door to my shop. She reminded me of the pastel characters in Beatrix Potter. I had grown up fiercely defending Arthur against bullies; the sight of Harriet's distress made me instantly angry.

"I don't get involved in politics," the woman told Harriet, then blithely fished through the cookie basket on Harriet's petition table and started to hand a second cookie to her friend. The cookies were shaped like zoo animals.

"No petition signature, no giraffe," I said, intercepting both long-necked cookies, which were wrapped in cellophane. I tucked them in my blazer pocket. I could not abide the parasites of the world. Every one of them was a Janine Tiber, filled with gall, grabbing my book. *Mine*, they said.

Not in this generation, I answered.

"What do you think you're doing?" the woman sputtered.

"Sorry, ladies, but there are rules of social activism around here. Comeon now, won't y'all sign our petition and help us out?"

"You can keep your cookies, bitch," the first woman retorted in a flat midwestern tone. I took a menacing step towards them. "What did you say?" I asked in a soft, icy voice that promised an old-fashioned walloping. The woman's brows shot up. Her friend said quickly, "Tiffany, she's not kidding," and pulled her into the crowd.

Harriet stared up at me like a pleased rabbit. "I'm glad you use your powers for doing good instead of evil, Supergirl. I wish I had your courage."

"Sometimes even to live is an act of courage," I quoted.

"Who said so?"

"Seneca."

"Oh. One of your Roman philosophers. He never had to protect gingerbread cookies."

I returned to my petition work. "Ursula, I need some background on you," called a reporter from the Atlanta Journal/Constitution. I had cultivated the media so much as a small bookstore owner hunting for publicity that I was on a first-name basis with half the reporters in town. "Terry, you don't need to know anything about me. It'll rate about two lines at the bottom of your piece on this rally."

"Yeah, but I'm thinking of freelancing an article to Atlanta Magazine on the in-town independent bookstore scene."

"There is no in-town independent bookstore scene. I'm the only one left."

"Exactly. And now you're fighting developers who want to put in a strip shopping center. The big bookstore chains couldn't take you down, but the malling of America might. Isn't that ironic?"

"I hate irony. I promise you, nobody's going to build a discount pharmacy and a video store on the same stretch of earth where Margaret Mitchell autographed a copy of Gone with the Wind in 1939 and Maya Angelou recited poetry last year. My bookstore isn't just a landmark, it's a sixty-year icon of the southern literary community. Nobody's going to sell hemorrhoid creams and rent out Adam Sandler movies where Truman Capote spent a whole afternoon sipping toddies and reading out loud from his books. I promise you."

"Background," she said again. "Don't change the subject."

I gave her the nickel spiel—president of the Peachtree Lane merchants association, president of the regional booksellers' association, scholarship graduate with honors of Emory, and I made certain to plug my back-room publishing empire, Powell Press, which consisted of two fledgling authors no one had heard of.

"More personal," she insisted.

"On a good day people tell me I look a little like Julia Roberts. On a bad day they admit they were wrong."

"Somebody told me your father runs some kind of artists' co-op in the mountains."

I fixed a long, quiet look on her. "He has tenants who call themselves folk artists. They live in what used to be his chicken houses, which he converted to crappy apartments after I left for college. His tenants cheat him, steal from him, and mooch off his generosity. One of them got arrested for selling redneck cocaine and the government nearly confiscated our entire farm. I told him to shut down the apartments or I wouldn't come home again. He didn't and I haven't. That was two years ago."

"Oh. Uh, I see. Sorry."

"I have to go, now. I've got rabble to rouse. I'll meet you for a glass of wine at the Rib Shack tomorrow."

She smiled awkwardly as I walked away. The mere mention of Daddy had put a knot in the pit of my stomach. My Atlanta friends vaguely realized I regularly sent money to a father and an autistic brother in the mountains, but they had never visited my home, and they had no idea that I was far from where I belonged, and that I had finally broken Daddy's heart, just as he had broken mine when Mama died.

After I'd bought the business from Edythe I installed a striped awning over the stoop and a handsome iron railing around the edges of its plain concrete block. I set out a small wrought iron café table and two heavy iron chairs, where I ate my meals, even in cold weather. I craved the outdoors, and if I shut my eyes, I was at Bear Creek.

During an afternoon break Dr. Cesara Lopez-Jones sat outside on the stoop with me, her aching pen hand soaking in a silver bowl of warm, mentholated water that I provided. Dr. L-J, as the public called her, was a bestselling author of self-help books and a nationally syndicated radio therapist. "This feels wonderful," she said.

"I put some old-fashioned salve in the water," I told her. "It's something I buy when I go home to visit." As if I had been home, lately. "A neighbor of my father's used it this way. He said it was the only thing that helped his arthritis."

"I must get a supply. What's the name?"

"It's Dr. Akins' Udder Balm." And then I confirmed, "It's meant for sore cow teets."

Dr. L-J's eyes widened, and she burst out laughing.

"Well, cows like it." She laughed, again. I took out a pack of cigarettes and lit one. She peered at me. "So you've become a smoker. Doesn't your pristine Gregory hate that?"

I smiled as I drooped my cigarette-holding hand over the stoop's railing. I'd let the cigarette burn to the filter without taking another puff. "There's nothing sinister about this."

"Any marriage date, yet?"

"We're in no hurry."

"I see. Well. He's out of town this weekend?"

"Presenting a paper."

"Out of sight, out of mind."

"Dr. L-J, you're prying."

"You bet. I've watched you become harder and more driven over the years. It worries me."

All right, this was going to be my personal counseling session, no matter how much I tried to avoid that fact. I looked at her squarely. "My love life is not important. But I *would* like some advice on my father."

"Ahah. Go ahead. The doctor is in." She leaned forward, set her wine glass down, and collected a handful of my homemade cheese straws from the platter. The pungent smell of mentholated udder balm filled my nose. Home.

I took a deep breath, and told her how things were with Daddy. That I had finally told him how I felt about Mama's death. That he'd looked at me as if I'd ripped his heart out, and we hadn't spoken since. Dr. L-J studied me sympathetically. "Honesty can be painful, but it's usually worth it in the long run. Not always, but usually."

I shook my head and chuckled wearily. "I'm tired of honesty."

"Did you say anything to him that you don't sincerely believe, then and now?"

After a dull moment, I exhaled wearily. "No. I've been mad at him since I was a little girl. Mad and hurt."

"Go see your father. Put your arms around him. Tell him that it's time to move forward. Just tell him you love him. You don't have to accept everything he does."

"Too easy," I insisted. "That won't solve the larger issues."

"Well, of course not. You have to learn to butt out of his business and accept him the way he is, and he has to respect your difference of opinion, and both of you have to compromise, and that could take the rest of your lives. But you can start the process, at least. Are you going to be happy if you don't try?"

"Listen, *happy* is a word I look up regularly just to see if I understand the definition."

"You're looking in the wrong dictionary. It takes work, trial and error, and risks."

"I'll drive up tomorrow and take him to lunch," I said slowly, my words already attaching themselves to anchors.

"And tell him you love him," she insisted.

"I'll have to think about that." I couldn't even repeat the words now, so I didn't know how I'd get them out tomorrow, but I'd work at it.

"Promise me," Dr. L-J growled.

I arched a brow. "You have my word that I'll try."

She laughed. "You are wrapped in steel. Aren't you suffocating inside that armor?"

"I've cut breathing holes."

We talked on for awhile, of fears and compromises and loved ones and communicating with the dead, that is, the memories of every person you represent in the world, hearing their voices as well as your own.

"You're pretty good at this advice business," I said.

She lifted her soaking hand and smiled. "My next book should be titled, *Teet Salve For The Soul.*"

We heard the chimes on the store's front door. I assumed one of my clerks had come in to use the bathroom. I got up and walked inside. "How's it going out there?"

Dr. Jonah Washington gazed back at me gently. Mr. Fred had died a few years before. In the past year Jonah had retired from teaching at Harvard and shocked everyone by moving back to his brother's homestead at Bear Creek.

And now, without explanation, he had driven two hours from Tiber County and stood in my bookstore. He was a short, rotund, brown-black man with a neat gray beard and pepper-gray hair—always a very dapper dresser in his photographs, but on that day he looked harried in old corduroy trousers with leather suspenders, a flannel shirt, muddy walking shoes and a rumpled windbreaker.

"Dr. Washington, I'm so glad you came to the rally!" Bewildered, I hurried toward him with one hand outstretched. Suddenly, something kind and sad in his face sank into me with warning. Suddenly, I knew. I stopped a few feet away from him, afraid. I lowered my hand to my side. "Is it my father, or is it Arthur?" I asked.

He spoke in a deep, resonant voice, the voice of souls forged in quiet sorrows. "It's your father," he said.

8

At the funeral home I cupped my hands around Daddy's peaceful, homely face and begged him to open his eyes. When he didn't, I rested my head on his chest and sang a lullaby to him. As strange as that sounds, it kept me from breaking down. I had Arthur to think about. I feared the depths of my own panic and despair.

Daddy's tenants told me he sank to his hands and knees without warning, while crossing the pasture just below the Bear to retrieve a ladder stored in the barn. As everyone ran to him he put one hand over his heart, turned himself, and managed to stretch out atop the soft winter grass. He had been planning to clean the house gutters, which were overflowing with autumn leaves, fallen tree branches, and the dried brown fringe of summer weeds that had taken root there. I knew what he had said before he went for the ladder, because every winter, when I was a child, he offered the house an apology. *Time to take your necklace off, old gal.*

Arthur was away in the creek hollow on one of his daily searches for any number of small wild animals and birds he called friends, and so he didn't see our father collapse. Just before Daddy went for the ladder he told the tenants to help him watch all the local Atlanta television stations that evening, in case I was interviewed at the rally. He'd called everyone he knew to brag about the event. He was always proud, always hoping I'd come home. He had his pride. I inherited it.

And so Daddy died where he most likely wanted most to die, under the gaze of the Iron Bear. Did it speak to him finally, the way Arthur claimed it could? I'd never know.

And I could never tell him I was sorry.

*

Arthur and I slept in Daddy's big bed that first night after he died, me wrapped up in a quilt atop the covers, Arthur huddled beneath them. We'd slept together many times as children when he was frightened or confused, which was often. When he'd gotten old enough I'd methodically explained to him about sex, sisters, taboos, and politeness. He understood. He had such an anxious sense of his own spaces and boundaries that he didn't want me to so much as brush a hand near him when he slept.

But now he burrowed his head against my shoulder and cried. My gently autistic brother was a shapeshifter. Usually he went through his days as a small, harmless mammal—a mouse, a squirrel, a rabbit—and sometimes as a bird, a snake, or a fish, rarely anything dangerous. More often than not, he was a bear cub. He was 22 years old and over six feet tall, slender, elfish, and beautiful, with a congregation of tender animal psyches inside him. That night, he was a heartbroken puppy. "Tell me stories about us," he whispered.

I retold all our legends for him, and for me. Erim and Granny Annie, Miss Betty, Mama and the snakes, Mr. Fred's encounter with me down at the creek, Daddy's salvation from the polio epidemic, and then the Iron Bear—how it came to be, how it came to town, and how Richard Riconni, a man we had never met, had looked into our hearts. This was Daddy's version of the Bear's story, not mine.

As I talked I stroked his hair, which was long and glossy brown, Mama's color. He cried for hours. After he fell asleep I stared at the ceiling, where the narrow, slatted boards of an old design seemed to sway in the darkness. I was looking for patterns, for answers, but there were none, or I didn't know how to see them.

The next morning Arthur pulled me outside to the Bear. He gazed hollow-eyed at the sculpture, holding onto its sides, his knuckles white. My skin crawled; he seemed to be lost in some silent, frantic communication. Suddenly he leapt back from the sculpture, his mouth gaping, his hands curled to his chest. He whirled toward me. "Sister, you went away," he said, his voice breaking. "You didn't want us, anymore. Daddy was sad. He cried. Where did you go? Where's *he* gone?"

For one irrational moment I thought, *What is that thing telling you about me? It's a lie.* "Oh, Sweetie, I'm sorry. I'm so sorry. I'll try to explain it all to you. All that matters is that I've come back. I took care of you when you were little and I'm going to take care of you, now. Don't worry."

He lifted both hands toward the Iron Bear. He trembled. A new torrent of words poured out. "Lonely lonely lonely. Mama Bear's so lonely. She's all empty inside her ribs. My ribs are empty, too. I don't know what I ought to do! Nobody loves her, anymore. She'll die! Just like Daddy!"

I held him in my arms, and looked up with weary disgust at the sculpture. I was ten years old, again, vowing to fight it in the name of common sense and Powell family redemption. *Liar, killer, thief of hearts.*

Daddy had stored his will in an empty fruit jar in a dresser drawer of his and Mama's bedroom, and it was very simple. *I leave everything I own and love to my daughter, Ursula. I trust her to take care of her brother, the farm, and the Iron Bear. I leave her all the good and the bad that our family has been and will be. I leave her my mistakes, my sadness, my faith and my love. She has her mama's angel looking over her, and the heart to make some sense of it all.*

*

Mr. John came to the funeral home every night. I suddenly appreciated his friendly, gray-fringed bald head, his hearty, put-women-on-pedestals manners, and his silk ties emblazoned with tiny Tiber Farms logos. He had only grown older, not different. "You call on me when you feel like it," he urged kindly. "I don't want you to think you're taking on your Daddy's woes without a friend in the world. I'm good for plenty of advice and assistance."

I'd never accept help from a Tiber, but I didn't tell him that.

Janine came by, too, signed the guest book, and pressed my hand with her cool, beautiful fingers. "Your daddy was certainly *unique*." As if unique were an ailment.

"He knew how to put up with people's weaknesses," I replied. "He even tolerated fake piety and polite bullshit." That was ungracious and uncalled for, but all I could think was that she still had her father, and that life was goddamned unfair. Plus exhaustion and grief had narrowed one channel in my mind to an unending refrain of the old Billy Joel song. *Only the good die young,* he sang in an obsessive chant. I blinked and Janine was glaring at me worse than before. I had spoken the words out loud.

"Nonetheless, I am so sorry for your loss," she said coldly, and walked off.

A few minutes later I glimpsed her peeling away in a late-model Jeep with chromed fog lights and a Tiber Farms logo on the side, her honey-hued hair floating, her slender control accented by a dark-blue executive suit dress. She'd take over as president of the Tiber chicken empire some year soon. Mr. John had raised her to do it, she'd earned a business degree, just like me, and she was now his second-in-command. She'd built a handsome house on a beautiful, wooded lot in town.

The weather turned freakishly cold on the day of Daddy's funeral—below freezing even in the afternoon. Church bells rang all over town as we drove from the stately Victorian funeral home off the courthouse square in a long procession led by the sheriff, with the cars' head lights shining. On-coming drivers pulled their cars over as a courtesy.

Finally the procession reached the steepled, white-brick grandeur of the Tiberville Methodist Church and its large cemetery. I stared. The cemetery was filled with people. Parked cars and trucks lined the road for a half mile on either side. I'd expected no more than two dozen old friends to brave the cold for the graveside service beside Mama's burial plot.

"What's happening?" I said aloud. Arthur and I were alone in my car, and Arthur hadn't said a word all day. He sank down in the seat and covered his face.

I saw colorful outfits, bizarre hats decorated with plastic flowers, large crucifixes held above aging heads, a brightly handpainted sign saying RIP Brother Powell, and another saying The Iron Bear Lives Forever, which made me shiver. Tears of gratitude rose in my eyes. These peculiar folk were part of Daddy's vast network of folk artists and crafts people from all parts of the south.

In the front of the crowd, standing just across Daddy's grave from Arthur and me, were John Tiber and a handful of elderly Tiber kin, all respectful, sincere, and extremely well-dressed. They stared at the rest in disbelief.

I caught Dr. Washington's somber gaze and nodded my thanks to him for being there. He nodded back. Jonah Washington had tremendous presence and dignity, with his jowly, bearded face composed behind his steel-rimmed glasses. This was probably the first time in the 150-year history of our families that a Washington had stood openly, up front in public, as a Powell's welcomed neighbor.

Daddy's five tenants were clustered nearby. A ratty bunch. I tried to ignore them. Arthur clutched my hand harder. He stared at the casket perched on rails and the artfully hidden hole beneath it. His beautiful face, so much like Mama's, compressed suddenly. His soft blue eyes narrowed until they squinted shut. I recognized the signs.

I raised on tiptoe and whispered in his ear. "What are you, Sweetie?"

"A gopher," he whispered back, his voice breaking. This meant he wanted to go underground with Daddy, or to at least confirm that underground was a safe world. My throat aching, I told him not to worry, that Daddy wasn't living underground. He squinted harder.

As soon as the minister finished his short sermon, a long-haired boy in the crowd lifted a corroded yellow trumpet to his lips and played a mournful refrain of Taps. Then an obese woman in a pink coat burst into a tearful, off-key rendition of Elvis's *Are You Lonesome Tonight?* A tiny black man cocooned in several sweaters and faded overalls waved a four-foot-tall cross made of sticks wound with colorful electrical wire. Another man played Amazing Grace on a flute, the sound so haunting I thought my heart would bleed through my skin. A teenage boy sang a morbid Alanis Morrisette song in a high voice. A man in a yellowed white tuxedo with a gold cummerbund loudly recited a short, awkward poem.

It was a circus of creative mourning, a glorious and appalling spectacle, a celebration of the whimsies that had defined my father's life. The minister, John Tiber, and the other Tiber relatives stared with their mouths open. Mr. John began to scowl. The others traded disapproving looks. I was torn between embarrassment and pride. I was the Uber-Powell of Bear Creek, the landlord, my brother's keeper, the owner of the Iron Bear.

No. I never felt I owned the Bear. I didn't inherit it.

It inherited me.

*

"One, two, three, *up*," Quentin ordered, as he and a three-man crew sent by an antiques broker attempted to hoist a six-hundred-pound slab of imported marble out the loft doors of the aging Brooklyn textile mill. He'd acquired the old mill when a salvage deal fell through, then converted the bottom floors into apartments, which he rented out. He used the entire top story for his own living quarters and business. There were days when he cursed that decision.

The marble was wrapped in a spider web of cables attached to the arm of a massive wench Quentin had installed on the building's outside wall. If they simply let the slab go, it would swing wildly out the doors and snap the cable.

"Another few inches. *Dese prisa,* " he urged. The broker's Hispanic crew, sweating, surged forward. Quentin fitted one shoulder under the slab and braced himself. Here he was not the heir to Richard Riconni's legacy and fortune. Here he was not a finely dressed businessman aiding his mother's cause. Here he became elemental—a creature of iron, flesh and blood wrapped in dirty denim and his own sense of order.

One of the men suddenly slipped and fell, and Quentin sagged, struggling to hold up that end of the marble alone. Its blunt edge pressed on the hapless man's chest. "*Socorro! Cuidado!*" the victim yelled, and began squirming.

Quentin went down on one knee, every muscle straining. "In the background, retired army master sergeant Harry Bodine Johnson, otherwise known as *Popeye* for his thick forearms and garrulous temper, bellowed, "You sons of bitches, *lift that motherfucker or I'll let it swing.*" He thrust the control stick on the wench's motor, tightening the cable by dangerous inches. Standing beside him, Hammer barked wildly.

Quentin thought his back would break. He could feel the strain grinding into his knee joints, his shoulders, his neck. *Have to change a static load into a dynamic load, and I need leverage.* He tried to ignore the shiver in his weakening legs. "Let it go, Captain, that's an order!" Popeye thundered, having never really forgotten that he'd trained a raw, homesick recruit named Riconni in boot camp.

But Quentin finally shoved one foot forward, found the fulcrum of bone, muscle, and determination he wanted, and inched the slab upward just enough. With a mighty explosion of breath, he and the remaining two men eased the marble out the doorway. It swayed gently in thin air.

Quentin sat down next to the man who'd fallen. They were both drenched in sweat. "*Muchas gracias,*" the man said breathlessly.

"*De nada.*" He wiped his forehead and got up, then helped the other man up. The man was shaking. Quentin did not display so much as a quiver. The crew gazed at him in awe. "Damn, Boss," the translator among them said. "You act like that happens every day."

"Anything a man can live through couldn't be too bad." Quentin fitted a cigar in his mouth then shrugged exhausted muscles in his shoulders.

But after the crew left with the slab safely atop their flatbed, he stretched out on the loft's thick wooden floor in a rare, empty space not occupied by inventory that included elaborate mantels, Grecian pediments, stacks of wrought iron fencing, and crates of hand-painted tiles. Hammer lay down next to him and snuffled his face. Quentin shook him gently by his shaggy yellow ruff. "It's a good day when nothing falls down. That's the point, isn't it?" Popeye came over and sat down on a crate, rubbing arthritic knees. Quentin shut his eyes and smiled thinly. "I'm getting old, Sarge."

"You're *making* yourself old, son, that's for damn sure." Popeye spoke in a slow Kentucky drawl that seemed soothing even when he was shouting obscenities. "You're gettin' bored and restless since your ol' daddy's work made you rich. What you tryin' to prove, that you're not his flesh and blood and you don't need his money?"

Quentin curled his hands behind his head and gazed at a ceiling crisscrossed with massive beams. The roof of the mill had a brutal simplicity that he loved. "I don't need any of it," he said.

It's only right for a son to inherit the benefits of his father's success, his mother insisted, and vowed the money was his. She talked as if he were part of his father's work, another piece she would manage dutifully. They never discussed her disappointments about his life, only her pride. But he knew she still wanted that MIT architect, that golden child for whom she had sacrificed, that boy who had worshipped Richard Riconni as much as she. And that boy was gone.

"Money isn't important as long as you've got a roof over your head and enough to guarantee it will always be there," he said to Popeye.

The old soldier snorted. "That something you read in one of your ass-suckin' books? I've fucked ten-dollar whores who have better ideas than that."

Quentin eyed him narrowly. The old man had never been easy to like. In the barracks one night during boot camp he'd snatched a book of Freud's writings off Quentin's cot. "You sick in the head, *boy?*" he'd thundered. "That why you're readin' about head doctors? You a goddamn pussy-hating fag, *boy?*"

Quentin had replied loudly, red-faced and angry, standing at attention. "Freud writes about *big dicks,* Sergeant! You'd know that if you read the book first!"

"You callin' me a *dick,* you Yankee *wop?*"

"Yes, Sergeant!"

For that smart remark he'd spent several weeks of boot camp in a virtual hell of extra duties and excruciating punishments. He'd never complained, never asked for mercy, and the impressed sergeant had said to him one day, *Son, you're the loneliest, toughest motherfucker on the planet, next to me.* And Quentin had nodded.

Twenty-two years later, Popeye grunted with the same crude devotion he'd demonstrated then. "You're a frugal SOB now, huh?"

"I know what I need to live."

"You know what you need to *die.* I coulda swung that marble outside. Yeah, so the cable might have popped and dumped it on their damned truck. So what? You got business insurance. You could buy those boys a *new* truck. You can't buy a new set of bones, though."

Quentin sat up wearily, flexing his back and arms. *"Beware the golden chains that bind. Your spirit moves freely in righteous solitude, alone.* That's something I read in a book of poetry, Sarge."

"Poetry, *shit*," Popeye answered. "You looking for answers in the pissin' end of the cow pond."

"It means be careful what you love. And who. Every person and thing you care about is a weight you agree to carry. You can't put it down once you pick it up."

"You're afraid that weight's gonna *fall* on your ass, and you keep testing to see if it will. And some day you *will* find out!"

Quentin smiled, got up, and said nothing. He'd stayed in the army for sixteen years, and had been on the short list for a promotion to major when he left after the Gulf War. Army life made it easy not to think, or to feel. He'd earned a basic engineering degree while in the service, had been stationed all over the world, had served as a peace keeper in several crises and had led men in battle. But after the mine incident in the Gulf War he'd known he didn't want to die, yet, at least not that far from home.

Now his life was about taking other people's memories apart, not his own. Depending on the point of view, he was either a glorified junk dealer or an antiques expert. He tore apart mansions, mills, factories— any building in which the parts were worth more than their sum. Then he supplied a network of brokers with everything from handmade eighteenth century bricks to Tiffany transoms.

He went to his office, a corner area defined by rows of file cabinets, office equipment, and a battered desk sporting a state-of-the-art computer, and began to check his e-mail. Most of his orders came in that way, meaning that he rarely saw customers in person. His business had become a carefully efficient and isolated process, like the rest of his life. He preferred it that way.

Next to the office, a double set of heavily carved Moroccan doors led to Quentin's living quarters. He'd turned one end of the huge loft into his own apartment, a handsomely simple place outfitted with salvage items he'd decided to keep. An eighteenth century plaster molding graced the wall above his bed. A weathered, worm-eaten, yet strangely beautiful mahogany archway framed the kitchen window. He'd covered the cracked and worn base of a stone fountain with a thick piece of plate glass to form a dining table. His tenants swore he had an artist's eye.

And he always denied it.

But his father had appreciated cast-offs, too, and Quentin never forgot that. "Those pieces bring something to you," Papa had said. "What they know, what they remember, the glory they used to have. They can talk, if you listen."

Quentin's tenants sometimes wandered up to admire and sketch items in the loft's enormous inventory. Most of them were young, and most were pursuing ragtag careers as artists or musicians. The irony of that never escaped him—that he had somehow managed to draw that kind of people to him. Only Popeye knew that when they couldn't pay their rent or needed help with their bills, they came to Quentin, and he took care of them.

Popeye followed him to the office with military determination, plucking a stub of chewed cigar from his shirt pocket then flinging it out the open loft doors before shutting them against the cold March air. He'd been born in the backroom of a Kentucky whore house and was raised by strangers so cruel he would never speak their names, even now. He'd joined the army right after World War II, when he was only sixteen. He'd never married, never had children, never called anyplace home. When he showed up to visit Quentin after his retirement, he looked like a lost soul. Quentin hired him as an assistant and gave him a small apartment downstairs.

Popeye pointed at him. "If you're such a hard SOB and you don't want to be weighed down, how do you explain the pack of half-assed kids you rent places to, and how do you explain a pair of no-accounts like *us*?" He pointed to himself, then to Hammer.

"You earn your keep," Quentin said, and never looked up from the computer screen.

"You're gonna end up like me."

"I hope so, Sarge." Quentin flicked a darkly amused look at him. "You're the biggest dick in the neighborhood."

He dodged the sergeant's stream of profanity, as the phone rang. Quentin lifted a hand for silence when he heard Alfonse Esposito's troubled voice. "Your mother's in the hospital," he said.

*

She was napping in a private room by the time he arrived at a Manhattan hospital. She'd fainted while meeting with a financial planner. Alfonse stood up from a chair beside her bed when Quentin walked in. Alfonse's dark hair was almost pure white, now, adding a cosmopolitan air of elegance to his rugged features and olive skin. He was a precinct commander and would be retiring from the police department in a year. His eyes were stern but worried.

"She's a trooper," Alfonse whispered. Quentin gazed down at his mother, her skin chalky, her eyes shut, and covered one of her hands with his atop the bed covers. He resisted an urge to test her pulse. "She wanted to leave straight from the emergency room," Alfonse went on. "I told her I'd handcuff her to a bed. They want to run a few tests." He lowered his voice even more. "Her blood pressure's above normal. Doctor says it's probably been that way a while. I suspect she's been hiding the fact from us."

"Absolutely," she murmured, and opened her eyes. She squinted. "Someone please hand me my glasses." Alfonse took a pair of slender metal frames from the nightstand. She slid them into place, and Quentin felt relieved. She looked wan and tired, but more like herself. He'd never gotten used to her contact lenses. "I'm fine. I think I hyperventilated over a discussion of mutual funds."

"I thought the money would keep you busy," Quentin said. "I thought you *wanted* to stay busy, now that everything else is settled. Would you like for me to hire a business manager to take care of it for you?"

"I won't let some stranger manage our family's future." She said that simply, without insult, but she meant it. She'd made it clear that if he wouldn't accept a share of his father's legacy, either financially, spiritually, or creatively, then he shouldn't be involved in the money. "You still don't respect what the money represents," she went on quietly. "You don't respect your father's memory."

Quentin walked to the room's window and stood with his back to her, letting her words settle in his gut. He'd never told her about his father's adultery, and he never would. Nor had he ever confessed his last conversation with Papa, and the guilt he still felt. "I respect *you*," he answered finally, "and I don't want you to spend the rest of your life worrying about every penny from the sculptures. If that's the case, then I'd rather take all the money and throw it in the East River."

"I have nothing else to live for," she said suddenly, her voice raw. Immediately she looked regretful for the outburst, and frowned. "I don't expect you to understand. Alfonse, would you please let me talk to Quentin, alone?"

"Of course," Alfonse said, but shut the door hard as he left the room.

Quentin turned and looked down at his mother pensively, then pulled a chair closer and sat beside her bed. "Will you *really* talk to me? Is it that hard to be open about what's bothering you?"

Angele fidgeted with the bed covers, a nervous movement so unlike her that concern curled through Quentin's chest. She clutched the material hard, became very still, as if aggravated with herself, and stared at the ceiling. "All right. I'm miserable. For years I had a mission in life. Now I have nothing to do. I don't even want to get out of bed in the morning."

"You've got a multi-million dollar estate to manage. You have plenty to care about."

"That's only money."

"You've achieved what you wanted. Papa's a star. People won't forget him. His work's on display all over the world. Retire, now. Marry Alfonse."

Her gaze jerked to him. "Alfonse?"

"You don't think I know about you two? I've known for years."

"He's only a friend."

Quentin considered this in rueful silence. He had spotted Mother at a corner deli having breakfast with Alfonse too many times to assume they merely met there. "You don't have to hide your romance. I don't disapprove."

"I will *always* be married to your father."

"He's been dead for over twenty years. He'd want you to be with Alfonse."

"I *am* with Alfonse. We're dear friends."

"Alfonse is crazy about you. You insult him by treating him like a second-class choice. Just now, didn't you see the look on his face? How does it sound to him when you say you have nothing to live for?"

"I'm being lectured about romance by a forty-year-old bachelor who has no family life." She knotted the covers again, exhaled deeply, and trembled. "What have I accomplished? All this success will never bring your father back, never make me feel I've done the one perfect thing his spirit demands, never restore whatever it was that stole your ability to care about him—to care about *anyone* in anything but a detached way."

"I have what I need. Let's talk about your problems, not mine."

"Oh, no. When I woke up after fainting I felt as if I had been in a dream, talking to your father. *Quentin's following the same path as me*, he said. *Stop him*. If you don't find some measure of real happiness you might end up, you might . . ." She stopped, pressed her fingers to her eyes, and composed herself. When she lowered her hands she was in control of herself, again. "Enough of this. Let me be clear. I don't know what you're searching for, but I want you to make some decisions about your future. All of the millions from the auction are yours—now or later, whether you wish it were so, or not. I would like to believe that the Riconni name and all it represents—including the money—will be passed along to new generations."

"You want me to marry someone just to start breeding?"

She stared at him. "I want you to find a woman who is worthy of you and of our name. I want you to marry her and love her the way your father loved me. I want you to have children. I want grandchildren."

Quentin hid a coil of anger. He'd promised himself as a young man he'd never be his father, and that included never having a child to betray, or who would betray him. "If it were that simple," he said, "I'd marry Carla."

Angele huffed. "My dear son, pardon me for being blunt—I will never say this in front of Alfonse, because he is well aware of his daughter's weaknesses, and they torment him—but Quentin, Carla is temperamental and frivolous. She's fiddled her intelligence and her youth away on shallow husbands and on *you*. If she didn't dote on her daughters I have no doubt she'd have thrown herself off a bridge over your lack of commitment, by now. She comes to you for money and advice, and you let her, and she lives in the fantasy that some day you'll marry her and turn into a good stepfather for her girls."

"She's an old friend. I help her when she needs help. I keep my distance from her daughters so they won't confuse me for a father figure. I have no intention of marrying Carla or anyone else."

"Then stop letting her hang onto you. Stop loaning her money and letting her be so convenient when you're not seeing some other woman. And yes, I do know you have your choice of women. You pick among your female tenants as if they were fish in a barrel. They're more than willing, but then you break their hearts and they move away. Carla's problem is that she can never make herself give up on you, the way the others do. She remembers the boy who seemed to love her, and confuses him for the man who can't love anyone. You're ruining her life in some misguided effort to be kind to her and to hold onto some memory of yourself you won't admit."

Quentin looked at her with the strained privacy a grown son affords a parent, but her mouth tightened with resolution. Over the years since his return from the army there had been periods of time when he and Carla were together, that was true. There was a warmth there, a comfortable pattern. "I don't sit around debating the meaning of my life, or where it's headed. I think that's pointless."

"You *cannot* go on this way."

He stood and abruptly. "Do you still like your brownstone?" She had bought a pleasant place in a better neighborhood some years earlier, when money began to come in from the sculptures.

"What in the world does that have to do with the discussion?" she demanded. "I'm very happy in my little place. I just wish there were more room for books."

"You could move anywhere you want. A penthouse in the city, here. A place out in the country. How about a house in Martha's Vineyard, or the Hamptons? With a boat dock. God, Alfonse would love that. Get rid of his old cabin cruiser and set him up with a yacht."

Mother gazed at him as if he were a pimp asking her to sell herself, body and soul. "You see me living in luxury and forgetting that your father ever existed?"

"No," he answered patiently, "I see you enjoying the life you earned." He hesitated, then, with tight restraint, "The life he deserted. He told me once that his sister made him promise to live two lives for her. That's what you have to do. Live the life he threw away."

She shut her eyes for a moment. When she opened them they glimmered with tears. "If I could only find some peace of mind. Something that I felt was more personal to accomplish in his memory. It's not about managing the money—I can do that. I *will* do it well, because I keep praying mine and your father's *grandchildren* will have wonderful opportunities because of it." She gazed at him pointedly. "But . . . there has to be *something*, something that would mean so much to him. I want to find out what that is. *I have to.*"

A nurse came in, fussed over her obviously agitated state, and suggested a tranquilizer. "I do not want medication meant to soften my outlook," Mother replied in short, even tones. After the nurse left Quentin took her hand. For once—this did not happen often—she let him hold it. He sat and looked at her with a son's grief. *Don't let her fall.* The memories that gnawed inside him asked for a sacrifice, not a gift. And he didn't know what that would be.

*

When he returned to the old mill that night he discovered Carla's white Lexus parked beside the entrance he used. She'd kept a key since their last turbulent round of togetherness, more than a year before. He found her naked in his bed, which didn't surprise him. Over the years since his return from the army they'd played this game several times.

"How's your mother?" she asked. "Pop says she just fainted."

"She has high blood pressure. She was ignoring it."

"Good. So she just needs to relax and take her pills."

Quentin said nothing to that typically Carla view of complex situations. He pulled an upholstered armchair across the floor and sat down a safe distance from the bed. "What are you doing here?"

She smiled. "I like to fuck rich men. I've been waiting since January to add you to my list."

She was tempting, he admitted it. The wild-maned Brooklyn beauty queen had become a sleek Manhattan businesswoman, running a salon that sold custom cosmetics. She lay upright against a mountain of his white pillows with seductive welcome. The bed's dark coverlet pooled around her hips. Her short, sophisticated black hair curved artfully around her flushed face. One hand lay along her stomach, and she stroked the skin just below her navel with one long, white-tipped fingernail, occasionally raising the hand to circle a nipple. "Look how cold I am in this drafty room."

He shrugged his leather jacket off and tossed it gently across her breasts. "Don't freeze."

She kept smiling but disappointment gathered around her eyes. "I'm not engaged," she said. "Yet." She had been dating a banker who was crazy about her and her girls, and she'd admitted to Quentin that she liked him.

"I told you that we can't do this, anymore," he said.

"Quentin. Please. I make the best efforts I can to find someone else, but I always come back to you." She scrubbed her hair away from her face impatiently, annoyed with her own façade. With a flash of the old Carla, who would have punched him, she said impatiently, "*Comeon.* When did your latest poor lovesick victim move out downstairs? A month ago? Oh, she was a smart one. Had a masters in art history, I heard. But even the smart ones aren't smart enough to catch *you.* So I just wait." She grinned and lifted her hands. "And here I am."

Despite himself, he was drawn to her when she was more honest. She antagonized him, seduced him, and often made him laugh, remembering with deep longing the easy sex and friendship of their youth. He liked her sassy little daughters, who looked like each other and like miniature Carlas, though each had a different father. He liked her lusty attitude toward life and men. But that was all there was to it, and he was tired. "I think you ought to marry the banker," he told her.

"Why?"

"Because he'd be good for you. He loves your girls. They like him a lot. They told me so. Comeon. Get dressed and go see him. Get naked in *his* bed."

She slid down on the mattress and crossed her arms behind her head, eyeing him shrewdly, taking a long, breast-lifting breath as she settled deeper between his gray flannel sheets. "I'd stop seeing him in a second, if you said the word. If you don't do something soon, I'll marry him."

"I'm trying to be a good influence."

"You haven't always felt so honorable."

"I know, but every time we go through this you end up hating me for a year or two. I'm thinking this time we ought to just skip the hating part. For your sake, at least."

"Quentin, hasn't anything changed since January?"

"Not really."

"Your mother's upset because you won't take charge of your family's future. You understand what I'm saying? For the Riconni name, Quentin. You have to get married, you have to raise children and give them a great life, be a great papa, make a great home, build up the family, hmmm? That's what you need to do with the money, no matter how you feel about it."

"We've been over this before."

"Comeon, Quentin, what's holding you back?"

"The money doesn't change anything."

She slowly pushed his coat and the covers down, exposing her long, smooth belly and a wedge of dark-brown public hair between slender thighs. "You're right," she whispered. "It doesn't change how much I want you. You're always here when I need you. I don't just come to you for money and sex. You know that."

Quentin nodded. He knew how easy it would be to slide into bed with her, to use up the cold spring night inside her sincere heat, but he set up boundaries so he'd never lose control of his passions. His passions, Quentin told himself, were simple: a woman who didn't really need him, the Yankees from April to July, the Knicks over the winter, a good cigar, a cold Scotch, and a well-written book. He stood. "You're welcome to stay."

She grinned. "Now, you're talking."

He picked up his coat. "I'll see you later." He bent swiftly, kissed her bare stomach just below the navel, looked into her distraught eyes, and apologized. "It's not your problem, it's mine," he told her.

Then he left.

At dawn he sat on the crumbling patio of an old Tudor mansion he was tearing down, with Hammer shivering against him in the breeze off the cold gray Atlantic ocean. He could see so far out there by the ocean, and that's what he wanted, someplace to see for miles, to have it all become clear.

He didn't like to admit that he was at a loss to build anything in his life. He wouldn't let the word *unhappy* rise in his mind, because it was self-indulgent. Hell, people were better off unhappy and knocking the joints from under buildings than following their goddamned artsy bliss at the expense of other people's lives.

When he'd come home from the army he'd gone to the old warehouse that still housed his father's sculptures. He'd stood in the middle of a jungle of grotesque iron and metal, gazing up at the warehouse's wooden beams and rusting metal roof, picturing how he'd dismantle each joist and lift off each decrepit piece of sheet metal, and then when the building was dissected he'd turn to its contents, exposed in the sun, and one by one he'd cut apart the old man's useless creations until he'd reduced everything to neat piles of nothing—no more warehouse, no more stockpiled artwork, no more memories.

He scanned the ocean, leaning forward, looking deeply into the pinks and golds of the universal dawn. There had to be an answer somewhere, something or someone—someone, yes, all right, someone out there worth dying for, someone scanning her horizon for him, seeking a mutual destination in the emptiness.

There had been more women in his life than he cared to think about, always left behind at some army base or moving out of the apartments he'd rented to them. He could barely remember their names. When he was in Iraq he'd suddenly begun wondering if there was any woman in the world he would never want to miss.

He couldn't imagine her.

9

"Your Daddy's tenants want to speak with you," Mrs. Green whispered to me behind one liver-spotted hand. She was organizing the supply of casseroles, fried chicken, and desserts brought by a long stream of neighbors. We would have food for a month.

I looked at her grimly over piles of paperwork on the kitchen table. "Tell them I'll speak with them after I finish these bills, please." I had found a stack of unpaid invoices in the kitchen drawer. The electricity was about to be turned off.

"Child, that won't do. You have to speak to them now." She was firm, she was a social leader. She had retired from running our local Quik Boy grocery after she and her husband sold it to a national franchise. The Quik Boy once sold everything from ammunition and boiled pigs' feet to whole homemade cakes and used paperbacks, thanks to an unending supply Daddy traded. Now it sold gourmet coffee and camping gear for tourists. My whole world was changing.

"They're a-waitin' on the front porch," she finished, and pointed. I grudgingly pulled a sweater around my shoulders and walked outside.

Five strangers looked back at me as suspiciously as I looked at them. Oswald T. Weldon was sixtyish, lean, leathery, with a Tennessee twang and old biker's kiss-my-ass attitude. A white handlebar mustache rode his upper lip like a furry sneer. He called himself a folk painter. His themes ran heavily to naked people cavorting through farms, fields, and flowers. His other theme, more disturbing, was abused children.

His wife, Juanita, was no more than 30-years-old, and came from some tiny farm village in Mexico. She barely understood English and was very shy. Next to them were a couple as plain as fieldstone. Bartow and Fannie Ledbetter were simply old—well past seventy, maybe even eighty. She leaned on Bartow and Bartow leaned on her, aided by a heavy wooden cane, his back grotesquely twisted by an old injury, so that he always bent sideways. He and Fannie had spent their lives working in a North Carolina ceramics factory before new investors closed the plant and sent the production jobs overseas. Now they were living hand to mouth on what they earned from their odd-shaped bowls and dishes and mugs. When I opened Daddy's kitchen cabinets, the Ledbetters' strange creations seemed like colorful little aliens, looking back at me as if they might pounce.

And last, there was *her*. Her, a mystery every time I saw her, and a threat I hadn't yet fully defined. I had noticed her crying at Daddy's funeral, and had seen her from a distance later, alone at his grave. With all seriousness she called herself by the New Age Native American moniker, Liza Deerwoman, an absurd choice since she was a thickening, middle-aged, green-eyed, platinum-white blonde. She must have been beautiful not that many years ago. Liza Deerwoman made glass. The shelves outside her front door were filled with perfume bottles, vases, and hanging ornaments.

She was colorful, herself. Today she was dressed in startling green chiffon—some kind of jumper—with a baggy green coat over it. She wore white silk ankle socks with loafers, and the socks were embroidered with tiny pearls. Her eyes were covered by green-rimmed sunglasses. "How are you?" she asked in a cultured, coastal voice that always surprised me. "Have you talked to your father in any of your dreams?"

What bullshit. I stared at her. "No, but I'm sure he'll call me when he gets time."

"Please don't be annoyed. I have a duty to tell you, even if you won't believe me. I've had glimmers of him. Feelings, really, nothing visual. A sense of deep peace. I believe he is at peace with the work he did, here, and he's gone on to—" her voice broke—"to prepare to do fine work in other realms. The fact that he left you in charge tells me he knew this was best for you. He knew you needed this chance to come home."

"Stop it. I don't know you, you don't know me, and if my father had something to tell me, he would have written it in his will." I couldn't take any more of her poignant babble.

The old couple shuffled forward. "All she's sayin' is that Mr. Tom was a fine, kind man," Mrs. Ledbetter said. Her gnome-like husband nodded, the movement reflected in his twisted body. "A good soul," he said in graveled tones.

Oswald Weldon snorted. He grimaced at me. "Let's get to the point, here. You plan to kick us out?" His deep, sarcastic, truck driver's drawl raked my ears. "You wanted to get the hell rid of us a couple of years ago," he went on, "and now you got your chance. Just say so."

"As long as you're honest with me, and trustworthy, you pay your bills and keep up your apartments I'm not planning to make any changes anytime soon."

"Thank you," Liza Deerwoman said softly. "I'm sure your father is pleased."

I looked at her with barely concealed disgust. *You New Age Blanche du Bois.* "As I said, I'm not planning to change anything around here. Not right away."

"People burn in hell on words like that," Oswald informed me.

"You can always leave, if you don't believe me."

"We wouldn't give you the satisfaction."

"Oswald, that's enough," Liza said, very quietly and with cool warning. He clamped his mouth shut and stomped down the porch steps. The others filed after him. I watched them go with amazement and dread. I controlled these people's homes, their businesses, their lives at Bear Creek. I was fairly certain that none of them could afford to move anyplace else.

What am I going to do with them? I thought desperately.

*

Arthur had rarely left the general vicinity of the farm and Tiberville during the course of his first twenty-two years, and almost never crossed the county line. Travel terrified him. His phobia was the reason Daddy never brought him to visit me in Atlanta. Arthur grew stone silent and rigid with alarm when forced to pass some invisible psychic boundary point.

Nest, he would say loudly in the car, a habit from boyhood when he'd gone through long phases of pretending to be a bird. *Nest*. He had to get back to his safe roost. And besides, he couldn't leave the Iron Bear. It was his surrogate mother.

Now, I lied to him. "Mama Bear started talking to me last night. She wants you to come live with me," I said. "She told me you'd be happy in my house in Atlanta. Mama Bear said she'll be fine here at the farm, and we'll visit her every weekend. I promise. But for now, I really need for you to come stay with me."

"Nest," Arthur said, wringing his hands.

I explained my plans for Arthur to my tenants the next morning, facing them crisply in a circle of straight-backed chairs set around the farmhouse's living room. I couldn't live at Bear Creek. My bookstore, my home, and my possibly future husband remained in Atlanta.

"Ursula, please don't take Arthur away," Liza begged. She held out her hands. "Arthur loves it here. This is his home. He'll be miserable in the city. He's accustomed to us, and we'll take care of him. I swear to you, if you'll just let Arthur stay you won't be sorry."

"It's out of the question. He needs supervision. I'm his sister. I'll take care of him."

"But Miss Ursula, you're not gonna help him by caging him up down yonder in Atlanter," Fannie Ledbetter said tearfully. "He's a sweet, wild child in his heart. He's got to wander the woods with the other creatures. He needs that Bear out in the yard. It talks to him, keeps him calm. I do believe it does. Liza's right. We're his people, now. You can leave him be."

I stood, furious. "You people are *not* his 'people,' you're not his family, and you're not *my* family, and you need to keep that fact straight. Go on about your business, and I won't interfere. But listen to me—I'm letting you stay on the farm out of the goodness of my heart, and because my father would want it that way. Don't ever forget that you're tenants, here."

They rose en masse with a certain hard-kept dignity and filed toward the front door. *I can't afford to be soft-hearted*, I thought. *I'll end up like Daddy.*

Fannie Ledbetter stopped and made one last effort to convince me. "That brother of yours'll go to the city because he loves you like nobody's business," she insisted, "but if you carry him away from this place you're gonna kill him, *mark my words*."

*

Arthur's face grew sadder with every passing hour. He paced the floors, he cried, and finally, just before dark, he disappeared. I went upstairs to Mama and Daddy's quiet, heartbreakingly empty bedroom, filled with cold, fading light, and I struggled not to give up and burrow inside the blankets of their old pine bedstead. I opened the lid of a huge quilt chest beneath one window.

"What are you?" I asked Arthur gently. He was curled tightly inside the big chest, a feat of amazing flexibility for his six-feet-two-inches of lanky arms and legs.

"A baby chick inside an egg," he said.

I sat down on the floor, reached inside the chest, and stroked his luxurious red-brown hair back from his face. It draped onto his shoulders. Daddy had let him grow it as he pleased, and Arthur didn't like to cut it. "Are you going to hatch?" I asked.

"Yes." His voice trembled. I knew at that moment that he had made up his mind to do what I'd asked—and that it was an act of devotion based solely on pure trust and adoration. He held up a shaking hand and I gripped it firmly. "Arthur, I promise you, you'll be

108

safe with me, and I'll take care of you, and I'll make sure you're happy."

He dragged my hand to the center of his ribs. "Hurts," he said in a small voice. "Daddy's here. Can't talk. Like Mama Bear." I rested my head on one arm along the rim of the trunk. "Hurts," I agreed. Silver shadows were gathering, the whole world had gone gray and quiet. "Daddy's here," Arthur moaned again, pressing our locked hands harder against his ribs.

"We'll take him with us," I whispered.

*

I bought a sofa bed and moved my brother into the tiny living room of my garage apartment. Gregory regarded Arthur the way he looked at specimens under a microscope. "I'm going to talk to some people," he told me as we sat on opposite ends of his pristine white couch one night. "See what kind of experimental medications they can suggest. We may be able to hook your brother up with a program that can help him. With help and support, he can live happily in a group home."

"Let's get something straight. My brother," I said in a low, even voice, "isn't ever going into an institution."

Stiff silence filled the perfectly deodorized space between us. We had not slept together in a month. The next day he left for a public-health convention in Canada. I was glad.

"You look tired, Boss," my clerk said at the bookstore.

"I'm fine." I went to the supply closet. Arthur napped sitting up, leaning against the cramped walls, his long arms laced around the handle of a mop. Pity filled me, and then, hatred.

The next morning, as if he knew, Arthur left.

I realized something was wrong when I went into the kitchen around seven and found his copy of *The Incredible Journey* standing on the table in the breakfast nook. Over the years, Daddy and I'd taken turns repeatedly reading the classic children's story to him, and he loved it. Alongside the book, he'd neatly stacked the new sweater and the Braves cap I'd bought him. Half-awake, I picked up the book and frowned at it, then walked down the hall to Arthur's room to see what he was up to.

The room was empty. I called the police. By the time the officer arrived at my door I was already working a network of friends and neighbors, marshaling a citizens' patrol, and about to leave the apartment myself on the search. "How do you know your brother ran away?" the officer asked.

"He *told* me," I said, and held up *The Incredible Journey*. A book about desperate, lost animals finding their way back home.

What had I done to him?

*

Arthur, who could lose all track of time and place even on the familiar turf of Bear Creek, tried to walk back to the mountains through the streets of Atlanta. The police found him two miles from my neighborhood, unconscious and badly bruised, with a broken rib. His backpack was gone, along with a change purse he carried, which had been stuffed with the five dollars I'd given him, even though he could never quite figure out how money worked.

After the emergency room doctors patched him up he was transferred to a private room at the hospital, and there he slept peacefully, thanks to tranquilizers and painkillers. I went into the bathroom, threw up, and screamed into a towel. What the attackers had done to him was like beating a lost puppy. And it was my fault.

Sometime after midnight, he woke up. One eye was swollen shut. The other filled with tears when I bent over him. I spoke his name. "I'm here, I'm here, it's okay," I whispered, stroking his hair. "I'm so sorry, Sweetie. I won't let anything happen to you again. I swear. I swear to you. I'm so sorry."

His bruised, swollen mouth compressed into a trembling line. He had to work to form words. I leaned closer to hear them. "Mama Bear didn't tell you to take me away from home," he said. Then he turned his head away and, sobbing in soft, pained mewls, said nothing else.

By the next day I realized his silence toward me wasn't temporary, and that we had a serious problem. Liza and the other tenants came to visit; she and Fannie Ledbetter sat by Arthur, spoon-feeding him vanilla yogurt Liza had brought. Liza knew his favorite foods, damn her. I watched from across the room, trying to catch his attention, thinking he'd give in, eventually. "Here, look at this, Arthur," I said lightly, pulling a can of root beer from Liza's blue macramé tote. "Your favorite." I opened it, poured it into a cup of ice, inserted a straw, and brought the drink to him with an urgent halo of apology.

His battered face tightened with fury. His right hand shot out. He slapped the cup, catching me off guard. The cup and its contents landed on the floor.

I stood there in disbelief. My brother had never been violent, before. The enraged expression on his face made him a stranger. He

110

did hate me. I saw that. "Arthur Powell, you behave!" Fannie said, gaping at him, while Liza looked from him to me, frowning.

Arthur began to struggle weakly, flailing his bruised arms. "Go outside," Liza ordered quietly.

I nodded. "I'm leaving the room, for his sake."

I went down the hall and sat on the edge of a stiff chair in a waiting area, clutching my knees. My little brother, who I'd diapered and fed and watched over and read to and defended when bullies picked on him, my brother, my only close family in the world, did not speak another word to me or anyone else from that day onward.

By the time Harriet Davies showed up at the hospital late one night, I looked the way I felt. Pale, hollow-eyed, my hair up in a ratty ponytail, wearing a pair of faded jeans stained with coffee and a black pullover with several unraveling threads dangling from the wrists. I'd forgotten about the zoning vote. I took one glance at Harriet's soft, dimpled, teary face, and I said, "We lost the vote, didn't we?"

"Yes." She crumpled on one of the hospital's vinyl sofas and sobbed. I sat down and put an arm around her. Peachtree Lane was doomed. I'd just lost my business. The leaden impact, coming on top of everything else, was too much for tears. I hugged her hard, squeezing because it comforted me, until she squeaked with pain and gently pried herself out of my frozen grip.

Gregory was due back the next morning. I paced the hall outside Arthur's hospital room, trying to think of solutions, trying not to think of anything else. About mid-morning, I glanced up and saw a vaguely familiar young woman walking my way. Then I realized I knew her—she was a technical writer for the CDC, which published a stream of reports and newsletters. I'd met her a couple of times at parties, with Gregory.

Strangely enough, I remembered her because she looked like me—tall, a brownish redhead, semi-slender, with blue eyes. "Is Gregory all right?" I asked quietly.

"Yes. Oh, yes," she looked startled, then halted a dozen feet away, her gray trench coat swinging around her rumpled blue pantsuit with stylish momentum, very dramatic. "I have to talk to you," she said. "About Gregory." Then she spun around and headed into an empty hospital room. I followed her and shut the door. My instincts for privacy were good.

She began to cry. And then, without warning, she spilled her lurid, heartfelt confession. She and Gregory had been lovers for almost a year, now. They didn't mean for it to happen, but it did, as usual in such stories. She loved him and he loved her, and he'd been trying to find a way to tell me so. "You've hurt him so much, forcing your brother on him, pressuring him to be a surrogate father to a grown man," she moaned. "He says it's the last straw."

"Excuse me, I need some air." I walked back into the hallway. The floor felt soft beneath my feet; I had to concentrate on the workings of my knees. I braced one hand against the wall and slowly made my way to the door of Arthur's room, walking as if the floor had tilted.

I called Liza out of Arthur's room. She took one look at me and reached out, frowning. "You need some rest," she said. I shook my head. "I want you to tell Arthur something. In a day or two, when he's released, I'm taking him back to Bear Creek. For good. Please tell him that. No more worries, no more experiments. I doubt he'll forgive me for what's happened, but at least he can relax about the future."

"What about you?" she asked.

Lights danced before my eyes. I would have to sit down soon and take some breaths, have to pretend I wasn't being pulled backward by the same hand of fate that had closed around Daddy when he was boy, the curse that kept Powells at Bear Creek without good choices or any foreseeable way to break the cycle of just-getting-by.

"I'm going back home, too," I said.

*

Everyone in Tiber County who heard the rumors or read between the lines knew I came home broke and jobless, my man had fallen in love with another woman, and because of me my own brother had retreated into shy and speechless torment. I rated a level of gossip equivalent to weddings, community awards, church events, college happenings, and a Rotarian lunch hosting the lieutenant governor.

My bookstore, like all the other shops at Peachtree Lane, sat empty. I'd packed and sold my inventory with a knife in my chest as every book disappeared from the shelves via a return box to its publisher or into the hands of yet another bargain-hunting stranger.

I deposited enough money in the Bank Of Tiberville to pay the farm's modest bills for only a few months. I had no more than the summer to set up housekeeping, concentrate on restoring Arthur's faith and voice, and find a decent job. I was afraid to leave Arthur alone, even though he wouldn't come in the house with me there. I had to stay nearby in case he suddenly needed me. He was already certain I'd deserted him, or didn't care.

Arthur couldn't or wouldn't speak, but moaned as he wandered around the farm, darting into the woods whenever I approached him, then sneaking into the house to dump food from the refrigerator or throw books off my shelves in the living room—acts of meanness that were totally out of character.

"He's acting out his grief and fear," Liza suggested to me. "Just give him time."

He slept in a tiny extra bedroom in Liza's chicken-house apartment, or he stayed with Dr. Washington at the dilapidated Washington homestead, a ten-minute walk away, through the woods. I began to depend on Liza, though I didn't want to. She looked after Arthur conscientiously, and she grieved for my father in a huge garden he and she had created behind the chicken houses. I walked up once and caught her crying, talking to him about seeds. *Thomas, I'm planting everything in good earth. That's all I can think to do.* I retreated before she noticed me, angry and sad that she seemed sincere, that Daddy had never told me he had feelings for her, and that she called Daddy by his formal name, which no one else, including Mama, had ever done.

The Ledbetters had installed a small herd of goats in the pasture, and had turned an old cattle shed into a shelter for feeding and milking. A dozen majestic Rhode Island Red hens and their rooster lived in a fenced yard, supplying everyone with big, brown eggs. Liza's mixed-breed gray cat, named *Eternity*, prowled everywhere, often showing up on the back porch wanting me to let her in, a clear sign that she—and Liza, too, I assumed—were accustomed to Daddy's hospitality.

But the old water spigots poked up from the earth just as they always had, the massive forsythia at the edge of the front yard would sprout next year just as it had this year, turning butter-yellow with tiny blooms every spring. The blue hydrangeas would always be blue. I knew every smooth inch of the two fieldstone steps to the back porch, and the three to the front porch, worn from generations of Powell feet.

The chicken houses had lost their lean, working angles over the years, going soft like old dancers. They bulged with ramshackle porches and crudely added rooms, odd doors, uneven windows, and unmatched metal awnings. The Ledbetters' small porch was rimmed with wooden shelves filled with their strangely shaped, softly colored pottery. Next door, Liza had transformed her porch into an open arbor, an incredible green bower she'd created with climbing roses, trumpet vine, and confederate jasmine.

The second chicken house, which sat only a dozen yards from its sister, had been divided into work spaces—Liza's glass-blowing studio, the Ledbetters' dusty kilns and pottery wheels, Oswald's gallery of weird canvases.

I thought constantly about the fire hazards, about the lack of insurance, about the thin line between my tenants, me, and disaster. The farmhouse was in no better condition than the chicken houses. What Daddy couldn't afford to fix he'd learned to laugh at and ignore. The pipes hummed and snored, half the light fixtures no longer worked, the floors sagged, the roof leaked, and the house was riddled with holes that let in furry visitors.

On the back porch I set a large white ceramic pot. In the pot was a tall, leafy seedling I'd started the year before from a peach pit of the Peachtree Lane tree. The old grandmother tree might not survive the developers' plans, but her offspring would establish a new peach tree dynasty in the mountains.

"You're going to survive, and you're going to grow," I told it, and myself.

By god.

*

Quentin drove upstate on a hot summer morning. Word had come that the warehouse was being sold by the latest in a series of absentee owners, and soon would be remodeled to serve as a distribution center for a furniture manufacturer. Pragmatic crates of recliners and cheaply veneered dining tables would replace his father's metal dreams and nightmares.

Once inside the building, Quentin went to the door of the old toilet, picked the padlock, and shut his eyes for a moment, remembering, and trying to forget. Then he swung the door open for the last time.

When he lifted his finger under the light switch he saw what a stranger would see—only a small, utilitarian space, with cracked tiles and yellowing fixtures. But when he got down on one knee and ran his fingers over the cold floor, he saw blood and his father's empty stare. He walked out shaken.

As he passed the shabby cubicle that had served as his father's living space, he stopped for a moment, breathing hard. He stared at its bare walls and the old stove and sink standing forlornly in a corner. When he was a boy he'd imagined his father there with the woman, servicing her in lurid detail. Now he only noticed how cold and depressing the place was, and he thought of his father always coming back to it after weekends at home, and how that must have felt.

Workmen for the new owner had dragged the old stove out from the wall a few inches, and had left crumpled bags of debris from a fast-food restaurant scattered on its blackened burners. The trash bothered Quentin. Papa had always been neat, disciplined, clean. Quentin knelt and gathered the garbage to discard. As he did he noticed what appeared to be dozens of pieces of mail on the floor behind the stove, covered in dust and spider webs. He pulled the appliance further away from the wall then reached behind and scooped up the materials.

Yellowed, stained, and badly rumpled, the long lost mail was mostly just advertising flyers and other junk, but Quentin plucked out a water bill and looked at the postmark. His heart twisted. This mail had been delivered only a few days after his father's suicide. Someone—probably Joe Araiza or one of Papa's friends who had helped take care of the place for awhile—must have tossed the pieces on the stove. They'd fallen behind it.

He stood angrily, wishing he hadn't found anything to draw him back to that time. He was about to drop the entire handful of papers into a garbage can without sorting the rest, when one letter fell to the floor. Quentin glanced at it with perfunctory disgust as he picked it up. But when he read the dimly scrawled return address he went very still, and frowned.

Mr. Tom Powell, Bear Creek Farm, Tiberville, Georgia.

He opened the old envelope carefully then eased out two pieces of notebook paper filled with the same script, showing hard crease lines from twenty-two years of folded secrecy. Next he removed a faded color snapshot. He held the items with his fingertips, the way an archaeologist might carry priceless sheets of Egyptian papyrus.

Hello to you, Mr. Richard Riconni. You don't know me, except what Mrs. Betty Tiber may have written to you. She is kin to me, and I helped her with the Bear. Now, sir, I am sorry to tell you that she has passed—rest her soul—and I have bought the Bear. It is sitting in my back pasture, as safe as it can be. I promise you, sir, it will stay here for good, and I will take good care of it. Me and my little daughter, Ursula. We know great art when we see it. We sent you a picture of your Bear in its new home.

Standing beside Daddy and the Iron Bear in the photograph, I smiled at Quentin, who was stunned, with a certain amount of solemn urgency. *I'm waiting for you, that child's smile said. This Bear is hard to hold still without help.*

10

I was alone at Bear Creek on that Fourth of July, the day of the storm. Liza, Arthur, and the others had gone to the Old Tiberville Independence Festival, an annual event celebrating not only the Fourth but also the founding of the town in 1850. Daddy and his tenants always rented booth space at the arts-and-crafts show. *Bear Creek Farm Artists Gallery*, Daddy's colorful homemade banner proclaimed atop the booth's tent poles.

I stayed at the farm, filling my time with a project that already had Oswald grumbling and Liza giving me wounded looks. I was fencing in the back yard. "I'm building a fence for a dog. I intend to get a dog," I told everyone. I just wanted to keep *them* out, and they suspected it.

I dug post holes, set and tamped and straightened the posts in them, measured, dug more holes, and was grateful for fatigue that kept a bay a restlessness so deep even the song of a robin made me feel lost. For weeks I'd tried to scrub, repair, and organize the home place into good grace, again, but the list of chores kept growing.

I didn't care how I looked; I wore a faded cotton skirt and an old white t-shirt. Barefoot, with my damp hair pulled up in a long curly ponytail, I toted boards to my posts and began nailing them into place. I still had half the fence posts to set, but I was bored with post-hole digging. The chicken wire would come last.

Black clouds rolled over the mountains and piled up in the sky behind the barn, and thunder began to rumble. I shivered and began to think I sensed some odd change in the air, even though I knew to beware the false portents mountain storms always brought with them. Every collection of Appalachian stories included storms, for good reason. They conjured magic and ghosts.

That day's storm seemed deeper, richer, more insistent than most, dredging up sensations. The air turned brisk with ozone like cold butter on my skin, making me feel slippery and anxious as I hammered long galvanized nails into the soft pine fencing. Yellow lightning began to flicker. A clap of thunder made me shiver. The blisters on my hands were bleeding, now.

A fat gray squirrel bounded across the yard. Her name was Lassie. She was an old squirrel, one of Arthur's pets, the latest of many orphans he'd discovered in the wild then tamed and raised.

Lassie was nursing her newest litter of two babies in the loft of the barn. I fed her a few sunflower seeds I'd stored in my skirt pocket. When she finished eating Lassie hurried to the edge of the yard oaks, which were darkening to emerald green in the failing light. She paused to assess the pasture between her and the barn, then went sprinting toward her destination, her fuzzy gray tail streaming behind her. I'd seen Arthur's pet squirrel's race that treeless distance a thousand times, and I silently counted the seconds from oaks to barn. The record was ten. With the wind pushing her, Lassie had a chance of breaking it.

A dark shape plunged from the gray sky. I saw the hawk a heartbeat before Lassie must have felt its talons break her back. In the next moment she was just a limp, dangling little form being carried skyward.

Oh, no, no, no, not this.

I ran out through the sheltering oaks, into the pasture, waving my arms, screaming, but that only made the hawk disappear faster over the forest at the pasture's far rim. I halted in shock, lightning flickering around me. This was unbelievable. This kind of thing could not be happening on top of everything else. Hawks didn't hunt during storms. Small horrors had been added to larger ones, small deaths were everywhere.

I sprinted to the barn, while the wind died down in an ominous way I should have noticed, just as I should have noticed the way the clouds had begun to twist, and how the light had gone gray-purple, as if filtered through a bruise. I had to get Lassie's babies, and bring them to the house. Arthur would take care of them, and he wouldn't blame the hawk for Lassie's death. The hawk had to live, too. Probably had babies of its own, to feed. Mothers had to be killers, for their children's sake.

No, he'd blame me.

Poor mama squirrel, I'm so sorry. So sorry. I'll take care of your babies. I can do that much. My mind whirling, I went inside the barn and climbed an old wooden ladder up about thirty feet, to the loft. Decades of sifted hay formed a thick mat on the loft floor. I found the young squirrels curled deep in the center of a snug nest of hay, twigs, and leaves Lassie had built in a wire egg basket hanging from a rafter. The babies had most of their fur and looked like miniatures of their mother. I spoke softly to them. *It's all right, you're coming with me, it's okay, babies.* They peered up at me in petrified terror.

The wind suddenly roared, making the heavyset old barn tremble a little. Now I looked up worriedly. I closed the basket's wire top, latched it, then turned to climb back down the ladder as quickly as I could.

At that moment a tornado flicked its thin, curving tongue down to earth about fifty feet away, slapping a pair of massive poplars. The tall trees uprooted and fell, hitting one side of the barn's roof with the force of giant baseball bats. Timbers groaned and gave way, nails shrieked as they were pulled from tough chestnut beams, and sections of the tin roof tore open like paper. I yelled and dropped to my knees on the loft floor, huddling over the squirrels and flinging up both arms to cover my head.

I was one second too late. A ripped board cracked me over one ear. I didn't faint, but I saw a universe of stars and lay very still for a while. By the time I recovered enough to sit up, the tornado had retreated and the world was starkly quiet, accented only by benign gusts of wind and spatters of rain. I dabbed my fingers in a thin stream of blood trickling down the right side of my face, then touched the hard, wet knot under my hair, setting off pain that throbbed through my entire skull. I checked the young squirrels. They had burrowed deeper into their nest and were safe. I envied them.

I squinted up at the sky through jagged beams, streamers of torn tin, and the leafy green top of a downed poplar. A few raindrops fell on my head, hurting like tiny, sharp rocks. Shaking, I crept to the far wall and looked out a gaping hole. A dozen feet below me, the second poplar tree lay atop the barn's lean-to. Under the roof of that crumpled shed, under the crushing weight of that giant poplar tree, I had parked my car.

My car.

I found some heavy baling twine, tied it around my waist, then anchored the basket of squirrels to my makeshift twine belt. I was climbing down the rickety loft ladder when its last two rungs snapped. I sprawled on my back. The squirrels, safe in their basket anchored to my stomach, made small, squeaking sounds. I untied the basket and set it aside.

Everything hurt. I was dizzy and covered in sweat. I began to laugh at the bleak craziness of life, then suddenly, with a force that surprised me, I sobbed. I cried for myself, my car, for Arthur, for Daddy, for poor Lassie and her motherless babies, for every creature and every ancestor of mine who had been caught up in the cycle of life and death at Bear Creek. When I finally quieted I shut my eyes and rested in a daze of surrender.

Suddenly, a cold, canine nose and warm tongue touched my face. I opened my eyes. Large, ugly, and covered in damp, shaggy, golden fur, an unfamiliar dog stood over me, wagging his tail as he began licking the blood off my right cheekbone.

I scooted backward, every muscle aching, until I leaned against the rough planks of a stall door, exhausted. The dog happily followed me, wagging its tail. "Either you're lost or somebody dumped you on my road," I said grimly. My new friend noticed the egg basket and began snuffling it, woofing softly. The unseen squirrels chattered with alarm.

Beyond the barn's broad open hallway, rain began to fall in sheets, pounding on the remnants of the roof, drowning out sound. The dog, unconcerned, licked my bloody hair. There was some purpose in all this, I told myself. I had been pretending to build a dog fence, so the universe had sent me a dog. "All right, you can stay," I said. I shut my eyes, again.

A few seconds later there came two sounds—heavy footsteps on the hard clay floor, and then the thump of my head hitting the planks behind me as I jerked back from the firm touch of a man's hand on my face. As I opened my eyes a dark-haired stranger dropped to a squat in front of me, balanced on one large hiking boot he planted outside my left thigh. He settled his other foot firmly between my knees. We were nearly nose to nose, and I drew a sharp breath from his effect.

He smelled of rain and good cigar smoke; he wasn't old, wasn't young, but I felt incredibly innocent next to him. It was his face—hard, handsome and serious, and his eyes, which were steel gray and very cynical. He wore rumpled khakis and a plain work shirt. He seemed very tall, even sitting on his heels.

"May I help you?" I asked absurdly. He didn't answer. Never taking his eyes off the rafters above us, he clamped one hand around my wrist. "Hold onto your basket," he ordered in a low voice, as if the barn were listening. Then he pulled me forward, levered me over his right shoulder, and staggered to his feet with me draped over his back.

Stars danced in my vision as he carried me outside. He set me down about fifty feet from the barn, with his arms around me tightly. Once I had solid earth beneath me I braced my legs and stiffened, insulted by his patronage, blinking hard in the rain. His dog huddled beside us, forlornly dripping water. The man gazed down at me with the sharpest scrutiny I had ever felt in my life. "Stop bleeding," he ordered.

"It took a tornado to knock a piece out of that barn," I announced, trying to step away from him. "That barn has been here as long as this farm, and it's built out of strong chestnut wood. We can certainly—" *Stand in there out of the rain*, I would have finished, except that at that moment another piece of the roof caved in, dumping thick beams, boards, and torn tin on the spot where I had been sitting sixty seconds earlier.

My knees buckled. The stranger caught me, and we sank to the ground, together. He held me in his arms as we both stared into the barn's jumbled hallway. Cold sweat and blood mingled with the rain on my face. "*Memento mori*," I murmured.

"What did you say?" he asked.

"Memento mori. It's Latin. It means—"

"Remember that you're mortal," he supplied.

Silence. We gazed at each other with stunned gratitude. Drops of rain clung to his eyelashes and mine, blurring my vision, uneasily melting us together. Yes, we knew we were mortal, and that we were very much alive, and together.

And there, in that moment, our past, present and future took an abrupt turn down a new path.

*

Quentin hadn't meant to lay his hands on the grown woman who had been the child in the photograph, or to be anyone's rescuer. I hadn't meant to be rescued. Yet we'd rewarded each other with a simple understanding of life and death we could only indulge in a dead language. Quentin introduced himself to me and was amazed when the Riconni name made me gaze at him with blue-eyed wonder.

The sky cleared and the rain became a warm white mist rising from the earth, sifting with ethereal grace through a patch of sunlight between us in the pasture. We walked among fairy circles of clover, serenaded by the low *coo* of a dove. My land welcomed him with all its mysteries and enchantments. He felt a little drunk, somehow taken by surprise, aroused by the land and by me.

"Your family name is as a legend, here," I told him.

I saved her life, and she's just grateful, he told himself, as we both tried to act as if nothing had happened.

When we reached the Iron Bear he stood for a long moment just looking at it. Then he circled the sculpture, studying, touching, pulling on a section here and there, as if he were only interested in testing its seams and structure. I stayed back and kept my distance, sitting in the grass a good dozen yards away. I watched him, mesmerized.

A rugged black sports vehicle of some kind sat in my yard, splotched with thick red mud from the dirt road. Before he'd turned into the tunnel of forest and flowers that led to Bear Creek he'd spent fourteen hours on an interstate highway headed down the eastern seaboard. He'd wanted time to study the territory, get the feel of the land and its people. He wanted to know what kind of people would set his father's abstract sculpture in their field and love it.

His city-raised dog, equally curious, sat on the Bear's concrete base with its attention riveted to the Ledbetters' small herd of goats and Daddy's chickens in the high-fenced chicken yard. The goats stared back. The chickens did not. Chickens are rarely curious and never impressed.

Quentin gazed up into the sculpture's massive face, those hollow, see-through eyes looking down at him, and he remembered the sculpture's effect clearly as a boy, or thought he did. *I was young, then, maybe I'm just reaching.* But a glimmer of memory rose in his mind, vivid and heartrending, and he was once again looking up, so far up, at the marvelous, half-formed *thing* looming in the shadows of Goot's garage. He saw the flash of his father's jaunty smile as Papa worked on it, his face streaked with grime and sweat, his big hands spread in joy.

"Balance," Papa had shouted. "It's all about finding the balance! And this one is perfect!" *Balance.* For that one, brief time, he had been perfectly in sync with himself and his son, his wife, his life, their love. Quentin's gaze remained riveted to the sculpture, now. He wanted to remember his father this way. He wanted to present this sculpture to his mother as an offering. Bare Wisdom. The Iron Bear. Those memories.

He turned away, met my intense and blatant scrutiny, and slid every emotion behind a shield. He liked how I filled out wet cotton. He wondered what, exactly, a hillbilly was, or a redneck, and if I qualified. He knew southern culture only through Popeye, books, and movies. As he gazed at me and then around me at the rundown but appealing farm shadowed by stunning, blue green mountains, his chest expanded with a strange sense of excitement. He wondered if I suspected how easy it would be for him to look at me the way I was looking at him.

He walked over. I sat up straighter, and he noticed. He pulled a photo from his pants pocket and held it out. When I took the old snapshot my breath caught. Daddy and I stood before the Bear so happily all those years ago, framed by Mama's straight-on vision of us as her hands fumbled with the camera Daddy had patiently taught her to point and click. There we were, preserved in a time when I'd believed my mother would live forever and my father's dreams would always be golden.

Now I looked protectively at my small, innocent self, then up at the amazing man who had carried my own memory back to me with such obviously conflicting emotions. *Tell me how we've known each other for so long,* I wanted to say, but wouldn't be that sentimental with him. With any man.

"You still say you don't want to see a doctor?" he asked brusquely.

"Yep. I feel fine."

"Mind if I look at the wound?"

"Go ahead. If you don't see sunlight, it's not that bad."

He uttered a soft, tense sound that might have been a laugh, then dropped to his heels beside me and probed my hair. "The bleeding's stopped. No sunlight." His hand grazed the side of my neck as he drew it away. My body contracted in a deep, pleasant breath, like a cat stretching. I got up and moved away from him as easily as I could without insulting him. "Thank you, then. I'll live."

He realized I'd pulled away from him, and he frowned. He didn't want any wariness on my part, any reluctance to cooperate. At that moment he was preparing to tell me what he wanted from me. Or at least, what he hoped he could buy.

He had to take the sculpture home.

*

We faced each other across the cracked Formica of the farm's kitchen table as the last glow of an ethereal gold-and-purple sunset filtered through the sink window and the porch door. Twilight cushioned the kitchen's poverty, burnished the dented aluminum cake cover on the pine shelves, softened the rust-rings from coffee cans that Daddy had painted and used as flower pots on the peeling ledge of the sink window. I clenched my hands around one of the Ledbetter's distorted pottery mugs, filled with wine. Quentin nursed a shot of scotch in a tiny, rose-colored glass Liza had made for Daddy. Between us on a table top, Oswald had painted a centerpiece of roses on the Formica for Daddy.

And then Quentin finished explaining that he wanted to purchase the Iron Bear and take it back to New York. He offered to pay me the sculpture's likely market value. "That would be two to three million dollars," he said.

I got up, pressing my bare heels hard onto the faded linoleum floor, finding my balance against all odds. "I need a few minutes to myself. Make yourself at home, you hear? When I come back, maybe I'll know what to say."

He stood, his face grim. He'd hoped for a simple reaction—shock, joy, and a quick agreement. The answer most people would have given him, and most women in a shabby farm kitchen, especially. But I looked as if he'd punched me. "Are you all right?"

"Fine." I forced a hard smile, and left the room. He listened for a moment, perplexed. *She's something different*, he thought, and walked outside to study the mountains in moonlight, lighting a cigar stub and smoking it briefly as he considered the wild beauty of the place, the stunning effect of the home his father's work had found by the strangest of luck. And what kind of woman was this Ursula Powell? An architectural ornament he'd never collected before?

He did not get involved in people's lives any more than he could help, mine included. Frowning at the turn this simple trip had taken, he went back inside, turned on the sink faucet, and doused the cigar in the water. A gushing sound came from beneath the wooden cabinet, and when he opened the door he saw a stream of water spewing from the drainpipe into a galvanized water bucket I emptied every day.

He debated that leaking drain pipe for a full minute, as if the mere act of caring about it would infect him with longings for the high southern country and barefoot redheads who wouldn't say yes easily. He emptied the bucket outside, replaced it, and closed the cabinet door. *I'm not here to fix her life*, he told himself. *She can do that herself, with the money I'll pay her.*

I made my way down a dark, narrow hall smelling of pine and cotton rugs to the house's only bathroom, a cramped and practical place across from the open door to a storage room where old glass kerosene lamps and boxes filled with canned vegetables crowded the shelves. There I took a beeswax candle from a dusty box, lit it with a match stored in a fifty-year-old baking soda tin, and carried the candle into the dark, windowless bathroom like an acolyte entering a chapel. The bathroom light hadn't been turned on for a month; the fixture had started sparking and I hadn't had time to prowl through a home-fixit manual and learn how to repair it. At any rate, I craved the soothing darkness.

I latched the door's plain metal hook-and-eye, then sat on the side of the tub in the dark, gazing at the yellow dewdrop of candle flame at the opposite end of the tub. Two to three million dollars.

Mama, Daddy? I didn't lose the faith. I just saw the cold, hard truth. In cash.

I couldn't hear my parents' voices, couldn't feel their spirit working in me, and wished they would give me a sign, the way Mama swore she saw crucifixes in clouds and plate-glass windows. I wanted some revelation to leave me frothing at the mouth in a fit of guiltless ecstasy. My head ached.

Yet I didn't doubt there was only one honorable way to honor my mother, take care of Arthur, and make peace with everything my father had sacrificed for his beliefs, and now, mine. Shivering, I got up and blew the candle out.

When I returned to the kitchen, full darkness had settled outdoors, the ceiling light was on and Quentin Riconni was studying the frayed cords of the light fixture over the sink. I sat down at the table, sinking, humiliated, a little angry. "Yes, the wires need to be repaired," I said grimly. "Yes, everything around here is in lousy shape. No, I don't need your help."

He inclined his head, then leaned coolly against a counter top and crossed one foot over the other. "I'm not offering it. I'm also not offering a bribe, or lying to you, or trying to con you. I'm just telling you what the sculpture is worth, and what I'll pay."

I shook my head. "It's not that simple. In a very real sense, the sculpture doesn't belong to me."

"I assumed you inherited it from your father."

I nodded. "But it belongs to my brother as much as to me."

"You have a brother?"

I explained about Arthur. His frown deepened. "But you're his guardian. You can do what's best for his future."

I gazed up at this hard-looking man who apparently had no understanding of kinship. "When my brother was ten old years old, he still hadn't spoken a word. We knew he was autistic and might never be able to talk. But one day he came indoors and out of the blue, he said to Daddy and me, 'Mama told me to come and tell you I got hurt. And she said not to play with snakes anymore.' He held out his arm. He had two punctures on his hand. A copperhead bite."

"So he talked," Quentin said calmly. "It happens."

"It wasn't just the talking. You have to understand, our mother came from . . . fundamentalist people. Their religion was strict, severe. They were snake handlers. She was bitten by a rattlesnake once, and would have died if my father hadn't taken her away from her family. So that day, when Arthur came indoors and said that she'd warned him about snakes . . ."

"He'd heard you tell that story."

"Maybe. Probably. We couldn't remember if we'd ever talked about Mama's past in front of him. As Daddy carried him to the truck he asked Arthur where he'd been when Mama spoke to him, and Arthur pointed to the Iron Bear. 'Mama Bear,' he said. He'd decided that the sculpture talked, or that our mother spoke to him through it. He's believed that, ever since."

I hesitated, then decided I couldn't escape, and quietly told Quentin what had happened to my brother in Atlanta. "I hurt him, I lied to him, I didn't take care of him well enough. So now his Bear is lonely and going to die, and he can't talk, anymore. That sculpture's the only hope I've got of getting through to him, again."

"I have a bad feeling you're trying to tell me something I don't want to hear."

I took a deep breath. I hurt all over. My very bones burned with disappointment, but there could be no equivocation, no wishful thinking or cool rationality, no practical brutality. "I can't sell you the Iron Bear," I said quietly. "Not for any amount of money."

He looked at me in wonder. He'd expected to negotiate, to pay more than his first offer, to be laughed at and investigated before anyone took him seriously, but the last thing he'd expected was to be told that his father's work meant more than money could buy. "Let me talk to your brother."

"That won't help. And I won't allow it. He's terrified of strangers."

"You need the money I offered you?" He asked that question with an admirable lack of irony.

I managed a laugh. "To put it frankly, I'm broke and I don't even know how I'm going to pay the bills in a few months. But this situation can't be fixed by money."

"I don't get the feeling the sculpture means very much to you—you don't seem sentimental about it. It should be easy to make a decision and convince your brother."

"You're wrong. A person can't be neutral about the Iron Bear. That's it's brilliance—that's why its effect on people is so strong. I'm sure that sense of provocation, that passionate vitality, that *life*, is why your father's sculptures have finally been recognized. If they're all like the Bear, they get down inside you and talk. You can't shut them up." I paused. "Would I sell it to you if Arthur agreed? Probably. I'm not a fool. That money would change the future for my family. But that's a moot point. I won't *have* a family if I break my brother's heart."

Frowning, he scrubbed his hands on a sheet of paper towel. With startling accuracy he lobbed the crumpled paper into a tin trash bucket Daddy had painted in bright blue and orange dots. The man had perfect aim. Men like him had a way of luring women into a dependent state that seemed far safer than it ever turned out to be.

"The sculpture belongs in a museum," he said. "Not a pasture. It was the definitive work of my father's career. It should be displayed where people can appreciate it."

"I've lived with it all my life. I *know* its power far better than you do. If you think it isn't appreciated out here in my woods, you're wrong."

"Will you sell it if I raise my offer?" he asked.

More than three million dollars? I got to my feet, shivering. He was torturing me. "Go back to New York, Mr. Riconni. You don't have a clue. You're not even listening."

He looked at me with shrewd curiosity, examining me as if I couldn't exist in nature. I understood that feeling. I'd stripped chicken carcasses to the bone, sliced apart the meat and blood vessels, looked at the sinews and broken joints. After a minute under Quentin's scrutiny, I knew how it felt to be in neatly carved pieces.

The sound of a car broke the spell. When I looked out the kitchen window I confirmed the headlights of the Ledbetters' ancient VW van, pulling a small trailer the tenants shared. The Ledbetters had driven everyone to the festival, towing the trailer loaded with boxes and canvases for the booth. They would go back for a second day in the morning. I turned on a pair of floodlights that lit the back yard.

"You're about to meet Arthur," I said.

"You've got my word I won't say anything about offering to buy the sculpture."

I looked at him for a long moment, then very quietly warned, "Your word better be good."

A few seconds later Arthur loped out of the darkness with Liza running after him. Hammer got up from his napping spot and woofed at them, then stopped as if he recognized a friendly dog in Arthur.

"I told Arthur about Lassie on the way home," Liza said breathlessly, as she reached the back door. She had called me to say they were packing up an hour ago, and I'd given her the news about the barn, and the squirrels. "Arthur, Arthur, calm down," she called, her voluminous blue peasant skirt fluttering around her like a bluebird's tail. Arthur's brown hair swung wildly and his pale, beautiful face constricted with misery. He made little pawing motions at his jeans and shirt, as if he were ready to attack as he bounded onto the porch. He swung the back door open with a bang, rushed into the kitchen, and stared at me with tearful fury.

I pointed to a cabinet and Arthur leapt to it. When he opened the cabinet doors the baby squirrels were perched atop their wire basket. They squeaked in alarm then dove back into their transplanted nest. Arthur made a cooing sound, gathered the basket in his arms, and headed for the porch door. I blocked his way. Oswald, Juanita, and the Ledbetters were judging my command of Arthur's situation, as usual, from the shadows of the porch. "Arthur, will you listen to me for one minute?" I held out both hands to my brother. "I couldn't do anything to stop the hawk. I tried. It happened too fast. I did try. I promise you."

He pushed past me and Liza, hurrying across the porch and out into the yard. I darted after him and grabbed him by one arm. "Arthur, we can't go on like this. You've got to talk. You've got to listen to me. I wanted Lassie to live, and I want you to live. You're my brother. I love you."

He swung around and shoved me, an act of violence so unlike Arthur that I knew it was all impulse, not malicious. I sprawled on my back, and a jolt of pain through my tender skull sucked the breath out of me. I was dimly aware of Liza bending over me, and then Quentin, who knelt and smoothed a hand over my forehead. His challenging presence made me sit up before he could help me. Arthur squatted on my other side, crying softly and pounding one of my knees with the back of his hand. "What are you, Sweetie?" I asked with strangled dignity, bracing both elbows on the ground and trying to ignore the sick bile rising from my stomach. "What kind of animal right now? Please tell me."

He made clawing motions in the air, and at his throat, pounded his hands against his forehead, then snatched one of my hands and held it to his cheek, as he rocked. "I'm *fine*, Arthur. I'm not going to die. I'm okay. Don't cry, Sweetie. Please, talk to me. I know you can do it. You don't need the Bear's permission. We still have each other. Please tell me what kind of animal you are. I want to understand."

He cried and rocked. Suddenly a deep voice intoned, "Arthur? *Arthur.* Look at me, pal." After a second my head cleared and I realized

Quentin was speaking to my brother. Arthur stopped crying and stared at him. Quentin held out one hand. *"You're a man,"* Quentin said. "And *a man* says to his sister, 'I'm sorry I knocked you down.'"

My brother edged back into the shadows like a crab, hugging the wire basket to his stomach and staring up at Quentin with his mouth open. "Don't be afraid," I said quickly. "Arthur, this is a new . . . friend. He won't hurt you." And to Quentin, "Don't force some brand of gentlemanly *machismo* on him. He doesn't know what you're talking about."

"Yes, he does." Quentin waited, his hand still outstretched. He wasn't threatening; there was nothing in his face but quiet and stoic patience. "Arthur, my name is Quentin Riconni," he said. *"And I'm the Iron Bear's brother."*

Silence. I stared at Quentin warningly. Beside me, Liza made a soft sound of awe. Arthur gasped. "I'm the Iron Bear's brother," Quentin repeated carefully. "And I'm telling you that Mama Bear would want you to *be a man* and say you're sorry for hurting your sister."

"Stop it," I ordered. "Arthur, it's okay—"

Arthur whispered, *"Brother Bear?"* Then he set the basket aside, got down on all fours like a bear cub, and crept to Quentin, giving him urgent, tearful glances as he did, and reaching up tremulously. Quentin remained on one knee, as if humbly waiting to be knighted. Arthur touched his hand, grew bolder, clasped it, then examined the fingers, palm, and knuckles as if checking for metal claws and wire tendons. Apparently, he found them.

Shivering with excitement, Arthur released his hand, then crawled over to me. "Did you ask him to come visit us?"

"I didn't, I can't—Arthur, I don't want you to believe—"

"Yes, she did," Liza supplied quickly, cutting her azure eyes at me to keep me quiet. "Arthur, your sister knew you wanted to meet Brother Bear and she brought him here especially to visit you. Because she loves you and she knew you needed your brother to help you and Mama Bear feel happy, again."

Arthur's eyes gleamed. He touched my face with a fingertip as tremulous as a leaf falling on my skin. I stared at him in teary surprise. He scooted away, grabbed his basket, bounded to his feet, and looked at Quentin. "I'll see you tomorrow!" he said loudly, then hurried into the night. Stunned silence settled on everyone in the yard. All the tenants stared at Quentin. So did I.

"My god," Oswald drawled finally. "Arthur's *talking.* He bought that horseshit."

Liza got to her blue-sandaled feet and gave him a firm glare. "Something special just happened here, and we won't make light of it. There are forces at work that shouldn't be ignored." Oswald grumbled but said no more. The Ledbetters nodded in unison. Juanita crossed herself.

Quentin offered me a hand up, and I took his aid again without thinking, but after I was on my feet I backed away from him. I needed to study him from a safe distance, to understand this man who analyzed people and barns with such merciless instincts for their weaknesses.

"You've made yourself a part of our lives, now," I said. "I'm not sure I want you to come back, but I don't have much choice. My brother expects you."

He nodded. He called to his dog. The tenants gazed at him as if the afternoon storm had conjured an Appalachian mountain spirit with a Brooklyn Yankee brogue. *What am I getting into?* he was asking himself quietly. He had not meant to prey on my brother's childlike faith, and it worried him to be depended upon so instantly, so trustingly. He hadn't meant to care about me, either. But he had to have the sculpture.

"I'll see you tomorrow, *Sister Bear,*" he said. And then he left.

11

I spent most of that night on my laptop computer, searching the Internet for art-world stories about Quentin's father and the new fame that had led Quentin to me and the Iron Bear. I found confirmations for all the basic facts Quentin had mentioned, and read one detailed account of the January auction that made my head reel.

I tried to sleep but just lay in bed, tossing under the old chenille covers, staring at the slatted ceiling. Arthur had *spoken*. My brother was recovering—finally—but I couldn't let him be caught up in some fantasy about Quentin Riconni, who was just a stranger passing through. The damage to Arthur's trusting nature might be permanent, next time.

But this man saved your life. The dilemma tore at me. I got up a few hours later, swallowing aspirin and drinking black coffee laced with dollops of rich sourwood honey. Still dressed in the jeans and t-shirt from the night before, my hair unbrushed and wild around my face, I drove Daddy's colorfully painted truck into Tiberville that morning. I intended to find Quentin at a local motel and restate my case. I had to tell him, as kindly as possible, to go back where he'd come from. To leave me and Arthur alone. To let us forget about him, which would be hard enough to do, already.

I stopped at the Quik Boy on the way and filled up a paper cup with black coffee, wanting to be hyper-alert around Quentin, who had already seduced my brother's friendship. The morning clerk at the Quik Boy was an old classmate named Rita. She looked at me oddly. The word was out. "Don't you know your Yankee's in jail?" she asked.

I left the coffee sitting on her counter.

*

He had risen early and gone for a restless walk in the bright spring sunshine, surveying this new terrain like a soldier. Hammer snored on one of the motel room's double beds. As he walked up the two-lane toward the square Quentin mused, *Pretty town. It's got good lines.* He mentally catalogued the shady, turn-of-the-century neighborhood, the graceful church steeples, the college campus stretching over rolling green lawns, and the gilded courthouse cupola peeking above the treetops.

He kept thinking about Arthur, and about me, a barefoot redhead who quoted Latin and turned down money on principle. I made him remember his boyhood's metal puzzles, something he hadn't thought of in years. And he caught himself wondering, *What if I were free to have her?* The thought startled him. *Free from what?* He didn't know.

Birds sang, a few lazy cars eased along the early morning streets, and somewhere in the distance, if he listened, he could even hear roosters crowing. A strange sense of calm settled in him. This quiet world was so *Mayberry* that he didn't know whether to admit he was charmed or pull back from it with wary restraint.

He ate scrambled eggs, bacon, and toast at the Tiberville diner on the square, amused as he pushed a spoon through the gelatinous bowl of steaming grits the waitress included without warning. He felt the stares of the locals and the curiosity of the suburban visitors who had driven up from Atlanta for the July Fourth festival.

How did they know he wasn't one of them? Quentin realized finally that the other men sitting at the diner's bar with him had doctored their hot cereal with the traditional salt, pepper, and butter, while *he* had experimented with sugar and milk from the coffee creamer. Men in tractor caps and hunting shirts glanced his way with tongue-chewing smiles. "Next he'll use some ketchup," one drawled.

"That's how we eat grits in Brooklyn," Quentin announced on his way out. Laughter followed him. People craned their heads to see where he went next.

He walked around the courthouse square, now cluttered with tents and concession stands, though it was still too early for much activity. Only a few arts-and-crafts vendors puttered around, preparing their simple canvas booths for the festival's second day. The Bear Creek Arts Farm banner stopped him. My father had painted it. Daddy's awkward but heartfelt rendering of the Iron Bear graced both ends.

I wish Papa had met Tom Powell, Quentin thought. Disturbed by the sorrow and regret rising in his chest, he turned away from the square and explored a narrow side street lined with shops. He noticed the *Open* sign on Luzanne Tiber's small antique store at the end of the lane. The simple mechanics of a mule-pulled seed spreader, displayed on the tiny patch of lawn, caught his eye. He walked down to study the archaic piece of farm equipment, then went inside to ask about the price.

Mr. John's older sister did not staff the store herself on a regular basis, but instead left the running to an elderly cousin, Mr. Beaumont Tiber. Mr. Beaumont was at least eighty, a little frail and hard of hearing. Quentin walked in to find him shaking, huddled in an old arm chair behind the store's roll top desk. He got to his feet, swaying. Apparently the sight of a tall and powerful stranger was more reassuring than not.

"Sir, *please* stay right here with me until the police come," he whispered to Quentin, darting frightened glances toward the door to a back room. "I've got a pair of young men back there who're in a *mood*, Sir, *an ill mood,* and I can't get rid of them. They pilfered a silver spoon from that basket over yonder, and I'm pretty certain they took an old compass over there, too. Just wait here for a minute, please-sir. I don't want to be alone."

"I'll wait," Quentin said, and leaned against a nearby counter with the quiet calm of a man who doesn't have to announce his capabilities. He trained his eyes on the back room's doorway. He had no intention of doing anything more.

The customers wandered back into the main room and halted at the sight of him, uncertain. Beefy and crewcut, with NASCAR t-shirts, crisp jeans and expensive running shoes, they quickly put on attitudes like cocky pro wrestlers. "I'm not giving you twenty dollars for these. They ain't worth it. I'll give you ten," one said loudly, dumping a pair of handmade iron tongs on Mr. Beaumont's desk. The tongs knocked over a plastic mug filled with iced tea. Mr. Beaumont moaned with dismay and began shuffling his paperwork out of the way while snatching sheets from a box of tissues.

The one who'd caused the accident backed up, looking disgusted. "Sorry," he said without much sincerity. Quentin walked over, picked up the tongs, laid them aside, and moved a stack of catalogs for Mr. Beaumont, who shook harder as he dabbed at the stream of light-brown liquid spreading across the old wooden desktop.

"You work here?" the other man brayed at Quentin, and his friend laughed.

Quentin set the stack of catalogs on a display case. "Just shopping. Thinking of buying some tongs." He picked up the tongs and put them on the case. "In fact, I'll take these. And I'll pay twenty."

Their laughter faded instantly. "What the hell you think you're doing?"

Quentin turned to the pair without any overt anger or threat, yet they both took a look at his face and backed up. He could hear the faint sound of a police siren, now. "I want the tongs, that's all."

After a tense moment, the leader snorted. "Shit, take them. I don't want the damn things anyway." He and his friend walked past Quentin and out the door. Mr. Beaumont wrung his hands. "Oh, they'll drive off and take my stolen goods with them. Luzanne will never forgive me."

"I'll try to keep them here until the police come."

"Oh, thank you, thank you, Sir, you're so kind. Bless your heart."

Quentin followed the pair outside to a gleaming, red, late-model truck parked with one brawny wheel atop the curb. "What the hell do you want?" the driver said loudly, as he swung his door open.

"I want you to wait here and have a little talk to the local cop." Quentin gestured up the lane, where a Tiberville police cruiser was only fifteen seconds from turning the corner off Main Street.

"Kiss my ass!" The driver started to climb into the truck. Quentin had visions of a police chase through the town square, which had begun to fill with a crowd for the start of the festival's second day. He took two long steps, sank his hands into the man's shirt, and the next thing the driver knew he was face-down on the ground. Quentin stood over him, with one foot planted squarely on the back of his neck. He pulled the man's extended left arm as high as it would go and angled it over the man's back, then twisted it just so. He held it by the wrist with one hand. "Move, and I'll break it," he said calmly.

With his other he slid his knife from his khaki's front pocket, and when the second man ran over, shouting obscenities, Quentin flicked the long blade out. The man froze with the knife posed under his chin.

That was the scene Officer Rexie Brown saw when he pulled up. Rexie went to high school with me, and I remember that he was large, simple, and liked to play football without a helmet. He found Mr. Beaumont passed out behind his roll-top desk. He pulled his gun, called for back up, and arrested everyone in sight.

*

I was more familiar with the Tiberville jail than I cared to remember. My stomach knotted as a deputy led me back to the holding cell. Quentin had his back to us and was gazing out a small, barred window toward the sheriff's personal garden plot. Short-termers wearing striped convict uniforms would be planting the spring seedlings, soon. Later in the summer, other prisoners would be put to work selling the produce at the Tiberville Farmer's Market. The proceeds went to a fund for needy families.

"I hope you like dirt and okra," I said.

He pivoted slowly. There was no doubt the man was handsome, no doubt the cool gray eyes and the slight sardonic smile had a startling effect. "Bless my soul," the deputy, a grandmother, said under her breath.

"I only eat okra with my *grits*," he answered.

The deputy unlocked the cell door. I stepped inside and she locked me in. "Thank you, Mrs. Dixon."

She arched a silver brow. "I've always told people you'd end up here, again."

After she left I sat down on a low steel bench along one wall. He sat down next to me. I arched a brow. "Do you always carry a switchblade?"

"It was standard issue where I grew up. I never lost the habit."

"When you pulled it, Mr. Beaumont thought you were about to cut somebody's throat. He's in the hospital having heart palpitations. They haven't gotten his side of the story, yet."

"I've told *my side* of the story. The police found what I said they'd find in my *friends'* pockets." He spread his hands. "Look, I mind my own business. I didn't come here to get involved, to strike up a reputation as a do-gooder, or to make any kind of point on behalf of my father's work. I just came to buy the bear sculpture."

"Then you better stop rescuing people."

"Sounds like you believe I'm innocent."

"You risked your own safety to pull me out of that barn yesterday. I can't picture you terrorizing old Mr. Beaumont."

He snapped his fingers. "Always trick old people, women, and children with fake piety. That's my rule."

"Oh, mine too," I said as lightly as I could.

His humor faded. He nodded toward the door. "What did that deputy mean when she said she always knew you'd come here again?" I said nothing, but looked at him firmly. He arched a dark brow. "I'm a nosy Yankee," he said.

I gave in. "I worked on the processing floor at the Tiber chicken plant as a teenager. I tried to unionize the employees. A real *Norma Ray* moment. I climbed up on a table with a *Union Now* sign. I got fired, so I went back the next day and put up union posters on the breakroom wall. When I wouldn't apologize and promise not to do it, again, Mr. John had me arrested. John Tiber. He's a cousin of mine."

"Your own cousin locked you up?"

"Yep. I bet you thought we just *married* our cousins around here."

The weak joke did nothing to lighten his intense curiosity. "How was it settled?"

"I apologized very humbly, and they let me go."

134

"Well. You were only a kid."

"You don't understand." I hesitated, again. Warning bells were going off in my defense systems. I was telling this man too much about myself, and I didn't understand why that seemed so necessary. I'd *never* told Gregory about the jail incident. "My father came here and insisted on being locked up with me. He wouldn't leave. I apologized to get *him* out of here. He didn't deserve the humiliation. He had enough humiliation in his life."

Silence. Finally, Quentin nodded at this information. "It's easier when it's just you. You can stand anything if there's no one else to worry about."

He understood. Shaken, I got up quickly and began searching through my purse as if I needed to find something. *Keep moving. He's in the salvage business. He's picking you apart to see what's valuable. He'll use it against you.* "I've never thought of it that way, but yes, that's true. Of course, the people you love should be worth the effort. And he was."

"I envy the way you feel about your father," Quentin said softly.

I halted, staring at him, wanting to know why he couldn't say the same about his own father. Suddenly I noticed long, raw welts on the inside of his wrists. I forgot everything else. Disgust boiled up inside me. Rexie had done that to him, with handcuffs. The clumsy redneck. "Jesus," I said with no charm at all. "Your wrists."

He glanced at them as if he'd just noticed. "It's nothing."

I opened my macramé tote bag and got out the can of udder balm. "Here." I sat down next to him again, scooped the soft, thick cream on a fingertip then bent over his hands, smoothing the ointment into each red mark. As I put the can away I met his troubled gaze and went still. We were sitting closer than I'd realized, or I had moved closer without noticing. We traded a long, silent look that made my heart race. "Thank you," he said.

"It's teet salve. I'm wearing some on the gash in my head, too. In the course of my life I think I've used it everywhere except my teets."

He laughed sharply, then stood and went to the window. He leaned against its narrow metal frame and surveyed me with dark amusement. "So. Do you plan to stage a sit-in on my behalf? No need. Just see if you can arrange bail. And take care of my dog."

"No. You're *my* Yankee. Everyone's already decided. I won't leave you."

He pinned me with another shrewd gaze, now touched with quiet admiration. I couldn't look away.

"You've got company coming," our grandmotherly deputy sang out as she came back down the hallway. I went to the cell bars as Mrs. Dixon led Mr. John to the door and unlocked it. He gazed at me with portly aggravation, then turned his eyes to Quentin with a deep scowl. "What have we here?" he demanded.

"He was only protecting Mr. Beaumont," I said quietly.

The door swung open. Mr. John marched inside and went to Quentin. "I know that. I do, indeed. Old Beau is finally calmed down and telling everybody who'll listen what a fine fellow you are. I may not approve of your methods but I'm here to apologize for your trouble and to thank you. You're a free man, Mr. Riconni." He thrust out a hand. "John Tiber."

Quentin looked from him to me for a few intense seconds, an awkward space of time that brought red to Mr. John's clean-shaven cheeks. "Your cousin?" he asked. I nodded, bewildered.

Quentin turned to Mr. John and asked softly, "Were you responsible for taking my father's sculpture off the campus of the college?" He captured Mr. John's attention with stunning ease, his voice a deep monotone, his hands resting casually by his sides. No fuss, no brag, no physical menace, just the pure, polished knowledge of his own character, his own purpose.

Mr. John lowered his hand. He blinked, startled. "Yes, I was."

"And you sold it to Tom Powell?"

"Yes."

"You would have sold it for scrap, otherwise?"

"I . . . yes."

"Were you responsible for the college lying to anyone who asked what had happened to it?"

Mr. John's face began to redden. "I was indeed responsible. Are you calling me a liar?"

"Yes. I just want to know why."

"My family founded this town, sir, and we are responsible for what comes into and what goes out of it. Including any so-called art." Mr. John pivoted and glowered at me. "Ursula Victoria Powell, will you explain our ways to this gentleman? I came here to thank him, not to be accused of crimes I never committed."

"He has good reason to want answers," I said as politely as I could. "It wouldn't hurt to apologize to the Riconni family. His mother grieved over the Bear for years. The college told her it'd been destroyed."

Mr. John stared at me as if I'd lost my mind. *"Now, listen here.* Your Daddy had a lot of foolish ideas, too, and I tried my best to set a good example that he might follow, but he never did. If I was hard-nosed about it at times, it was for his own good, just the same as I'm trying to be firm with this fellow here for his own good. I am *not* going to apologize for *anything.* I came here to make a noble gesture on behalf of Beaumont, and now I find myself being insulted!"

I stared at him. *Foolish ideas* rang in my head. "Mr. John, you might want to sit down," I said through gritted teeth. "I've got some news. Richard Riconni's sculptures are valuable, now. *The Bear is worth a fortune.*"

Mr. John gaped at me, then at Quentin. "I don't believe it," he said.

Quentin nodded. "What you think or believe is beside the point. Any apology you have to offer is beside the point, too. I came here to buy the sculpture and take it back where it belongs. This is business, not family sentiment. I just want the truth."

Mr. John snapped to attention. "If that sculpture's worth a good deal of money, then you better believe, Sir, that my family deserves a large piece of the credit—*and* the money."

"What?" I advanced on him with slow, even steps, incredulous. He glanced at me and frowned. "Mr. John, you don't mean that."

"I most certainly do. Miss Betty paid for that sculpture. She commissioned it."

"You sold it to my father!"

"A tepid and informal transaction, at best." He looked at Quentin. "What is its value, now?"

Quentin gazed down at him as if he were an amazing insect, something so biologically basic that an observer could only marvel at its crude threat before quietly crushing it. This was how he had looked at the men he'd confronted at the antique store. "The price is part of a private negotiation with the Powell family."

"I see. So you say, Sir."

"I say you'll never get a penny of the money. I say you'll spend the rest of your life in court fighting *me* over it, because if you dispute Ursula's ownership I'll hire lawyers to defend her case."

Mr. John was an aging bulldog who didn't back away from anyone. But an expression came over his face that said he knew, he *knew* he'd met trouble. "I was only making a point, not insisting on a course of action," he said.

"There *is* no negotiation," I put in. "I'm not selling." I was so upset over Mr. John's betrayal. Warts and all, he was someone I'd trusted. "How you could say you have a right to the Bear? How could you do that to me, to my father? You *know* the sculpture would be long gone if it weren't for him. *You know that.* Would you really take me to court over ownership? Sue me? Do you know what people in this county would say about you if you did that? Do you know what it would do to your good name? Your business image?"

Mr. John waved both hands and sighed, having the good grace to begin to appear embarrassed. "I spoke in anger. I was thoughtless. You know I don't want to hurt you, Honey. We'll talk about this later, when we've calmed down." I had hit him in his public image—a vulnerable point.

But I was not calming down. That teenager who'd been willing to go to jail had only matured, not mellowed. I stepped closer. "Daddy was kind to you. He put up with your high-handed attitudes. He always said you're a good man who's done a lot of good for the community, even when you behaved like a petty dictator. He believed in passive resistance. He had more patience than Gandhi, *but I don't.*"

"A petty dictator? Is that what you think of me?"

"You took advantage of his good nature, and you let your family turn their noses up him over feuds that happened at least fifty years ago. You patronized him and bullied him, and you called it 'doing it for his own good.' That won't work with me. I understand the Tiber mentality far better than Daddy did. I've seen it in professors who were too smug to consider new ideas. I've seen it in business people who could justify anything to make money. I've seen it in publishers and book reviewers who refused to give avant garde writers a chance, simply because *they* want to be the ones who defined the standards for the rest of us. I didn't come back home to play the same old games, Mr. John. You're not dealing with my father, you're dealing with *me,* now. You'll get my respect by earning it. I expect the same courtesy from you and every other Tiber. Don't you *dare* try to take advantage of me!"

"Ursula, you're agitated. Just calm down—"

"You can't keep me quiet the way you keep other people quiet." I was *boiling* inside, old wounds opening, pus oozing out. "The money you made my daddy pay you for the Iron Bear could have gone to medical expenses for my mother. It was Daddy's choice to spend that money, but it was your choice to demand it. I don't know if she'd be alive today or not, regardless. And I don't know if Arthur would have

138

been born without a handicap. But I know you shouldn't have asked for a lousy two hundred dollars you didn't need from my father, who loved that sculpture and had earned the right to it a thousand times over the years. *You helped kill my mother and hurt Arthur.*"

Mr. John looked furious, but also stunned. He blinked, he shook his head. Finally he caught his voice and thundered, "I'm so ashamed of you and so wounded by your remarks I don't know what to say. You're talking the same kind of nonsense your Daddy used to talk. Same song, just a different verse. Air-headed Powell nonsense. I've always held you up to Janine as an example of strong-minded, hardworking, bootstrap ambition. My wife, rest her soul, used to insist that you'd never be a lady. But I always believed that once you polished off your rough edges you'd be as fine and admirable as my own daughter. I'm very disappointed in your ungracious attack. *What kind of effect has this man had on you?*" He jerked his head toward Quentin.

I recognized a useless battle of ethics and philosophy, here. My head hurt, the barn was ruined, my car was gone, I had the dilemma of Quentin to deal with—the sculpture, Arthur's future, the enormous sum of money I'd turned down but secretly wanted and desperately *craved*. I stood in a jail cell with raw nerves and tangled hair stinking of mentholated udder balm because I couldn't afford a doctor's visit. It made no sense to badger the one Tiber relative who would come to my aid if I were desperate for help.

I looked into Quentin's eyes. He thought I was incredible at that moment. Beautiful. Strong. I saw that. I took a deep breath. Oh, what the hell. "I'm disappointed in *you*," I told Mr. John. "And let me tell you something about Janine. I hope to God I'm *never* like her. She's a ruthless *bitch*."

I didn't mean to call my cousin a bitch, especially not to her own father. I didn't like the word, and never used it ordinarily. Like everything else that day, it just came out. The real me. Mean as a snake and twice as cold. A crazy Powell who burned the few ramshackle bridges that led to security. I stopped talking, completely empty of words. I grimaced.

Mr. John's eyes filled with tears. *With tears.* "I am broken hearted," he said softly, with a certain degree of melodrama that was, nonetheless, sincere. He walked out. The cell door stood open in his wake. After he left the hallway I realized I was shaking. I sank down on the metal bench and put my head in my hands.

Quentin sat down beside me, his face carved in thought. *I want her.* It was as if he'd been walking through a gallery of half-formed images all his life, searching for the one, key element that made sense of so many things that happened to him, that said answers *did* exist. *Her. She's the key.*

That idea was too new and foreign to last long in its clearest form. Instead it found its way through another channel. The energy we'd generated in that room, the karma or essence or fall-out from childhoods built on hard realities—all of that had settled low in his body with primitive ease. And at that moment, his one consuming wish, filled with affection and greed, was to strip off his clothes and mine, and get inside me as quickly as possible.

"Are you all right?" he asked. His voice was stern. His willpower was in full force.

I nodded and straightened up. "I have to live here. I have to find some way to make a living in this community, and get along with people, and take care of the people who depend on me. Now, that's going to be more difficult. But I made my choice. It had nothing to do with you."

"That's not true, but I appreciate the pardon," he said.

I looked at him, shaking. No weakness. *Show no weakness in front of this man.* My research said he'd been a career soldier, *a war hero.* He didn't have to prove his strength of character, that was obvious. It only made me more determined to prove myself to *him.* I could not tell him to go back to New York and leave us alone; the situation was already too involved for that. Had I known what he was really thinking about me I might have shaken harder.

Or I might have simply held out my arms to him. *I've been waiting for you, no matter what,* I would have said.

12

"In town the Tibers are saying the Bear's worth a lot of money," Liza whispered as soon as I got back to the farm. "You can't sell it, Ursula. *You'll kill your brother's soul.*"

"I know," I answered wearily.

When Quentin came by later that afternoon he found a crowd of two-dozen neighbors and all five of my tenants waiting enthusiastically to thank him for being a hero on Mr. Beaumont's behalf. Of course the neighbors' main purpose was to learn all about this interesting man who'd come from Somewhere Else. He was a new local legend in the making. "I want to say I was here at the beginning," one man told me.

Quentin immediately directed me into my own kitchen and shut the door. "I have nothing to say to these people. I don't want anyone's gratitude." To himself he thought, *I just want to buy the goddamned sculpture and get out of here before it gets more complicated.* We were awkward with each other after the jail scene. It had been very intimate and emotional in unspoken ways we both recognized. He was suddenly embued with a deep brooding that went beyond his ordinary restlessness.

"It's too late to save your privacy," I said grimly. "Word's gotten around about your mission and the value of the Bear. One of my tenants already told me she heard."

"They've heard the price?" Quentin asked.

"No. Just that it's very valuable. Before long somebody's going to tell Arthur why you're really here. You have to make nice with this crowd and keep them away from him until I can decide what to do. They want you to answer questions about your father's career. That's all."

"I'm not here to be a tour guide. My father's career ended twenty-two years ago. Thanks to my mother's back-breaking work, he wasn't forgotten, and also thanks to her, publicity finally overtook common sense. People decided to pay a lot for his work. That's all there is to it. You and I need to talk to Arthur. Tell him the truth, and work with him on the idea of giving up the Bear. I believe I can persuade him to let me have the sculpture. And then you won't have any money worries. Everything you love here—and you do love it, I can see that—will be safe."

I wanted to shout, *Don't you understand? I can't sell the damned sculpture,* but he never seemed to hear that. "I'll talk to him when I feel the time is right. Not now. You don't realize what's going on, out there in the yard. These people brought pictures of themselves beside the sculpture. Pictures to show *you.* At first the Bear was just a joke to them—'Oh, that crazy Tom Powell's put that ugly thing in his pasture!' But somewhere over the years it became a part of their lives. There have been marriage proposals beside the Bear, and weddings, and christenings. People bring their houseguests– their 'good company' they call it—out here to see the Iron Bear. They bring their children. And their grandchildren. And those children seem to understand it. They climb on it, they talk to it, and they say it talks back. To these people, you're a part of what makes the Bear special. They want to know about you and your family. Please, try. Just answer their questions."

There was a long moment when he looked down at me without answering. Everything I'd told him seemed like a fairytale; he believed he'd never understand that kind of reaction to his father's work. The glimmers of his own mesmerized memories were a child's dreams. Safe fantasies from a time before the truth eroded them. "It's only metal," he said.

He walked out to the Bear with the group trailing him. His manner was stiff, not ungracious, but brusque. He regarded the sculpture as a thing with a price tag. I gazed at the scene in dull wonder. Who was this stranger who'd already begun to change my life? I'd peeked into the cab of his vehicle and seen a half-dozen books scattered on the passenger seat. They were much-read, much-loved volumes of fiction and poetry and engineering. I had shivered with delight.

He was a booklover, a scholar of Latin, a warrior, a businessman, a mystery. A gossipy, art-magazine profile I'd found on the Internet said Richard Riconni's son had given up a full scholarship to MIT to join the army. Why? And why was he so uncomfortable discussing his father? I knew that Richard Riconni had committed suicide long ago. I did not know what had led to his death.

Suddenly I saw Arthur creep out of the woods, watching Quentin with gleaming eyes from a distance. I went over to him. He stepped back in the shrubbery, still wary of me on some level that wouldn't let him be too friendly. I halted, miserable. "I knew Brother Bear was a hero," he whispered loudly. I was so glad to hear his voice, but so afraid it was only a temporary improvement.

"Sweetie, do you think Mama Bear is happy to see him?" I ventured.

Arthur nodded fervently. His brown eyes were large and sad. "But . . . she wants him to *give* her *something*. I haven't figured out what, yet. It's important. She's gotta have something so she'll never feel lonely and scared, again." He touched his chest, over his heart. "How can she make it stop hurting? That's what Brother Bear came here to fix. What does she want? I bet he knows."

I looked at my only brother, my only family, my shapeshifter and soothsayer, and wanted to cry. *It's you she wants. A good heart and faith. I'm going to lose you forever.*

The visitors gathered around Quentin. Their voices, rich with mountaineers' drawls, soft vowels sliding over hard bedrock, politely inquired, one at a time. *How many sculptures did your daddy make? Did he know he'd be famous? Where did he do his work? Which sculpture was his favorite? Did he make more bears?* And on and on, each receiving a pragmatic answer filled with facts but little emotion. Until finally, someone said, *You and your mama must be so proud of him.* And Quentin looked at the person, an elderly woman with large, worn hands and hopeful eyes, and he said as gallantly as he could, *We must be.*

*

Quentin raised a 35 mm camera as utilitarian as everything else about him, with scuff marks on the rim of the lens and a wide leather carrying strap bearing the marks of Hammer's puppy teeth. We were alone at the sculpture the next morning, standing knee-deep in an ocean of grass that undulated in a slow breeze. The Bear seemed to float on that green, inland sea.

Mother will be interested in everyone and everything here, he told himself. He thought of how he'd tell her the news, the look in her eyes as he explained how he'd found Bare Wisdom and maneuvered to purchase the sculpture. The photos would enthrall her, although he knew she'd want to fly back with him immediately and see for herself. *This is Ursula Powell. You'll like her. She's smart, she loves books, she's strong. Family means everything to her. You two have a lot in common.*

He told himself he was only taking photos for his mother's sake.

I stood back with Hammer sitting beside me, watching as he circled the sculpture and snapped it from all angles. "Come here," he called, waving me over. "I need pictures of you with it."

I gave him a sardonic look but sat down on the old concrete pad. "Smile," he ordered drily.

"Why? So you can prove to the folks back home that hillbillies have teeth?"

"Absolutely."

I bared my teeth at him, and he chuckled. After he took the picture he sat down next to me. We looked up at the Bear, which was surrounded by a half-dozen small, white butterflies who didn't suspect its existential power. Quentin blew out a long breath, and the butterflies hurried inside the Bear's ribs, as if seeking protection. Maybe they did know.

"One of my earliest memories," I told him, "is of going to visit the Bear with my father when the Bear was on the lawn of the administration building at Mountain State. And I remember sitting on Daddy's shoulders one sunny day—it must have been summer—I remember the beautiful flower beds on campus, and there were butterflies everywhere. They came to us—those butterflies flocked around Daddy and me and the Bear as if we were flowers. It was incredible—like a fairytale—I was up so high, and surrounded by these beautiful little creatures. Daddy said, *Don't scare them, because they're the tiniest angels.* He said they'd come to whisper all the news of heaven and earth to the Bear, because the Bear couldn't leave that spot to get the news firsthand. So that was how the Bear knew all about the world and everything in it, Daddy said.

"Suddenly something startled the butterflies, and they all fluttered inside the Bear's middle, just like now. And I said, *Oh no, the Bear ate the news angels.* Daddy laughed, and I'll never forget the *feel* of his laughter under me, like this current of . . . of love and joy. He told me that every wise soul was a butterfly eater. I had no idea what he meant at the time, but now I do."

At the end of this sentimental confession I looked at Quentin shyly, but he was watching me so gently I knew he understood, or wanted to, at least. His face growing pensive, he looked away, toward the mountains, squinting against the sunshine and his own memories.

The warm, damp heat of the earth rose around us, bringing the scent of our own skin, the fertile pasture, the mountains waiting for time and new children to squeal at their heights, birds singing old praises, insects whirring secret languages. He scanned the vista around us, and I watched him with my heart in my throat.

"The Bear's got a helluva view," he said, and he included me in that view as his gaze slowly came back to my face. "Maybe it does know something we don't know."

*

Sunlight streamed through the barn's broken planks and ruined roof, illuminating Arthur's mink-brown hair like a halo as he looked down anxiously from the barn's loft, where he had barricaded himself. Quentin cast troubled glances at my strained face. *She's tearing her heart out over this. She's trying so hard to hold her family together.*

"What kind of critter are you, Sweetie?" I called up carefully.

"An owl." Arthur hunkered down on his heels and wrapped his arms around his knees, then gazed at us without blinking.

"Why did you decide to climb up in the barn all of a sudden? Don't you remember I told you it wasn't safe?"

"I got a feeling I had to see things from up high. So I can understand."

"What gave you this feeling?"

"I heard Oswald say Mama Bear costs money."

"I think you heard Oswald tell Bartow Ledbetter that the Bear is worth *more* than money. He meant that nobody can put a price on Mama Bear. That's good."

"Why is everybody talking about money? Do you have a secret?"

I hesitated, agonizing over every word. Quentin said under his breath, "Let me talk to him."

"No. He's on the verge of a full retreat. I have to talk to him. Not you." To Arthur I called, "I *do* have a secret. And I'm about to tell you what it is. It's a surprise."

"Like when Daddy died? You don't want me to go back to Atlanta, do you?" His large dark eyes stared at me, but there was nothing placid or owlish about them. He looked horrified.

"Oh, no, Sweetie, no. It's nothing bad. I promise you. I won't make up any stories about it. I'll tell you the truth."

"How will I know it's the truth?"

"You have to trust me."

He was silent. Big tears slid down his face. "I don't know how, anymore."

His plaintive confession stabbed me. As I struggled to speak Quentin laid a hand on my arm. I glanced at him and nodded.

"Arthur," he said. "Watch." He dropped to his heels. We stood beside the barn's collapsed lean-to. My car, an old brown Mercedes sedan, was bashed under heavy chestnut timbers, strips of torn pine plank, and long pieces of the barn's rusty tin roofing. I'd bought the sedan years earlier for two thousand dollars from an Emory classmate who had broken her foot kicking it after the latest in a series of expensive engine problems. I put a Chevy engine in it, and it had run ever since. Now, my hybrid car was flattened.

Quentin felt around in the air between timbers and then under the car. I looked at this strange behavior in amazement. So did Arthur, craning his head. "Brother Bear?" he called in a worried tone.

"There. I've got one." Quentin thrust one large hand into a space between the jumbled boards, as if catching something. He pulled back his closed hand and studied it. "It's in there. I can feel it moving. I didn't hurt it."

"What is it?" Arthur called, craning his head more. I found myself bending over to look, then straightened quickly.

Quentin stood, holding out his closed hand. "It's one of the creatures who live in the air between things. Between rocks and the ground. Between the boards of the barn. Between the parts of the car. When I was a boy I called it a *Tween*. Because it lived *Between*."

"A Tween," Arthur repeated in awe. "What does it look like?"

"I don't know. Tweens are invisible."

"What do they do?"

"They hold the world up. Every part, every piece of every thing is held together and held up by Tweens. If you know how to make the Tweens happy, nothing falls down."

Arthur unwrapped his arms and pointed down at the lean-to's crumpled roof. "I see them! There and there. There are hundreds of them! Gazillions! They're not real happy, though. We're all in a mess. That's what they're saying."

Quentin opened his hand. "Go on, it's all right, go do your job," he said to the Tween, then blew on it softly. He made a show of watching some invisible thing fly back into the rubble. I found myself tracking its supposed route with hypnotic fascination.

"Are all the Tweens good?" Arthur called.

Quentin hesitated, gauging which answer would work best, then shook his head. "You have to be careful with Tweens. Some are bad-tempered. The bad ones make extra space and push things around. They make your structure weak. When you see too much emptiness, there's usually a bad Tween involved."

"We've got a few really bad Tweens around here," Arthur said somberly.

"Don't be scared of them. I know how to keep the Tweens happy. It's really simple. If you lie to a Tween he'll let the things you love most fall down around you. Am I going to lie to you, Arthur? Ask the good Tweens."

My brother bent his head and sat, deep in thought. I faced Quentin. "Where did you learn that wonderful story?" I asked softly.

Until that moment he hadn't considered where the idea came from, it had just come, drawn out of him by some strange alchemy produced by a need to comfort me, my brother, and himself. He looked at me like a man with amnesia, as deep in thought as Arthur, seeking his identity. *Papa told it to me,* he realized suddenly, with a quick mental picture of his father patiently showing him how to stack the clanking pieces of his homemade metal building set. "My father thought it up to keep me distracted while he worked," he said, then turned away, his jaw clenched. "Brother Arthur? What do you think? What do the good Tweens say?"

Arthur raised his head. His somber gaze went to me. "The good Tweens want to know what's the secret you want to tell me."

I took a deep breath. "It's not really a secret. *Mama Bear belongs to you.* Do you understand that? She's your property. You're the only one who can take care of her. Whatever you say about her, that's what happens. Understand? You love her and you're her protector." He nodded, but with an incredulous and guarded tilt to his head. "Okay," he said slowly.

"But Quentin and his mother love Mama Bear, too. In fact, Quentin's mother thought Mama Bear had been taken to the junk yard and cut up for scrap metal a long time ago. She's so happy to know that Mama Bear is okay."

"Mama Bear's still held up by the good Tweens." Arthur looked at Quentin, who nodded.

"Quentin would like to take Mama Bear back to his home so that his mother can love her just the way you do."

Arthur shot up like a rocket. Legs braced, hands clenched by his sides, he stared down at us. My heart stopped. Beside me, Quentin said in a low voice, "I'll climb up and get him, if I have to."

I held up both hands. "Arthur! It's your choice. Don't you remember what I just said? Mama Bear's not going anywhere unless you think she needs to go."

Arthur trembled. He pointed at Quentin. "*Brother Bear.* You think she'll die if she doesn't leave here? You think that's why she's so lonely?"

"I don't know. You have to decide what's best for her, and tell me. That's all I want to know. It's your choice."

"I don't own her. She makes up her own mind."

"All right, then, you're going to have to interpret for me."

"Maybe she wants to go. I've got to think about this." He swayed on the lip of the loft's sill. One wrong step and he'd fall twenty feet into the jagged debris of the lean-to. I was scared out of my mind. "Arthur, sit down."

"I have to talk to the good Tweens that hold her up, and see what kind of bad Tweens are around!" He took a rattled step forward. The toe of his tennis shoe now hung over the sill's edge. Quentin raised a hand. In a deep and commanding voice he ordered, "The Tweens only respect a man who takes care of his *own* spaces. Be a man. *Sit down.*"

My brother dropped to a squat with the speed of an unplugged toy. His eyes were soulful yet determined. "*Like a man,*" he said. I sagged with relief. But then Arthur's eyes lit up and he pointed at *me.* "Sister! I see a great big *bad Tween* right in the middle of you and Brother Bear."

I rubbed my forehead. Quentin had created a whole new fantasy world for Arthur, one that quickly became aggravating. "I don't see a Tween," I said.

"It's a *mean* Tween," Arthur insisted, louder. "It came out from under the lean-to. It's floating in the air between you and Brother Bear."

"I'll get it some iced tea and a cookie. It's not mean. It's just hungry. Calm down." I faced Quentin. It was amazing that Arthur hadn't gone into hysterics—or voiceless shock—over even the suggestion of selling the sculpture. But that was only a temporary reprieve, I felt. I was both angry and grateful to Quentin. "If we don't get him down from there the Tweens are going to cart my brain away to an asylum."

Quentin crooked a finger at him. "Arthur, come down. I want you to move slow, and be careful. If you do that—and don't fall—I'll show you how to get rid of a bad Tween."

My brother hopped up and crept from sight, placing every footstep with melodramatic care. Quentin and I walked to the front of the barn and waited as he picked his way down the loft ladder and then through the piles of beams and debris. Quentin grasped him by one arm, helping him crawl nimbly over the last beam.

Arthur faced us with electrified energy. "Okay, now you get rid of the bad Tween. I gotta understand how they think, so I can decide what to do about Mama Bear. I don't want the bad Tweens to get mad at her." He shifted from one foot to the other, wringing his hands. "Chase it off!"

I reached for him. "Sweetie, sssh, calm down—"

148

He jerked away. "The Tween's right in front of you!"

Quentin faced me. He took me by the shoulders. "Trust me on this," he said, and before I realized what he intended, he kissed me lightly on the mouth. Dazed, I simply stood there. He had eaten an orange at some point in the day, and his lips were still flavored with it. I knew, at that moment, that when I was an old woman I would lift a wedge of orange to my mouth and still remember him.

"*You kissed my sister,*" Arthur said in an awed voice.

He nodded. "I chased off the bad Tween."

Arthur gasped and scrutinized some spot in the air before us. "You did!"

Quentin gave me a half-smile that mocked us all. I stared at him, not yet capable of registering anger at the intrusion or resistance to the sensations that swept through me like nothing I'd ever felt before. "You're about to find yourself *between* a rock and a hard place," I warned.

"I've been there more often than I care to remember. I don't mind the pressure, and I don't think you minded the kiss." There was the slightest touch of ruddy color in his cheeks, beneath the shadow of fine, afternoon beard stubble. He frowned and rubbed his jaw as if the softness of my face had polished his. *A mistake, a goddamned reckless mistake*, he was thinking.

"I have to go off and think about the Tweens and Mama Bear," Arthur announced, then headed for the woods at a lope.

I looked at Quentin, then away. "He thinks slowly. He ponders important questions for hours, or even *days*. The color of a bird's wing, the shape of a snail's shell. What to name a squirrel. You've asked him to make a decision that changes his entire universe. Don't expect an answer right away. And don't expect the answer you want. He'll think and he'll agonize, but in the end, he'll never decide that his Mama Bear wants to go with you."

"I'll take that bet," Quentin said.

In the spaces between our lives, the Tweens were gaining control.

13

Get Arthur's answer and settle this negotiation before the situation falls down around us all. Quentin's plan for the day was simple when he left his motel room the next morning. At the Tiberville Diner, just off the square, he parked in the midst of muddy pick-up trucks and service vans. His Explorer's New York tag drew curious glances from the blue-collar men striding inside for a quick breakfast. The men nodded to him, even though he was a stranger, and said *Mornin' there, how you doin'?* There was no choice but to nod back and answer.

He rolled the Explorer's windows down and locked Hammer in the back compartment. Hammer slurped happily over a bowl of dry dog food and a bowl of water, after uttering one deep, ferocious bark at a large, rust-red hound dog sitting majestically among the ladders in the bed of a painter's truck nearby. The hound merely wagged its tail. *Mornin', there. How you doin?*

Quentin took a corner booth where he drew less attention. He spread out a collection of local history books and tourists' pamphlets he'd purchased, and after placing an order for waffles, sipped black coffee and continued methodically working his way through the information. It was a crash course in Powell and Tiber history, including the story of Erim and the lost Annie, which he read twice. In the more recent pamphlets, which detailed notable events and milestones, there was not one mention of the Iron Bear. That fact began to gnaw at him, even as he dismissed it.

"Gawd, you're just like Ursula," the waitress said, grinning a gold-toothed grin when she delivered the waffles. "Got your nose stuck in a book all the time. What you reading?" She pecked a long fake fingernail on a tome of Tiber County stories, and snorted. "That's Tiber tall tales, right there. You read that, you'll think Tibers walk on water and the rest of us can't even swim."

"Can't even go wading," a man at the counter amended, and others guffawed. And before Quentin could inject even a word or question, his fellow diners began to tell him their own version of the county's history. He heard the news of my family in colorful detail, including the story of the Bear's arrival, and how my father defended the sculpture from that day forward. By the time they finished with the night of Miss Betty's death and the confrontation between Daddy and

Mr. John, Quentin had let his food go cold and forgotten, his hands quiet around his empty coffee mug.

He went to the cash register to pay his bill, and a stocky older man swiveled on a counter stool to study him with narrowed eyes. "Hear you and Ursula Powell set John Tiber's ass in a crack the other day," he said. The man wore a Tiber Poultry work shirt. The other diners grew very still and quiet, watching.

Quentin looked from the logo to the man's eyes, expecting trouble. "That could be." Amused respect spread over the man's face. "Then you fit *right* in with the Powells, mister. They been dogging Tibers since god was a youngun'. Keepin' them as straight as anybody could. Glad to see you takin' up the cause."

"Well, Albert, after all, his daddy did build the Bear," a trucker in overalls commented. "It's in his blood to stand up for what he believes in."

Quentin laid his check and money on the cash register. The waitress handed it back. The diner's owner swiveled from a sizzling griddle. He held a long spatula in one hand and a determined expression in his eyes. "Your breakfast is on the house, Mr. Riconni," he said. "It'd be an honor."

Quentin thanked him, nodded to the others, and walked outside in warm, flower-scented air. Beyond the end of the parking lot, the land fell in great forested swoops into a valley dotted with houses and tiny roads. In the distance, green mountains shimmered in shadows and sunlight. The sky was the bluest he'd ever seen. Paradise was an easy illusion, some days.

He took a deep, troubled breath, and exhaled.

*

I was in town that morning, too, minding my own business, trying to concentrate on the simple task of filling a grocery cart at the Piggly Wiggly. Almost every mountain town had a Piggly Wiggly, and ours was little different from the rest—small, modest, and no-nonsense. You couldn't buy wine or beer there, or the makings for sushi, or even a fancy spinach salad. It was a meat-and-potatoes grocery store, and I was debating the price on a two-pound package of cheap ground chuck when Janine Tiber pushed her way through the swinging metal doors from the store's warehouse area.

She carried a mahogany-veneered clip board with a stack of notes atop it. A half-dozen exquisitely business-suited men and women followed her. I glimpsed Rolexes, Gucci scarves, and diamond cufflinks. Janine looked sleek and autocratic in a handsome linen suit and matching pumps. Her blonde hair, as always for business, was pulled back in a gold clasp at the nape of her neck.

I cursed silently. I wore leather sandals, faded cargo shorts, and a Faulkner t-shirt I'd won in a raffle at a booksellers' trade show. William Faulkner stared somberly from the background of my breasts. My hair still smelled of udder balm.

"Piggly Wiggly is one of Tiber Poultry's major customers in this region," she was saying, as she walked. She was leading a tour of investors. Rumor had spread that when Mr. John retired in a year or two she intended to expand the company. Janine halted when she and her small army came down my narrow aisle. I stood next to the Tiber section of the meat coolers, blocking the entrance with my cart. Her eyes glittered. "Good morning."

"Morning." I nodded to the group, which stared back. "Give me a second and I'll move out of your way." I began maneuvering the cart to avoid a display of beef jerky on the opposite side of the aisle. I bumped the jerky. A wheel jammed. I shook the cart and nudged the wheel with my foot. Janine said nothing, but her mouth puckered with impatience. My face burned. I bumped the jerky display again. Several vacuum-sealed packets of Spicy Joe Jerked Beef toppled to the floor. I squatted and began gathering the damned packets.

"Are you a regular customer of Piggly Wiggly?" a woman in a red-silk power suit asked.

"All my life." *And in this hellish parallel universe, too.* I stood, grasping handfuls of jerky. I began putting the packets back on their holders. No one, especially Janine, lifted a finger to help.

"Let's do a quick customer interview," the red-silk woman announced to the others. She stepped closer to my cart. "Do you purchase Tiber Poultry products here?"

I put the last beef jerky on the display. I'd had enough. I looked at Janine, then at Red Silk. I said bluntly, and honestly, "I don't eat chicken."

Janine's eyes flared. Red Silk arched a brow. "Oh? Why?"

"My father was a Tiber contract farmer. I grew up shoveling chicken manure and burying dead chicks. We ate chicken because it was all we could afford. The annual income for Tiber contract farmers runs just above minimum wage after you factor in feed, utilities, and labor. Of course the farmer usually has little choice, because his chicken houses are built with loans from the Bank of Tiber, which is, of course, controlled by Tibers. He's got mortgages to pay, so he can't complain too much. It's a government sanctioned form of indentured servitude." I smiled. "I swore that once I was set free, I'd never eat chicken, again."

The group gazed at me with stony-faced resentment. I hadn't told them anything they didn't know, I'd just embarrassed them. Across the aisle, a gaggle of women, including Mrs. Greene, Juanita, and Liza, stood listening behind the frozen-foods case, with their carts nosed together like metal cows communing at a water trough. Liza applauded. "Be strong and stay inside the light," she called softly.

Why am I asking for trouble? I have so much already. I had lost my mind. Quentin had taken it. The Tweens had helped him. This news would spread.

Janine was furious. "I apologize for inadvertently subjecting you to our local politics," she said to her group in a voice that could have cut a buffalo wing. "I assure you this is a matter of personal disagreements, not a serious issue that causes any ill will or controversy in our dealings with our contract farmers. In fact, Tiber Poultry is considered a beloved part of the community, and we treat our employees like family."

"That's right. I'm her cousin, and she treats *me* like an employee," I said.

After that remark, I saw war in Janine's eyes. She could have strangled me. "Let's move on," she announced smoothly, then detoured her group around me and led them to the store manager, who hustled them down a distant aisle. Five seconds later she strode back to me. She tossed her clip board into the meat bin and put her hands on her hips.

"First you publicly insult my father, and now *me*. Oh, I've heard all about your *visitor*, your knife-wielding New York *thug* who's waving money around and claiming the Bear is valuable art. He's obviously convinced you that you're going to get rich off that piece of junk. Is that what this is all about? Poor white trash Ursula, still trying to prove she's not a Nobody and certain she's found a sugar-daddy to fund the effort. You couldn't gain anyone's respect with an Emory scholarship or a masters in business. You failed as an entrepreneur, your publishing company is a joke, you came home broke, your brother's going to end up in an institution, so all you can hope for now is a lucrative hand-out from a *gangster*. Congratulations. You're continuing the Powell family tradition of no-accounts and n'er-do-wells."

I put my open hand on her face, and pushed. She staggered back and hit the Spicy Joe display. It careened on its cardboard side. She tripped and sat down on it.

Beef jerky went everywhere.

*

Quentin studied me through the bars of the holding cell, where I sat on the metal bench with my hands in my lap and my back very straight. "Do you mud wrestle, too?"

"Only with my cousins. You didn't have to come here. I can get myself out."

"Not this time. I had to pay the store for the damage to the Spicy Joe display."

I stared straight ahead. "Thank you."

He leaned against the bars with one foot crossed over the other and his hands lounged in the pockets of his trousers. His nonchalance was feigned for my sake, I believe. "You're welcome."

The deputy, Mrs. Dixon, shook her gray head as she unlocked the door and swung it open. "I think I'll just give y'all the key." She wandered back down the hall, and left us alone. Quentin crooked a finger at me. "Come out, Xena, Warrior Princess. You're free. No bail. Charges were dropped. Your Tibers obviously like to have their cousins arrested and then turn them loose as a show of family kinship."

I stood up. "It's a southern tradition."

As I walked out the cell, Quentin straightened, and his expression grew serious. "This happened because of me, I hear."

"In part."

"I'm sorry. People will forget once I'm gone. That'll happen as soon as Arthur lets me have the sculpture."

Anger boiled inside me. "I have bills to pay and tenants who depend on me and a brother who's more like a child than a grown man. I have to make the future safe for him. But that doesn't mean I like what I have to do. And I don't enjoy being charged with assault and going to jail! People *won't* forget!"

He listened without any outward reaction, his somber gaze never leaving my face. *She can't let herself depend on anyone. God, I want her to trust me.* "I'm going to make it worth your while," he said. "When you're rich, people won't give a damn about today."

"You don't know this town, and you don't know *me*. So please, save your shitty promises."

The air froze. If Arthur's bad Tweens existed, they were trapped in the crystal layers of ice we generated. "I don't make promises I can't keep," he said quietly.

"Don't make me any promises at all."

The door at the end of the hall clanged open. "Y'all coming, or you plan to set up housekeeping?" Mrs. Dixon called.

We walked out of the small, utilitarian brick building in tense silence. When we stepped outside we met a small crowd. My tenants rushed forward. Arthur was with them, clutching Liza's hand. He stopped, breathing hard, his eyes wild with fear as he looked from me to Quentin.

"He thought you'd be locked up forever," Liza whispered. "He was afraid you'd died and no one would tell him."

I tried to touch him, but he pulled back. "I'm fine, Sweetie," I said wearily.

Arthur bounded to Quentin. "Brother Bear." His voice cracked. "You wouldn't let anything bad happen to my sister, would you?"

He trusts me, Quentin thought with a silent groan. "Your sister can take care of herself."

"No, the Tweens almost got her, yesterday and again today! Just like they'll get Mama Bear if I do the wrong thing. But you won't let anything bad happen. I just know it. As long as you're here we don't have any big empty spaces!" He threw his arms around Quentin and gave him a hug. Quentin stood there with grim reserve, finally raising a hand to clasp my brother's shoulder and gently pry him away. My heart sank.

Arthur had found a hero, and he thought Quentin would stay forever.

*

Hospitality demanded I offer Quentin a place to stay at Bear Creek. To my dismay, he accepted. "The closer I stay to Arthur, the sooner he'll make up his mind," he reasoned.

He phoned the old sergeant to tell him about the delay. Popeye was the only person who knew Quentin had found the sculpture. Since Quentin often spent time on long jaunts out of state to buy and dismantle properties, no one else yet thought his absence was peculiar. But there would be questions, soon.

"What the hell are you doing down there?" Popeye growled. "Making time with that mountain gal?"

"Negotiating."

"Aw, sure. She pretty?"

"Sarge, stop digging."

"Not married or anything?"

"Stop."

"You go ahead and piss on my questions, but I smell the answers. Lemme warn you, son, you let a mountain woman get her legs around you and she'll squeeze your soul out. Gals in those mountains grow up *tough and hungry*."

Quentin brushed off the sarge's typical bluster and revealed nothing about the situation. *I'm the one who's hungry around her,* he thought.

He refused my grudging offer to stay in the farmhouse—I would have given him Daddy's bedroom—and bunked in a shabby, half-furnished apartment at one end of the second chicken house, where the tenants had cordoned off space for their studios. Dust sifted through the wall vents from the Ledbetters' pottery wheels and kilns. The added heat from Liza's glass furnace made the apartment's two tiny rooms swelter. The window air conditioner was broken; only one burner worked on the small stove, and the toilet tank leaked.

This is a test, he thought grimly. He opened the door and one small window, set up an electric fan I gave him, and spent as little time there as possible. It was all he could do to resist working on the place. And on me. *She hates me being here. She watches me all the time.* He was right about that. I had no intention of letting him near Arthur without my supervision. Or near *me*, again.

Arthur followed him like a puppy, often silent, simply studying him with sorrowful adoration, pondering the Tweens that Quentin had revealed to him and the decision we'd asked him to make. He paced and huddled, polished the sculpture with his bare hands, couldn't eat, grew quieter. He turned pale any time Quentin tried to draw him into a discussion about the future.

I could put an end to this, I began to tell myself. Just tell Quentin to go, leave us alone, as I should have done at the start. But then what would I say to Arthur? He'd think Quentin had died. Everyone could die at any time, in my brother's fragile world. The dilemma made me toss in my own bed at night. I woke from a dream about being homeless and finding Arthur beaten to death beside Mama and Daddy's graves.

Darting outside in the warm moonlight, I took deep breaths then squatted by the yard spigot, splashing my face and neck with ice-cold well water. Kneeling there, barefooted and dressed only in a thin cotton gown, I looked up and saw Quentin crossing the pasture. I stumbled to my feet.

He walked to the sculpture and stood facing it, looking up into the thick, ursine face that his father had cut from huge cast-iron pots my father collected. His shoulders were hunched; even in the moonlight his silhouette conveyed both strength and defeat. He was so alone. I pressed my hand to my heart and slipped quietly to the edge of the light beyond the tree-shadowed backyard.

I'd listen, if you could tell me. I'd tell you, if you could listen.

He turned his head my way. There was no doubt in my mind he saw me in that sheer gown, my hand over my heart as if pledging allegiance. For one bone-tingling moment I thought he was going to walk to me, but instead he pivoted and walked slowly back to his own door.

We never mentioned it.

*

"What is he saying to that thing?" Quentin asked. We watched from the porch the next evening as Arthur huddled on the Bear's concrete pad, hugging his knees and rocking, his mouth moving in some obviously fervent conversation, lost in some lonely world.

"He talks to the sculpture every day around sunset. It's his habit. When he was a child it comforted him. But now he says *he's* trying to comfort the Bear. I asked him this afternoon if he was any closer to a decision. He told me the Bear is still thinking."

Quentin leaned back in an old Adirondack chair, his eyes troubled. "Do you talk to it, too?"

I hesitated. Everything I told him about myself felt too intimate. "Everyone who's around the Bear for very long starts to talk to it. You can't help yourself."

Quentin frowned. He'd never talked to any of his father's sculptures, never felt they were *really* alive. This bewildered him and made him feel more isolated than he realized.

"Do you understand what the Bear means to us?" I asked.

"Childhood memories. I understand that."

"It's not that simple." I moved from my own chair to sit on the steps near his feet, looking up at him as if in prayer. If I could just make him understand. Maybe there could be a friendship between us, between our families, something Arthur would hang onto no matter what happened about the sculpture.

"I don't know what my father would say to you, but I know he'd want to do what was *right*," I said in a fervent tone, my hands gesturing, almost brushing the material of his trousers, almost ready to touch him, to reach for his own hands, which lay open, palm up, on his knees. He leaned forward—frowning, listening intently, those large silver eyes never leaving my face. "Life was hard, here. Daddy didn't have a lot of choices. He learned to appreciate what he had—in fact, he *celebrated* what he had. He was a righteous person. Truly, purely righteous. He believed in the integrity of sharing. He'd share with you, I'm sure." I hesitated. "I was angry at you the other day at the jail because I behaved foolishly. And because I *do* want your money. I want to lord it over every damn Tiber in the county. My father would be ashamed of me."

I started to turn away, hiding my emotions and changing the subject, but Quentin touched my shoulder with just his fingertips. "No, he wouldn't feel that way. You made him proud. There's nothing wrong with wanting money to take care of your home and family."

Looking up at him helplessly, I said, "Are you psychic?"

"Not even a little. I just can't imagine any man not being proud of a daughter like you."

Warmth rushed through me. "My tenant, Liza, says she's spoken to Daddy in dreams. That's bullshit. I don't really believe in that kind of thing, but still. I've tried to dream about him. The worst thing is, when I *do* dream about him, I can't speak. Or I talk but I know he can't hear me."

"And you wake up in a cold sweat with your throat raw."

I stared at him. "You *are* psychic."

"I've had that kind of dream."

I hesitated. Then, "Tell me about your father."

"I don't like to talk about him. There's nothing to say—and obviously I can't say it even in dreams. He's been gone a long time."

"Was he kind? Did you love him?"

"None of that matters."

"But you still dream about him?"

"I try not to."

"Then how do you live with what you can't change and can't explain?"

He frowned. "I get up each day and forget he existed."

"It's not that easy to shut yourself off. To stop caring."

His eyes narrowed. He studied me as if I were deliberately provoking him. "Practice makes perfect."

That glib remark brushed me away like a butterfly. I tossed up both hands in disgust. "I read an article that said he committed suicide. All right? I *know* what happened to him. I can imagine what it did to you and your mother."

His eyes darkened. *All right, she wants to know, she thinks she can imagine?* "He shot himself in the chest. I found his body. I can still smell the blood. I can still see the hole over his heart and the little pieces of his skin and his shirt splattered all over him. I can remember how cold he was when I put my hand there. I can see the look in his eyes. How alone he was when he died. *That's* how I see him in my dreams."

I looked away, stunned, ashamed of myself for prying. I fumbled with one hand and brushed his by accident. It only seemed natural to slide my hand across one of his open palms as a show of apology and sympathy. I had no idea how he'd react.

But he curved his other hand over mine and turned my hand in his, then linked his fingers through mine. "Sorry to lay it all out that way." His voice was gruff, his grip gentle and electric.

I faced him, again. "It didn't occur to me that you were the one who discovered him. I wouldn't have asked."

"I just don't like to talk about him. I never think about him without remembering how he died. Nothing I can say will change it."

I shook my head. "*Silence is the worst enemy of hope.* I can't remember who said that. Plato, maybe, or one of the saints. But it's true."

He sat back slowly and released my hand. A shield returned. "I respect you. Don't ruin it with the kind of advice I could get off a fortune cookie." The tone of his voice sent a chill down my back.

One of Mama's favorite sayings rose in my mind. I hadn't thought of it in years, but suddenly she was there beside me, firm and plain, warning the godly side of me. *You don't hold a snake. The snake holds you.* Quentin had drawn me in, only to shut me out. I got up. "Making friends with me and Arthur is just a necessary maneuver to you, isn't it?" I asked quietly. "You say what you have to, you do what you have to, it's all calculated. You don't want us to know you, and you don't want to know *us.* You think we're just quaint hicks. You have no real respect."

"That's not true, but I'm here to do business, not share sad stories or analyze my father's life. You need to keep that in mind."

"I will, from now on." The tenants would be walking over, soon, for dinner. I had a huge pot of stew on the stove, and potato salad in the refrigerator. I had to set the table, be the lady of my father's house, and now, my own. "Excuse me." I walked inside. The hot evening sun couldn't prevent an unnatural shiver.

*

Quentin lay on the small, cheap bed of the apartment that night, grimly replaying our conversation. He had left the apartment's door open to fight the stale air and heat, with an outside screened door latched. Moths fluttered against that screen. The window fan pushed warm, wisteria-scented air—the faint aroma like grapes—over his naked body. He linked his hands behind his head and gazed out a narrow window at a sky of brilliant stars undimmed by city lights. Hammer slept on the simple tile floor by the bed, twitching and breathing hard as he chased memories of a gray rabbit he'd spotted in the pasture.

It's so easy to forget who you are, here, he thought. Her hand on mine. Her blue eyes wide open and not as worldly as she thinks. She hasn't traveled that far, hasn't hated her own life that much. But we're alike in so many ways. The same cloud over us. Growing up poor. Loving parents who didn't always make sense. Losing the one who kept the family in one piece. Never forgetting.

He groaned under his breath and shut his eyes.

I didn't want to hurt her, but she got too close.

14

After that, every moment I spent in Quentin's company was a push-pull of conflicting emotions. I saw flashes of humor, kindness, deep intelligence, but always that stony overlay, that impossible wall. I knew I hid behind a simpler version of that armor, but I felt very vulnerable around him.

I escorted him over to the isolated Washington homestead and made introductions. We sat on the porch with the professor, sipping iced tea from crystal glasses and eating slices of a pound cake I'd made. Dr. Washington pointed to the porch hammock where my brother slept most nights. "Perhaps you can explain something Arthur's been hugging in his slumber."

Arthur made the hammock his bed so often that I'd outfitted it with a thin cotton quilt and pillow. Dr. Washington pulled a dog-eared copy of a Hemingway's Old Man and the Sea from under the pillow. "He's been holding this as if it were a security blanket. Ursula, is this something from your father's bookshelves?"

"It's mine," Quentin said. "I left it on the seat of my Explorer. It disappeared."

I winced. "I'm sorry. Arthur's not a thief. He just wanted something of yours as a keepsake. Like a talisman." I looked at Quentin coolly. "Whether you want it or not, you're one of his *Tweens*, now. Holding up his world."

"Whatever he wants to believe is up to him. Leave it." Quentin tucked the book back under the pillow.

When I tried to thank him, he shook his head and instantly changed the subject. "Mind if I look at your barn?" he asked the professor. The Washington barn was a two-story architectural oddity built of thick-hewn logs. The top level was twice as large as the bottom, and perched on the smaller bottom like the top of a giant wooden mushroom. Its overhanging floor made a covered walkway on all sides of the bottom level, which had once provided stalls for the Washington milk cows.

"It's a cantilevered construction style," Dr. Washington said. "Rare, around here. My brother Fred always took such pride in it."

"Dutch, isn't it? I read about barns like this in eastern Tennessee."

"Yes."

"If you ever want to sell it, let me know."

Dr. Washington gazed at him curiously. "What would you do with an ancient log *barn?*"

"I'd bring a crew down, dismantle it piece by piece, take everything to New York. Sell it to a buyer who'd reassemble it."

"I was of the impression that you dealt in fine period architectural pieces."

"I do. The craftsmanship on the iron work alone makes your barn special."

"I admit to you I didn't always care about that barn, but I'm wiser, now. My great-great grandfather hand-forged every nail, every hinge, every hook. One of his children wrote that he believed he put the spirit of African strength into every piece he forged. His work was a testament to his heritage and his pride, even though he was a slave for much of his life."

Quentin listened with quiet respect. "I'd say he was an artist."

"Interesting. I suppose he was."

Quentin walked over to the barn, stepped into the shadows under its looming second floor, and ran his hands over massive iron hinges along a cattle stall door.

"An interesting man, himself," Dr. Washington said to me.

I blew out a long, frustrated breath. "I read in an article that his father taught him all about metalwork. He likes iron, if nothing else."

"He clearly appreciates history, yet he's bluntly unsentimental. So many contradictions."

I could only nod in agreement.

∗

I can't do this, I can't just sit here, Quentin conceded as another day stretched out with no sign that Arthur's intense musings would reach a conclusion, soon. He and I had used up most of our reasons to avoid each other or at least to stay busy in each other's company. He had studied Liza's glass-blowing techniques and the Ledbetters' pottery skills. He'd adjusted an unbalanced pottery wheel for the old couple and rewired the electrical outlet on their largest kiln. He'd sketched a suggested new window for Oswald's small painting studio, and had stood nearby, making serious commentary as Oswald finished an erotic forest portrait, titled Peckerwood, for lurid reasons the rest of us pretended to ignore.

I'm already involved, he told himself. *What could it hurt to stay busy?*

The farmhouse invited him inside as if it had a voice. He imagined that voice as feminine and very southern. My voice, in fact. The house, with its plain comforts and old woods, wrapped itself around him every time he stepped through the kitchen door. He inhaled the aromas from generations of hearth fires and home-canning, baked cornbread and fried apple pies, old cotton curtains and scrubbed linoleum. He had watched me at breakfast one morning, kneading biscuit dough in a wooden bowl that had been carved by my great-grandmother, and the blood rushed through him as if my hands were on his body. He'd had to step outside and shake his head in grim amusement over his own stark arousal. A barefoot woman in baggy, cut-off overalls massaging biscuit dough had that kind of effect. Work, hard physical work, was the only answer. His demons could be sweated out.

Quentin walked into my living room with a tool belt over one big shoulder and a look that burned the clothes off my body. "Time to fix your pipes and make your outlets work," he said.

I stared at him from behind my office desk. Powell Press was now headquartered there in less-than-professional splendor. Morning glories crept inside the window screens and a small chipmunk darted in and out of the soot-stained fireplace. "I beg your pardon?"

He held up his hands as if to say, *Look, they're empty.* "I need something to occupy my time while Arthur drags this negotiation out, and you need repairs done around here."

I knew he had grown up working at a garage, and that he had a degree in engineering. I knew he worked with his hands as well as his mind, tearing homes and mills apart with a surgeon's precision. But he did not *build*, and he did not settle in one place, and the thought that I'd be surrounded by his handiwork after he left brought a pang of sorrow. He'd be everywhere I looked in my own home, and nowhere. "I appreciate your offer, but no. Thank you, but I can't accept."

He mulled that statement as his gaze went to the walls crowded with bookshelves and office equipment, the old sofa and claw-foot end tables pushed aside for boxes of my authors' unsold books, the general shabby, shoestring appeal of my work. He walked to a bookcase filled with my father's favorite volumes. Selecting a thick text on modern art, he flipped through the pages, frowning. "I wish I'd met your father. I'd ask him what you were like before you decided not to depend on a man. Any man."

"I don't just feel that way about men," I corrected as lightly as I could. "I include women, children, pets, and inanimate objects. You're one to talk. Old bachelor."

He shut the book and tucked it back into place, then slid a toothpick from his shirt pocket and eyed me while chewing the tip. "Old maid," he deadpanned.

"Would you like to hear a polite southern-girl excuse? *If it ain't broke, don't fix it.*"

Quentin nodded at the hearth. The chipmunk had suddenly appeared. It saw us and zipped back into a hole in the wooden baseboard. "You like running a kennel for cute rats?"

"Look, the truth is, I can't work in here with you making noise in the house." I tapped the desk. "Believe it or not, this is my business, and I make, oh, a whopping hundred dollars a month at it. I'd really like to be able to declare that steady income when I apply for food stamps."

"Tell me about your work." He sat down in an old wooden chair near the fireplace. He looked so good, there, so right. I blinked away the image. "Welcome to the Powell Press publishing empire." I pointed to boxes stacked in one corner. "My warehouse." A bookcase filled with books and files, computer mailing lists and promotional materials. "The marketing department." A work table covered in boxes, labels, and rolls of packing tape. "Shipping department." I pointed to the floor where he stood, in front of my desk. "You're on my loading dock. Watch out for forklifts."

"I'd like to read the two books you've published."

"Oh?" Secretly pleased, I picked up a pencil. "Then you've come to the right place. You're talking to the sales rep."

He got up. I gave him the books, and he left with them under one arm. I settled back at my desk and put my head in my hands.

An hour later, Liza hurried in. "Did you know that Quentin is working on your barn?"

He nodded at me from the loft, where he and Arthur were clearing broken planks and beams. One of the baby squirrels darted out of his shirt pocket and leapt to Arthur's shoulder. "I'm infected with squirrels," Quentin said dryly.

"Sounds painful."

"I need something to do. This won't bother you, will it?"

"What does a man do now?" Arthur said loudly. He held one end of a short plank; Quentin held the other.

"We're going to angle my end out the hole in the wall and toss it." I watched as they maneuvered the board and dropped it with a woody rattle atop a pile outside the wall. Arthur's new hobby, besides pondering the sculpture's fate, was asking Quentin for instruction on this creature, *a man*. When Quentin wasn't Brother Bear he was the epitome of manhood, and Arthur mimicked him desperately. I had never seen anything like it before. My brother was finding a way to slip past the invisible bonds of autism. Thanks to Quentin, who didn't want to care.

"What does a man do?" Arthur asked again, picking up the end of a heavier beam.

"A man doesn't let go of that sucker unless he wants to drop it on his toes," Quentin told him, and grabbed the opposite end. They guided the beam out the hole. Arthur held on with the somber concentration of a monk studying sacred texts. "Now a man let's go," Quentin told him. The beam fell with a satisfying thud. Arthur smiled. Quentin gave him a thumbs up. There was so much gentleness in him. Arthur saw it, and suddenly, so did I.

I looked up at Quentin Riconni and, without warning, without common sense or logic, without the space to hide the idea even from myself, I thought, *I really want to love you.*

*

The phone rang and I answered it dully. "Daddy passed out with chest pains yesterday," Janine announced.

Is he all right?"

"He'll do. The doctor put him on new angina medication and tranquilizers. He's been under a lot of *stress*, lately. I wonder why. He wants to see you for lunch tomorrow. Clearing the air might make him feel better. Will you come?"

"Yes."

"Thank you."

"Janine, I'm sorry I pushed you."

"No, you're not. But I'll make a pact with the devil if you'll be nice to my father at lunch."

"I'll take that invitation, Beelzebub, and thank you."

She hung up.

*

Tiber Crest, a large, plantation-like estate a few miles west of town, had become the family's centerpiece in the 1960's, after Mr. John and Janine's mother received the land as a wedding gift and built a huge, white-columned house. Among Tiber employees, the estate was jokingly known as Rooster Hill.

My drive into the estate on a winding paved lane took me past acres of old apple orchards parading up terraced hillsides bordered with pristine white fences. Decorative black beef cattle grazed in lush, pastured glens. As the road reached the main house, a flock of stately hens and roosters carved from marble peeked at me from among beds of azaleas and laurel. A lot of people in the mountains decorated their yards with faux critters—deer, geese, an occasional bear cub carved in silhouette out of plywood—but marble chickens were a Tiber specialty. Tibers took their yard art seriously.

The three-story, white-columned house at Tiber Crest sat grandly atop a hill that looked due east toward town. As I drove into the stone courtyard I heard the college's noon chapel bells, carried like a recital on the high mountain breeze. On any clear day the house's occupants could sit on one of several upstairs balconies and glimpse the steeples of the churches, the courthouse, and the college administration building. Not that I had ever had that chance. During the rare times when Mr. John had forced Janine to invite me to a birthday party—and Daddy had forced me to go—Janine had relegated me to her B-list, meaning I did not go up to admire Janine's fluffy bedroom and personal balcony.

Tricky Stuart, a fellow B-lister, opened the mansion's double doors as I reached for the bell. She grinned at me. "Hey, Bearclaw." My nickname from high school. "Hey, Tricky." Her given name. She wore a blue-polyester pantsuit as a maid's uniform. We'd grown up comparing calluses and grotesque dead-chicken stories. Her parents still made a living as chicken farmers, and had mortgaged themselves well into the new century with five new chicken houses. Tricky and her husband lived with them and helped run the business, supplementing their income with Tricky's job at Tiber Crest. She was struggling to raise four children, and do it with style. She wore her coal-black hair with a blonde skunk streak, a gold-capped molar flashed on one side of her smile, and hard, no-bullshit expectations were carved into her eyes. "How's your New Yorker?"

I handed her a double-handful of yellow roses Liza had cut for me to bring. There was no point addressing any of Tricky's comments. They were a ritual, the shorthand for telling me her place in the social order, and mine. "My New Yorker's rebuilding my barn," I said. "I think he's putting in a subway."

She launched into a whispered account of everything the Tibers were saying about Quentin (troublemaker, bad influence, uppity outsider) as she led me down a hall hung with gilt-framed portraits of notable dead Tibers. Since all Tibers considered themselves notable, it was a long hall. I read a nameplate on an unfamiliar portrait, and stopped abruptly.

The portrait's subject had rich-looking, copper-brown hair, done up elaborately. Her buxom body had been straight-jacketed in an elaborate turn-of-the-century gown that looked as if she were planning a cruise on the Titanic. Her face was stately. She looked a little like Daddy and me, and for good reason.

Bethina Grace Powell Tiber gazed down at her kin with soft blue Powell eyes and the hint of unhappiness in her smile. I had never seen anything except one grainy photo of her as a child, taken from a tintype. Daddy had kept it in a frame on the living room lamp table. The woman who linked modern-day Tibers and Powells did not look like a crazy hoyden, a wicked adulteress, or in more brutal terms of eras past, a nigger's whore. She looked lovely and sad. "Tricky, where'd this painting come from?"

"Mr. John had it hung last week. It was brung down from his old Aunt Dotty Tiber's house in South Carolina. Esme inherited it from old Dotty, and Esme loves the picture, and Mr. John and Janine are trying to make Esme feel at home, so they put it on the wall for her. Bless her sweet, silly heart."

"Who's Esme?"

"Mr. John's niece. William's daughter. You know—William—the brother that got killed climbing some mountain way back when. They say he was one of the Powell throwbacks, like Miss Betty. Moon-gazer. Wanderer. That's what they say around here." I vaguely recalled that William Tiber had died in a climbing accident in some exotic land when I was a girl. "I never knew he was married, much less had a daughter."

"Wasn't married. Got some girl pregnant. She turned over their baby girl after the doctors said it wasn't right in the head. Dotty raised her. Esme. Now Dotty's passed on and Esme's here. Nineteen years old and her engine don't quite fire on all cylinders, you know? I guess you'd call her mildly retarded. Well, don't call her that around *here*. Around here she's got 'special needs.'"

I was still recovering from the portrait. This story of a second stranger in the house made me look around as if I'd been invited to a surprise party and more people might pop out at any moment. I couldn't help wondering if Mr. John had hung our notorious relative's portrait as a message of reconciliation. Tricky kept up a stream of trivia, rhetoric, and gossip as we walked through to a bright, flower-filled sunroom on one back corner. Mr. John, dressed in a golf shirt and white trousers, looking pale and a little wan, rose from a patio table and motioned for me to sit down. No hugging, no jovial, booming, Ursula girl! Which had become his habit over the years.

We sat down over iced tea and chicken salad with yeast rolls, and looked at each other sadly. "How are you feeling?" I asked.

"Uh. Doctor's got me on new angina medication. Guess I'll tick along a little easier, now."

"How's Janine?"

"Her pride's sore."

"I'm sorry about what happened. And for the record, Quentin Riconni didn't intend for his meeting with you to turn into a fiasco, either."

He scowled at Quentin's name. "I'll try to be fair and give him his due. That's better than him giving *me* a heart attack." I nodded. Mr. John suddenly pushed his dish away and leveled a stern gaze at me. "It breaks my heart to be at odds with you. I promised myself I'd look out for you and Arthur after Tommy died. I want to make up to him for not including him in my family in a more respectful way. Am I such a mean old man that you can only hate me?"

"I don't hate you at all. I wish things were different."

"Well there, now! Don't you know that Janine and you have a lot in common? Smart and fine-looking young women, hard workers, ambitious. Your advantage is being more practical, because you weren't pampered the way her mama pampered Janine. You don't know how many times I've held you up as an example for her. I fear I've made hard feelings between y'all because she resents my admiration for you."

"I've always envied *her*."

"Then you two should be able to sit down and make amends, shouldn't you?"

"I'd love to have to heart to heart with Janine, sometime." *When hell freezes over and pigs fly.*

"Wonderful!" He began to polish the tea spoon with his napkin, frowning at it, studying glimmers of his own reflection. "Has Quentin made you a solid offer for the sculpture?"

I froze. "Mr. John, if you intend to sue me for a share of the sculpture's value, I want to know *now*."

He laid the spoon down. "Please forget what I said about that. It was nonsense spoken in anger. I *despise* your Iron Bear. The fact that it's valuable and that Richard Riconni's work has become so reputable is the greatest irony of the entire mess." He winced. "*Irony.* Even my puns can't escape the thing's influence."

"A deal's not likely to happen, at any rate. It's up to Arthur, and I don't think he'll give up the Bear."

"But you'd let it go if he agrees? Really?"

"Yes." The word sounded hollow. I felt empty, inside. "For the amount of money involved, I'd be irresponsible *not* to sell it."

"Good for you. I know you want to make something of yourself and that wild old farm of yours. You've got to keep Arthur together, too, body and soul. But you don't need some scruffy outsider poking around, making you idle promises and causing you grief. If the sculpture's so valuable, collectors would offer you just as much money as he does. Get rid of Quentin Riconni, for your own sake."

"I can't do that to him."

"What if he turns out to be no better than some of those shiftless folks who took advantage of your daddy?"

"He's not that type."

"How do you know? I hear he's charmed you. I hear he's a regular wizard in Arthur's eyes."

I spent a moment folding my linen napkin, bending its Tiber monogram out of shape between my fingers. "He's a good man, at heart."

"Well, so am I. Haven't I proved that to you and your folks a time or two?"

I nodded. Liza had confided to me that he'd intervened on Daddy's behalf in the terrible situation two years earlier. When federal agents arrested Daddy's tenant for dealing drugs, and found some of his stash in his apartment at the farm, Mr. John had used his influence to ward off a DEA confiscation of Bear Creek.

Watching me, Mr. John sighed. "I knew Tommy had no idea one of his tenants was a criminal. I couldn't let a scandal like that mar his family name. We're related."

He always considered the Tiber reputation. Nonetheless, I owed him some humility. "I never thanked you. I'm thanking you, now."

"No thanks needed, Honey. You see? We're family? So just humor me and listen up about Quentin Riconni."

The humility phase ended quickly. I stiffened. "You were right then, but you're wrong, now."

"Now, listen here—"

"I saw Bethina Grace's picture in the hallway." Changing the subject was a good option.

Mr. John gazed at me impatiently. "It's time to put that past to bed. Time to say Powells and Tibers are proud to be kin."

"Good. I'd like a favor from you."

He scowled. "Just ask, Honey."

"I'd like for you to write a letter of apology to Quentin Riconni's mother. Tell her you were the one who had the sculpture removed from campus and you told the college to let people believe it was destroyed."

He stared at me. His mood was now ice cold. "*Never.* And if that's the only reason you came to have lunch with me, today, then just go on and—"

Tricky ran into the sunroom. "Esme's took the golf cart, again!"

Mr. John slapped a hand on the table. "Close the gate!"

"I already done that, but she's headed down the driveway and you know she's going to be upset when she gets there." Mr. John lumbered to his feet, his face grim. "You've heard about my new guest? My niece?"

"Yes."

"Well, she's grieving for her Aunt Dotty and homesick for South Carolina, and she keeps trying to run away."

I stood. "In a golf cart?"

"She's slow-minded. About golf cart speed. Tricky, get my car out."

"I can catch up with her faster than Tricky can," I said. I ran out of the house, got in Daddy's truck, and drove quickly down the winding lane. I saw the golf cart idling in front of the tall ornamental iron gate at its forested intersection with the public road. Esme Tiber's delicate blonde head was bent to the steering wheel. Her shoulders shook.

I walked up to her slowly. She was sobbing so hard she hadn't noticed my arrival. She was barefoot, dressed in pale blue shorts and a Minnie Mouse t-shirt, with flowery canvas luggage piled beside her. On the back of the golf cart, where bags and clubs are usually carried, she'd inserted the framed portrait of Bethina Grace.

"Esme?" I said in quiet wonder. She gasped and straightened, scrubbed eyes the soft blue color of old jeans in a sweet, heart-shaped face, then yelled, "Bethina Grace! You're alive!"

"No, my name is Ursula. But I'm a relative of Bethina Grace's, just like you. I'm your cousin."

"My cousin Ursula. Ursula. Ursula. Oh!" She clambered out, a nineteen-year-old child whose slow, tinkling voice made me think of a fairy on tranquilizers. Despite her tragic eyes and tear-swollen face she threw her arms around me in a hug. I had no choice but to hug her back. "I'm Esme, Esme Tiber, Esme, Esme," she chanted against my shoulder. "Can you open the gate?"

"I'm afraid not. Why do you want to leave?" She stepped back, her lower lip crumpled, and I grasped her hand as if she were indeed a child. "Are you homesick?" She nodded fervently, trying so hard not to cry that she made soft snorting noises.

I squeezed her hand. "My brother gets homesick when he goes very far away. I understand." She stared past me at Daddy's colorful truck, her eyes widened, and she was distracted. "What is *that?*"

"*That,*" I said dryly, "is a magic Powell-mobile."

She darted past me and ran to the truck, where she stroked her fingers over a cartoonish black bear strolling with angels and dinosaurs across the right fender. She whirled around. "Are you the Iron Bear lady?"

"I suppose so. I live at Bear Creek. And that's where the Iron Bear is."

"Miss Betty!"

"I'm not Miss Betty, I'm Ursula."

"No, no, I'm talking about Miss Betty and the Iron Bear and how it went to live at Bear Creek. Aunt Dotty told me stories from the time I was little. I have the book."

"The book?"

She ran back to the golf cart, unzipped one of her bags, and dug through a jumble of clothing and shoes, then tossed a small, pearl-handled revolver on the pile. She kept digging in her possessions while I gingerly picked up the gun. A quick check showed no bullets in the chambers. I exhaled in relief. "Esme? Is this yours?"

"Oh, yes." She was still searching for something. "Aunt Dotty gave it to me. I can shoot targets." Tibers were all gun-loving hunters and sportsmen, so it didn't really surprise that even the most tender among them had a passion for fire-power. I laid the revolver aside.

"Here!" she exclaimed happily. She pulled out an old black scrapbook with Betty Tiber's name embossed on one corner in fading gold. "Miss Betty's book! Aunt Dotty gave it to me."

We sat down on the side of the lane and she opened the yellowed scrapbook. In it were dozens of pictures and articles, all about the Iron

Bear. "That's my father," I said, and pointed to a newspaper photo of Daddy painting the Bear during its vandalized campus years. "And that's me." A snapshot of Miss Betty's showed me at about four years old, straddling the Bear's head as if I were riding a circus elephant.

Esme Tiber gaped at me. "Will you auto . . . auto—" she struggled with her mental thesaurus—"*sign* the picture?"

Despite some embarrassment on my part we got a pen from my purse, and I autographed the picture across one corner. She hugged the book to her chest. "I made up a lot of stories about the Iron Bear. It was my friend when I was a girl. Now it's my *only* friend." Tears welled in her eyes.

"That's not true. You'll get used to living here. It's a wonderful place. And you'll make a lot of new friends."

"Like you? Can I come visit you and the Iron Bear, please? Please, please?" Her eyes were lonely and hopeful.

What was happening to me, today? Tibers were surrounding me and luring me into their lives. "Why don't you ask Mr. John if Tricky could drive you over to visit sometime?"

"Oh, I will!"

"But you have to promise not to run away anymore."

"All right!"

"How's about I back up the driveway and you follow me in the golf cart?"

"Okay."

Esme Tiber might not be the smartest chicken in the flock, but she was Mario Andretti behind a wheel. She zoomed up the driveway after me and careened the cart to a stop in the courtyard, where Mr. John and Tricky were waiting. "I'm going to visit the Iron Bear and Ursula soon," she announced. "I won't run away again. I promised Ursula!"

Mr. John's expression was dark. He drew me aside. "I will *not* have her visit there as long as Quentin Riconni is in residence."

"I'm sorry, then." Stiff with dignity, I thanked him for lunch. He gave me a sorrowful but curt nod. I drove down the lane in a daze. Even though he'd told Tricky to open the remote-controlled gate for me, I had to wait for the pulleys to ease its two wings apart. A peculiar panic came over me, a claustrophobic *squeeze* that made me breathe hard. I couldn't stop thinking about strange, sad little Esme, who was trapped more than most people by her own shortcomings and her family's conventions. Now she was caught in the unfolding complications of my situation with Quentin.

As soon as I could, I stamped the truck's accelerator pedal and zoomed onto the public road. Free. Free of the snake.

Or only wishing.

15

It was mid-afternoon. The sky over the mountains had bloomed gray with promised rain. The air weighed on me, humid and heavy. Quentin had gone into town, taking Arthur and the grudgingly respectful Oswald with him, to purchase nails and other hardware for the barn.

The barn was debris free, now, and he'd begun, with Oswald and Arthur's help, to replace the rafters. I said nothing, made no protest, because the work kept us away from each other. Arthur seemed to be suspended in Quentin's aura, fascinated by the manly duties he mimicked. Arthur was still totally unable to tell us what his beloved Mama Bear had decided about her future.

The kitchen phone rang. I answered it with one damp hand, then continued toweling a large cast-iron skillet I'd used to cook sausage at breakfast. Cooking had never been one of my habits when I lived in Atlanta. Since coming home I'd turned into a southern Martha Stewart, devoted to making Arthur's favorite meals.

"It's Harriet," a voice said sadly.

I set the skillet down quickly. "How are you?"

"I'm managing the fine china department at the Perimeter Rich's store. I miss my shop." She went on to tell me how my other former neighbors were faring and where they'd found jobs. "I just had to let you know. Demolition starts next week at Peachtree Lane." She began to cry. "I went to see the old shops. Ursula, they're like old people on death row. You probably don't want to go."

My heart sank. I leaned my forehead against the wall beside the phone and shut my eyes. "I have to," I said.

*

I was on my way to Daddy's truck. I'd changed into a long, sleeveless dress Liza had made for me from a bolt of rose-print cotton fabric I'd found in the attic. Mama had stored it there in a box, wrapped in waxed paper. To our amazement, only the outer layer of material was rotted and bug-eaten.

"She'd want you to make something from this," Liza said. "I've always felt her spirit in this house, and always known it was very loving and positive."

"I can't sew. I only do hems and buttons."

"I'll make it."

I looked at her with mixed affection, but finally agreed. Now I was glad to have the dress. Today I felt the need to wear talismans, mementos. I wanted to dress up in honor of the old shops' passing.

I heard a car coming. A bright red Corvette rounded the last turn in my dirt road and pulled into the farmyard. I frowned and tossed my purse into the truck's driver seat. I didn't recognize the visitor.

He was a fat, wall-eyed man with a jowly face. He pried himself out of the Corvette, gave me a big grin, then brushed invisible lint from his golf shirt and slacks. He wore a lot of gold jewelry—pinkie rings, necklaces with crucifixes, thick ID bracelets. "Morning. How do?" he drawled.

"Can I help you, Sir?" He nodded, sighed, then retrieved a black leather briefcase and set it on the Corvette's hood. He adjusted a pinkie ring then stuck out a hammy hand. "Joe Bell Walker. I'm here to see Tommy Powell."

"I'm his daughter, Ursula." We shook.

"Do tell? I've sure heard about you. He's mighty proud of his chillen."

"Mr. Walker, I hate to tell you this, but my daddy died in January."

"No!" To my surprise, he leaned against the car, bowed his head, pulled a white handkerchief from his slacks, and wiped his eyes. I stood there in miserable silence, focusing my gaze on the yard oaks, wondering what kind of friend he was. He owned too much finery to be one of Daddy's artist cronies, and had too much flash for a local.

"Lord, lord," he moaned. He asked me what had happened, and I explained in gentle detail. "Lord, lord, lord," he repeated, then put his handkerchief away. He waved one gold-trimmed hand at the Bear. "You take care of Tommy's chillen for him, you hear?" he called.

"Mr. Walker, are you an artist?"

"No, Hon, but I do appreciate art, and I done a lot of shopping amongst your daddy's co-opters. My wife and daughters love them perfume bottles Liza makes." He reached for his briefcase and sighed. "But I'm here on business, today. I'm a collector for the Donahue Financial Institute."

I took a step back, my mouth open in silent horror. The so-called Donahue Financial Institute was infamous throughout the mountains. Old Man Donahue and his sons were rumored to have run gaming halls for the Dixie mob until the 1970's. In the last two decades their clan had established a reputation as notorious loan sharks. This tearful fan of my father's was a knee-breaker. "Did my father take out a loan?"

"Yes, Miss, he sure did. About two years ago he borrowed ten thousand dollars, not counting interest . Said he was cleaning this place up after that unfortunate business with the drug bust. Said he had some tenants who couldn't quite foot the rent—these folks he's got here now—they're good and decent and he was determined they'd stay, but they couldn't come up with full pay and he didn't want them to know he needed the money. So he got himself a loan."

"How much does he still owe, with interest?"

"Five thousand, Hon. I been lettin' it slide since winter. He hasn't been able to make no payments—he told me things were down in the art business. His folks couldn't give him a dadblame cent of rent. But they sure pitched in when he needed them. Miss Liza handed over some jewelry and the Ledbetters sent a whole set of nice crockery to Mr. Donahue's wife, and Oswald threw in his spare motorcycle, but it just ain't enough, Hon. I mean, there's *rules*, and your Daddy knew that when he signed for the money."

I fought a rising tide of nausea and fear. "What did my father use for collateral?"

"Three acres of land, Hon. Surveyed off the front of your farm, here."

Daddy had been desperate, if he'd risked Powell land. In the 150 years of our turbulent history, we had never, ever, lost even an inch of the original homestead.

"I've got some papers here, Hon. If you go ahead and sign then I'll get the deed worked out."

I forced myself to think. My head spun. "I can have your five thousand in cash by tomorrow."

"Well!" He gazed at me in pleased surprise. "You sure?"

"Absolutely. I'll bring it to you in the morning, before noon."

"Whew." He slammed the briefcase, handed me a business card, and wiped his forehead. "That's a load off my mind." He pulled out a stylus and a handheld computer, and made a note. Even good-old-boy kneebreakers had gone high-tech.

"I sure am sorry to bring you this news," he finished. Joe Bell Walker looked stricken. "And I hope you get the money to me. Cash, now, you hear?"

"I hear."

He put a hand over his heart, and told me goodbye. As he drove away my knees gave out as if he'd cracked them. I leaned against the truck. Daddy had needed money; he'd tried his best to improve the old homeplace and protect his favorite tenants. He'd wanted me to be proud of him. This was right after I'd scalded him with my shame and anger.

Three hours later I sat at a desk among the gleaming shelves and display cases of Atlanta's most reputable silver dealer. She was a discreet older woman dressed in a tailored outfit of blue wool, with a fine strand of pearls at her throat. I'd heard that she went into the silver business after her husband died, because she'd had to sell her own family silver to make ends meet. We'd become friendly over the years, as I scrimped and saved to put together my proud heirloom collection, the first silver set any Powell female had owned, the set I would give to my eldest daughter some day, and her to hers. Now that collection sat in cardboard boxes around my feet.

"Dear, I hate to see you do this," the dealer said in a dulcet Old South voice.

"You know how it is, sometimes."

She nodded. When she handed me a check she rested a blue-veined hand on mine. "I'll hold your silver for a month, and you can have it back for what I paid you."

I thanked her but walked out knowing that the silver was gone forever. Rain had begun to pour down. The day was ending, growing darker. I should go home, give myself a break, get drunk.

I drove to Peachtree Lane.

*

I'd have given her the money, if I'd known. If she'd asked. But she'd never ask. Quentin drove into Atlanta, looking for me. Liza had confided to him about Joe Bell Walker; she'd caught me in the farmhouse living room, packing my silver, and I'd had to explain.

Goddamn blood-sucking loan shark, just like the bastards I grew up with, he thought. He maneuvered his vehicle into a narrow lane of traffic on the crowded interstate. But all she had to do was tell me. I'd have given her whatever she needed. We could have called it a small advance on the Bear.

He frowned, thinking about my attitude, then cursed under his breath.

She doesn't want to owe you. Not for money, not for herself. She has you figured out. Cash and carry. Keep it impersonal. So she did. You want your life to operate this way? You got it.

Quentin guided the Explorer up an exit ramp and onto a city street. Slow gray rain slid down the windshield. He started the wipers and rolled his window up tight. The scents and colors of a rainy day had always made him feel the world was empty and he had to move through it alone. He drove faster.

Maybe I don't want it this way, anymore.

*

Rainy southern evenings in the summertime were a dangerous sauna, melting even the strictest inhibitions with wet heat. The sensual steam made people kill or seduce, scream under full moons, or channel their wildness into tent revivals where sweat, sex, and salvation smelled the same. Heat fogged the truck windows. The windshield wipers said *Fool, shush, Fool, shush, Fool.*

The day had melted into wet shadows when I parked in one of the spaces that nosed up to the broad sidewalk at Peachtree Lane. Around me, the residential streets were quiet and empty, the weeknight house lights glowing in the lonely mist. Not many blocks over, in the house I had helped him renovate, Gregory and his new *me* were probably scrubbing a sink or spritzing disinfectant on his squeaky clean floor.

The lot beside the shops had already become a jagged landscape of plowed-up concrete. The pecan and peach trees were gone; a hole existed where the peach had stood, and the pecans were just low stumps in the sidewalk. Unsheltered by greenery, the shabby line of old brick shops look vulnerable and naked. Their tall palladium windows had been removed and the openings boarded over. Worst of all, ten towering feet of hard chain-link security fence enclosed the whole block. I clutched the unexpected fence and pressed my face against it, staring at my shop like a parent separated from an injured child. I wanted to squeeze myself through the wire the way soft butter passes through a sieve.

I returned to the truck. I drove around back where the dumpsters used to sit, eased the truck into low gear, inched the front wheels over the curb and nuzzled the fence with Daddy's pink-painted bumper. The fence swayed. Clearly, its steel posts had not been set deeply, so there was no real concern for trespassers. A sign from god.

I pressed down slowly on the truck's frayed accelerator pedal. A section of fence buckled with satisfying surrender, giving the truck's grill a coy slap before it flattened under my wheels. I got out, took a small ice cooler from the truck's cab, then climbed the steps to the stoop outside my shop's back door. Only then did I see that a large clasp and padlock had been added by the demolition contractor.

178

I pounded the door with a fist, then went to the back windows and tried to pull the boards off—even considered, for one wild second, ramming the shop's back wall with the truck. The slow, warm rain trickled down my face, the darkness grew around me.

I heard a thick engine prowling the narrow street that bordered the parking lot. The sidewalk oaks and a row of tall lilac shrubs hid me and the truck from casual view, but then came the unmistakable sounds of the vehicle circling the block and turning back, moving slower as it approached the back lot. A high-powered police cruiser, probably. *The law*, as old mountain folks said. Someone had spotted the downed fence, and me, and had called the law.

I wiped my face and climbed back onto the stoop to meet my fate as a vandal and trespasser, clenching both defiant hands around the ornamental iron railing I had lovingly shellacked each year with black, rust-proof paint. A love for iron was in my blood, though I never thought of it that way. I just held onto to the least giving structure I could find. If the law had come to carry me away, I'd have to be pried off.

Quentin drove up. I gazed at him with honest relief.

"Raising hell like a good Rebel?" he called in his deep voice, the voice of Brooklyn boxers and old movie gangsters, enough to make a nearby magnolia tree drop the last genteel white pedal of its summer blooms like a startled handkerchief.

I nodded. "And kicking a little symbolic corporate behind."

He made his way across the street jungle of flattened fence and uprooted steel posts. A yellow street lamp clicked on, and the seeping evening mist settled on his dark hair like tiny jewels. His very presence was large and reassuring. All I could think was, *I'm glad he's here.*

"You're always hanging around buildings that are about to fall down," he said.

"So are you." He climbed onto the narrow stoop, then halted beside me. "Liza told me where you were headed. And about the silver."

"She thinks I need a shoulder to cry on. She's wrong."

"I didn't come here to offer any body parts." He lifted a hand, and when I didn't indicate I'd disagree he touched just the back of a knuckle to one of my cheeks, tracing the bone, where he caught a drop of rain that might have been a tear. Then he turned and studied the padlocked door instead of me, while I gazed blatantly at him. "You want to go inside?"

"Yes. I just want to see my old shop one more time."

"Give me a second." He went back to his truck, then returned with a powerful flashlight and a pair of slender gadgets he cupped in one hand. I held the light while he slid them into the keyhole of the padlock, and I heard it click. He pulled the lock off, flipped the latch back, I pushed the door, and it swung open. The engrained scent of old wood, paper, leather, knowledge, the essence of books rushed out on dark air. I inhaled deeply. "Thank you."

"Thank a guy named Lockhead. He taught me to do this when I was twelve years old. Want me to wait out here?"

"No. Come in. This store has wonderful ghosts."

He gave the cooler at my feet a curious glance, then picked it up. Carrying it, he followed me into the cozy labyrinth of small rooms still fitted with bookcases. Even bare, they had a certain warmth and personality. The creaking wooden floor echoed with our footsteps. I caressed the shelves and the faded rose wallpaper. He turned the light from the wall to my gently rose-flowered dress. "Bookstore camouflage," he said. "Pretty smart for hunting books in the wild."

I choked on a laugh. He set the flashlight atop the old oak counter that remembered sixty years of sales, readings, authors, readers, and joy. "F. Scott Fitzgerald leaned on this counter when he visited the original owner in 1945," I said. "I have her picture with him. And last year, F. Scott Shey leaned here when he visited *me*. He won the Nobel Prize for physics. I have a picture of me with him. There's such a spectrum. Such continuity."

Quentin nodded. "Okay, so that covers the F. Scotts. Tell me about everybody in between. Get it out of your system."

"That could take awhile."

"I'm in no hurry." He leaned against the counter, webbed in shadows, sharing my sorrows quietly. The rain soothed me, and I was glad it was just us, him and me, sheltered in this old haven on its last few days of existence.

"I had a little ceremony planned," I told him. I knelt by the cooler on the floor, then looked up at him with an idea. "In the back room I left an old wooden bench. Its cushions are torn and it wasn't worth saving. Will you pull it in here? It's heavy—and about six feet long."

"Your wish is my command."

If only, I thought, as he left the room.

We sat on the bench, sharing a bottle of champagne and a delicate, long-stemmed glass Liza had made. Flickering light bathed us from two tall, wide candles I'd placed on the bookstore counter. Quentin took his turn sipping the chilled champagne from the glass as I opened a book of poetry I'd brought. A few long swallows of the liquid had already driven away my artificial dignity. My stomach was warm, my muscles relaxed. I was ready to speak to the bookstore.

"I really couldn't decide what to offer in honor of your spirit," I said aloud, gazing around the room. "So I looked for something in the classics, to sum it up for me. I took this from Ben Jonson." I bent my head over the book. "*A lily of a day is fairer far in May. Although it fall and die that night, it was the plant and flower of Light. In small proportions we just beauties see; And in short measures life may perfect be.*"

I lifted my head, took the champagne glass Quentin held out, and raised it to the deeply shadowed room. The shop was so quiet, not even the hum of a light fixture breaking its silence, just the sound of rain on the roof. There could have been no world outside the boarded-over windows. Oddly enough, that felt fine. Even Quentin looked content. I nodded to the old store. "You made a lot of people's lives perfect inside these walls. Including mine. Thank you."

My voice wavered on the last words. I sipped from the glass quickly, then turned and set up on the counter behind us, next to the bottle. "No more for me."

"May I see your book of poetry?"

I handed it to him. "It's a collection," I said. "A little bit of everything."

"How about something from Macbeth?" He browsed through a section of Shakespeare with skilled reference, then read in a low, melodic baritone, "*Life's but a walking shadow, a poor player that struts and frets his hour upon the stage and is heard no more; it is a tale told by an idiot, full of sound and fury, signifying nothing.*"

I groaned lightly. "Oh, how perfectly *you*. How morbid."

He arched a dark brow. "*All* poetry is morbid."

"It is not." I slid closer to him and flicked the pages in the heavy, hardcover volume as he held it. "There. Ogden Nash. Very sweet." I read, "*The turtle lives 'twixt plated decks, which practically conceal its sex. I think it clever of the turtle, in such a fix to be so fertile.*"

"Hmmm. All right, a compromise. Something Masefield wrote." With a glint of humor in his eyes, he thumbed through the book. "Let me have wisdom, beauty, wisdom and passion, bread to the soul, rain where the summers parch. Give me but these, and though the darkness close, even the night will blossom as the rose."

"Roses," I teased. "You only thought of that because of the rose wallpaper."

"No, because of you and your dress." He nodded at the faded roses softly aligning themselves down my body. "You're beautiful."

We grew quiet, trading a look that made me feel unwound, settled, open. He looked down at the book, again. "Let's go back to Shakespeare." He emanated a visceral heat I couldn't resist. I bent my head next to his, then shut my eyes for a second, enjoying the scent of his clothes, his hair, his skin. His shoulder brushed mine and I didn't move away.

He cleared his throat. "He jest at scars, that never felt a wound. But, soft! What light through yonder window breaks? It is the east, and Juliet is the sun." His voice caressing me, he continued through the entire famous soliloquy. No man had ever read to me, before. At least, not since Daddy had read to me, as a child. I watched him, enthralled, feeling renewed and alive for the first time in months, no, years. Years had gone by since it had been that easy to simply feel.

Quentin was vividly aware of my breath on his cheek, the scent of me, the need in my eyes, the easy intimacy that had melted us together over spoken words and silent desires. He had grown hard beneath the book, reckless, starving. When he finished he raised his eyes to mine, intense and searching, dark in the candlelight. "Don't look at me that way. Get up and walk out of here right now."

I shook my head. "I can't walk out on the way you make me feel. I just want *more*." And then, on my low sigh or his—I don't know—I kissed him. I was trembling when we eased apart. I looked into his face and saw my own emotions mirrored there—the danger, the impulse, the lust. And perhaps the love. Whether it was my wish or his reality, I had no idea.

"I'm giving you one more chance to leave," he said.

I kissed him, again, and this time he took charge. He touched my face, slid his hands into my hair, drew my tongue into his mouth and tasted me with his own. Suddenly we were both frantic and rough, tangled together, consuming each other.

We shoved the bench cushions onto the shop's scarred wooden floor and used them as pillows. Delirious, rough, quick, silent, we worked in unison. Stripping our clothes away, moist skin open to touch in the hot, sexual air, his hand on my breasts, then his mouth. I stroked him as he stretched out atop me. And finally, as I looked into his face, he kissed me very gently, a lull in the storm, and I urged him inside my body.

We merged and flowed as easily as the rain on rich earth.

*

The stars were out when we arrived back at Bear Creek. I'd had a long drive home, alone in my own truck, to clear my mind and fill it with a misery so deep I could barely focus on the road. *You'll spend the rest of your life wanting him, again.*

He was thinking the same agonized thoughts about me, but I didn't know it. We crossed the dark, misty yard without touching. I lit a kerosene lamp on the rail of the porch and sank gingerly onto the creaking porch swing. Quentin sat down on the porch steps, a dozen feet from me. Hammer bounded out of the darkness, his tail wagging. He looked subdued when neither Quentin nor I offered much petting.

"We need to talk," Quentin said.

"I know."

"I'm eight years older than you."

"Only eight years? You'll have to think of a better argument than that."

"Old habits die hard."

I kicked off my sandals and pushed the porch floor with my toes, rocking slowly, the rhythm so sensual that after a second I stopped. "I have old habits, too. I've always gone my own way. I've tried so hard to stay clear of serious relationships."

"What was your doctor like? The researcher. Liza told me a little about him."

"Gregory? Very clean. Very dependable."

"But he cheated on you."

"I think I knew he would, some day. I knew I'd never marry him."

"You must have loved him in some way. He did something for you that made you stay."

"If you mean sex, you're wrong. Not that it wasn't pleasant, but it's always been a resistible urge, to me." I paused. "Until lately. I've never thrown myself at a man, before."

"I thought I seduced you," he said with weary humor. "When I told you to stop? I was lying."

Those gallant words warmed me to the bone. "You have an ability to pinpoint connections and relationships. Structure, I mean. Spaces and joints and systems. You've got a feel for it. It's a creative instinct. You saw what I wanted and you gave it to me."

"That's not being creative. That's being a man."

"I think you're an artist, at heart."

183

"No."

I squeezed the next words out with painful effort. "You have a woman in New York? You must. More than one, I expect."

He told me about Carla Esposito, bluntly, honestly, and without saying they had no future. "We've been friends since we were kids," he concluded. "She comes and goes."

Friends who have been sleeping together most of their lives, I mused in dreary silence. "This isn't just a friend. This is a woman you *love*." I spoke without accusation, just stating what was obvious, to me.

"No."

"What do you call love, then?"

"Someone I can't live without."

There was a long pause between us, with no indication that his someone might someday be *me*. I stared hard into the darkness beyond the low pool of lantern light. "That's how I define love, too. Probably why I've always run from it, and I may never *stop* running. My parents loved each other that much."

"So did mine."

"Too painful."

"Yes."

I took a deep breath. "My life is here. This place. I'm a Powell. This land owns me. And Arthur. Arthur can never live anywhere else."

"You need someone who loves this farm as much as you do." Quentin pulled the stub of a cigar from his shirt pocket, then jabbed it in the dirt of my potted peach tree seedling. He seemed to be telling me he'd been raised with pavement beneath his feet and didn't appreciate the sanctity of dirt. I watched the light on his dark hair, his tired profile, his hardening eyes. I watched him in silver silence, hurting inside.

He was no better off, though I didn't guess it.

She could say I might be the man's she's looking for, he thought. If she believed it, she could say I might learn to belong here. If that were possible, and she wanted to believe it, she could say so.

Hammer raised his head and barked softly. Quentin and I looked at the forest path beyond the forsythias in the side yard. At first the only sound I heard was the low singsong of frogs from the creek bottoms, but then came the distinct rustle of feet on twigs.

I stood and went to the edge of the porch. "Arthur?"

He slipped out of the darkness into a patch of moonlight. He held something in his hands. "Brother Bear?" he called.

"I'm here, Arthur," Quentin said.

"Sister Bear?"

"Right here," I said.

"I know what Mama Bear needs. I've finally figured it out."

I caught my breath. "What is it, Sweetie?"

He emerged farther into the moonlight, silver shimmying on his brown hair, his face as pale as cream. He stepped forward again then stopped, swaying as if he'd come to a revival. The bulky object in his arms weighed him down. "She's got nobody like her. Her own kind. That's what you think too, isn't it, Brother Bear? You gave Ursula a kiss the other day to chase away the Tween because she's lonely, too. Like the Bear."

Quentin stood. "I kissed your sister just because I like her."

"Mama Bear needs a kissing friend. She's so lonely—if she doesn't feel better she'll . . . she'll die!" Arthur caught a tearful sound in his throat as he held out the mysterious object to us. "It's so bad to be alone. She'll die if she's not happy! Just like Daddy died! But you can help her!"

"Easy, easy, Arthur," I crooned, moving down the steps. He backed away and I halted.

"Tell me what you want me to do, pal," Quentin urged gently.

"She needs a friend! If that doesn't make her feel better, then she can go live with you."

"You mean that? You'll let me have her?"

"Yes. If she's not happy even after she gets a friend. We have to see, first. All right?"

"All right, Arthur. Whatever it takes. We'll find out." Quentin and I traded puzzled frowns.

"I brought you the first piece of her friend!" Arthur said. "I found it in the barn where we've been working. Daddy put it up high, but it fell back to earth. Because he wants us to use it!" Arthur knelt and laid the item at Quentin's feet, then bounded up and began backing away. "A bone!" he exclaimed. "I'll look for more parts tomorrow!" He turned and trotted into the night.

Both Quentin and I stood there for a moment, trying to sort through the perplexities of my brother's request. "Let's see what he brought," Quentin said. I went inside and turned on the porch lights. When I came back Quentin had dropped to his heels beside two long rectangles of ornamental ironwork with pronged feet, bound together with baling wire for easy storage. "These look like the base for an old sewing machine table," he said.

"They are. The sewing machine is long gone. It was my grandmother's, and then my mother used it. Daddy hung the pieces of the base up in the barn loft. He meant to make a tabletop for them. He never got around to it."

"What does Arthur think I'm going to do with them?" He propped the heavy pieces against his bent knees and scrubbed rust from their tops. "What does he want?"

Suddenly I understood. I sat down on the rain-soaked ground, just sat down, and lifted the two heavy iron pieces onto my lap. I looked up at Quentin bitterly—defeated, angry, lost. What my brother wanted was impossible, just as wanting Quentin was impossible. We'd all end up losing our hearts, our voices, our hope. "He wants you to build another Iron Bear," I said.

16

After a sleepless night, the hot morning sun burned Quentin's eyes. It beamed through a fat pine tree, illuminating Tiberville's small, whitewashed Catholic chapel. Clay pots, bursting with gaudy petunias, lined the chapel's front walk. A short, graying priest, dressed in a collar, a black shirt, and jeans, was sweeping that walkway. His chubby beagle stopped snuffling in the chapel's neatly mowed lawn long enough to bay at Quentin as if he were a fox.

"Morning, Quentin," the priest drawled. "I've heard a lot about you. I know who you are."

This kind of reaction no longer surprised Quentin. "Father, I'd like you to hear my confession. But I have to warn you, I haven't been to church in years. I'm rusty."

"Oh? Well, no time like the present to oil your conscience. Come on inside. I'm Roy. Father Roy." They shook hands.

Quentin reassessed his decision as they walked up the path of old-fashioned flowers. He couldn't imagine elegant and cosmopolitan Father Aleksandr growing petunias, wearing jeans, or owning a beagle. Or being named *Roy*. It just seemed too *comfortable*. Yet a priest was a priest, and this morning, when he felt twisted inside, he sought comfort in the traditions of his boyhood. "Where are you from, Father?"

"Mississippi. I grew up two miles from Elvis's birthplace. Around here, that's the same as rubbing shoulders with a saint."

"Maybe Saint Elvis is my best bet."

Father Roy laughed.

*

I went to the bank, then drove the sleepy, forest-shaded back roads to the next town. I waited in the lobby of a small brick office building, staring blindly at Jerry Springer on a corner television, along with two other bedraggled *clients* of the Donahue Financial Institute. "You ought to beat *the e-ternal tar* out of her puny little ass," one said to the combatants on the screen.

Life was dominated by petty nonsense, disappointments, and humiliations, broken only by rare moments of transcendent victory and joy. Last night, in Quentin's arms, had been one of those special moments. Reality had returned, now.

Had the world been akilter all these years without a second Iron Bear to measure our lives against silent fates? Arthur thought so, and now nothing would do except to build one—and it couldn't be done. I'd spent a large chunk of the moonlit summer night in a rocker on Dr. Washington's weathered, honeysuckle draped front porch, watching my brother sleep, smiling and dreamless, in the hammock.

When he woke once I whispered, "Arthur, are you sure you need a second Bear?" and he murmured, "You can't make babies without two," before dozing off again, snuggled in a cool muslin sheet and the profound serenity of his decision. Like a tribal shaman he planned fertility and harvest, symbolic riches to sustain us and our land.

When Joe Bell Walker arrived with a box of glazed donuts in one gold-pinkied hand, I followed him into his office and laid a bulging envelope on his desk. "Five thousand, in cash. Twenties. Sorry. The bank teller was sadistic."

"I'm kinda *sad* myself over the way you've treated me." He shook his head and arched his eyebrows. "You pulling my leg? I been paid already."

"When? How?"

"Got a call from a feller early this morning. Friend of yours. Quentin Riconni? Met me at the donut shop, handed me the money. We had a little talk." He scowled.

I stared at him. My mind was bleary, I'd barely slept, my body was tender, I felt numb. Quentin was paying me off. Telling me our bonds could be converted into simple cash. "Good enough," I said, and picked up my packet. I had to get out there, to be alone with the misery crawling through me.

Joe Bell cleared his throat. "I just want to say something, here. You send a man like that to see ol' Joe Bell Walker, then you're sending a *message*. You're a tough lady. I sure underestimated you. But I didn't fall off the turnip truck yesterday, myself. So just lemme be clear on this. *No hard feelings, okay?* I don't want any trouble from his kind."

"His kind?"

"You know what I mean. Italian. New York. Us boys down here, we got our territory. Those fellers up there, they got theirs. Never the twain shall meet. Let's keep it that way. If you're under that kind of protection, we're sure gonna respect it from now on. Okey dokey?"

He thought Quentin was in the Mafia. I wanted to laugh, or cry. I ought to tell Joe Bell the truth, but I just nodded my acceptance and walked out, carrying my money. I'd earned that five thousand dollars on the floor of an empty bookstore.

*

Quentin and I walked out in the pasture and stood before the Bear. "When are you leaving?" I asked. I was stone cold about it.

His shuttered expression weighed me down for a moment. I dared him to tell me he wasn't planning to get as far away from me as quickly as possible. Men tended to give gifts when they felt guilty. "Today."

There. Done. Not so hard. You cut it sharp, clean. Keep breathing.

I nodded my approval. "Please don't call, don't write, and don't come back with a new offer. Arthur will recover sooner, that way. I'll think up some fairy tale to explain why you can't do what he asked."

"Stop it." Quentin took me by the shoulders. "You know why I can't build a second sculpture—I'm not a goddamned artist. I never told you I was."

"I understand. I realized from the look on your face last night that you have no intention of doing what he asked."

"Even if I wanted to, I couldn't. *I'm not my father.*"

He'd spent most of his life trying to prove that, and this was the ultimate test. "I understand," I repeated.

"Stop agreeing with me."

"I just want to put an end to this fantasy before it's completely out of control."

"I still intend to buy the Iron Bear. I'll *find* someone—a trained metal sculptor—who can copy it for Arthur. I'll have that imitation built. And I'll bring it back here. He'll like it. He'll trade with me. You'll see. I'll do whatever it takes to get the original sculpture. You have my word I'll make this deal work." He released me and stepped back.

I shook my head. "My brother doesn't want a *copy* of the original. And he doesn't want some stranger to build it. He wants a *second, unique* Bear. In his mind, you're the *only* one who can build it. And it has to be made just like the first—from things we gather in this community. Our memories. Our talismans. Our junk. Our cast-offs. The pieces of us we want to throw away. Whatever you want to call them. *But only you can make what he asked for.* I know you can't do it—or won't. That's why you have to get out of our lives *right now*, before he gets hurt worse."

This rationale sank into Quentin like acid. *She's right, admit it, you can't win this way. Admit it.* He looked down at me with such brutal frustration that he seemed to be in pain. I clenched my hands behind me to resist touching him, clinging to him. "We'll try it my way, first," he said between clenched teeth.

My heart sank, and then I was angry. I walked a few feet away before I faced him, again. "Demolition and salvage, that's your style. No permanent home, no permanent relationships. You've never *built* anything in your life, have you? You just tear things down."

"Any salvage and demolition expert can knock a building into pieces," he said slowly, pinning me with his gaze. "But I'm the only man in the business who can *take one apart*."

"You believe your father's work is all hype and no substance. You talk about his sculptures as if they're pieces of metal engineered to fool people looking for some deeper meaning. All right. If they're so simple, then creating one ought to be easy for you."

"No. *No.* That's my answer."

Silence stretched between us. He was quiet, emphatic, and uncompromising. I believed he'd return to New York and realize the futility of his own plan. Then that would be that. "Goodbye," I said.

He walked to me, reached out, and cupped a hand against my hair. When he drew it back, the tiniest white butterfly perched on his fingertip. His troubled gaze held mine. "They'll bring you the news as soon as I know it."

And then, after being a part of my life for three weeks and six days, thirteen hours and twenty-seven minutes, and changing my life forever, Quentin left me.

*

"Where'd Brother Bear go?" Arthur asked frantically, just as I knew he would. "*He didn't die, did he? You're sure he didn't die?*" I saw the terror in his eyes. We stood atop a granite overhang that protruded like a hat brim from a ridge above Bear Creek. We'd played under the blue shadows of the tallest trees a thousand times when we were children. The granite ridge was one of the most beautiful spots on the farm.

I'd brought him there to lie to him, something I'd sworn I'd never do, again.

"He's gone to his home to work on the idea for your Bear. He'll be back, but working on a Bear takes a lot of thought. I can't say exactly when we'll see him, again."

Arthur paced, wringing his hands. "He's got to build a friend for Mama Bear. He has to. He just has to."

"Sweetie, here's what we'll do. Every day we'll come over here, and we'll set a pebble on this rock to mark the day. As long as we keep counting the days, we'll be getting closer and closer to the day when he comes back." The rock cairns of ancient lands had probably started this way, built on sorrow and hope.

Arthur stared at me urgently. "As long as we have rocks, we have days?" I nodded. He bounded off the overhang, scratched in its crumbling fringe for a few seconds, then held out a handful of small rocks. "How many is that?"

I counted out seven and told him to throw the rest back. "That's enough for the first week." He put six in the pockets of his shorts, very carefully brushed leaf mold from a flat spot on our granite stage, and laid the seventh pebble there with solemn ceremony. "I'm counting on you, Brother Bear," he whispered. "I know you'll come back."

I wished I believed it, too.

A big brown UPS truck lumbered into the farmyard the next afternoon. The driver unloaded several large boxes. As he drove away I stood there staring at the return address of the silver shop in Atlanta. "This can't be right," I told Liza and Fannie Ledbetter, who had wandered over in curiosity. I opened the boxes and found my entire silver collection inside. Finally I discovered a handwritten note from the shop owner, my genteel and sympathetic counselor in the fineries of a southern lady's survival. *Sometimes, it is quite appropriate to accept a gift from a gentleman. Your friend is indeed, a gentleman.*

"Quentin did this for you," Liza said in soft awe. "Oh, Ursula."

"He's a fine man," Fannie Ledbetter agreed.

I carried the boxes inside, sat down among all that cold, beautiful silver, and cried.

PART THREE

17

I can put the idea of her out of the way, here at home. Her voice, her eyes, her body, her thoughts. How she felt around me, and how she made me feel, Quentin told himself after he returned to New York. He'd always been able to divvy up his everyday life, concentrate on specific tasks, and let troubling circumstances fade into the back of his mind. This had worked every time he wanted to forget a woman.

It didn't work, this time.

New York and its boroughs suddenly looked different to Quentin, made of the wrong kind of mountains, not quite real, anymore, a place full of rented spaces and tiny rooftop gardens, of public property and little privacy. No forest kingdoms, there. Not one single Riconni in the history of the family in America had owned land, to Quentin's knowledge. He kept thinking of me and of Bear Creek, then shoving the thoughts away.

"All right, Joe, tell me what the problem is. I knew on the phone you didn't like this plan." He and Joe Araiza sat in the worn wooden booth of a sports bar in midtown Manhattan, where Joe managed a prestigious sculpture gallery.

His father's former student, now middle-aged and stocky, brushed a hand over his fading, sandy hair before grimly downing a shot of scotch. He slapped the glass on the table and leveled a hard look at Quentin. "I don't like what you've asked me to do. I want to know what you're trying to accomplish with this crazy idea about faking your father's work—"

"I want a companion piece for Bare Wisdom. Not a copy, but a similar sculpture. You find me a sculptor who can do the job. You make the connections. It's that simple."

"I need to know why you want it."

"I have my reasons."

"Is this for Angele?"

"Indirectly. I don't want her to know until I'm ready."

Joe spread his hands in dismay. "Ready? Ready to foist off a copy of your father's masterpiece on her? You want to convince her Bare Wisdom still exists?"

"*No.* It's not about lying to her. It's not about faking a copy. I told you." The accusations gnawed at Quentin and brought a harsh glare to his eyes. Had his reputation become so cold-blooded that even Joe Araiza thought him capable of deception?

Joe glanced at the look on his face and leaned back. "All right. I shouldn't have put it that way." He exhaled and rubbed his receding hair line, then slumped forward with his elbows on the table. "Quentin, what I'm getting at is this: You don't know what you're asking for."

"I want a skilled artisan to do a contract job. That's all."

"Your father was an *artist*. You can imitate his work, but you can't *recreate the magic*."

"Just interview the best people and pick one. Hire him and send me the bill."

Joe sighed. "All right. But do you know this will be a *massive* job for any fool willing to try it?"

"I don't believe that. The structure's already determined, the basic design's in place. It's just a matter of working with the metal and improvising on the concept."

"*You* understand what you want, obviously. Or you think you do. Why don't you build the sculpture yourself?"

"I have a business to run. Sarge doesn't have the kind of personality you leave in charge of your front office. When he has to deal with a broker you get the feeling he doesn't know whether to salute or yell *Drop and give me twenty push-ups*."

Joe mused over this excuse while frowning at him. Then he sighed. "Your father once told me that he spent *months* working on the bear sculpture—and he tore it apart at least a half-dozen times in the process. Plus we only have a few old photographs and sketches to work from. It'll take time to find the right person. You don't realize how daunting your father's reputation is. Or how much blood, sweat, and tears he put into every piece."

"I remember the blood."

"God, I shouldn't have said that. Sorry."

A fractured mood silenced them both. Quentin sat back, took a sip from his own shot glass brimming with scotch, and studied the tiny pool of amber liquid. Liza Deerwoman had confided to him that she believed in water-gazing to communicate with the dead. She said she'd spoken to Tom Powell that way, and that he wanted me to *give* the Bear to Quentin, if Arthur would let it go. She hadn't dared tell *me* that.

Quentin found himself staring deeper into the glass. What would you say to me, now, Papa? Go back to Bear Creek and give it all a try?

Love a woman as much as you loved Mother? Or give up, the way you did? Do I have to follow your footsteps all the way to the grave?

"Quentin? Are you all right?"

He set the glass down and laughed sharply. "Hire a sculptor for me, Joe. If I get the result I want, you'll be glad you went through this."

"Tell me something. You've never given a damn about your father's work. Why now?"

Quentin smiled thinly. "I still don't give a damn."

*

A week passed, and then another. He began to concede that it could be months before a sculpture was designed and finished. He picked up the phone to call me, then stopped. Slow news was no news. It would only make matters worse. He lay in his bed at night remembering how we'd been together on the floor of the old bookstore.

Give it up. Ursula was right. You'll ruin Arthur. Stay out of their lives. Forget her. He slept badly, took too many risks for his own safety at salvage sites, and sat brooding at his office desk on too many hot, smog-choked summer evenings. *You could do it. Build the sculpture for her. For Arthur. For yourself.*

But he didn't know a damned thing about the pattern of his father's thoughts, how he had planned and started a sculpture, which of his random visions transformed cold metals into provocative life. What kind of alchemy did a man need, to perform that godlike result? *I can't go that deep for Papa. Can't stand to look that long into his heart.*

He dug inside a storage box, searching for a few of the metal toys, as if they might hold some clue to the mechanisms of his father's ideas. Instead he came up with something his mother had packed long ago: A handful of smooth, gunmetal-gray ball bearings, like dark steel pearls. Papa had bored the finest small holes through each one, and linked them with heavy cord. They had served as his rosary.

For one of the few times in his life he was stymied by a situation he could not reduce to the scattered sum of its parts. That kind of void was his nightmare, and a reason, for example, that he avoided taking airplanes, though no one in the world knew that. He didn't like so much thin air around him.

Brooding over a decision, he visited mountainous junkyards, barges floating heavy under demolished cars, salvage yards stinking of human garbage. He sorted through the trash of the industrial universe, trying to see shapes and forms the way he imagined his father doing, to hear his father's voice offering guidance among the creaking steel and sad decay. He carried the rosary in his pocket, touching it often.

It didn't help.

"What happened to you down there in Georgia?" Popeye demanded. "Somebody knocked the shit out of your attitude."

"Leave me alone," he said quietly, as he lifted a wrought-iron garden gate and slid it into a shipping crate that had to go out the next day. Popeye stared at him. There was a soft threat in his tone, a deadly emptiness that had always been concealed, before. The old sergeant was filled with affectionate concern. "Cap'n, get drunk, get a woman, pay her to fuck your brains out. That'll solve most of your problems."

Quentin mulled the advice more than the old man ever expected. But he knew of only one dependable antidote to every uneasy thought. He called Carla.

*

Carla glowed with pleasure, teasing and joking, touching his hand often as they ate a catered dinner of lobster and steak in his dining area beneath a turn-of-the-century gas chandelier he'd restored. His rare invitation had all the earmarks of a new beginning, another intimate phase in their relationship. She fully expected to spend the night. He fully expected to let her.

She talked all through dinner about her daughters, how they were doing so well in private elementary school, how she'd begun taking them to the ballet and the opera—they wouldn't grow up with no culture, no, they weren't stuck in Brooklyn. "They keep asking me when their Uncle Quentin will come to visit, again."

"How about this weekend? I'll take them to the zoo."

Carla stared at him. He'd never taken her daughters on an outing, before. "Are you . . . all right? What's happened to you?"

"You don't want me to take them to the zoo?"

"No, I'm thrilled. It's just . . . odd. You've never wanted them to like you."

"That was for their own good. Maybe I'm trying to change."

"*Quentin?*" Smiling, incredulous, she got up, came around to his side of the table, and sat on his lap. "That southern buying trip really gave you a new perspective. I like it."

A dull thread wound through him, but he nodded and held her around the waist as she planted small kisses across his face. "I'm going to put on a special outfit I brought," she whispered. "You wait out here until I call you."

"Sounds interesting."

She kissed him lightly on the mouth, hopped up, and disappeared into his bedroom. He sat staring into space. Take her to bed and get it over with. This could be a good life. If you don't want to be alone anymore, you've got Carla. Simple.

He heard a crash, and a shriek. He strode into his bedroom. It was a wide, airy space fronted by huge brick-rimmed windows, always uncovered, even at night. He found Carla standing before one of them, where a tall brass floor lamp reflected her fury in the glass. She clutched a handful of photographs. One of his dresser drawers lay on the floor. "*Who is she?*" she demanded, thrusting out a picture of me kneeling beside Hammer with my arm around him.

"Why are you looking through my dresser?"

"Because I knew you were hiding something from me."

He held out his hand. She backed away. Her black hair fell over her face as she tossed her head. Her eyes glittered. "There had to be *some* reason you're acting so strange. This is it." She shook the photographs. "You took a dozen pictures of this woman. That's not a coincidence. That's not casual. You've never taken that many pictures of *any* woman, before. Including *me*."

"This makes no sense. I invite you here, I offer to spend time with your girls, and you assume I'm seeing another woman?"

"Yes! It makes perfect sense! You're using *me* to avoid *her*. Goddamn you. Goddamn you, Quentin. I knew this was too good to be true." She sank down on the window's wide sill. Her shoulders slumped. He sat down beside her, took the photographs, and laid them aside. "I don't have a life with her," he said quietly.

"You already *do*."

"No. You and I have a life. We've had a long past. Maybe we have a long future. I'm trying to make some decisions. I'm forty years old."

Tears slid down her beautiful face. She wiped them away with a rough swipe of her hand. "Forty years old and forced to consider the fact that one day you'll be a lonely old man like Popeye. Getting desperate. Settling for a comfortable situation with me."

"I'm telling you the truth when I say what you see in those pictures isn't my future. It won't work. I'm not capable of *making* it work." He paused. "Here's the only fact I can guarantee: I care about you."

She uttered a hard, sharp groan and looked heavenward. "Mother Mary, he *cares* about me. Isn't that the most romantic thing you've ever heard? He doesn't love me, he doesn't keep a dozen homey pictures of me in his dresser, but he might be willing to marry me someday because I'm so freakin' *familiar* to him."

He stood and walked to another window, shoving his hands into his trouser pockets, staring bleakly at a landscape of aging industrial buildings being converted to apartments and lofts, like this one. The world he remembered was fading away. His mother, growing old, still hadn't forgiven him, though she didn't suspect his real crime. Carla, finally dropping the veneer of hope he'd subconsciously encouraged all these years, would find someone else, probably the banker she still dated. This time, her marriage would be permanent.

She dried her eyes and walked over to him. They looked out on the night, together. "I want you to *love* me," she said. "I want you to believe you can't wake up happy every morning without me here. I want you to tell me your life won't be complete unless you and I have a baby together. I want you to say no one else can make you feel the way I do."

After a moment, he put one arm around her shoulders, then pulled her to him for a deep hug. She cried into the crook of his neck, then pushed herself away. "See you around," she whispered. He walked her to the elevator, but she waved him off when he tried to escort her downstairs to her car. "I'm on my own," she said. "Finally."

*

Two more weeks passed. Popeye grunted as he tossed Quentin a wrinkled manila envelope folded tightly around a pliable block of contents. "I found this under your travel-sack of dogfood in the back of the Explorer. You missed it when you were unpackin'. You been careless, lately. It's not like you."

"I have no idea what that is." Sitting at his desk, Quentin pulled out his knife, flicked the blade open, and slit a piece of twine tied around the packet. When he opened it, twenty dollar bills cascaded out, along with a folded sheet of Powell Press stationary.

Yours, I had scrawled there. *Ursula*.

Popeye read my note over his shoulder before Quentin could lay it aside. The sergeant eyed him with abrupt understanding. "I don't know what you did to the lady, Captain, but *damn*. She's bribing you to come back."

*

"Alfonse says you and Carla had a very serious disagreement," his mother reported. Quentin made a vague sound of no-comment while he hung the jacket of his suit on a chairback and sat down to face her. He'd taken her to Sunday brunch and now shared a small, lace-draped table in her brownstone's parlor. She always invited him to Sunday tea, as if enough tea and gentility might erase the past. "Alfonse could make a second career as a snitch," he said.

"Is it true about Carla?"

"Now, wait a minute. I want to tell *you* something. Alfonse snitches for me, too. So I know you haven't been back to the doctor for a check-up, the way you promised."

"I take my blood pressure medication. I feel fine. No more whining."

"I hear you've been talking to a publisher about putting together some kind of memoir on Papa."

"Yes, something very personal, very warm."

Quentin set the cup down. "Don't do it," he said quietly. "You'll never make strangers understand what happened to him."

"When I still don't understand it myself? Is that what you're saying?"

"*Let him go*, Mother."

She slammed a hand on the table. "How can I? Have you?"

"Yes."

"No."

Quentin pushed the acidic tea away. He felt sour inside. "His reputation as a man who killed himself is a fact we can't change. You can't redeem the way he died."

Her lips tightened. "I'm not going to discuss this with you. As usual you've attempted to divert the subject away from your own unhappy situations." Angele stroked a fingertip over the fine frown lines between her brows. "I despise learning about your life through gossip."

"I'm sorry. You only have to ask." He looked at her sadly, wishing they still had the kind of camaraderie that encouraged long talks.

She pressed a spoon into the dark, fine leaves of Earl Gray, strained the last bit of liquid into one of a series of china teapots Alfonse had given her on her birthday over the years, then laid the silver strainer aside on a gaudy, bright-yellow spoon rest with mermaids painted around the rim. No matter how much china and silver she set out, she always used the mermaid spoon rest. His father had won it for her at a Coney Island carnival game, when they were dating.

"Was Alfonse correct about there being a problem?" she persisted.

Quentin stirred lemon juice into his cup. "All right. Yes. Carla and I had a discussion. It's over."

"You mean 'over' as in temporarily, as usual?"

"No. Over for good, this time. She won't be waiting, anymore."

His mother's troubled scrutiny contained shock. "I can't say I've ever thought that Carla was the perfect match for you, but I've never doubted she *loves* you, or that she would have been devoted to you as a wife. Are you sure you want to give up on her?"

He smiled. "You'd settle for a practical marriage and some grandchildren?"

She stiffened. "Have I ever settled for less than the best? Either from myself or from the people I love?"

Quentin lifted the delicate tea cup into his thick, callused hands, again, cradling it carefully inside his palms. He could barely fit his forefinger through the handle. He sometimes wondered if she looked at him and thought, *His fingers would fit if he had become an architect.* "Remember that you told me I had to stop ruining Carla's life? That's what I did."

"She told Alfonse you have another woman. Someone you met on that buying trip you took through the south." Angele paused, frowning. "Someone special, Carla said. Or at least particularly photogenic."

Quentin silently filed away Carla's small betrayal. Careful, now. No details. He didn't want his mother to piece together any names or possibilities. She had an encyclopedic knowledge of trivia surrounding his father's sculptures. The Tiber name, Tiberville—any mention of that or anything related to it, would alert her. As long as there was a chance he could bring Bare Wisdom home to her as a surprise, he wouldn't risk spoiling it.

"I met someone interesting on my trip. I'd rather not talk about her. It's not what Carla thinks."

"I see. You're full of secrets, lately. A friend saw you in Joe's office last week. Is this something to do with your father? I could barely believe it, since you've never taken any interest in Joe's work on his behalf, before."

"I've known Joe since I was a kid. It's not that strange to have lunch with him. That's all it was."

"Quentin, what's going on? This mysterious woman? The meeting with Joe? Tell me the truth."

"It's nothing sinister. Can't you trust me?" He paused, then added quietly, "I think I've earned that right."

"Can't you trust *me*?" She gazed at him with tears glimmering in her eyes, then looked away. "Someday I hope you'll even tell me what your father could have done to deserve the way you feel about him."

Quentin sat back. He would not tread in this area, ever. "The woman I met?" he said abruptly. "She speaks a little Latin, she has a masters in business, she used to own a bookstore. She runs her own small publishing company, now. She has this sweet younger brother who's autistic or a little mentally retarded, it's hard to say which. There's just the two of them, and she takes care of him. They live on a farm in the mountains—the most beautiful land I've ever seen in my life. She has some tenants there—artists, craftspeople. They've turned some old chicken houses into apartments. It's an amazing place. She's amazing."

By the time he finished, Angele was leaning toward him, enthralled. "You can't . . . you can't tell me about this wonderful sounding woman and make me believe there's nothing to hope for. I've never heard you talk about anyone like this, before."

"There's nothing else to say."

"Oh, *Quentin*. At least tell me her name. At least give me that much."

He hesitated. Then, very quietly, he said, "I called her *Rose*."

18

Forty two rocks. Arthur and I stood atop the granite overhang, gazing forlornly at the large mound of pebbles, while a chilly September rain drizzled through the treetops and dampened us despite rain slickers and big straw hats. I felt as if my chest was being scraped from the inside. "Brother Bear must have died," Arthur moaned in a small voice. "He would have come back by now."

"No, Sweetie, he's fine, I'm sure. I'm sure. We've got a lot of rocks left." I pointed to the ground all around.

"If he doesn't come back Mama Bear will never get anybody to love. I'll never know if she wants to keep on living here. She'll die." He shuddered. "I'm afraid I'll die, too. I'll go be with Daddy and Mama. Do you think Mama will recognize me?"

"You won't die. I promise. Come with me." I led him to the edge of the huge, flat rock. "Let's fill our pockets with pebbles. We'll take them home and put them in a jar, and then we'll take out one every day. And when the jar is empty, if Brother Bear still hasn't come back, *then I'll go to New York and get him.*"

Arthur gaped at me. "You can do that?"

"Yes, but only when the jar's empty."

Arthur absorbed this complex plan and hope sprang into his eyes. I'd bought him and myself just a little more time. I'd have to decide what to do when we took the last rock from the jar. Arthur spread his arms and flexed his fingers in wide arcs as we walked the soggy trail back to the house, loaded down with hard, stone faith. I looked at him anxiously. "What are you doing, Sweetie?"

He shut his eyes. "I'm flying to New York," he said.

*

It was a bright blue day, just a little crisp. The leaves had only started turning red on the dogwood at the edge of the front lawn, and everything else still looked like summer. "I hear somebody comin' down the road," Fannie Ledbetter called.

I ran to a living room window and gazed out the front of the house, my heart in my throat. But it wasn't Quentin. Slowly, a golf cart trundled into sight around the curve in the dirt road. I got one glimpse of delicate blonde hair and a piquant face, and I groaned.

Esme Tiber.

She had finally outsmarted the gate at Tiber Crest. The golf cart was packed with her luggage and the portrait of Bethina Grace. As she clambered out of the cart with her hair in disheveled streamers, Fannie, Liza, and I surrounded her. Her face was swollen from crying, and she looked terrified. "I never really ran away, before," she moaned, and began to shiver.

I put an arm around her. "It'll be all right. You come inside and rest." I introduced her to Liza and Fannie, as I tugged her toward the house. Her gaze darted around. She began to perk up. By the time we reached the porch she spotted the Iron Bear in the pasture.

"*The Bear*," she squealed. She shrugged out of my arms and burst across the yard, then into the pasture and up to the sculpture. I followed her quickly. She stood below the Bear's abstract snout, petting it as if it were a large dog. "Oh, Bear, *Bear*," she cooed in her funny, fairy-queen voice, smiling. "When I was a little girl I made up stories about you. Whenever I was lonely, there you were. Whenever people made fun of me, you *ate* them right up. Whenever I was scared, you sat down beside me and *purred*." She looked at me, shivering, smiling, then hugging herself. Tears slid down her face. The traumatic five-mile trip from Tiber Crest to Bear Creek, on public roads at a top speed of fifteen miles per hour, had taken a toll on her. "Bears *can* purr," she whispered.

I held out a hand. "I believe it if you say it's so."

"No one *else* believes me. I'm the family idiot. Everybody came over for a party the other day, and I heard somebody say, *Esme's a pretty little idiot.* I know what an idiot is."

I felt so bad for her, this beautiful, permanent child. "Well, this is a special place," I said. "Bears *do* purr, here."

She laughed. I took her to the house.

I couldn't get Mr. John on the phone, and left a message for Janine at the Tiber Poultry plant. In the meantime, I fixed Esme some hot tea and let her take a nap on my bed. Liza and I sat in the kitchen debating what to do with her. "Surely Mr. John will let her visit," Liza said. "After all, Quentin's no longer here."

I looked at the jar of pebbles on the window sill. Only a few remained. I had enough trouble looming over me without a confrontation over the runaway Esme. Arthur burst into the house. He'd been on one of his woodland jaunts. Leaves clung to his long brown hair, and he dropped a flowered cloth tote bag on the table. It bulged with his daily collection—interesting pieces of bark, the bony white shells of long-dead tortoises, birds' nests, and other nature mementos. But his eyes were fixed on the ceiling. He looked stunned. "There's someone upstairs," he whispered loudly. "I saw her from outside."

"It's a visitor," I assured him. "She won't hurt you. She's a cousin of ours who moved here this summer from South Carolina. Her name's Esme."

"I saw her at the window! Looking at me!"

"She must be awake," I said to Liza. "I'll go check."

I went through the house with Arthur traipsing right behind me. I halted. "Now, Sweetie, Esme has had a bad day, and she's a little sad and worried. We don't want to startle her. You go back in the kitchen and wait—"

"Mickey!" Esme's twinkling voice called out the name. She stood on the bottom step of the staircase, staring at Arthur. Her cheeks were pink. Her eyes glowed. She pointed at the t-shirt he wore beneath a floppy blue jacket. Mickey Mouse smiled out in faded splendor. Esme was wearing a pullover sweater. She wriggled out of it, then pointed to herself. She wore the Minnie Mouse t-shirt I'd seen the day I met her. "Mickey!" she said, again, and pointed at Arthur.

With a look as sweet as her reflection in his eyes, he put one hand over his heart and pointed at Esme's t-shirt with the other. "Minnie," he answered softly.

*

"She could have been killed on the road," Mr. John said angrily. "She could have been run over by a tractor trailer!"

Janine, who stood beside him on my back porch, made a shushing gesture with her hands. "Daddy, she got over here all right. Let's not go hunting for trouble. Look at her. She's fine. This is the happiest she's been since she moved to Tiberville."

Esme and Arthur lolled around the Bear, laughing, pointing at each other, circling the sculpture as if they were playing a game of hide and seek. I stared at Janine, amazed that she wasn't ranting at me, too. "Esme told me how much she loves you," I said.

Janine raised her chin. Dressed in a cool black jacket and tailored skirt, she looked very severe. "Don't bother to hide your astonishment, please. I can see it quite clearly. Yes, Esme and I are very close. I've always been like a big sister to her. I'd have moved her into my house, but I'm away too much on company business."

This was a side of Janine I'd never seen before. Actual compassion. Tenderness. Generosity. While I considered this startling revelation

Mr. John turned to me with no grace at all. "You encouraged her to come here," he accused. "You put ideas into her head about the sculpture."

"She grew up hearing about Miss Betty and the Bear."

"Only because her Aunt Dotty encouraged it, too. Which was fine when Esme lived three hundred miles from here." He waved a hand at me. "I'm not going to have her running away over here to worship that *thing*."

"Daddy," Janine sighed. "She has nothing else to occupy her time. She needs a friend. Look at her and Arthur. Arthur's harmless. It wouldn't hurt anything to have Tricky drive her over to visit." Janine flashed a stony look at me. "For a *supervised* visit."

"Daughter," Mr. John said in a tight voice. "You're not in charge of our family quite yet. I'd like to talk to you in private." They walked to the edge of the yard. I made a pretense of not watching them, but watched anyway. From Janine's exasperated expression and the considerable amount of hand-waving on Mr. John's part, it was clear they still disagreed.

He won. "Daddy's got a huge problem with this whole situation," she told me as we walked out to the Bear. "And he's just morose in general, these days. Getting old. Letting go of the family business. Afraid I'll make changes he won't like."

"I could suggest some changes neither *one* of you would like."

"Don't push your luck."

"Look, Esme's welcome here. If you can work things out, have Tricky bring her back. She may run away again, otherwise."

"I'm afraid she was born to wander and think up strange ideas. Must be the Powell in her."

"I saw the gun she carries. She was born to shoot at people, too. That would be the Tiber in her."

Janine and I traded acerbic looks. She spoke gently to Esme, and Esme's shoulders slumped. Esme turned to my brother and, trembling, touched a fingertip to his t-shirt. "See you later, Mickey."

He stood there gazing at her sadly. "Don't forget what I told you about the Tweens."

She nodded. "I'll be on the look-out."

As they were preparing to drive away in a luxury town car with a Tiber Poultry vanity plate on the front, Mr. John paused long enough to say, "Quentin Riconni's deserted you for good, I take it?"

The humiliation burned me to the bone. "I wouldn't say that."

"No, *you* wouldn't, but everybody else in the county is wondering. Honey, it's for the best. The man was a rough character, and obviously not the kind who *sticks*."

After they drove away, I turned around and met the embarrassed gazes of Liza, Fannie, Bartow, Juanita, and Oswald. "He'll be back," I swore.

But I didn't believe it, either.

*

Two days later, Esme escaped again, this time in Tricky's old hatchback, which Tricky left parked with the keys in it. She made it two miles down a back road before she crossed an intersection without looking. A Tiber Poultry truck, delivering a load of new chicks to a contract farmer, clipped the hatchback's rear bumper and spun the little car into a ditch. Esme ended up with a fractured wrist, a mild concussion, and numerous bruises.

"Don't tell Arthur," I warned everyone at the farm, and hurried to Tiberville's recently inaugurated hospital. Esme was resting in the Betty Tiber Memorial Wing. Mr. John confronted me in the hall. "You will *not* go in to see her. I forbid it! All she's talked about is Arthur this and Bear that, something about air fairies or elves or such nonsense—"

"Tweens," I supplied.

"*Tweens.* The Bear is held up by Tweens, she says, and now she's decided that *she's* a Tween, and that she has to come over and do her part to hold the damned thing up! I won't have that damned sculpture ruin my family!" He was yelling at me, now, *yelling* while nurses and Tibers ran up to him with their hands out. *Be quiet, please, calm down.* Mr. John ignored them all. "No one ever gave me the opportunity to laze around believing in Tweens! A man has to protect what he's been given! And I *will* make certain my niece stays away from that sculpture!"

"I'm sorry, but you're wrong," I said. Then I turned and left. I heard him sputtering at me even as I walked down the hall. I left a spray of golden mums, cut by Liza from Daddy's garden, on the desk of the front lobby.

*

"I bet Esme would like ice cream," Arthur noted, as he licked a tall chocolate cone. "When she's coming back?"

"I'm working on it," I said. One more small lie. Esme would come back. Quentin would come back. Or I'd go get him. Mama Bear would stop feeling so lonely. Arthur would be safe and happy, his sense of security, restored. We'd prosper at Bear Creek. I knew how to accomplish every bit of that.

Lies. All lies.

On that cool autumn afternoon we sat around a wooden picnic table with Dr. Washington and all the tenants. A Saturday excursion for ice cream had become our habit. I spooned vanilla from a paper cup. The tiny, moss-tinged concrete building behind us sported a rusted yellow sign saying Big Mountain Sweets. It sat in an oak grove near the proprietor's home and ten-cow dairy barn. Big Mountain Sweets had provided homemade ice cream to Tibervillians for fifty years. This particular outing was my treat, to distract Arthur from asking me when Esme Tiber was coming back.

"Ah, paradise," Dr. Washington sighed, dipping into a scoop of strawberry-laced ice cream. "Brings back childhood memories."

Oswald eyed him with redneck diplomacy. "They let Coloreds eat here when you was a boy?" It was not said unkindly.

"Yes, as a matter of fact. There was a special table." Dr. Washington nodded to a spot along the wall of the building. "It was only for us. My brother Fred and I thought we were royalty. We were too young to know the difference."

"I'm so glad the energy of that time has improved," Liza said.

He smiled ruefully. "Has it? My son, up in Boston, said he imagines me wearing overalls and picking cotton. I took some care to explain to him that we don't grow cotton in the mountains, but he maintains that it's how he sees my life here. My daughter is convinced she'll come to visit and find me wandering in the woods with a Klansman's noose around my neck, despite the fact that the Klan hasn't been active here for forty years. I keep trying to convince them to bring their children and visit, but they won't."

"Have you told them Mr. John is pushing for you to become president of Mountain State College?"

"Oh, I've told them. They think I'm gilding the situation to reassure them." He laughed. "Some days I feel a wicked urge to send my children a photo of myself barefoot, in overalls, with a straw hat on my head and a piece of hay between my teeth, with a burning cross in the yard behind me and a bag of cotton over one shoulder." He laughed harder. "My children would faint."

"Why did you come back? Seriously."

His expression grew solemn. "Because I owed it to Fred. If I don't re-establish our family here, there will be no more Washingtons in

Tiber County. This is our home place, our womb. It's where our ancestors realized this family had true freedom, even though they were slaves. Land is freedom." He paused, smiling dryly at his own sentimentality, then added in a melodramatic Tara brogue, "We'll always have the land, Katie Scarlett O'Hara."

I nodded.

As I drove Arthur back home that day I began to feel that something was out of place. Something felt *wrong*. The others had gone to the Piggly Wiggly, so we were alone when I turned off the county road at Daddy's brightly painted Bear Creek mail box. Frowning, I guided the old truck along the rutted dirt road. Arthur fidgeted next to me. "Sister, *stop*," he said. "The dirt looks funny."

He was right. The road itself was bothering me. I stopped, got out, and scrutinized wide tire tracks that had chewed up the soil and gravel. Arthur craned his head from the passenger window. "We got big company," he said.

Indeed. The old road carried the signatures of visitors like fingerprints. The fresh tracks indicated some large, heavy, double-wheeled vehicle had come through. I felt a wild rush of hope, then realized Quentin didn't drive anything the size of a cement truck.

"Sweetie, I'm going to play a game," I told Arthur. "You want to play?"

"Sure."

I drove a little further but stopped out of sight of the house, cut the engine, and got out. "I'm going to surprise our visitors," I said. "You stay here and surprise anyone else who comes down the road. Don't get out of the truck, though. Just wave at them."

"Okay, but this is a silly game."

"I know. I'll be back in a few minutes."

When he looked the other way I slipped an old revolver from under the truck's seat. I had no idea why I was so suspicious, although rural people are raised to reach for their guns before they step outside on a dark night, or when a stranger rolls into their yard. I told myself I'd listened to too much of Liza's chatter about spirit guides giving her hunches. If I had spirit guides, they were probably laughing their ethereal asses off at the sight of me slipping through my own woods with a 45-caliber pistol in one hand.

What I saw when I crept to the edge of the clearing shocked me so much I didn't move for a minute. A crew of four men were working feverishly to cut the Iron Bear apart. They'd set up oxygen and acetylene tanks near a truck the size of a moving van. Sparks flew from their cutting torches. They'd already severed the sculpture's head. It lay on the ground.

They're killing the Bear. The next thing I knew, I was striding from the forest, the revolver raised in one hand. "Get away from her, you sons of bitches," I yelled, and fired at the sky. They jumped and jerked the visors upward on their welding helmets. I advanced on them with the revolver now pointed right at them. They threw their helmets and torches in every direction then ran, disappearing into the woods.

I fired two more shots into the air. Breathing hard, I stood with my legs braced apart as the shots echoed off the mountains. I stared at the beheaded sculpture. The men had only just begun to cut a second section apart. I saw score lines on the metal skeleton, but no further damage.

Still, the Bear's head lay on the ground. I wanted to sob.

"No!" Arthur's voice became a long wail behind me. I spun around. He'd followed me from the woods. Now he rushed past me and fell to his knees beside the sculpture's head. *"She's dead,"* he screamed. *"The Tweens got her."* His mouth worked in convulsive misery. His eyes rolled back, and he collapsed.

*

The October wind curling off the ocean was frigid. Standing in what remained of the upstairs floor of a beachside mansion that had once belonged to a Vanderbilt, Quentin braced himself beneath the collapsing weight of a massive mahogany fireplace mantel. He stood on the remnant of a second-story portico thirty feet above a marble patio. His crew scrambled around him, yelling and cursing as they hurried to re-fit the tangled chains of the block and tackle they'd been using to hoist the huge, decorative mantel when a hook came loose. Popeye bellowed at him from the ground. "Let the damned thing fall! Let it drop! Captain! *Move!*"

Sweat poured down his face; sinews bulged in his throat; he hunched over double beneath the leaning wood. The buckle on the canvas web of his tool belt dug into his thigh through his work pants.

"We got it, Boss, we got it!" his foreman called, and suddenly, with a whir and rattle of pulleys and chains, the weight lifted off his back. He sank to his knees, gasping. A minute later his crew began pounding him on his pained shoulders.

Coughing, he got up, staggered inside, and went down a shivering wooden construction staircase, holding onto the safety railings because his legs shook. Popeye met him at the bottom, in what had once been the mansion's foyer. "I've had it with you!" he yelled. "I won't watch this kind of shit any more! What's the matter with you, son? Are you trying to get yourself killed?"

Yes. Yes, I think I am. The words crept into Quentin's mind like snakes. The old sergeant climbed into a truck and sped off. Quentin walked outside and sat down on the remnants of a low stone wall. He had scared himself, this time. Some kind of destiny was at work, here. Somebody was trying to tell him something.

A high-pitched beep emitted from the dusty cell phone on his belt. *Your conscience is calling,* the snakes hissed.

His hands shook as he put the phone to his ear. "Quentin?" a soft, New Orleans voice said with quavering distress. "It's Liza Deerwoman."

He stood up. "What's wrong?"

She told him. Ten minutes later, he was driving to the nearest airport.

19

Arthur lay in a bed at the new hospital, tranquilized into a stupor. I had several stitches in my forefinger where his teeth had clamped convulsively. The knuckle was swollen to the size of walnut. I'd rammed my finger into Arthur's mouth to keep him from choking. My brother had suffered a seizure.

The whole county was in an uproar. It only took an hour or two for the sheriff to determine who owned the deserted truck at Bear Creek. He unearthed the names of the four men, who were from North Carolina. There the FBI caught one man immediately, and he wasted no time spilling every detail.

He and the others had been told that everyone at the farm went for ice cream and groceries every Saturday. They didn't expect me and Arthur to return early. After all, their information had come from a source who knew us well.

The men had been hired by Mr. John.

I sat by Arthur's bed, staring at the floor. Fannie lumbered into the room. "Go get yourself some coffee, child," she crooned, and patted me on the head with a comforting hand that knew a piece of clay would break when fired too hard. "I'll keep time with our po' sweet boy."

I nodded and got up. I wandered down the hall to a waiting area and stood at the window. Arthur's doctor wanted to call in a psychiatrist. "Your brother's suffered so many traumas over the past ten months that he's in real danger of a major, long-term illness," she told me. "You may want to consider placing him in a facility for treatment."

"My brother's not going to leave my sight," I answered. "If I have to turn my house into a mental ward and take care of him myself twenty-four hours a day, I will."

The doctor looked at me patiently. "Now, that's not sensible, and you know it."

"In my family," I said with slow emphasis, "being sensible is not considered a virtue."

Lost in thought at the window, I didn't hear Janine walk up. "Ursula, please don't refuse to talk to me," she said in a voice so shattered I barely recognized it. I pivoted slowly, keeping my expression shuttered.

Tissues protruded from the side pocket of her hounds tooth blazer. Coffee stains speckled her jeans. Her skinned-back hair was held by a lopsided barrette, and her eyes were red-rimmed and hollow. She struggled for a moment. "I am . . . I am so ashamed. For Daddy. For our family. For me. Our oldest, dearest friends are turning their backs on him. The respect that generations of my family has earned is permanently tainted."

"Are you asking me for sympathy?"

"No. No. Just . . . I can't really explain what he did, but I have to try. I know this much: He wanted to get rid of the sculpture so it wouldn't tempt Esme to run away, again. He acted out of concern for her. Yes, it was a crazy and vicious thing to do. He knows that. Yes, there's no excuse. But Ursula, he turned himself in at the jail. He's sitting there *in a cell*, like a common criminal, tearing his heart out over what happened to Arthur. He told his lawyer not to ask for bail. He says he wants to be punished."

I searched her tormented expression. "I don't want him prosecuted. I don't want any charges filed against him. I'll tell them."

She put a hand to her throat and stared at me. "You'd do that for him?"

"It's time a *Powell* let a *Tiber* out of jail."

She sank down on a sofa, with her head bowed. I remained standing. There was dignity in offering mercy, in taking the high road, but I was not so noble that I'd sit beside her. "Everyone's saying you have a perfect right to demand justice."

"I do expect justice. But not this way." A warm sense of serenity and purpose flowed through me for that moment. I was doing what I knew to be right, what Daddy would have done.

"I'll never forget this," she said. "Thank you."

"I have to go back to Arthur, now."

"Wait." She raised her eyes to mine. "You may not believe this, but I've been planning to improve conditions for all the Tiber employees. Better pay, benefits, fairer treatment. That includes the contract farmers. Now that potential goodwill may be ruined." She struggled with her voice for a moment. "This . . . horrible thing with the Bear and Arthur has stirred people up. They're talking about going on strike at the plant."

I stared at her. *Business and image above all. Always a Tiber.* "You want me to talk to them for you?"

"Oh, Ursula, would you?"

"Absolutely." *But not the way you think.* "I'll help them work up a list of demands for those new benefits and terms. Then they'll have a solid starting point for negotiations."

Her enthusiasm dimmed a little. "You'll have them asking for the moon."

"Good. You can meet them halfway. There'll be lots of space to share."

She sighed. "Whatever you want. All right."

For the first time in our lives, we shook hands.

*

I sent the tenants home from the hospital. I wanted to be alone with my brother. Arthur looked up at me with bleary, vacant eyes, and did not speak. I combed his hair, sang lullabies to him, and promised him it would be easy to repair Mama Bear. His expression crumbled. Slowly, he shook his head. Then he turned his face away.

After he fell asleep I walked blindly into the hall, pulled his door shut, and leaned against it. *What am I going to do?* Failure swirled through my thoughts. I was so tired, and almost out of money, and terrified. I had never felt more hopeless in my life. My injured hand ached. I cradled it and closed my eyes.

A minute later I heard strong, heavy footsteps on the hall's tile floor, but didn't open my eyes to see who owned them. Some orderly or janitor, some harried physician on his way to his afternoon rounds. I didn't care. I only wanted the intruder to pass by as quickly as possible, and leave me to my own bleak thoughts.

A large, coarse-skinned hand touched my face, then curved along the side of it, palming my cheek. I opened my eyes quickly. Quentin looked down at me with stark concern. I caught the front of his shirt with my good hand and gazed up at him as if he couldn't be real. His clothes were covered in the dust and grime of a worksite, although he'd scrubbed his face and hands in an airport men's room. Beard shadow darkened his lower face. The strain of recent weeks showed in his eyes, as gray as steel. His was nobody's beauty. I had never seen a more wonderful sight in my life. *He had come back.*

Neither of us said a word. His fingers pressed possessively against my cheek. There were no words for my feelings, now that he was there, or at least none I'd admit. I didn't throw myself at him. I managed to keep my pride. I simply raised my uninjured hand to his hand along my face, covered it, and squeezed with fervent welcome.

He lifted my other hand and studied it, frowning. I let it rest gratefully atop his palm, like a wounded bird.

Quentin thought, *If I'd stayed, this wouldn't have happened to her. Arthur and the sculpture wouldn't be damaged.* He raised angry, determined eyes to mine. I slumped a little. "Arthur thinks Mama Bear is dead."

Quentin lifted my chin with his fingertips. Never turning his gaze away, he looked straight inside me, and me inside him. "Then we'll bring her back to life."

*

He stood before the broken sculpture, alone and unprepared for the rush of fury and grief that hit him. *I'll put it back in one piece again. It's not ruined. I'll take care of it, Papa, just like I took care of everything else.* But the other one. The other one—invisible, waiting to be built— lurked in the place that fostered nightmares and unspeakable regret. *I'll take care of that, too, to get what I want,* he thought. *For Mother. For Ursula. For Arthur. For you, Papa, god damn you. This is the last time.*

One more testament, then the debt that had tormented him for so many years would be paid.

*

Everyone said he'd come back for my sake and his family honor. It was widely accepted that some measure of man-to-man confrontation with Mr. John was inevitable.

Juanita, who had barely spoken ten words to me since I'd known her, rushed into the hospital cafeteria where I was buying Arthur's favorite yogurt. Oswald's shy wife, who had been a worker at the Tiber plant before she married, hugged a colorful sweater over her denim jumper and spouted an anxious stream of Spanish. "Slow down," I begged, translating slowly. She gulped. "My friends just see Quentin drive into the parking lot at the plant."

I handed her the yogurt and hurried after him. Tiber Poultry was only a two-minute jog from the hospital. Heads turned on every corner as I ran past.

The processing plant loomed beyond the town railroad tracks like a brick beehive. Refrigerated tractor-trailers sat at wide loading docks on one side of the building. A line of refrigerated freight cars waited for loading on a side spur of the train track. The parking lot was filled with employees' cars. I groaned as I darted by Quentin's rented sedan in a parking area for visitors.

"*You let him go on in?*" I accused the lobby receptionist, a high school classmate of mine.

214

She raised both hands in defeat. "Mr. John said if he showed up, to let him by. Go see for yourself."

I was astonished. I strode down the main hall of the plant offices toward a pair of darkly paneled double doors. The staff was clustered in open doorways, staring at Mr. John's office. "We haven't heard anything violent," someone called to me. "But he hasn't been here long."

When I reached the doors, I halted. For a second I listened, heard nothing myself, considered knocking, then pushed my way inside. Mr. John sat in an arm chair in one corner, before a large picture window that framed a postcard view of Tiberville. Quentin stood opposite him, gazing out the window, too.

Both of them turned their heads when I burst in. Mr. John looked haggard and old, his graying hair just a white shadow over his balding head. He had always been a pristine dresser, always in silks and linens proudly embossed with the Tiber logo. But now he was a portly old man in a golf shirt and rumpled trousers. His eyes, behind heavy bifocals he wore in private, were red-rimmed and swollen. He had obviously been crying only seconds before I entered the room. When he saw me he put his head in his hands. "Oh, Honey," he moaned. "I didn't mean to hurt you and Arthur."

"Too late for that," Quentin supplied. His expression was simply cold, and a little sad. "We've come to an agreement," he told me. "There'll be a bronze plaque put on the campus at Mountain State, where the sculpture used to stand. I want it to tell how the sculpture was commissioned, and who was responsible for it. Betty Tiber. Tom Powell. Richard Riconni." He paused. "And I'll receive a letter of apology to present to my mother."

Mr. John raised his head and looked at me. "Is there anything, anything at all, I can do to make this up to *you?*"

"I want the two hundred dollars you made Daddy pay you for the Bear. I want it donated to the March of Dimes."

"Yes."

"And I want your permission for Esme to visit Bear Creek whenever she wants."

He nodded.

"That's all."

His face crumpled. "I would give all my money, everything, to turn back the clock."

"So would I," I whispered, on the verge of tears, myself. "I'd set it back more than twenty years. The Bear would stay on campus. And I'd save my mother's life." I looked at Quentin. "And you could save your father's." The look that came into his eyes was hard and poignant, taking little, a raw wound. Yet he nodded.

We left Mr. John sitting there with his own regrets. We took ours with us.

*

Arthur sat listlessly in a lawn chair as Quentin, Oswald and I, standing on ladders, guided the Bear's head back into place. Dr. Washington and the tenants watched anxiously. The abstract iron head hung from the hoist of a huge tow truck designed to pull tractor-trailer cabs. The operator was the son of a neighbor who had insisted on helping. It seemed that everyone in the county had come to visit and offer assistance in the few days since Quentin's return.

"Another inch, that's it, hold it there," Quentin called from atop a wooden ladder leaning against the Bear's shoulder. He waved the rest of us away, pulled a welding visor over his face, and ignited the slender welding torch he held in one thickly gloved hand.

Don't look at the torch, just look at the pretty sparks," I called to Arthur. At my quick nod, Liza hurried over to him. "Look at the lovely fireflies, Arthur," she crooned, dropping down beside his chair in the browning pasture grass.

He said nothing. When Quentin had entered his hospital room the first day his eyes brightened. *Brother Bear,* he whispered. *I knew you'd come back. I still had rocks.* Then he sank back on his pillow and whimpered, *But it's too late. Mama Bear's gone.* And nothing either Quentin or I could say to him would shake his conviction.

Quentin touched the tip of the torch to one of several dozen fissures between the sculpture's body and head. Sparks cascaded around him like small fireworks. Slowly, fresh metal scars began to heal the Bear's wounds.

Arthur huddled deeper inside the light quilt I'd wrapped around him, though the late-September day was mild. I moved to stand behind him, stroking his hair back from his forehead. "This reminds me of the day Daddy brought the Bear home," I told him. "He welded her feet to the metal stobs he put in the concrete. Mama and I sat right about here, watching the sparks that night. It was the most beautiful thing. Wouldn't you like to hear that story again, Sweetie?"

"No. It makes me sad, now." He shivered under my hands. I went around in front of him and dropped to one knee. "Why, Sweetie?"

He looked down at me with tragic eyes. "Because Mama Bear can't talk to me, anymore. She's not coming back. We need to have a funeral for her."

"*No*. No, she's just fine. Look at her. She's almost her old self. The good Tweens are helping Quentin fix her." Arthur frowned, thinking this through. His hands lay limply atop the quilt. I gently gripped one of them. "Sweetie, the Bear doesn't live by ordinary rules. Cutting her apart can't kill her. She lives up *here*." I pointed to my head, and then to his. "And she's still waiting for Quentin to give her a friend of her own kind to love."

He listened intently, but only sighed.

Liza and I guided him indoors for a nap late that afternoon. He slept in his boyhood bed under a down comforter Mrs. Green had loaned us, because Arthur had admired the comforter at her house, once.

Quentin finished restoring the Bear just after sunset. In the cool, pink-and-purple dusk the last sparks showered to the ground, the brilliant flare of the welding torch vanished. He climbed down from the ladder. We stood there, just the two of us, in the wistful semi-darkness poets and mourners call the gloaming. The Bear gazed at us, and beyond us, as grandly as before. I hugged myself. "The difference between Arthur and me is that I grew up wishing I could tear this sculpture apart," I confessed. "I thought I'd always feel that way. But I'm glad to see it put back together."

Quentin went very still beside me. The slope of his shoulders said he was bone tired. He tucked his welding gloves into the waistband of his trousers like forgotten gauntlets. "I'm worse than you. I always wished I could tear apart *every* sculpture my father made." His troubled tone made me gaze at him sadly. "It makes no difference now," he went on, "but there was a time when I loved everything he touched."

You still do. It's so obvious, I thought. I faced him, reached out a hand, then just as quickly brought it back to my side. An almost imperceptible angling of his body said he'd felt the incomplete caress. I kept my distance, and he didn't encourage me. But the raw tension was there, the deep and urgent stream of awareness always circling us, swirling between our bodies, filling the night, our dreams, the simple acts of conversation and cooperation. "Why did you come back?" I asked. "Why did you change your mind about building a second sculpture?"

Because of you, he thought. "I have a responsibility to this situation. I started it."

"I see."

"There's no other solution." He'd already told me about his father's former student, Joe Araiza, and Joe's unsuccessful efforts to find a suitable artist to create another sculpture. He jerked his head toward the Bear. "I still intend to buy this thing. If it means slapping together some kind of copy for Arthur to love, then so be it." The last shimmer of light caught his most cynical smile, making me think he was still as cold-blooded as ever. "I might even ask for a discount," he warned, "now that it's damaged."

We were back to business. I feigned a laugh. "No way. You fixed it beautifully."

We walked toward the house. I frowned. "What if Arthur doesn't care, anymore? The circumstances have changed. He's not insisting you build a friend for Mama Bear, now." Quentin put a hand on my arm and brought us both to a stop . We stood in the side yard, screened by tall camellias and crepe myrtles, whose foliage broke up the light from the windows. In that fractured darkness I could see the taut line of his jaw. "Are you giving up?" he asked.

"I'm offering us both an easy way out. We could talk to him. You might be able to take the original, *now.*"

"Is it that unpleasant to be around me?"

"Not if we keep our hands off each other. That's not easy." Silence. The look that came into his eyes, and I'm sure into mine, almost brought us together *then.* I took a step back, weak-kneed. "I wouldn't want Arthur to think you're *permanent.* I can't risk adding that fantasy to his repertoire."

"I agree. But I promised your brother I'd do a certain job, and I intend to do it. If the sculpture's effect is as powerful as everyone around here seems to think, then it'll lure Arthur back."

"You know it won't be easy to build another one."

"It isn't going to be a work of art."

The fact that he'd returned, that he was determined to try, made the enterprise itself a rare masterpiece. I looked at him pensively. "I think you'll surprise yourself."

I told him goodnight and walked inside. We had no comfort zone, no rules, no familiar questions. We were a flexing cocoon containing two strangers trying to transform each other. He lingered outside my windows in the darkness, shielded by the faithful old shrubs, looking up into the light.

20

He called Popeye and told him what he intended to do. He would spend the autumn building a second sculpture, hoping to make a trade. The old Sarge shocked him. "Son, you been needin' to do that all your life. Don't worry about business up here. I'll put on a smiley face and keep it rollin'." He paused. "Just don't pick up more than you can carry, dammit."

Next he called Joe Araiza and canceled the search for a sculptor. "Change of plans," was his only explanation.

Joe sounded more curious than angry. "The mystery deepens."

"It's complicated, but you'll understand eventually."

"Where are you?"

"I'm doing some work out of state."

"Somewhere down south, again? You're buying? You're doing some salvage work?"

"Joe, do me a favor. Don't ask questions, and if my mother comes to you with questions of her own, don't tell her anything."

"I've been dancing on thin air with her for weeks. I've perfected my technique."

"Keep dancing, then."

Quentin settled back in a chair in his motel room after those conversations. He continued to hold the phone in his hand, thinking he should call the front desk and book the room for the rest of the month, at least. He had no desire to set up long-term housekeeping in the tiny chicken-house apartment, as before.

I should stay here in town. Treat this project like a job. Go out to the farm, work, come back here every day. Eat my meals at the diner, and sit in this room, alone, at night. Stay away from temptation. From Ursula.

He spent some time looking around the antiseptic motel room, trying to convince himself that his efforts to live there would make any real difference between him and me. On the lighted sign outside the Tiberville Methodist Church he'd read the weekly words to live by: THERE IS NO SUBSTITUTE FOR A STRONG SPIRIT.

He put the phone down, closed out his bill, and drove to Bear Creek.

*

As October began and the mountains went from green to a patchwork of gold and red, he set up a base camp next to the Iron Bear. He pitched a large green army tent on a platform he built at the edge of the oak grove, and installed a small, pot-bellied stove Dr. Washington dug out of storage in his top-heavy barn. The stove pipe angled through a vent in the tent's roof like the silver spire on a small church. He hung lanterns from the tent's ceiling, and carpeted the floor with braided rugs he bought at the Tiberville Flea Market, where he also bought an old, whitewashed wooden table and a heavy arm chair that just needed to be refinished. He didn't refinish it, but when he set it next to the table the combination worked. He placed a laptop computer and a small printer on the table, alongside a tall stack of textbooks on art theory and design.

He arranged his clothes and other possessions—which Popeye shipped to him, along with Hammer, who seemed thrilled to be back—in an old armoire he found in town at the New and Used Furniture Barn.

He ran a power line from the farmhouse's circuit box, plugged in a miniature refrigerator and a pair of hot plates, but also dug a fire pit outside and set up a cooking area for a cast-iron skillet and a coffee pot. We were all mesmerized. Even Arthur crept outside to watch. It was still clear that he adored Quentin. Most days, watching him work was the only incentive that got Arthur out of bed.

But everyone else gawked at Quentin's elegantly utilitarian camp, too. Bartow Ledbetter leaned on a cane with the bushy-browed scrutiny of a gentle troll. "I guess he spent a lot of time learnin' how to live outdoors in the army. He may not be no artist, but he's got outdoor livin' down to a art."

"The army doesn't let you put rugs on your tent floor," Oswald snorted. He turned to me. "You sure he's not *gay*?"

"I'm sure," I said.

Next he used my discarded barn timbers to construct a high base for a large bed at the center of his tent. He filled that bed with a luxurious mattress, which he then outfitted in flannel sheets and a collection of heavy, colorful quilts I loaned him from the Powell quilt chest. Atop this bed he placed a half-dozen fat pillows.

Finally, he leased a portable toilet and had the delivery men set it discreetly behind his tent, shielded from indiscriminate sight by a rough wooden screen he built. He'd return to the chicken house apartment to shower, but otherwise, he would be self-sufficient at the edge of my pasture. Him and the Bear.

"I want to buy a used truck," he told me. Oswald and I took him down to the Tiber County Auction, where we mingled with farmers, merchants, tobacco-spitting bikers, and women in skin-tight shirts bearing slogans. *Back Seat Mama. Do It With Four On The Floor. Tune Me Up And Grease Me.*

He bought an old National Guard convoy truck, stripped of its olive green cover and painted a lovely shade of primer-rust-red. "What do you need something that big for?" Oswald demanded.

"To haul sheet metal and scrap iron." Secretly, he just liked the plain majesty of commanding all that horsepower and riding high across the earth, viewing it from a tall perspective. He proceeded to buy welding equipment, power cords, an anvil, tongs, hammers, grinders, sanders, other tools I could not recognize and more, plus a large boom box he hung from the bottom limb of an oak. He tuned it to a pure jazz station in Atlanta.

He accomplished all of his buying, building, and decorating in an amazing two weeks' time, and then he moved in.

Early one morning, I walked out there to share biscuits and bacon with him. The weather verged on a mild frost, so everything had a glittering sheen in the dawn sunshine. A coffee pot steamed atop his campfire. His chimney pipe puffed fragrant pine smoke.

Quentin sat in his armchair by the fire, with Hammer lying sphinx-like beside his feet, dozing. Quentin's dark hair was still ruffled from sleep. The maturity in his face and the bits of gray at his temples only made him look better. He was dressed in old jeans and a flannel shirt over a thermal one. He stretched his long legs in front of him and crossed them at the ankles, without looking up from the book he was reading. I squinted at it and realized in surprise it was one he'd borrowed from me. One of my authors.

My senses filled with the brisk, pine-scented air, the aroma of the coffee, the pride of seeing him read a Powell Press book, the comfortable scene, how well he fit there, and him, most of all, *him.* Desire for him. Every *bit* of me wanted to slip inside his world and into his homemade bed, under the quilts that had warmed several generations of Powell wives and husbands.

I stopped in the middle of the path. I cradled the forgotten bacon-biscuits in a tin bread pan covered with a dish towel. I was drunk with emotion and need. When he looked up, my face flushed and I looked away. He laid the book aside and stood. "Spying?" he called.

"Yeah, that's it." My momentum restored, I took a deep breath then walked into his campsite and nodded at the book. "Tell me what you *really* think of *The Strangled Willow.*" It was, after all, a difficult collection of essays on women's emotional connection to the environment.

"I like the parts about women having sex with trees."

"That's called magical realism. It's a metaphor about nature."

"No, *Moby Dick* is a metaphor about nature. *The Strangled Willow* is a book about women being a *little too interested* in the wrong kind of roots."

"Pshaw. Men never get the point of the book."

His humor faded. "That's not true. I respect it. I respect your judgment in picking the author, and I respect the way you published it. And your other book, too. You're very good at what you do."

"Oh, pshaw," I said, again. He held out a hand for the biscuits, and as I gave the pan to him our hands touched and our eyes met. The mood was suddenly so heated, so tender, that either of us could have seduced the other, at will. A thousand moments tempted us every day—a shared look, the slow motion of his hand passing mine over a meal, the way he leaned back contentedly in front of the crackling logs in my fireplace on the cool evenings, the way I walked on the balls of my feet around him.

He exhaled, and I realized I'd been holding my breath, too. "I'll have to have a talk with your little teenage peach tree," he said with melodramatic rebuke. "Find out if it's got a crush on you. Or vice versa." The tree, which had dropped all its leaves for fall, was now a robust four-footer. I'd planted it in layers of chicken-enriched soil beside Daddy's garden spot. It would be a giant.

I feigned disgust. "You leave my little *friend* out of this."

"Friend? *Jail bait.*" He arched a brow at me. "Cradle robber."

I couldn't help laughing. I couldn't help myself at all, around him.

I hurried back to the house. He never took his eyes off me. His thoughts churned. Every impulse wanted to overwhelm the rules he'd set for himself long ago. *Never love what you might lose.*

*

I asked Janine about Esme. "She's about like Arthur," Janine confessed wearily. "Depressed by everything that's happened. Afraid that her world's falling down around her. Hurt. She's still got a cast on her wrist. I'll bring her to visit when she seems to be up to it. Right now she just cries at everything."

I drove to Tiber Crest, taking along a box of Liza's peanut-butter cookies for Esme. When I rang, Tricky swung the ornate front doors open with a grimace and a smile. "Guess you know Mr. John's not here right now."

I nodded. "I heard Janine sent him on a cruise."

"Yeah. All them islands in the Bahamas. He didn't want to go. She sent a couple of his old-man cousins with him. Like parole officers, he said."

"Maybe I'll see him when he gets back." He had written me a long, apologetic letter, and had already presented Quentin with a more formal one to give to Angele. *Will you come to see me?* he'd added at the bottom of his letter to me. I had not answered. The quality of my mercy had been strained as far as it would go, for then.

"You oughta come visit him when he gets back," Tricky lectured. "Yeah, he's a high-handed old bastard, but he's just about ruint himself and his family reputation with what he did, and he knows it. Janine says he's officially in retirement *now*. She's took over running the business. He *is* being punished."

This made me feel bad, but I wanted to have no sympathy for Mr. John. "Look, I came here about Esme. Janine said I could visit her."

"Sure, but she won't come out of her room. Her nerves are shot, the doc says. She's taking mood pills, but it ain't helpin'."

"I'll sit outside her door, then."

"All righty, all righty, comeon in, Bearclaw." She paused, looking at me with glittering eyes. "You're meetin' with the board of the growers' group next week, I hear."

"That's right. I've been working with them on a new standard contract with Tiber Poultry. It's just about finished. We'll present it to all of you at the November meeting."

She put a hard-worked hand on my arm. "It's gonna make a big difference to me and my kin. To a lot of folks in this county. Thank you. Your daddy'd be proud."

"Thank him. And thank the Bear," I said quietly. She gave me a puzzled look but led me up a handsome staircase to the second-floor bedrooms. I knocked on a pristine white door. "Esme? It's Ursula."

I heard soft footsteps and other noises. She knocked back. "Hello." Her voice was wan.

"I brought you some cookies. Janine told me peanut butter are your favorite. Liza made these. May I come in?"

"I get shaky when I open the door. I c-can't."

"Okay, then let's sit down on either side and talk."

"You're . . . you're funny. Sit on the floor?"

"Yep." I sat down cross-legged and wiped my hands on the legs of my jeans. "I'm going to eat a cookie." I rumpled the aluminum foil, scuffed the cookie box on the polished heart-of-pine boards, and made loud *hmmm* sounds as I chewed. Esme's shadow filled the space at the door's bottom. I heard her settle, there. "You could slip a cookie under the door," she said.

I did. We ate in companionable silence. "How's Arthur?" she whispered. "I heard he's been sick."

"Yes. He misses you. He needs a friend."

"I heard—" her voice broke—"I heard some of Uncle John's friends say nobody in my family could ever go to Bear Creek, again."

I groaned. "*No*. Honey, that's not true."

"Uncle John's so sad. I know what he did to the Iron Bear. It's all broken up, now."

"No, it's not. We fixed it."

"You did?" Her voice brightened.

"As good as new. I just wish *somebody special* knew how to fix Arthur."

She moaned. "I . . . I could. I know I could. I'm just afraid to go outside. People get runover when they go outdoors."

"Arthur feels so bad that he won't go many places, either."

"Oh, Arthur!"

"Janine and I have an idea that might help him. I think it's something you could help with, too." I told her our plan, and she grew very quiet. "I'll try," she said in a shaky voice. "For Arthur and the Bear."

"Good." I pushed several more cookies under the door, and told her I'd leave the rest on a hall table. As I walked back to the truck I heard a sad little tapping sound. I looked up. Esme waved at me forlornly from her window.

She wore her Minnie Mouse shirt.

*

Quentin and I stood on the manicured back lawn of Miss Betty's grand old home, which was now occupied by her daughter, Luzanne. Luzanne kept glancing up at the windows. Mr. John's eldest sister clutched plump, liver-spotted hands beneath her jowly chin. "I hope this works," she whispered.

I whispered back. "I'd say it already has." Arthur perched on the rim of the backyard's bubbling fountain, craning his head toward the house. He had not moved in five minutes. "Sweetie, come on," I called. "We're going in the shed, now."

"I'll wait out here," he replied, without taking his gaze from the mysterious windows.

"He's seen her," Quentin surmised. "Come on. Let's keep up the pretense."

"I'll go in the house and see what I can encourage," Luzanne said, then hurried up the steps of the back veranda with all the speed her eighty-year-old knees could muster.

I sighed and followed Quentin into the dim light of Miss Betty's former garage, now a storage shed. We'd told Arthur we might find a memento to use as part of the second Bear. I had something in mind, but wasn't certain it still existed.

The shed was crowded with modern metal shelves, and the stone floor was covered in musty carpet squares. Boxes and forgotten trunks had been stacked head-high. Dust motes floated in the air. I caught the remnants of a spider's line with my fingertip and moved it aside. "Luzanne said if what we're looking for is still here, it's probably piled in the corner over there."

Quentin wedged his body between jumbles of unwanted chairs and lamp stands. "Let's look for Atlantis and the lost city of the Incas, while we're at it. Anything could be hidden in here."

I went to a corner across from the window and, with his help, spent several minutes methodically moving boxes and ancient yard tools. The space was close and warm. We could hear each other breathe, and there was no way to avoid body contact as we worked. "There," I said finally, both relieved and disappointed.

We looked at a baby tram that had lovingly conveyed all of Miss Betty's children and grandchildren early in their lives: Her lost daughters, her saved sons, her favorite grandson, Mr. John. The tram's leather top was falling apart, its metal frame was badly bent, it was missing two wheels, and the satin interior was yellowed and torn. It must be over a hundred years old but still had a sweet grandeur about it.

"Miss Betty rode in this when *she* was a baby," I explained. "It belonged to her mother. Bethina Grace. So it's a Powell antique, too." Quentin examined the decrepit item with a deep frown. "I might be able to use a piece of the frame in some decorative way." He hesitated.

"I can't build a structure out of trivia like this. I expect to buy scrap steel and cast iron for the main skeleton."

I could see his concern. Turning mementos and junk into an elegant and inspiring work of abstract sculpture was his father's talent, not his. He was just beginning to comprehend how obsessive every decision must be. I tried to make it easier. "Well, we'll just take this tram on the off chance you can use it. If not, well, it was headed to the county dump, anyway. After all, we're only here to pretend we're looking while Arthur and Esme coax each other into the open."

Quentin scrubbed a hand over his jaw and shook his head. "You think what's between them is all that powerful? They only met once."

"They're soul mates."

He arched a brow. "They're *cousins.*"

"Kissing cousins. So distant it doesn't matter." I looked at him. "What have you got against romance?"

"It takes too much simple faith."

"You're saying people who want romance in their lives are simple-minded?"

"No. It just deserves a full commitment, which most people aren't willing to make, including me. Why play at it?"

"Your friend Carla must love it when you talk this way." I turned my back to him in that cramped space, that cool and provocative light, so he wouldn't see my expression. I began shuffling through odds and ends on a shelf. "Are you're looking for other candidates like her? Let's see. The personal ad would read: *Wanted. Devoted, long-term, hassle-free women willing to be called 'friend.'*" I rattled old watering cans loudly, shoving things aside. A box tilted precariously on the shelf above me and Quentin stepped closer to me, catching it. "What *are* you looking for?" I persisted. "No hearts-and-flowers, obviously."

He maneuvered the box back into place. His thigh pressed against my hip. "I gave up on hearts-and-flowers when I was old enough to realize most women want money and a car."

"That's not true."

"No, but it sounds better than playing games."

Without warning, even to myself, I pivoted angrily. We were only inches apart. "*Do you just want someone to fuck?*"

He clasped my face between his hands. "I want *you.*" No clear answer, really, but deadly effective. He kissed me, and I didn't stop him. We wound ourselves together, pressing against the shelves, struggling for every ounce of sensation, violent and gentle at the same time. Containers and boxes tumbled around us. I felt him hard against

226

my stomach and writhed in response. He slid his hands down me, while we tore at each other's mouths.

We heard Arthur shriek outside, and broke apart instantly. By the time we ran into the garden he'd cornered Esme. She crouched behind a large hydrangea shrub, peeking out, white-faced, through large patches where frost had already taken the leaves. Luzanne hovered nearby, wringing her hands. "Oh, they've just gone *wild*."

Arthur crouched on the hydrangea's other side, as if he might either pounce on Esme or run away as fast as he could. "What's wrong with you?" he asked sadly. "Are you scared of me?"

"No. I'm just an *idiot*," she moaned. "I can't even run away right. I got run over."

"I got run over, too. Just in a different way."

"I'm scared of *everything*."

"Me, too," he confirmed hoarsely. "But Quentin's teaching me how to be a *man*. I bet *you* could learn how to be a *woman*. My sister could teach you. Quentin says she's *all* woman."

"How can I be a woman? I don't even know how to cross the road!"

"I don't care. I'll stay on one side of the road with you."

"Is Mama Bear dead?"

"I'm not sure. I thought she was, but maybe she's just sleeping until her neck gets well. When I was in the hospital, my neck hurt and I didn't want to talk at all. I fell down and hurt it having a fit, you know. But now my neck is fine."

"Maybe, if Mama Bear gets better, *we'll* get better."

He nodded, then inched around the shrub, still crouching, and tentatively held out one hand toward her. She crept toward him on all fours, hesitant, trembling. Then, slowly, she lifted her hand, and they touched fingertips. As if some spell had been broken, they scrambled across the remaining space and huddled together with their arms around each other.

Luzanne began to cry. "There *are* miracles."

I nodded, then met Quentin's troubled gaze. We'd only made the chasm between us more painful. *All woman*, he had said? He was right. "I want what we've just seen," I told him. "Hearts and flowers."

His expression said I'd never get them, and I turned away.

21

Tricky began to drop Esme off at the farm every morning and pick her up every evening. Sometimes Janine substituted as a chauffeur, but clearly did not like having to be humble around me. The contract I wrote for the growers' association left her quietly foaming at the mouth. We were in negotiations.

Arthur and Esme clung to each other for mutual encouragement. Though Liza and the Ledbetters entertained Esme with their studio work, she spent most of her time sitting with Arthur at the edge of the pasture, somberly watching Quentin. I watched Quentin, too, wounded but still under his spell. I relived every moment and every nuance of our most recent encounter, scolding myself for the weakness.

He bought a load of scrap metal and iron then began sorting, shaping, cutting. I wondered at this methodical piecework. Could he imagine where each piece would fit? Did he expect to put a sculpture together as if it were a giant jigsaw puzzle? Or was he simply avoiding the day when he would have to begin to create something whose sum was far more difficult to achieve than each of its parts?

Several weeks passed as this disjointed work progressed. I needed heavy labor to take my mind off the growing tension. I got out Daddy's chain saw, sharpened the blade, changed the oil, and began cutting up the huge poplar trees that had fallen on the barn.

Quentin had never seen a woman do work like that, before. *Look at that. Look at her!* he thought with stark pride. *This is why her family has survived here. Because of women like her.*

I glanced up more than once and found him moving limbs for me, or stacking the sectioned trucks of the trees, so avoiding him had backfired on me. When I sat down on a stump with the quiet chainsaw across my knees and a file in one gloved hand, preparing to touch up the blade, he said, "I could do that for you."

I squinted up at him. "Why? I can do it, myself."

Other men, including Gregory, had withered under such blunt competence, but Quentin simply nodded. "You need a better file, then." He brought me one of his.

At night I lay alone in my childhood bed, covered in old pink chenille but no longer innocent. He touched my breasts, eased my legs apart, whispered in my dreams, filled me with chaos. I had duties to uphold as the ruling woman in my own house. I could not allow myself to love a man who wouldn't stay with me. A chorus of tough southern belles whispered, *You need a loyal husband around here. Loyal to you, loyal to your family, loyal to your land.*

I added, *Good in bed, smart, and romantic. Politically, socially, and religiously compatible.* And he had to want children. Arthur and I were the last of the Powells in Tiber County. One of us must reproduce. I found myself crying over that, just laying in the bed in the dark crying with fury over being the end, the last, the only.

And loving the wrong man.

*

Dr. Washington showed up on my doorstep one afternoon, a walking stick in one hand, a bulging cloth tote bag in the other. "I'm here to see the editor and publisher of Powell Press," he said primly. I invited him in, and we sat in chairs before the living room fireplace. "Welcome to another exciting day at my company." I waved at the mostly unneeded office set-up. The squirrels sat on my desk, eating peanuts from an open jar.

He set the cloth tote on the hearth and pecked it with the tip of his stick. "I have a project for you."

"Oh?"

"Inspired by Arthur." He smiled. "It's good to see him looking lively, again."

"He's a long way from being all right, though.".

The old professor clucked his tongue. "Most of the human beings in the world are constantly searching for pathways back to their own good graces. I came back here to find my own path, and you will, and Quentin, and Arthur, too. I only wish my children would try."

I kept staring at the bag of mysterious items. "We'll think of something to get your family to visit. They'll change their tune as soon as they come here."

"These wild mountains *are* easy to love. I just don't know what it's going to take to *get* them here."

"I know you're lonely at your farm. Mr. Fred was, too."

He sighed. "That's why I like having Arthur around. Here's what I meant by *inspiration.* Do you know what I've been doing since last winter? I tell him the stories I told my children when they were little. Stories I concocted about growing up here. He likes them. He's a wonderful listener."

"Children's stories?"

"Oh, just silly little tales." He tapped the bag. "I was telling Quentin about them some time back and he convinced me to make tapes. So here they are. I'm hoping you might listen to a few and tell me if they're publishable."

Now I looked at the bag with greedy excitement. God help me, my marketing hat settled firmly into place, and I could see the headlines in Publisher's Weekly and The New York Times, to name only two. *Acclaimed Historian Pens Magic For Young Readers. Retired Harvard Professor Is New Star In Childrens' Fiction. Powell Press Tops One Million Sales With 'Stories From Bear Creek.'*

"Stories From Bear Creek," I said aloud.

His eyes gleamed. "A potential title? You don't even know if my funny little tales are any good."

"I'm betting they are." I began to gesture enthusiastically, setting up invisible priority lists. "First, I'll transcribe them. Then I'll send them to a bookseller I know who specializes in children's books. She'll give me some good feedback. Oh, and I know a wonderful illustrator in Atlanta who's been looking for a project to—" I halted. Reality sank in, and my hands floated heavily into my lap. "Dr. Washington, if your stories are good, then what I'll do is recommend them to editors at some of the best publishing houses. You deserve to have your work presented well. I don't have the money to do that. It wouldn't be fair to you or your stories."

He frowned. "But I specifically want *you* to publish them. If need be, I'll fund the costs myself."

"No, please. You have no idea how much money it would take to do a *good* job publishing and promoting your book. It's out of the question. You need a major publisher with a lot of money to invest."

"I'm assuming that financing won't be an issue for you. Don't you expect to sell Quentin the Iron Bear?"

I sat in dull silence for a moment. "I have my doubts that plan will work."

"Explain this tangled rationale to me, again."

"Arthur says he can't let the Bear go to New York unless he's convinced it—she—will always be lonely here without my father. He says giving her a friend may make her want to stay. If she's still not happy when her 'friend' is built, then she can go. So all of my financial prospects are based on Arthur's whimsy. For all I know, Quentin will build the second sculpture and my brother will say, 'Yes, that's exactly what Mama Bear needs, and now she's happy.'" Meaning she stays. No sale."

"Do you really want to see the sculpture leave here?"

My shoulders slumped. "No."

"All right, then I confess. When Quentin talked me into this project—" he indicated the bag of tapes, again—"we agreed that it had to be a Powell Press book. Ursula, you and I are family, in a sense. We'll never know what became of Nathan and Bethina Grace, but that bond is between Powells and Washingtons forever."

I nodded. "And I'm proud of it."

"Indeed. I am, as well."

A quiet admission of mutual acceptance after more than a century and a half of silence. Both he and I took a moment to look away, blink, clear our throats. "My stories, if publishable, simply must be done by you. I'd consider it an honor."

"I'd be honored to publish them. If I have the money."

He nodded. "We'll leave it at that, for now."

I walked out to Quentin's campsite that night, carrying the bag of tapes. "I've started listening to these," I told him. He looked at me over a smoky cooking grill strewn with steaks—two for him, two for Hammer. "Are they good enough?" he asked.

"They're wonderful. I know you're responsible for suggesting it to Dr. Washington. Thank you."

"You'll have the money to publish them. To publish any book you want. You have my word."

One last, lone butterfly, who had somehow escaped the cold weather and the autumn frosts, fluttered lethargically toward the Iron Bear, and lit inside its ribs. *What's the news on this man's generosity?* I asked silently.

Easy to give, late in the season, when you can't fly away, it answered.

*

Quentin Riconni, the son of sculptor Richard Riconni, is the resident artist at Bear Creek this fall, and he's designing a companion piece for the Bear! We hope to interview him. This notice was published by a local newsletter called *Outside In*, which billed itself as the monthly journal of mountain folk craft and outsider art. Daddy had helped to start it.

When Quentin read that he'd been anointed a fellow artist, he told me very quietly that he never wanted to see another word published about himself or his plans. I called the editor, who had been a dear friend of my father's, and explained as best I could. "Is he shy?" the man asked.

"No, he's just not an artist. He's an engineer. He doesn't want to mislead people."

"How's he going to build a sculpture as creatively complex as his daddy's, then?"

"I don't know," I admitted.

How can these people just assume I know what I'm doing? Quentin thought. His father's legacy was so strong, the Bear's effect so potent, that strangers were willing to accept his own reverence on faith. He feared the local publicity would generate more media, and word might get back to New York.

When he went into town, people left gentle, hand-drawn cards on his truck's windshield, containing photos of themselves or their kin with the Iron Bear. *God bless you and Ursula for keeping up the good work,* they said.

Admirers came to the farm so often that he began to head for the woods with Arthur in tow every time a car rumbled into the yard. They pinned notes to him on the big canvas army tent. And then, without warning, old friends and neighbors began to show up at Bear Creek carrying contributions for the new sculpture—ancient car axles, discarded hand tools, rusty iron cookware. Each present came with a personal story.

Arthur and Esme studiously pondered the junk pile in the pasture every day, often sitting beside it cross-legged for hours. Quentin stared at the hodgepodge with growing unease. When he analyzed his father's sculpture, he saw, of course, that its bones were made from a dozen scrap sources. Yet each piece had been cut, shaped, and machined into something unique, the essence of its original form. *How did Papa fit all that together to make something coherent?*

He spread every piece of collected junk in a circle around his camp and the Iron Bear. He set aside, he tore apart, he selected like pieces and collected them in different piles, then resorted them into other piles. Like a scientist contemplating a Frankenstein project or a paleo-archaeologist plotting the skeleton of some animal no modern eye had ever seen, he looked for patterns in strange bones. He even commandeered my wrecked sedan one day and towed it to the worksite.

He began to sketch—drawing constantly on thick yellow pads he kept to himself. I made a point to avoid blatantly peering over his shoulder when he was nearby; since he rarely took time to come to the house and ate the food I brought him standing up, my honor wasn't tested very often.

"We have to go on a hunt for more bear parts," Arthur announced. He took Esme by the hand and they walked through the woods to Dr. Washington's. I followed them an hour later, curious.

"They're sitting in the old corn crib pondering a keg of nails," Dr. Washington told me solemnly, as we stood outside his barn.

"Maybe Quentin can make a porcupine."

He laughed. I peered into the barn, where I could just make out Arthur and Esme's bowed heads over a pile of rusty nails. "I'll come back and check on them again, later. You're very kind to my brother, and I appreciate all you've done."

"Arthur is finding his way in the world without a father, slowly but surely, just like Quentin, and like you. He'll be all right."

I had my doubts.

*

He couldn't put it off any longer. He had to begin building a sculpture.

The Iron Bear cast weird shadows across the pasture in the firelight. Quentin rose in the middle of the night, sweating and dreaming of his father with bloody hands. He hoped that starting a fresh fire would chase the memories away, but it didn't. *I'm surrounded by ghosts*, he thought, looking at the piles of scrap and cast-offs that circled the camp, shifting shapes in the high blaze. Some of them seemed to move, or to gaze at him with hollow eyes, the way the Iron Bear always did. *What are you waiting for? I know you*, it said. *I own you. Until you find yourself in me, I always will.*

His father's sculpture had finally spoken to him, just as he'd always feared it would. He doused the fire, took a long swallow from a bottle of scotch, and sat the rest of the night in untempered darkness, daring the jagged shapes of his past and future to come after him.

*

I woke up at dawn, my heart racing. I slept with a window open most nights, even in the cold autumn air. Outside my screen came the shushing sound that woke me. I hurried to look, somehow knowing that this was one of Quentin's noises.

I was right.

Out in the pasture, he was digging a foundation for his sculpture. He'd stretched lines of twine in neat grids outlining a 12-by-12-foot site for the concrete pad. The lines were perfectly parallel to the ground and he'd attached them with surgical precision to small pine stakes. Beside him sat one of the farm's deep metal wheelbarrows with the garden hose draped over it, and a gray pile of rocky concrete, waiting to be mixed. Nearby lay a carpenter's level and a plumb bob. He would measure everything. Every detail had to be perfect.

I threw on some clothes, peeked into Arthur's room to check on him, then went downstairs to make coffee. Arthur's squirrels, now brawny teenagers, scampered around me, taking nuts from a bowl on the counter.

When the coffee was done I hurried outside carrying two cups, and trailed by the squirrels, who met Hammer in the front yard with fearless chatter. He and they caravanned behind me across the frosty grass like a coffee-presenting procession. "Good morning," I called to Quentin. "How can I help? I'm good with concrete. I helped my father build the first pad, although frankly his engineering standards weren't as high as yours."

"You can't help me." He kept digging.

I watched him with concern. "How about a coffee break? Followed by a biscuit break?"

"No. I need to get this part done. I don't want a crowd. I'll finish pouring the concrete before everyone else wanders out here." He raised his head to scowl at me and I almost gasped.

He looked haggard. Even building the foundation had set off some altered state, opened some door he'd never wanted to open. Distracted, he plunged his shovel into the dirt askance. It hit one of his taut lines and neatly cut the twine. The ends jumped back like startled kittens. He cursed loudly and obscenely, which was not at all like him. The squirrels ran. Hammer whimpered. I stood there assessing this dark side of his personality, seeing so much pain I'd never imagined.

"You don't have to work on this alone," I said. "Whatever's driving you, you can talk to me about it. I swear to you, whatever you tell me will never be repeated."

"It's not your problem."

"Oh, yes it is. This is all about my family and my family's future, as much as yours. And if you don't trust me, then we have nothing. Not even friendship."

"We have nothing, then," he said.

After a stunned moment, I simply turned and walked back into the house.

*

Two days later, Arthur ran into the kitchen. I was fixing lunch. "He's made a paw," Arthur exclaimed. "The first paw!"

234

I walked out to the worksite. Quentin raised up from the concrete pad, a welding torch in one gloved hand, a welding helmet pushed up to reveal his face, already streaked with sweat and grime despite the cool air. On the pad, anchored by the rebar, stood a paw-like conglomeration of metal pieces.

"It's alive," he said.

I refused to offer help, though he looked worse every day, and I was worried. "Lunch is available if you want it," I said, and left him at his own misery.

You wanted to make her back away from you, and she has, he told himself with bleak satisfaction. He wearily turned his attention to the dismembered limb before him. *Now it can stalk me, just like Papa's sculptures stalked him. Let's see who survives.*

*

After that day, Quentin belonged in spirit and fact to the mystery of his father's lonely work. No one could help him, and no one could get in his way. He performed the most methodical, painstaking labor on the new sculpture—cutting, hammering, shaping pieces of metal into curves and angles, fitting, welding, fitting again. The sculpture progressed from paws to complete legs.

He decided suddenly that none of it looked right. He fired up a torch, and cut everything apart. Bear Two vanished, leaving only empty concrete stained with Quentin's sweat and a few antenna-like prongs of rebar, waiting to anchor the next version.

"Where'd Bear Two go?" Arthur asked worriedly.

"Back to Iron Bear heaven," Esme offered.

This disturbed him profoundly. Bear Two, as he called it, had not spoken, yet, so he didn't know if it was the right friend for Mama Bear or not, but he knew this much: Quentin hadn't even given it a chance.

22

I asked Liza to help me transcribe Dr. Washington's tapes, having learned that her skills from some past life enabled her to type at whirlwind speed. We holed up in the house for a day and tag-teamed the effort at my computer. I liked having her in my office, for company. She realized something terribly wrong was happening between me and Quentin, but she didn't pry. Her extravagant blonde hair and odd outfits – baggy white overalls and a pink sweatshirt, that day—had become a familiar and comforting sight.

During a break I couldn't find her, and wandered upstairs, searching. She was so lost in thought she didn't hear me. I glanced into Daddy's room. She was standing at the foot of his bed with her head bowed. I backed away but stepped on a creaking board, and she heard. When she turned, I saw tears on her face. She wiped them away quickly. "I'm sorry."

The suspicion I'd harbored for months just slapped me in the face. "Were you sleeping with him?" I asked.

She nodded.

Something irrational boiled inside me. *Goddammit, all I ask is a little peace of mind inside my own home.* "How long did this go on?"

"More than two years."

"He should have told me. I had a right to know." I didn't, really, but I spoke out of anger and hurt.

"He *wanted* to tell you. We both did. But you didn't know me—or anything about me. You wouldn't have approved. He didn't want to drive you further away."

"That's no excuse." My voice rose. "I have a right to know who's screwing my father in my mother's bed!"

Her face blanched. "Ursula, please—"

But I was already headed downstairs. I strode out the kitchen door, grabbing a coat and a knapsack I sometimes carried on walks. I had to get away from the images of her and Daddy, rising in my mind.

*

I sat by Bear Creek, in a spot thick with matted autumn leaves, where a finger of the water seeped among exposed tree roots and smooth boulders. Quentin found me there and sat down beside me. I held my notepad on my lap to feign activity, but no doubt he could tell

I'd just been sitting there, crying. "Everyone was afraid you'd been eaten by a bear," he said.

"There haven't been any bears here for decades. And black bears don't eat people."

"I told them I'd check, anyway."

"How's Liza?"

"Upset. And worried about you."

I stared into the quiet, naked forest, broken only by groves of evergreen laurel and a few large pines. "I was cruel. I've calmed down, now. It was just a shock. Thinking of her and my father sharing the bed I was born in."

"You don't have to explain. I'm an expert on being cruel when everything closes in on me."

"Look, Quentin, you don't have to say—"

"I hated the way my father lived his life. He was gone from the time I was eight years old. My mother's life centered around supporting his ambitions. There was never enough money, and when he was at home he never looked hard enough to *see* how badly we were doing."

I took a deep breath. "I grew up the same way, the only difference being that my father didn't leave home to chase his dreams. He chased them right here." I looked down at the notepad in my lap. "I guess I'm no smarter. Talk about a fantasy. I come to this spot to draw sketches of a house I'll probably never build. But I can picture it." I gestured behind me. "Up there on the top of the ridge, looking down on this spot."

"Will you let me see your drawings?"

"Don't laugh." I handed him the sketch pad and he opened it slowly. He studied my rough pencil drawings of a handsome house of deep porches and wide windows, somehow old-fashioned and familiar and warm. "It'd look good with a fieldstone foundation and shingled siding," he said, with clear approval. "What's this?" He pointed to an area where I'd scribbled *SEA VIEW*.

"A spot for a special bay window looking over the creek. You know, the creek goes to the river, and the river to the sea. So it's a sea view." I felt my face growing warm.

"I like it. I know the perfect window for it. I've got one in my inventory. It came out of a villa by the ocean. It's a huge oval with stained-glass trim by Tiffany."

I managed a tired laugh. "I think that would be worth more than my entire construction budget."

"Think big, Rose."

Silence. I stared at him. "Rose?"

He looked uncomfortable. "My mother gathered enough information to wonder about you intensely. I gave her a name to chew on. Sorry."

"No. I . . . I like it. It's all right."

He looked back down at the sketches. "If you want blueprints drawn, I can do them for you."

"You can?"

"I'm a civil engineer. That's architecture without the glamour." He'd leave for New York one day and never look back, but we both wanted to pretend we'd stay in touch. "I'll think about your offer," I said.

He broke a twig between his fingers and held the two pieces out. "Draw. Short end says we'll both get what we want."

I plucked a piece of twig from his fingertips. He held up his half. "Short end," he said. "We win."

I tossed my half away. "Never put your faith in wood. It rots."

"I'm putting my faith in *you*. You know what you've got here. You're holding onto a paradise by its short end, and you know it, and if you have to beg, borrow, kill or steal, you'll never let go. Liza ruffled your idea of home today, but it's still home."

The cool creek air, moss and remnants of fern and quieting autumn life, his appeal, this moment, his heartfelt words, filled me with sharp nostalgia for futures unknown. "Sometimes I think you like it here, yourself."

We were silent for a minute, his cool silver eyes boring into me, me staring back, hot-faced. "You believe that for both of us," he said softly. "I like the way you believe in things."

*

"Please talk to me," Liza said. She met me on the back porch.

I tossed my knapsack on a wall hook. "It's all right. You just caught me off guard. Sorry I hurt your feelings."

"Nobody could take your mother's place. Your father knew that. He and I never talked about marriage. I'm not making any claims, but I did love him—I still do—and I believe he loved me. I've come to think of this farm as *my* home, too."

I took a deep breath and said nothing. Daddy should have put her in his will, made his wishes clear. If only fathers would do that about everything their children still needed to know, to hear. *Dear Daughter, here are all the instructions I always meant to give you and all the things we needed to settle between us, so you can get on with your life and stop wishing we could talk to each other even one more time.*

Liza watched me worriedly. "He never forgave himself for what happened to your mother. I didn't take her place. She was always here, with us. I knew that." I sat down on the porch swing, and she sat down beside me. "He loved you so much. He understood your feelings."

"I couldn't change him. I shouldn't have tried. If you only love someone after they've changed to suit your tastes, then what did you love about them to begin with?"

"That's always the question, isn't it?" Her voice broke. "When I met him I knew I'd found a man who was true to himself. No false goodness. No false pride. Take it or leave it, he was the purest soul I've ever met. I work so closely with fire that I'm a little capricious about small burns. I have the scars to prove it, too." Her softening face constricted in sorrow. "Thomas was the only man I ever knew who didn't leave a single ugly mark."

"You'll always have a home, here. I'm sure that's what he'd want. But it's what I want, too."

Tears streamed down her face. She wiped them away and faced forward, pulling her hands into her lap. "I owe it to you to tell you about myself."

"No, there's no need—"

"I come from New Orleans. I was not a good person, there. I was a party girl when I was young, and I had a serious drug habit. I was married twice, both times to rich men who treated me badly, and I let them. I had a child with my second husband, but I was a drunk and a drug addict, and the baby died from complications. That changed me. I gave up everything. Even my real name. I wanted to be someone new."

After a moment I said, "How long ago?"

"It's been ten years."

"Did my father know all about your past?"

"Yes. I told him. He said—" her voice broke—"he said that was just an old layer of my life, one I'd painted over a long time ago. *It makes you who you are today*, he said. *And I love that person.*" She hesitated. "I thank you for taking a chance on me—and on the other tenants."

We sat in silence for a minute, letting everything sink in. I was still thinking about Quentin, too, with an uneasy feeling in the pit of my stomach. *If we could only hurry to the people we care about and tell them what amazes us about them, and how wrong they are to believe the worst. If they'd only listen.* "Are you glad to know about me?" Liza asked. "Or do you wish you'd gone on just wondering?"

"I already knew who you were."

"What do you mean?" She looked at me anxiously.

I got up. "You're the second woman my father loved. He didn't choose his loves lightly. That's all that's important."

The beatific look on her face said *thank you.*

*

The next day I knocked on Oswald's lurid pink door. Taking chances. Trying to believe in the people around me, as if I could build up steam to help Quentin.

Oswald appeared to feel as wary as I was. We sat across from each other on a plaid couch under one of his paintings, a huge naked woman standing in a cornfield. The ears of corn bore a distinct resemblance to penises. I pretended not to notice. "I have a manuscript for you." In my hands were the neatly transcribed pages of Dr. Washington's stories. I explained what they were about. "I want you to read these and let me know if you can illustrate them. You could start with a few trial sketches to see if we can come up with something that works."

He was nearly speechless. "Oh, hell, I'll give it a try," he said, finally. For all I knew he'd draw naked toddlers skewering monsters with sharpened crucifixes. But the next day he handed me a sheaf of sketches in which graceful black children played among the handsome farm setting of Dr. Washington' Bear Creek tales. When I showed the beautiful drawings to Dr. Washington and everyone else, we all looked at each other as if this new Oswald had emerged from some crusty shell, like a crayfish.

The world was changing.

*

It was time, Arthur decided, to share his secret with Esme, and see if she approved. Down in the creek bottoms one warm afternoon just after Thanksgiving, he and Esme sat on a large log, idly kicking piles of fallen leaves. Between them, spread on one of Mama's faded, hand-embroidered kitchen towels, perched the last of the peanut butter cookies Liza baked for their daily sojourn to the wilds. Esme darted flirtatious glances at him, knowing that when they both reached for the last cookie some handholding would ensue.

240

Suddenly she heard loud, rhythmic footsteps, and gave Arthur a worried look. "That's my heart beating for you," he answered with all the gravitas of a bad actor reciting a line. Quentin had told him that when he couldn't think of anything else to say, to say his heart was beating for her. Excited by the coming revelation, he stood, unafraid. No animal in his woods was frightening to him, or frightened of him. He knew, according to the legends, who and what had always lived in the hollow of Bear Creek.

The tall evergreen laurel began to wave wildly. Without any warning, a large female black bear and her cub shuffled from the thick green shield and halted, gazing at Arthur. He took the cookie from Esme's trembling hand, approached the bears without the least inhibition, broke the cookie into two pieces, and laid it on a rock. The mother and her cub ate the pieces eagerly. The female bear weighed several hundred pounds and easily could have mauled Arthur. Instead, she licked his hand. He scratched her behind the ears, then did the same with the cub.

Arthur returned to the log and sat down beside a wide-eyed Esme. "That's Granny Annie and her little boy," he explained calmly. "She found him." Spirit bears and real bears were the same, to him. All were Powell family. "Are you scared?" he asked Esme.

She looked up at him with trusting eyes. "Not if you tell me it's all right."

His chest swelled with pride. He sat down in the cushion of leaves, and Esme sat beside him. He put his arm around her, and then they kissed. "This is how you chase the bad Tweens away," he told her. "The bad Tweens got Mama Bear. We can't let them get Grannie Annie and her son."

Esme stared at the mother and cub. "What do you mean? What's going to happen to them?"

"I don't know, exactly. I just know bad things happen to bears when they get around people. Iron Bears and regular bears, too. We've gotta figure out how to save them."

She nodded earnestly. "I'll help." They bent their heads together.

So the bears had returned to Bear Creek—or had never left. We were converging on the sharpest winter in a decade, filled with the poignancy of endings and change, even more than winters usually are. I looked for my namesakes, Ursa Major and Minor, in the night skies. The constellations shifted into place, and so many paths, long forgotten or dreamed only in the hardest sleep, began to forge into one.

*

December arrived. Bear Two evolved into four paws and legs again, then disappeared, again. Quentin grew quieter and angrier, more frustrated every day.

Arthur kept his own vigil, hovering nearby while Quentin worked, listening feverishly as Quentin instructed him about women, life, and how to weld. Quentin built legs again, then took them down. This set was number five. We were all on edge now—me, Arthur, the tenants, and Quentin, worst of all. We got an early snow, just an inch or two, but it formed a nasty, icy slush. Quentin worked without stopping, his face and hands growing chapped, his breath making white clouds in the air, the muddy slush spattering the rubber boots he wore.

Four paws, four legs, and the beginnings of an underbelly emerged next, although none of it looking remotely like a bear. When she came to pick up Esme one day Janine gazed unhappily across the field, where the scene had taken on the appearance of a strange carnival. Sparks flew as Quentin finished cutting what was left of my sedan's axle apart. "Is he doing this just to prove that he can?"

"I don't think he has much choice. It's become an obsession."

"Well, it's sucking everyone else into its black hole." She sighed as we watched Esme and Arthur sitting together contentedly in the cab of Quentin' truck. "What are *they* doing?"

"Esme's been learning to drive it. They just go up and down the dirt road. One of us rides with them. She's actually progressed very well. She can shift gears like a pro."

"I don't understand why she has this fascination with mechanical things, but I suppose it's harmless."

"Better than playing with guns."

"Oh, we never give her any bullets."

"Isn't that sweet," I deadpanned.

She frowned. "Fuck you, and your growers' contract, too."

"Aren't you glad it's settled? It was a nice compromise. Admit it."

"It'll do. Daddy hates it, but he's resigned to the situation."

"How's he doing?"

"Not well. He's playing a lot of golf. He *hates* golf."

"You ought to find him something else to occupy his time."

She turned to me hotly. "Don't give me any more advice on running my family or my business. I've had your praises crammed down my throat since we were little girls, and since Mother died Daddy

242

has become your biggest fan. Mother was a snob, all right? He was just a rich, small-town nobody to her, and she always acted as if she'd married beneath herself. He adored her but she gave him a hard time about a lot of things—including his ties to your family. He wants to make up for keeping your family out of our social circle all those years. But you know what? *I don't give a shit*."

"Ditto, cousin. But look—we should be able to mend some fences, and get your daddy back to his old self."

"I'll work it out in my own way."

On that note, she marched over to the convoy truck, opened the driver door, and gazed up at Esme. "Breaker, breaker, Comeon," Janine drawled with exaggerated truck stop drama, as if talking over a CB radio. "Is that my cousin Esme at the wheel of that big rig? I don't believe it. Over."

Esme blinked in confusion. "I can drive this truck *anywhere*," she said merrily. "You'll be surprised."

She and Arthur smiled.

*

Just after sunset one evening not long before Christmas I began putting up ancient strands of holiday garland on the living room windows. My arms ached from stacking a ten-foot-tall mound of firewood on the back porch. I had ordered more propane for the room heaters and gotten out all the quilts. The house was filled with the scent of cornbread baking in the oven. Turnip greens simmered in a pot on the stove, with stewed apples in a casserole dish next to them. My omelet pan hung on a kitchen peg next to my grandmother's iron skillet. Liza was setting the table for dinner. I was trying to secure my nest not only for the winter, but against some unseen doom that haunted my thoughts.

"Come quick!" Arthur shouted. His eyes were glazed with fear as he dashed into the house. "Quentin's beating up his Bear!"

Liza and I ran outside. Quentin was slugging at the latest half-finished sculpture with a sledge hammer. Small pieces of metal flew in the fading light, but the larger sections were too strongly welded. He couldn't break apart something he'd built to outlast everything but his own frustration. He looked wild and enraged.

"Stop it," I ordered. "Quentin, I said *stop!*" He staggered to a halt like a beaten boxer, drenched in sweat, steam rising off him in the cold air, the long hammer hanging in his hands. "I'm starting over, again. Just stay out of my way."

Arthur began crying. "You're killing it. Killing it. And I *liked* this one. It's got good feet."

I put my arms around my brother. "He's not killing it. I'm going to talk to him and everything will be fine. Go in the house with Liza. Okay? Liza, take him inside and fix him some dinner. Don't let him come back out here tonight."

"Comeon, Honey," she crooned, and led Arthur away.

I hurried to Quentin and held out both hands. "Give me that sledge hammer."

"This one isn't working, either. Just leave me alone and I'll tear it apart like the others."

"You don't have any perspective, anymore. This sculpture is fine. You're the one who's being torn apart." I eased my hands between his and gripped the hammer's long handle. "I'm asking you to calm down and talk this over with me. Please."

His shoulders sagged. He tossed the heavy hammer aside, then sat down wearily on the concrete pad. I crouched in front of him and took his dirty, blistered hands tightly in mine. "You're making yourself sick over this. You've lost weight. You don't sleep right, you don't eat right, you've got half-healed welding blisters all over your arms. You look like hell and I haven't seen you smile in weeks."

His mouth crooked slightly beneath exhausted eyes. "Are you just trying to flatter me?"

"I'm sorry I ever agreed to this idea. It's destroying you."

"I haven't been killed by the damned sculpture—yet."

"Don't talk that way." My voice rose. I stared at him, suddenly understanding something. "You *want* it to hurt you. Quentin, why? What do you think you did to your father to deserve this guilt? What's happening to you out here?"

"I remember my father more every day." He spoke slowly, struggling. "Every goddamn day out here in the cold, every burn mark, every drop of sweat—he comes back to me a little more. Things he said, things he did when I visited him at his warehouse. Teaching me to play cards, telling me what to say to girls, teaching me honor and self-discipline, showing me how to be a man the way he believed a man should be."

"Good. Those are wonderful memories."

He shook his head. "I also remember him sitting in front of a fan on a hot day with his head in his hands, dripping sweat. He'd have little cuts all over his hands and blisters from the welding torch. And he'd sit there like he didn't have the energy to move. It wasn't just physical exhaustion. It was his heart. His soul."

He was also describing himself, lately. "You never realized how much his work took out of him?"

"Not the way I've learned by trying to copy him." He scrubbed a hand over his hair, and I noticed a burn welt at the edge of his forehead. He had welts and scrapes all over his hands and arms, too. "I'll be right back," I said. I ran to the house and returned with a can of udder balm. "You need teet salve," I said.

He stared at me then laughed darkly. "You think that heals everything."

"It's a start." I took his hands, one at a time, and massaged the thick ointment into them. I pretended to examine his palm.

"You read palms? What do you see?" He spoke with the acidic tone of a non-believer. I didn't believe in palm-reading either, but I took the opportunity to skewer him. "Fear of responsibility. Fear of commitment. Fear of sleeping with only one woman the rest of your life. The usual."

"No." He turned his hand inside mine, closed it around mine, and looked at me quietly. "Fear of dying," he corrected.

A heartbeat passed in measured silence. I said finally, "Tell me why."

"Men in my family die young. Always have. Killed in wars, or on the job—" he hesitated, a cynical appeal coming to his mouth—"Riconnis have a death wish, maybe. My father saved himself the trouble of wondering how he'd go. Have to give him credit for taking charge."

I stared at him. "If I believed—" I had to stop and clear the knot in my throat, and then I said loudly—"I have to believe there is a way to change a family's traditions, or fate, or stupid bad luck or poor judgment—whatever you want to call it. I *am* going to change my family's future. And you're going to change *yours*."

"As long as I work on the sculpture I've got a chance of understanding who my father was. Every time I tear down a sculpture and start over it's because *I still don't know.*"

"You may *never* understand why he killed himself."

He raised his head. His eyes burned into me. "You're wrong." He hesitated. The secret he'd held inside himself since he was eighteen years old had never been dragged out of him, before. *She deserves to know who I am*, he thought. "I broke his heart. *I killed him.*"

I went very still. "Tell me how." The story poured out of him. The woman who'd become his father's predatory mentor. His father's adultery. The unpaid bills, the struggle, the stolen cars. How it had all led to that confrontation in a cemetery, that brutal revelation of a son's loss of faith, and a father's tragedy. When he finished he sat with his head bowed. Relief coursed through me. I could comprehend guilt. I could help him.

I took his face between my hands, and lifted it. "There are so many times when I go off by myself and cry about *my* father. I hurt when I think about all the things I'll never get to say to him. I expect years from now I'll *still* hurt. It was like that with my mother. Even now— and it's been over twenty years—I pick up the phone in the kitchen sometimes and think, *I should have called the doctor.* It's something I have to live with. I asked Dr. L-J about that once, and she said, *Who told you you'd go through life with no unanswered questions and no regrets? Half the answer is learning to live with the questions.*

"You do your best, Quentin, you make mistakes, you learn, you go on stronger than before, so you don't make the same mistake, again. The trick is that we grow up telling ourselves we'll never make our *parents'* mistakes, but then we realize we're making a whole set of our *own*. Nobody warned us."

He shook his head. "I owe him."

"He owed *you*, too. It's not a matter of who made mistakes, of who hurt the other. It just happened."

"I can't tell my mother. I've never told her what I said to him. And I never want her to know about the woman. But because of that, she can't understand why I don't worship my father the way she does. That secret's been a wall between us since I was a boy."

"All you have to tell her is that you *do* worship your father. Because it's true." Denial rose in his eyes. I went on quickly. "Everything you're doing here is for *him*."

"No," he said quietly. "It's for you."

I kissed him. It was quick and easy, a soft press of my lips against his mouth, then drawing back. He shut his eyes then opened them slowly, savoring me. I saw nothing to promise that one word I'd spoken had changed his feelings, but I kissed him, again. "You're wrong," I whispered. "But I like the way you believe it."

We stood. The light of a rising moon cast mysterious shadows from the Iron Bear and its tormented, half-finished companion, their shapes as unfathomable as the destiny that had brought us together. There was only one way Riconnis and Powells would ever have met in

246

the world, and we stood before it. Our future was evolving or ending. We could not know which, that night.

He and I went into each other's arms, and after awhile we walked together to the tent. He built a fire in the pot-bellied stove. I pulled the covers back on his bed. The night was closing in, it would be cold, but not between us. He came to me. I put my hands on his shoulders, his on my waist, then sliding around me. I hadn't answered his dilemma, I'd only opened a door to answers which might never come. I knew that. "Make it easy to forget," he ordered in a low voice.

"You do the same for *me*," I whispered.

We made love like thieves after pleasure has become its own kind of stolen virtue. He moved over me and I moved over him, our hands linked, our breath rough and sweet, sometimes intensely silent, at others whispering commands and compliments. All during that long, turbulent night it *was* easy to forget there would be hard decisions.

The second sculpture would never be finished. I wouldn't let Quentin try, anymore. I didn't know what I'd say to Arthur, or how he'd react.

All I knew, throughout that night, was that I loved Quentin Riconni and I would always love him, even when he left me.

23

The mother bear and her cub had come to some understanding with Arthur, who told them it was time for them to move where they'd be safe. Quentin's misery and violence toward the second sculpture confirmed the plan. This was no place for bears.

And so, under the light of the moon, during some brief period when Quentin and I slept with the stove-fire crackling and quilts pulled over us like a cocoon that muffled all sound, Arthur coaxed the bear and her cub into the covered back of the convoy truck. Soon Esme trundled down the dirt road behind the toy-like lights of her golf cart. Carrying a knapsack with her gun and a package of cookies in it, she kissed him, then climbed, trembling, into the truck's driver seat. He settled beside her and squeezed her hand.

"It's a long way," he admitted.

She swallowed hard. "But we'll be fine. And the bears will be fine, too. And after we do this, everybody will know that we're a man and a woman. Not idiots."

They drove very slowly, carrying their precious cargo away from Bear Creek.

*

He was not the same man. Quentin knew that, even if the change was too new to be examined. A foundation had been put in place but needed more time to settle into its full strength. Still, he had a deep sense of focus and structure that suddenly felt right. *I want to wake up like this every morning,* he thought. *With her.*

"I need to go back to the house before Arthur gets up," I whispered. I was already half dressed when Quentin stirred and opened his eyes. Dawn had begun to seep through the tent's translucent canvas. "If I go now, he won't realize I spent the entire night with you. You come to the house in a little while and eat breakfast with us. All right?"

He sat up, exposing an irresistible expanse of darkly-haired chest and stomach. I trailed a hand down the center and he grasped it, tugging. "Get back in bed and give me thirty more minutes," he ordered in that gruff, seductive voice men have when they're sleepy and aroused.

Sisterly duty warred with womanly need. Both won. I unbuttoned my flannel shirt, watching him watch the movement of my fingers.

"Give me fifteen minutes," I countered with a seductive voice of my own, "and make it as good as thirty."

When I finally returned to the house I found two items Arthur had laid prominently on the kitchen table, as a message. One was a magazine picture of several black bears. The other was *The Incredible Journey*. It lay open on my table, just as Arthur had left it at the beginning of the year, in Atlanta.

I raced upstairs to confirm that my brother was not in his bed, then, bile rising in my throat, I shoved his bedroom window up and yelled for Quentin, the tenants, the whole world, to come and help me find him before something godawful happened, again.

*

"Bear tracks. Big bear. Little bear. I'm picturin' a mama and cub." The sheriff's tracker squatted over the paw prints that led up the dirt road and disappeared behind the imprint of the truck's rear tires. "Arthur led them up here and got them in the truck somehow."

Janine spoke loudly and with growing horror. "*And then Esme drove out of here with the truck full of bears?*" Deputies, forest rangers, Tibers and neighbors were crowded around us on the road. Mr. John had collapsed with chest pains when he discovered that Esme was missing in the middle of the night. He'd been taken to the hospital. Janine looked as if she might explode. She whirled toward me. "My cousin is somewhere in these mountains on a public road driving a four-ton vehicle *with bears in the back.*"

I looked at her wearily. "Quentin and I searched the main roads heading north out of the county right after I called the sheriff. Esme and Arthur made it that far with no problem. I'm sure they're driving slow, and it's just a matter of spotting them."

"What makes you think they've gone north?"

"He's taking those bears to higher ground. That's the only direction he'd go."

"But you have no idea when he and Esme left. They could be halfway to Virginia by now! Or down a ravine where no one's noticed the wreck, yet!"

That mental image, which I'd been trying to avoid, weakened my knees and sent the blood rushing from my head. Quentin caught me by one elbow and steered me out of the crowd. "The sheriff's organizing his own search. He's already called for help in other districts. There's nothing else we can do here. We need to get on the road again and look for ourselves."

"Quentin, I don't have a clue where he'd take those bears."

"We'll figure it out. Your brother's methodical. He has his patterns, and so does Esme. Come on."

We climbed into Daddy's truck. I called to Liza out the open passenger window. "We're going to find Arthur."

She ran over. "*How?*"

I shook my head. "Patterns."

*

Several hours later we'd traversed the length of two main routes that led across the rugged mountains between Tiberville and North Carolina without seeing any sign of the convoy truck. "Esme would never take a highway, or the interstate," Quentin said. "She's not that brave." He swung the pick-up into a convenience store lot and refilled the gas tank. I got out.

I leaned against the truck's hood scouring a map of the mountains I spread there, while I gulped a carton of milk Quentin forced on me. He leaned over the map, too, and began tracing lines with his fingertips. His eyes narrowed in concentration. *How does Arthur think? How does he hold his world together? What connects his spaces?*

I pounded a fist on the map. "There are too many back roads into these mountains."

He pushed my fist aside and planted his fingertip on Tiberville. "Help me find Bear Creek on this map. Does it show it?"

"No, but I have a county map that does." I retrieved that map from beneath the truck's seat and spread it on the hood. Quentin bent over it, pulled his knife from a trouser pocket, opened the blade, and used it as a pointer. "This is the creek, this blue line?"

"Yes. Why?"

"All of Arthur's landmarks direct him back to the creek. He's shown me his method when we walk in the woods. It's how he never gets lost on the farm. He can get lost anywhere else, but not there. He uses the creek like a compass."

"I don't understand your point."

He traced the curving line north to the map's edge. "Bear Creek doesn't originate in Tiber County?"

"No, it comes from a spring in—" I halted, thinking. My heart raced. I pulled the county map aside and frantically searched the larger one. I gasped and planted my finger on a spot far from where we were. "A spring high in the Ridge Mountains." I looked at Quentin. "And Arthur's been there, before."

He kissed me on the forehead. "*Patterns.* Let's go."

*

"Yeah, I noticed that big ol' army truck in the woods back yonder when I got here this morning," the grizzled proprietor of the Ridge Mountain Grocery told us. He spoke through a wad of chewing tobacco, as he shuffled a box of computer discs atop his store counter. His laptop computer, perched on an antique barrel with *Lula Brand Stone Ground Grits* still visible on its side, displayed the bloody screensaver for some violent, medieval video game. "I was planning on calling the law to look into it," he mentioned as he continued sorting his CD ROMs, "but I hadn't took the time, yet. Too busy playing a few rounds of Dragon Quest with a network of ol' boys up in Canada."

We told him the truck belonged to Quentin, and we'd be back for it, later. "I thought it was part of some kind of army maneuver," the store owner called as we walked out. "Cause the army brings their ranger boys up here to train." He guffawed. "I get their schedule from a feller down in Florida who sneaks a peek at the camp commander's e-mail."

I pointed to a narrow, rutted trail heading up the side of the mountain. "Take that jeep trail," I told Quentin. He steered Daddy's ancient, protesting truck up a path that left the paved road and all pretense of normal travel behind. We crested a plateau and the road vanished. Around us was nothing but forest. A deer path no wider than our shoulders led off along a shoulder of hills. "This is as far as we can drive. Now it's about a six-mile walk due east to the site of the spring. It'll take us a good two hours."

"Let's go, then."

We hiked east. The December day was cold and clear, the temperature only in the low forties according to a thermometer I'd noticed outside the store. We were in some of the highest mountains in the state, too, and when we cut across exposed ridges a brittle wind hit us. We both wore thick jackets and gloves, but I had to cover my exposed ears with my hands . In contrast to our grim and hurried mood the views were serene and stunning, the mountains falling asleep for the winter under their mantel of gray and evergreen.

The morning was gone and the sun was heading west by the time we entered the deep glen I remembered. In the center, canopied by the graceful green fingers of tall firs, a spring bubbled among jumbled boulders. The air was damp, clean, and cold. Ferns, sheltered from the frost, gently brushed our legs as we walked. The mountains' steep namesake ridges rose around the glen as if it were the center stage of a theater. It was a perfect place for elves and bears.

Arthur and Esme clambered down from a rock and ran to us, smiling. The bear and her cub ambled along after them. "Why did you do this?" I asked, as they threw their arms around us.

"We wanted to show people we could do something important," Esme explained. "I drove and read the map and Arthur remembered how to follow the trail here!" It *was* amazing to realize that my brother had gone on this adventure and even now looked very relaxed about being so far from home.

"I'm a man of the world," he proclaimed. Then, with a joy that only the outcast creatures can know, he said simply, laying a hand over his heart, "I won't be lost, anymore."

A shiver of pride and excitement crested down my spine. Granny Annie has finally found her little boy and brought him home. After all these years.

*

The four of us sat on a rock ledge beside the spring, watching the mother and cub. Arthur sighed. "Grannie Annie will still be living on Bear Creek, up here. It's her home. And she'll be safe from the bad Tweens."

Quentin said quietly, "Brother Arthur, I know I scared you, yesterday."

Arthur looked at him sadly. "You're building a Bear you don't even like. But you shouldn't kill it."

"I know. Maybe I'm not meant to build your Mama Bear a friend."

"Maybe not." He paused, his mouth trembling. He took Esme's hand and clutched it for support. "I can live without Mama Bear, if she needs to go to New York."

Done. After all we'd gone through, he sat proudly at the head of Bear Springs, having rescued our bear legacy on his own and put an end to months of uncertainty. Quentin could go, now. Buy the Iron Bear and take it to New York. Never come back. I froze, inside, and couldn't make myself look at Quentin's face.

"Am I still Brother Bear?" Quentin asked him quietly.

Arthur nodded. "You'll always be Brother Bear."

The bear and cub lay down beside the spring. Esme said, "This is a good place for bears, isn't it?"

I recovered enough to carry on as if the strangest victory didn't taste like defeat. "They'll be fine. They have lots of water, lots of oaks full of acorns, and meadows covered in blackberries. There are caves near here, too."

Arthur looked at them sadly. "I wish we could visit them."

"You don't have to. Granny Annie will always be watching over us. That's what Daddy told us, and he was right."

Tears crested in his eyes, but he nodded. "And it's easy to follow the creek home when you're lonely."

In the poignant silence that followed, Quentin looked at me and said, "That's what we need to do, sometimes. Just go home." I had no idea how he meant that. I was dying, inside. He put an arm around Arthur. "Let's get back to the rest of the world before they decide we're *all* lost."

Esme shook her head. "We've been trying to leave, but the bears won't let us."

Arthur nodded vigorously. "They keep following us! I been trying to talk them out of it for a long time, but so far they don't understand that this is their home, now."

"I told them they already ate *all* the cookies from my knapsack," Esme explained. "And I even put it on top of that big rock over there so they'd stop thinking about it." She squealed as the cub suddenly clambered up that rock and headed straight for her sack. He flopped down with the bag between its paws and began chewing on some bulky object inside. "My little gun's in there!" Esme cried. "He could get hurt!"

"It's not loaded," I soothed.

"Yes, it is! I didn't think I'd have to shoot anybody, but I thought I might need a few bullets."

"Jesus Christ," Quentin said. The cub lay on the rock directly in front of us. He wrestled with the knapsack and gnawed the loaded revolver. Quentin rose to his feet slowly. "Everybody up—don't startle the cub—and move out of the line of fire."

I pulled Esme to her feet, while he urged Arthur. "Run, over there," Quentin said, pointing. Arthur grabbed Esme hand and took off. Quentin whirled toward me, deliberately putting himself between me and the cub as he reached out to grab my hand. Too late. Fate, destiny, or simply the doomed chances in our combined legacy had finally found us.

The bear cub bit down just so, and the gun fired.

Quentin staggered but didn't fall. I heard the bullet zip by my left arm, and I saw the right side of Quentin's jacket move as if a hand had slapped it from inside.

Esme screamed. She and Arthur dropped to their haunches and held each other. Quentin and I traded a look of stunned disbelief. His expression conveyed dark wonder, at first. *So this is how it's meant to happen.* He reached inside his jacket and brought his hand out, covered in blood. "I should have known I'd be shot by a bear," he said.

I launched myself at him, snatching the jacket open and uttering a garbled cry as I saw the neat hole and its bloody apron in his flannel shirt, just below his rib cage. The bullet had hit him in the back and passed all the way through.

"Sit down," I ordered, and it scared me when he did so without arguing, his knees buckling. I slid an arm around him too keep him from falling. We slumped on the ground together. My mind blank, all I could think of was *Put pressure on the wound,* a tidbit I recalled from every shoot-em-up novel I'd ever read. I unbuttoned his shirt and gagged when I saw the small, pulsing wound on his right side. When I reached around his back I found blood there, too, and when I looked I found the entry wound on his right side, as neat as a hole bored into metal. I leaned into him with a hand pressed tightly to each spot.

His eyes were half-shut. The pain had hit. Arthur crawled over to us. There was blind terror in his stare. "Brother Bear," he whispered. Behind him, Esme moaned and sobbed. Quentin scowled at him. "Brother *Arthur!* Get up off your knees. Get up. Don't forget everything I taught you. You've got to be a man, remember?" Arthur wobbled to his feet. He trembled and looked at me wildly.

"Go back to the store where you left the truck," I told him. "Walk as fast as you can, but don't forget to pay attention to the trail—don't get lost. Tell the man at the store that we need help, and show him where we are on the map. Esme, you help him. I know you two can do it, together. I'll take care of Quentin. Now go. Go!"

He whirled and ran to Esme, helped her to her feet, and they disappeared down the trail at a trot. My ears still rang with the gunshot, but now the electric drone of fear joined it. Quentin and I were alone. Only seconds had passed in that convulsive moment of time. Breathing hard, Quentin said, "You should go with them. They'll get lost."

"No. He'll find the way back, and he'll get help. He couldn't have done it six months ago, but now you've taught him how to take care of himself—now he's pretending to be *you*, and that part of him is going to take care of you."

"I'm telling you, you better leave me and go help him—"

"I'm not leaving you. Have some faith."

"I don't like the way you believe in things at the moment," he said.

I wouldn't admit that I had visions of Arthur panicking and Esme sinking into total hysterics, both of them lost, wandering, while Quentin lay at the start of the Bear Creek waters, his blood slipping down that path to the ocean, some unimaginable fate bleeding him to death to ensure the futility of Riconni and Powell destinies. I felt his blood seeping between my fingers already, and I kissed him desperately.

Even the bears had disappeared.

24

I don't want to leave her, he was thinking.

I helped him walk to a high meadow nearby, where I could build a fire. He lay down on a bed of leaves I pushed together and put on a good show of comfortable lounging, drawing up one knee, draping his left hand atop his stomach. Neither of us said much. *Admit nothing worse can happen, and it won't.* "Stings a little," he lied, when I asked him how badly he hurt. His face was white, his teeth clenched whenever I caught him unawares. When I touched him, his skin was too cool.

I pulled off my coat and then my wool shirt, which I cut apart with a pocket knife. As I bound him around the middle with long strips of the material, he pretended to admire my thin undershirt. "Hey, no bra the next time I get shot." His voice was strained.

"I'll strip and dance naked if the distraction will stop your bleeding."

"I'll take you up on that when I feel better."

I pulled a rotten log to his feet. "Prop your feet up. It does something good for your circulation. I can't remember what." I could barely remember my own name, at that point.

"Keeps blood going to the heart," he supplied. "Why don't you get a fire going, and then hike out of here? I'll be fine. See if you can catch up with Arthur and Esme."

"Because the fire won't last without me tending it." *And neither might you*, I didn't say.

I put my coat over him but he pushed it aside. "You'll freeze. Put that back on."

"I'm moving around, and I'm perfectly warm. Who's the nurse, here?"

"I'm the one who knows why blood flows downhill. Now put on your coat and get that fire started, and get out of here."

I dropped to my knees beside him and took his face between my hands. "Goddammit, will you stop saying that? Do you *want* to be left alone?"

"I don't want you to watch me die."

I could see memories in his eyes, see his father in a pool of blood. Riconni's had a knack for dying in combat, dying in accidents, putting guns to their own chests in despair. Powells had a knack for fading away. Disappearing, wandering off, daydreaming into nothingness. But not this time—not for him, and not for me. I bent my head to his. "I'm not going to watch you die. You're not *going* to die. You're not."

When I drew back he whispered, "Just because I want you to leave me doesn't mean I want to leave *you*."

I took him by his shirt collar with fierce hands and kissed him as I tugged the collar closed and buttoned it. "Don't look back and don't look ahead," I ordered. "Just stay right here."

I put my coat over him then scratched leaves, twigs, and fallen branches into a pile. He fumbled a cigar lighter from his pants pocket and gave it to me. I got a small flame going and rushed around the perimeter of trees, picking up fallen limbs, snapping the smaller branches off trees, gleaning every source of fuel I could find. "I'm going to build the biggest bonfire in ten counties," I promised. "It'll warm you up and send a signal. Park rangers will notice before long. You just rest."

He shut his eyes. I watched him for a long minute, then looked at the deepening afternoon sky. I calculated it would take Arthur and Esme at least two hours to walk back to the road and the store. Then some time for them to explain to the man playing Internet games, and time for him to call for help, and for that help to mobilize. Then another two hours for rescuers to reach us on foot. A total of at least five hours. It would be dark, then. Five hours of Quentin bleeding in the cold, maybe bleeding to death.

And he knew it.

Memento mori. Remember that you are mortal.

*

"There are things I have to say," he whispered. I huddled beside him with my head on his shoulder and one arm over his chest to keep him and myself warm. A part of me wanted to shush him, to ward off doom by not acknowledging the possibility. He turned his head. His lips moved against my face. "I love you," he said.

Pearls of cold sunshine, fading on the horizon, clustered in my veins. To have him say that, the promise in those words, was the hardest joy I'd ever known. The world had no fairness in it, if we had come to this point only to end. I tightened my arm over him and pressed my face close to his. "And I love you. I've loved you since the day you carried me out of my own barn."

"I wish we'd had longer."

I lifted my head and looked down at him, begging. "Don't say that. You're going to be fine. There are certain things I *won't listen to you say*."

"I look ahead, I see you there. I look behind me, I see you. You're inside me, you're around me. I've never had that before, not with anyone." He paused, searching my eyes. "Would you have married me?"

"Yes." Crying hard, I kissed him. "And I *will* marry you. *I will*."

"Tell my mother I love her. She's my rock. I never went too far away for her to bring me back. I don't want her to die over this. You tell her. Tell her to *live*. To marry Alfonse. Yes. She has to marry Alfonse. My dying wish. He'll take care of her."

"You tell her, yourself."

"Tell everyone else I loved them. The man I told you about—the old sarge? Popeye. Tell him. Whoever you think ought to hear it. Tell them. Even if you're not sure I do. Use your own judgment. Take care of Hammer. I want him to stay with you. And treat Arthur like a man. Don't forget."

"I can't listen to any more of this." I hunched closer to him.

"You tell them," he insisted, kissing my eyes, my nose, my mouth as I moved my face to catch his caress. "How I know what love is, now."

*

Several hours later he had almost stopped talking, opening his eyes occasionally only when I insisted, growing paler, his skin so cold, even though I kept the fire going. I was freezing, then sweating, in agony and fear, my clothes splotched with Quentin's blood, my hands scratched raw, my face singed with careless fervor each time I poked and prodded the bonfire.

Dusk was falling and I had searched every easy area around us for limbs to burn. Sometime after dark, if no help had come by then, the fire would go out. I lay down beside Quentin, again, burrowing under my coat, wrapping my arms around him.

"Ursula," he said in a voice so weak I could barely hear it. I leaned over him anxiously. "I'm here," I promised. I'm *here*." He opened his eyes. The distance in them—seeing too far away, then focusing on me with effort—terrified me. A look of wonder spread over his face. "*I understand why he did it*."

Tears slid down my face. Now he heard his father's voice whispering to him in the fading light. I didn't want him to listen, I didn't want him to follow that voice. "Hold on, Quentin, please. Please don't give up. Please. He isn't telling you to stop fighting, the way he did. He wouldn't do that. He wants you to live."

"He thought he . . . set us free. No more loving him. No more pain."

I forced back a sob. "He was wrong. The love never ends. Do you hear me? The love never ends. You know that, now."

He shut his eyes, frowning, then relaxing. I frantically pressed my hand over his heart. My hands had gone numb with cold. I couldn't feel his heartbeat, or maybe I could. *There.* No? *I can't be sure. Oh, god.* He would die, drift away, and be gone before I even realized.

Panic began to take over. Fear crawled into my mind and assumed dark shapes, and I began talking out loud to drive those shapes away—promising to embarrass him with peculiar grief rituals if he died, loudly detailing each and every one. Then I began to describe the children that would never be born unless he lived.

"The first one will be a girl," I told him. "We'll name her Angela Grace—no, wait, that sounds like a stripper for Jesus, but I'm trying to use your mother's name. Our second daughter will be named after my mother—Victoria. Okay, that can be her middle name, although I wouldn't mind calling her Vick. Vick, not Vicki. Let's go back to Angela Grace. She'll have a temper. We'll have to teach her not to clobber her Tiber cousins. She'll be smart. I start reading to her right away. And you'll teach her how to see patterns in people and places and barn roofs. She'll grow up to be an engineer. But as for Vick, Vick Riconni will be the quiet type, very sensitive, an artist, like her grandfathers . . ."

Five children. Ten. Fifteen. My teeth chattered; I was croaking out words in a voice like an old woman's, and finally sagged to a halt. I touched his icy lips. His face was so peaceful. The sun was setting, the sky splashed with the deepest gold, purple, and pink, the bonfire lifting sparks into the first stars of the night, fireflies floating away, like his life. Reality became garbled with despair.

Concentrate, concentrate—hold him there with magnetic obsession, the weight of tears, the force of love, link my pulse to his, be inside him and close the torn place, this man I had come to love so completely. A thousand ancestors had sacrificed to bring us to this point. Our fathers must be watching, listening, and they could not let it end like this, I wouldn't let him die. *Concentrate.*

I heard something, and lifted my head. I saw two gleaming eyes creep over the rim of the world, parallel and focused on us, on Quentin, in the dusk, and around them a shape, round and earthen, dark, rising against the sunset. A ghost, or real. A spirit we couldn't escape. Annie searching, still, for her own kind? Life, or death? I shielded Quentin ferociously and looked back over my shoulder with enraged terror, daring the mysterious vision to be real. *I won't let him go. I've always known you were out there—and he knows, too. But now it's different, we're different together.*

I screamed a challenge, and heard a roar in return. The dark, ursine head and fateful eyes rose higher, swinging up over the horizon, becoming a great, lumbering Iron Bear, my namesake constellation, Ursa Major, coming to life to hunt for life, climbing down from the sunset, hovering, growling, singing deep songs in the firmament of night.

And then, *transformed.*

I realized blades of steel, the whir of a giant engine, the slow settling of a machine. The helicopter sank to earth as gently as any butterfly. Arthur had found angels with metal wings.

Just in time, they said later. Just in time.

*

I stood like a statue outside the waiting room of the intensive care ward. A nurse had given me a set of green scrubs to replace my bloody clothes, and Liza had brought me a sweater, before hurrying back to the farm to care for Arthur and Esme. They were shaken but all right. Tibers had invaded Bear Creek. Everyone celebrated Arthur and Esme's intrepid hearts—sweet saints, rescuers, the keepers of all bear-kind. For Quentin, they prayed.

I heard footsteps coming around the corner from the elevator. Two pairs, moving quickly. A tall, stately, white-haired man in a suit and long coat rounded the corner. He held the arm of a slender yet straight-backed woman with graying brunette hair. Her heavy black coat swung open as she maneuvered a brass-handled cane to assuage her limp. Quentin had told me, once, that his mother never let the leg slow her down.

I met her desperate, searching eyes as she came to me with one hand outstretched. We knew each other immediately. I grasped her hand in both of mine. "He's not awake, yet. They say it'll be morning before we can talk to him."

"I have to see him."

"I'll take you."

"I'll wait here," the man said with quiet dignity. This must be Alfonse Esposito, I thought. She turned to him. "No, you come, too. You're family. He needs you. And I . . . I need you, too."

A gleam came into his eyes. He accompanied us down the hall and through the double doors of the intensive care ward. One of my Tiber cousins, a nurse who headed the ward, gave me a discreet nod that said visiting hours didn't apply to one of her own. We eased into the tiny room where Quentin lay, connected to a spider web of tubes and machines. He'd been through surgery and slept now in some deep state below dreams.

He looked terrible, I knew. Ghostly white, with an oxygen canula taped beneath his nose and all those machines recording his life forces as if the technology controlled him. Angele's small hand clenched mine, then released. She uttered a soft sound of despair. I stood back, with Alfonse.

She leaned her cane against the bed as she moved to Quentin's side. Her hands trembling, she touched his face and stroked his hair. "Do you know how much I love you?" she said. "And what a good son you are? No, you don't know, because I haven't told you since you were a boy. Forgive me, *forgive me.*" She kissed his forehead then laid her cheek against it. Her voice faded into a fervent whisper. "You *will* live. You *are* your father's son, and he knows what you've been trying to do for him the past few months. He's so proud of you. And so am I. Quentin." She lifted her head and, crying, looked down at him. "*Your mother and your father love you. We're a family, again.*"

*

"Do you hate me for getting him into this?" I asked her during that long night, as we sat in the waiting room.

"His papa got him into this," she answered quietly. Then she reached out and cupped my chin in her hand, turned my face toward her, and added softly, "You got him out." Her eyes filled with tears, and she smiled. "Hello, Rose."

I shut my eyes, and she pulled my head to her shoulder. I curled my feet under me and sat there like a child. A little while later, Mr. John walked into the room. Angele and I straightened, gazing at him in disbelief. He wore only a blue hospital gown, white socks, and a thin robe with a Tiber Poultry logo on it. One of the disconnected wires of his heart monitor trailed over the neck of his gown. Within a minute, frantic nurses would track him down.

I introduced him to Angele. He clasped her hand and bowed over it gallantly.

"How is Quentin doing?" he asked me gently.

"We're waiting for him to wake up, and that probably won't be until sometime tomorrow."

"He'll live. He's strong. No doubt like his father." He cleared his throat. "It takes a long time for me to learn anything new. I can't say that I'm not impressed by the turn our Bear has taken, in terms of money value. But it's more than that. People are devoted to the thing, and I seem to be on the wrong side of that crowd. I can't say I'll ever love the sculpture, but I do love what it represents to the people I care about." He held out a hand to Angele, again. "I sincerely hope you'll forgive me for any wrong I've done to the sculpture and your husband's memory. And I'm praying that Quentin will be all right."

She took his hand in both of hers, raised it a little, and gave it a hard squeeze of acceptance. "I accept for Richard. And for our son."

Mr. John turned toward me. "I wish your daddy were here tonight."

"Daddy knows what you want to say to him, and so do I." I got up and hugged him. "It's all right." Mr. John looked at me with a pensive smile and tears in his eyes. "I'm getting smarter," he said. "Some people see the light, but that wasn't good enough for me." He paused. *"I had to see the bear."*

I smiled. We heard the cardiac nurses running up the hall. Two of them passed the waiting room door, spotted him, and wheeled around. "Mr. Tiber!" one said sternly. "We're going to handcuff you to your bed!"

"You've been busted," I said.

"Oh, well." Mr. John looked at me with a trace of jaunty freedom. He chortled when the nurses grabbed him.

*

When Quentin woke up the next afternoon I was beside him, waiting. I leaned over him, kissing his forehead, his nose, his mouth, and then his mouth, again, lightly. He blinked in sleepy confusion, shut his eyes for the next kiss, and opened them with a frown at the confused sensations. I murmured his name, stroked his face, told him where he was, and how he was, and what had happened on the mountain. He never took his eyes off me, but I could see him going back and forth in the channels of memory, trying to rebuild those lost hours. The doctors had warned me that people who came so close to dying could be affected in profound ways.

"If you're lost, I'll help you find your way home," I promised, frightened but trying to remain calm.

"Home," he whispered. The web of confusion cleared from his eyes and suddenly he returned, warm and fully alive, looking up at me as if I'd been gilded with a miracle, too. "People won't get to gossip," he murmured. I realized he meant I couldn't embarrass him, as I'd vowed to do by the fire. He was alive, and he planned to stay that way.

"Oh, they'll *still* talk about you," I vowed with tearful reproach, then laughed, cried, and kissed him. This time he kissed me back. I saw my reflected devotion in his faint smile, the kindness in his raw-boned face and features, so pale and tired, his jaw covered with dark beard stubble, the blue circles under his eyes saying he'd been on a long, hard trip but come back home wiser. He was once again nobody's beauty but mine, and I'd take him, then and always.

25

It's a blessing to know who you love, and where you belong, and what you're willing to die for. Wonderful pieces can be salvaged from damaged hopes, and new foundations can be created from even the saddest memories.

He had come back from the mountaintop.

We all had.

I took Angele to the farm, and we walked across the pasture. "Oh, Richard," she said brokenly, happily, as she looked up at the Iron Bear. "Quentin is recuperating in a hospital room filled with flowers and cards from the people who've come to know him, here. They've brought gifts and food to him. They've showered him with love. And they've told *me* how much they've come to respect him in such a short period of time. They've told me their stories about Bare Wisdom, too—what it means to them. It has a purpose here, Richard. It is a *marvel*. It represents everything you ever wanted your work to be. It's changed people's lives. It's where it belongs. I've decided it *must* stay here." She hesitated, then reached over and took my hand. She gave me a look of deep affection before she gazed up at the sculpture, again. "And our son will stay here, too. He's found someone to love, someone very special. And now, this is where *he* belongs."

*

We rested before fireplaces and under deep cover through a cold, beautiful winter spiced with more snow than usual. I put a king-sized bed in my room at the farmhouse, and the bed filled the small room from wall to wall with its snug warmth, its comfort, its love. Quentin's bullet wounds became pink dimples on his right side, front and back, just below his rib cage. I couldn't help thinking that some giant animal had taken him in its teeth, tasted him, then let him go.

He settled into the farmhouse as easily as any Powell ever had, and became as comfortable a sight for visitors. The house loved him, and he loved it back. Like my omelet pan hanging next to my grandmother's iron skillet, he thrived in the spirit of progress. The old sergeant, Popeye, showed up with suitcases and crates, including the Tiffany window, which we set up on the back porch to admire.

"What am I supposed to do up in New York without you, Captain?" he asked Quentin. "And have you got *any idea* what the hell *you're* gonna do with yourself down here?"

"I was thinking of renting a warehouse in the industrial park John Tiber's building outside town. Maybe collecting a few salvage knickknacks to re-sell."

"You gonna start your business all over?"

"Not unless I've got an assistant to help run it and yell at me when I try to carry too heavy a load."

"Rent your warehouse, then, because I'm your man and I'm hired." Popeye returned to New York to care for the mill building and its tenants for the rest of the winter. Quentin would keep that property and find a manager to handle it for him. He would never leave his struggling tenants, those young artists, with no reasonable place to live and work. He would put a plaque outside the building. *Ars gratia artis.* Art for the sale of art alone. And beneath those words. *In Memoriam, Richard Ricconi.*

As he grew strong again, so did I. I unpacked boxes filled with Mama's old canning jars stacked in the storage room. When I opened a jar of green beans that Daddy had cooked the summer before he died I dipped my fingers into them and ate a pliable, tender green piece, crying and smiling. Daddy and Mama were still with me, a warm hug in the kitchen, a wise whisper in my ear; they provided food for me again, now that I had finally come home in spirit as well as body.

On a day in March when the weather was clear, Quentin and I drove back to the spring on Ridge Mountain, taking Arthur and Esme with us. We saw tracks, but the mother bear and her cub did not find us, or we, them. "You think they're afraid of people after what happened with that gun?" Quentin asked.

I nodded. "I hope so, for their sake."

"They'll be safe because they're scared of us?" Arthur asked, his face wistful.

I put an arm around him. "They'll be safe because you and Esme took care of them. And they know what's best, because of you."

"Being a man is hard, sometimes," he said, but then Esme smiled at him, and he was reassured.

We left them pondering a squirrel's nest high in a white pine. Quentin took my hand, and we walked to the meadow where we'd waited for rescue. He dropped to his heels and prodded traces of the charred logs from my bonfire. "Seems like forever," he said.

"It was."

He pulled me down beside him and we sat with our arms around each other, looking out over the mountains. "This was a helluva place for a marriage proposal," he said. "Why don't I ask you again?"

I watched the winter sun, dazzled by the day's brightness, then turned my face toward him and shared that sunshine in my eyes. "I'm waiting."

"Ursula Powell, will you marry me?"

He got the same answer as before, and this time, he smiled.

*

When the first purple crocuses peeked out of the ground in late February Quentin ordered a load of lumber and built a twenty-foot-tall screen around the half-finished Bear Two. "I'm going to finish it, but I don't want an audience," he admitted. He put on his welding mask, and began, very slowly and patiently, to work and rework the sculpture, now hidden behind a pale wall of pine board.

Angele hurried down from New York. She and I decided to say nothing, just to wait and see how he progressed. She sported a small engagement ring on her left hand. "Getting engaged at my age," she said grimly, shaking her head at the enormity of it. "What am I thinking?"

"Some day you'll be a grandmother," I promised. "You have to set a good example."

"I'll tell my grandchildren their grandpapa would say, *Never give up what you love*. Any of it. Never give up."

"It's a deal," I said softly.

I spent the last of winter with Angele, Liza, Arthur, and Esme by my side, and all of us watched over Quentin. Most days we sat by the Iron Bear or shivered under the oaks as we listened to the hiss of his welding torch and the clank of metal behind the screen he'd built. On days when I sat out there alone I passed the time reading and making notes on Dr. Washington's Bear Creek stories.

I sent a copy of those stories to Dr. Washington's son and daughter in Boston, and one day in April he looked up from his morning coffee to find two airport limos delivering his children and grandchildren to him. He excitedly brought them over to the farm the next afternoon, and they had tea with us.

"What is *that?*" the grandchildren exclaimed when they saw the Iron Bear in the pasture.

"Comeon, Esme and me'll show you," Arthur said, and soon he, they, and Esme were playing tag under the Bear's quiet gaze.

"The Bear's caught their imagination," I said to Dr. Washington. "They'll come back."

His eyes shone. He nodded.

The tenants and I opened Bear Creek Gallery that spring, in town. Fannie and Bartow volunteered to manage the quiet, colorful shop, with help from the rest of us. Daddy's vision had a home on main street, now. Framed photos of him, the Iron Bear, and Miss Betty decorated the wall behind the sales counter. The shelves were filled with Liza's glasswork and the Ledbetters' pottery. A room in back displayed Oswald's controversial work, but up front, in a small but pleasant corner near the door, were the early samples of his illustrations for Dr. Washington's book. The first week, he sold five small paintings of the graceful Bear Creek children. I had a feeling his career as an artist was about to take off in a way he'd never expected.

*

"It's done," Quentin announced one morning in mid-May. He stood in the kitchen covered in sweat and grime, the welding helmet in one hand, a look of painful satisfaction on his face. I ran to him and we kissed, we swayed, he dropped the helmet and lifted me off my feet. I cupped his face between my hands, and hugged him, hard.

"I want a celebration," I said.

He laughed.

*

Quentin knocked down the pine enclosure one night, then draped the sculpture with Arthur's help. Bear Two was now covered in heavy canvas. Arthur's eyes glowed with intrigue and pleased secrecy. My brother and I stood between the new and the old, the Iron Bear and its hidden progeny.

"Is Mama Bear still lonely?" I asked.

Arthur took my hand. "She misses Daddy, and she won't ever stop. But she's got a friend, now, and she knows sometimes it's okay to feel lonely. She told me and Esme she's happy."

"She's been talking to you a lot lately, hasn't she?"

"She always talks. Just sometimes I don't know how to listen." He cuddled my hand to his cheek and looked at me without wavering. "I love you, Mama Bear."

*

We opened the gate wide. People flowed into the farm all morning, on that Saturday in May. Angele and Alfonse were there, and Harriet Davies, and there were more Tibers than I'd ever seen, before. Mr.

John greeted and hosted his kin as if there had never been a time when Tibers did not tread on Powell soil. Dr. Washington had a place of honor under a shade tree, and with him was his eldest grandson, a teenager who planned to visit his grandfather for the summer. They would take a blacksmithing course together at the college. Washingtons would forge iron and renew their anchor to mountain bedrock.

"How do I look?" Quentin asked upstairs in my bedroom, our bedroom. I smoothed the lapel of the fine dark suit he'd bought; I straightened the silk tie he wore. "Wrong," I said. "You look all fancy and just plain *wrong* for the spirit of the idea."

He smiled. "So do you." I was dressed in a pretty silk dress with hose and matching pumps. We stripped, put on jeans and t-shirts, and then, as we started for the door, he handed me a tiny, beautifully wrapped gift box. The ring inside it glittered with a cluster of diamonds. I leaned against him with my head on his shoulder as he slid the ring on my left hand.

Out in the pasture, a bluegrass band played under a sunny sky, and the crowd—as colorful as the throng at Daddy's funeral—ate barbecue under a long, catered tent. Arthur and Esme huddled under the oaks, watching like excited children and whispering to each other. On a platform with a microphone we hosted speeches, odes to the Iron Bear, impromptu poetry, songs, Elvis impressions, and tears. Father Roy led a prayer.

"Quentin's visited his chapel several times," Angele whispered to Alfonse proudly. "And Ursula goes with him. My grandchildren will have the church in their lives, no doubt."

Alfonse tucked her arm inside his and smiled pensively at her. For years he had wished that Quentin, whom he'd come to think of as a son, would marry Carla. It was a relief to put that hard, hopeless idea aside. His daughter would marry her banker, and be happy. And he, Alfonse, would be happy with Angele Riconni Esposito, with Quentin as a stepson.

Janine stood beside me for a time, watching from the sidelines. "I've got so many plans to improve Tiber Poultry. Maybe you should come to work for me."

I laughed. "Oh, I'll be working *on* you, instead."

"I'm afraid of that." She gave me a rueful look. "Is Quentin going to build more Bears?"

"I don't think so. He'll be busy with his salvage company, of course. And we're planning a house on the ridge overlooking the creek."

"What will you do with the farmhouse?"

"I'm going to let Liza live there."

"I see."

"She'll be the manager of the artists' studios. We're going to expand. Build a gallery, and all that. We'll be doing a lot of building. But not more Iron Bears."

Janine looked at Daddy's colorfully painted truck, now sitting in a place of honor in the middle of the garden, near the peach tree. She blanched. "Expand the art projects?"

I laughed. "I'm my father's daughter."

When the grand moment came, Quentin stepped to one front corner of the canvas cover over Bear Two. I went to the other front corner. "This is for you, Papa," he said so low that only I could hear him. "And for you, Daddy," I whispered. We pulled the canvas back and off, let it fall then walked to each other and linked hands.

The crowd stared at Bear Two, applauded, gasped, snickered, and shook their heads—all the typical reactions a five-ton work of junk-art sculpture receives. "Goddamn," Mr. John said, but when Janine draped an arm around him, he sighed with resignation. Standing nearby, Angele pressed her hands to her wet eyes and smiled at the sculpture. "He didn't build a copy," she told Alfonse. "He built a *son*."

Quentin and I looked up at the soaring ribs of iron rebar, a head made from an engine block, tangled sides of iron fencing and so much else. Inside Bear Two's see-through shell hung Liza's gift—a gleaming heart of interwoven glass, fragile yet beautiful, a stark contrast to the hard iron around it, yet utterly protected and hopeful, beating without motion to the rhythm of its future. Bear Two was alive and well—ugly, handsome, awkward, graceful, sweet, appalling, kind, cruel, clearly provocative and totally bewildering.

"What do you think?" Quentin asked.

"It's *perfect*," I said.

*

I walked out to the Iron Bear that evening just after sunset and sat at its feet, alone, surrounded by yellow daffodils and the low, silver mist rising up the hollow from the creek. I finally understood. No one ever said life would be easy. Daddy, Mama, Richard—they'd all made it look that way for a time—the miracle of creation—but life was hard, it demanded sacrifice and faith. "It's up to me to deal with you," I said aloud to the Bear, "not for you to deal with me. I don't hate you, anymore."

I heard the back door open and shut. Quentin stepped out in the yard, looking for me, silhouetted by the golden glow of light from the house. I raised a hand and waved. He walked toward me, his stride peaceful, his path certain in the mist. *Happy*, he thought. Happy. It was that simple to sum up.

A tiny white butterfly, hurrying somewhere safe, fluttered past me and went inside the Iron Bear, then on to the second sculpture, where it bobbled inside then perched delicately on a slip of iron. It folded its wings for the night. I watched with surprise, then looked at Quentin, and thought of our future. I put a hand to my heart. The message had been received. I had a talent for recognizing small miracles, now.

The news from heaven and earth was good.

I stood, and walked to meet him halfway.

Readers' Guide Questions

1. Ursula and Quentin struggle to come to terms with their respective fathers' intense devotion to unusual art. How to you feel about "modern art" and other non-traditional types of painting and sculpture?

2. Have you ever been disgusted or even just bewildered by a sculpture displayed in a public place?

3. Quentin's father's obsession with artistic success leads to tragedy. Do you believe in the image of the tormented starving artist? Do you think artists have to suffer for their work to be good?

4. The bears featured in the book are Black Bears, who are not generally dangerous to people. Have you ever had an encounter with a bear? Do you see them as noble creatures or just big, scary moochers?

5. If you could be a successful artist, what would your favorite subject matter be? Why?

6. A major theme of the book is art versus money. Do you think the two are mutually exclusive? How do you feel about art that is deliberately offensive (such as religious themes some see as sacrilegious?) Who should decide what's acceptable?